BLOOD ROSE REBELLION

ROSALYN EVES

BLOOD ROSE REBELLION

VOLUME I

ALFRED A. KNOPF   New York

THIS IS A BORZOI BOOK PUBLISHED BY ALFRED A. KNOPF

Text copyright © 2017 by Rosalyn Eves
Jacket art copyright © 2017 by Agent BOB

All rights reserved. Published in the United States by Alfred A. Knopf,
an imprint of Random House Children's Books,
a division of Penguin Random House LLC, New York.

Knopf, Borzoi Books, and the colophon are registered trademarks of
Penguin Random House LLC.

Visit us on the Web! randomhouseteens.com

Educators and librarians, for a variety of teaching tools, visit us at
RHTeachersLibrarians.com

Library of Congress Cataloging-in-Publication Data is available upon request.
ISBN 978-1-101-93599-6 (trade) — ISBN 978-1-101-93600-9 (lib. bdg.) —
ISBN 978-1-101-93601-6 (ebook)

The text of this book is set in 12.5-point Bembo.

Printed in the United States of America
March 2017
10 9 8 7 6 5 4 3 2 1

First Edition

To my sister, Jenilyn—
my first reader and my first fan

But often, in the din of strife,
There rises an unspeakable desire
After the knowledge of our buried life;
A thirst to spend our fire and restless force
In tracking out our true, original course;
A longing to inquire
Into the mystery of this heart which beats
So wild, so deep in us—to know
Whence our lives come and where they go.

—MATTHEW ARNOLD, "THE BURIED LIFE"

CHAPTER 1

London, April 1847

I did not set out to ruin my sister's debut.

Indeed, there were any number of things I deliberately did *not* do that day.

I did not pray for rain as I knelt in the small chapel of our London town house that morning, the cold of the floor seeping into my bones. Instead, I listened to Mama's petition for successful spells and sunshine. Peeking through my lashes at Catherine's smug face, I yearned to ask for disquiet, disorder, and torrential downpours—calamitous words that might have eased, a little, the restless crawling in my heart. But I swallowed the words unsaid. Even should God heed such a treacherous prayer, my father would not. Though Papa's weather magic would cost him a headache, my sister would dance under clear skies.

I did not argue with Catherine when she banned me from the ballroom where she and Papa laid the final grounding for her illusions while Mama supervised the servants. "You'll break my concentration and spoil my spells," she said, though it had been years since I had spoiled anyone's spell, accidentally or otherwise.

But then I did not go to the schoolroom, where I was expected to improve my sketching while my brother, James, studied his Latin. Instead, I lingered (Mama would say loitered) in the lower hall, watching the servants scurry back and forth with their brooms and buckets and cleaning cloths, in feverish preparation for the ball. I did not rest, as Catherine did.

Because of those omissions, I was in the hallway when Lord Frederick Markson Worthing came calling. I heard Freddy's signature knock—two short, three long—and my heart leapt.

Barton reached the door first and sent me a cross look down his long nose. He accepted a small white visiting card from Freddy, and I slipped into the open doorway.

"Lord Markson Worthing!" I smiled up at him, remembering just in time to use his formal name. "Won't you come in?"

I didn't have to look at Barton to know his brows were lowering. Our butler disapproved of forwardness in general and of me in particular.

Freddy returned my smile, his gloved hands tightening around the bouquet of roses he carried. "Thank you, Miss Anna. Only for a moment. I don't want to leave my horses standing too long in this wind." In truth, Freddy had no need for horses. As a Luminate of the order Lucifera, he could compel the carriage with spells. But he preferred the aesthetic of his matched bays, which drew the eye and required less effort to maintain than magic.

Barton led us upstairs to the Green Drawing Room, so named for the ivy pattern sprawling across the wall and the deep emerald drapes. "I will notify your mother, Miss Anna."

Freddy and I sat on matching high-backed chairs near the window. Freddy leaned toward me, nearly crushing the roses he held. He smelled of tobacco and cinnamon.

"I hoped I might see you."

My face grew warm as I met Freddy's intent gaze. I had first encountered Freddy only a few days after we arrived in town for Catherine's Season, to launch her into Luminate society. As the son of an old school friend of Papa's, he had come to pay his respects. But though he had talked to Catherine, he had *looked* at me. Two days later, our paths crossed by accident in Hyde Park, and after that, by design. My maid, Ginny, might suspect the frequency with which Freddy appeared during our errands about London, but she was the only one who knew of our involvement.

There was no one in the world I liked so well as Freddy. I admired the way his honey-colored hair curled a little above the collar of his coat. I adored his eyes, which were not really grey but a band of blue around a center of brown. And I loved him for the way the corners of his lips trembled when he was impassioned: when he spoke about his plans for a seat in the Luminate-led Parliament, or his dreams of a salon in London where Luminate could mingle freely with artists, poets, politicians, and scientists, where wit would trump magic, and ideals would matter more than money.

There was little room in the real world for people like me, but there might be room in Freddy's. We would be a good match, equals in passion and intelligence. I would bring the money his family lacked; he would provide the magic *I* lacked.

"I have something I want to say to you. Will you be at the ball tonight?"

"I am not yet out," I reminded him. *And Mama does not trust me around magic.*

"Then meet me. In the herb garden, at midnight."

The heat in my cheeks deepened. I rearranged my skirts, pretending a composure I did not feel. "Very well."

"Good girl." Freddy stood then and adjusted his top hat. "I must go." He thrust the flowers at me, roses of a red so deep their centers were almost black. The petals spilled over my fingers like blood.

I watched him walk away, admiring the straight line of his back. In the doorway, Freddy spun around to face me. "The flowers are for Catherine. See that she gets them, will you?"

※

"Anna?" Grandmama stood in the doorway, her fingers tight around her cane. "Has Lord Markson Worthing gone already?"

I looked up from the flowers. "He couldn't stay. His horses were waiting."

"And you were alone with him this entire time?" Her

mouth was pursed, her Hungarian accent more pronounced. First Barton, now Grandmama. At least Grandmama's disapproval stemmed from affection.

My shoulders lifted a little. "He left these for Catherine." I held out the roses and wondered if Grandmama would guess how much hid behind that small truth. Though it was customary to bring flowers to a debutante, I could not fathom what Freddy meant by asking me to meet him at midnight but leaving me with my sister's roses.

"Do not shrug. It is not ladylike." Her dark eyes studied my face, guessing at my discontent. "And do not pine so for Luminate society, for the magic and the dancing. You are enough just as you are—and you are not yet seventeen, szívem. Your turn will come."

"Mama would hide me in the country if she could."

"Your mama loves you. She is afraid for you, is all."

I did not believe that. Mama was afraid *of* me, of my strange lack of magic and my caprices. My fingers found a missed thorn on one of the roses, and I snapped it off.

Grandmama sighed. "Give me those flowers. I will take them to Catherine. You should go upstairs before your mama finds you."

I relinquished the roses, but their scent followed me down the hall like a promise.

)(

I sat on Catherine's bed, hugging my knees to my chest. As children, we had often sat on Mama's bed, watching Mama transform through the artifice of her maid from an ordinary mother into something resplendent and strange. I did not know if Catherine was thinking of our old habit when she summoned me or of flaunting her debutante status.

Catherine's maid attached a small coronet of pearls to my sister's mahogany hair. Catherine surveyed her reflection in the ornate mirror, smiling at the effect. Her image seemed unfamiliar, her usual severity softened by the glass and the late-afternoon light. Behind her, I could see the smaller circle of my face, a pale smear of flesh with dark holes for eyes.

I disliked mirrors. Sometimes when I looked at them aslant, I caught an uncanny doubled image, as if I were not one person but two—as if I were a stranger in my own skin. I never knew if such reflections were a by-product of my lack of magic or merely a defect in my vision.

Catherine must have seen something in my look to distrust, because she whirled suddenly. "Anna, you will be good, won't you? You know how much tonight means. I have worked so hard for this moment."

I did know. Catherine was almost frightening in her single-mindedness, and the only thing she wanted more than a dazzling marriage was a position in the Circle, the elite group of Luminate who governed all magic. If her debut spells were suitably impressive, she might be invited to apprentice with one of the Circle members, lifting her into the highest echelon of Luminate society.

"What would I possibly do? I won't be anywhere near you." *Except at midnight, in the gardens.*

"Strange things happen around you. You're so very . . ." She paused, searching for the right word.

"Quixotic? Unconventional? Immodest?" All those, and

worse, had been hurled at me by exasperated governesses in the past.

Her brows drew together, a faint tuck of disapproval. "You'll never get a husband with that attitude."

"Perhaps I don't want one." My eyes dropped to the soul sign glimmering above Catherine's collarbone: the illusion all full-blooded Luminates learned to craft upon entering society, evidence of their magic, just as their jewels witnessed their wealth, and their titles their lineage. Hers was a white rose with fire in its heart. I thought of the sign I would craft, if I could: a peregrine falcon, perhaps—fierce, swift, and strong.

Catherine could not know how galling it was to live in our world as I did. Every noble-born came into their Luminate magic after their Confirmation at age eight—except me. Without magic, everything about me was suspect: my lineage, my quality, my education, my very self. I had no hope of belonging to Luminate society unless I could marry into power, but as Mama frequently pointed out, no one of any position would choose someone so flawed. I would have no fancy debut, as Catherine would, because it would serve no purpose. Yet my noble blood barred me from seeking an occupation among commoners unless I wished to cut myself off from my family.

Until Freddy, I had not realized I might *have* a future.

My sister ran her fingers along the rim of the cut glass vase now holding Freddy's roses. "Lord Markson Worthing will be there. He has been so attentive lately." She glanced at me from under her eyelashes, a demure trick I could never hope to master. "I know you like him, Anna. But you should understand he would never look at you. Not seriously. His father intends him to marry *me*."

My hands curled tightly on the coverlet of Catherine's bed. What was it Freddy wished to tell me? That he loved me—or that he meant to court Catherine? I did not think I could bear it if he married her. She only cared for his name and his title and his family.

She did not deserve him.

⋊

At ten minutes to midnight, I set down my book of poetry and smoothed the sleek coils of dark hair around my ears. As a treat, James and I had been served some of the supper dishes in the schoolroom: lobster, dressed crab, rice croquettes, tongue sliced so thin it was almost transparent, pastries, cheeses, pulled bread, and iced pudding. James had eaten himself into a stupor and was now snoring on the rug, a book of fairy tales long forgotten beside him. I covered him with a quilt and crept down the stairs to my father's library.

I hesitated in the doorway, listening. Were I an Elementalist like Papa, capable of manipulating wind and light, I could set a spell on the air to tell me whether anyone lurked nearby. As it was, I had to rely on my own senses. Beneath the distant echo of voices and music, I heard only the quiet spit and crackle of fire in the grate, so I plunged into the room, crossed the carpet, and pushed my way out the large French doors into the garden.

A gentle breeze caressed my cheek, part of the wind charm Papa used to keep the smoke and fog of London from our garden. I closed my eyes and took a deep breath, smelling green and growing things. After the threatening sky of the afternoon, the evening had come on clear. Papa did not often use his magic, but when he did, his handiwork was always finely wrought.

I followed a little-used path toward Grandmama's herb garden. I loved her garden, especially in summer when the air was sharp with mint and basil. Even in winter I loved it: the bare, orderly plots waiting for spring, the neat circular walkway around the center.

The garden was empty when I arrived. The darkness of the night crept up my arms, settled under my heart. Freddy was not here.

A gust of wind brought with it the scent of roses from the ballroom, and I shivered. Perhaps Freddy was having difficulty getting away or negotiating the garden in the darkness.

Footsteps crunched on gravel behind me. My heart thumped, and I crouched down below the shadow of the hedge. I could not be seen. I was not supposed to be here.

A man's low voice sounded; it was not Freddy. "There's fighting again in Manchester, bloody lower classes demanding access to magic. Why can't they simply accept the order of things? If they were meant to have magic, they'd have been born Luminate. There's no magic in common blood. Riots and petitions for magic will not change that."

A pause, then a second voice. "The commoners questioning is bad enough. But they say Arden is a heretic, wants to do away with the Binding."

"Madness. How can he not see that breaking the Binding will undo the very social order that supports us?"

The hair at the nape of my neck lifted. Why should these

men link Papa with the worker riots? He was no heretic. He believed in the sanctity of the Binding, the great spell that held all magic in a vast reservoir of power, accessible only to those with Luminate blood.

"So I've heard. But his younger daughter's Barren and his son's nearly so. What more would you expect from such a family?"

"The elder daughter is comely enough. I hope for her sake her blood runs truer than her sister's."

My cheeks burned as the voices muted, moving out of range. I tried to push the conversation from my mind. I hated that people could speak so casually of my family, dismissing us—*me*—as so much gossip.

A fresh wind plucked at my hair and sleeves, and I smelled tobacco and cinnamon. My heart lifted; Freddy had come. I straightened and turned to face him. I was tall for a girl, nearly of a height with Freddy.

He took my hand, linking my cool, gloveless fingers with his gloved ones, and led me to a bench. "I'm sorry I was late. I was held up talking with Lady Dorchester."

I smiled down at our joined fingers. Lady Dorchester had three single daughters, each more homely than the last.

Freddy cupped my cheek with one hand, rubbing his thumb along the curve of my jaw, across my lips. His light touch left a powerful tingling in its wake. I lifted my face to his.

I was absurdly aware of how close his mouth was to mine, of the fluttering of my pulse in my throat, of the cold stars overhead. My eyes slid shut. Freddy bent his head and laid a kiss like a prayer on my mouth.

My whole body sang, sparks dancing from my toes to the crown of my head.

I did not know what to do with my hands. They fluttered upward, brushing tentatively against his chest, until Freddy captured them with his.

Freddy broke the kiss first, drawing back to grin at me and then tugging me closer.

I laid my cheek against his shoulder, the stiff fabric of his coat cool under my fingers. Delight bubbled inside me, like champagne, and I pressed my lips together to keep from giggling like a schoolroom miss. "You wished to speak with me?"

"I . . . I only wanted to see you. To hold you, like this." I felt him smile against my hair.

My mouth curled in response, though only the darkness saw it.

"I heard voices," Freddy said. "You weren't seen?"

"No." I remembered the conversation I'd overheard, and the bubbles in my stomach popped all at once. I drew back. "Freddy, why is there rioting in Manchester? And who are the heretics? I thought they were those protestors we saw in Hyde Park, wanting to be rid of Luminates entirely, but one of the men said my father was a heretic. I don't see how that is possible."

Freddy was quiet for so long I began to fear he would not answer. At last, he drew a deep breath. "I'm afraid you wouldn't understand." He dropped a kiss on the tip of my nose.

Perhaps the kiss was meant to convey his affection, but all I sensed was the patronizing note. "Let me try to understand."

In the distance, a bell tolled the quarter hour. Freddy turned toward the house; the faint light thrown our way illuminated the smooth planes of his face.

"We should go."

"Go?" For a moment my mind raced with wild ideas of flight to the border, to Gretna Green, where runaways could marry without a formal license.

"I promised your sister I would watch her performance."

"Oh."

When I did not move, Freddy held his hand out to me. "Come. Surely you wish to see Catherine's charm-casting?"

As Catherine's charm-casting was unlikely to be anything less than perfect, I had no wish to see it. Freddy and I had never talked of my magic—or lack thereof—but he must know. Everyone knew, even strangers in my father's garden. He should have guessed how much it would pain me to witness what I could never have. That he could not see my reluctance, somehow, led a cold fear to curdle in my breast.

Besides, I had no way to enter the ballroom unseen.

As if he read my thoughts, Freddy added, "I'll sneak you inside."

It seemed churlish to keep refusing. I stood, my long skirt falling in heavy folds around my ankles. "Very well."

Freddy muttered a spell, his hands inscribing an arch in the air. A shimmering bit of air split like a torn seam: a portal. I'd never seen one performed before. Only the Lucifera Order could manipulate space, and my family were Elementalists or Coremancers.

When I hesitated—spells were sometimes unpredictable in my presence—Freddy took my hand. "It will be all right."

At his touch, a kick of excitement sparked through my body, tamping down my momentary fear. Freddy tugged my hand gently, guiding me into the portal. The light blinked in and out around me, and then we were through. We stepped out of the portal into a shadowed alcove, partially screened by a potted tree. I wondered if Freddy had spied this out beforehand, prepared for just such a contingency.

The room was stiflingly hot after the garden, despite the rose-scented breezes that circulated. Tiny droplets of water, like so many winking jewels, hung suspended above our heads by Papa's magic, joining and then separating in intricate patterns over the assembly.

Peering around the tree, I saw Catherine in her white gown at the heart of the room. My parents and grandmother were nearby, my father's face flushed with wine, my mother's pale with tension. Mama knew, as I did, that no matter how lovely Catherine was, failure in this moment would compromise her marriage prospects. No nobleman would want a wife who could not ensure that his heirs carried magic. *Except Freddy.* Though we had not talked about marriage in so many words, Freddy had often hinted at it. His willingness to overlook my lack of magic only confirmed my belief in his open mind, his generous heart.

With a final squeeze of my hand, Freddy strode forward to stand by my father, and Catherine's face lit like a bonfire. As Catherine closed the distance between them and rested her hand on his arm, spikes of dread shot up and down my spine.

My father spoke. "Lords, ladies, exalted members of the Circle." He nodded to a small cluster of men and women standing near my sister, tonight's chosen representatives from the powerful coterie who controlled Luminate magic. "Thank you for joining us. This is a momentous occasion. It is the night my daughter Catherine leaves behind her girlhood and becomes a woman, the night she becomes a full Luminate of the Elementalist Order. I trust you shall be as dazzled by her debut spell as I have been all these years raising her."

While Papa spoke, Catherine cast her eyes down to the floor and a becoming blush suffused her cheeks. I knew my sister well enough to suspect the blush was charmed. When Papa ceased speaking, Catherine lifted her head. She closed her eyes and began chanting. I couldn't hear her words, but I could see the delicate gestures of hand and wrist as she laid her spell. The scent of roses intensified, and the lights in the room dimmed, all save a gradual brightening around my sister. The showmanship was part of the performance.

Catherine opened her eyes, and her illusion began to coalesce around her. Like Papa, Catherine was an Elementalist capable of manipulating wind, water, light, and fire. As her ability to manipulate light was particularly strong, illusions showed her skills to advantage. She'd taken roses as her illusion motif, an appropriately feminine choice that reflected her chosen soul sign, the white rose glittering at her throat. The air behind her shimmered with giant roses, a tapestry of red and white and pink superimposed upon the air. Before her, a steadily increasing glow became a tableau: a beautiful golden-haired maiden, asleep on a bed, a bower of thorny roses surrounding her. I deemed the Sleeping Beauty an obvious choice, but it pleased the crowd. I heard gasps from ladies standing near me, and then a ripple of applause ran through the audience.

Another illusion joined the tableau: a young knight who rode toward the maiden, only to be ensnared by the roses. The knight faded away, the faintest hint of a skull hanging in the air to mark his passing. I waited, wondering how Catherine would conjure the young prince who finally rescued the maiden.

More gasps, then laughter. I couldn't see, at first, what the focus was. I scanned Catherine's face, and then my family behind her. Finally, my gaze fell on Freddy, and fear ran cold fingers down my neck. This illusion was not all empty air and light. Catherine had drawn a crown on Freddy's head and placed a gleaming sword in his hand. When Freddy, at the urging of the crowd, stepped forward to the tableau, the thorns fell away from his sword.

My sister had made Freddy a part of her performance. With all the care Catherine had taken for her spells, there could be nothing impromptu about this. She had planned for it.

Practiced it.

Something snapped in me. As the maiden in the tableau opened her eyes and raised herself toward Freddy, I opened my mouth and shouted, a wordless cry that filled the entire hall. Fury pulsed through my blood, seeming to catch at the very air around me.

A thunderclap of silence followed in the wake of my shout.

Then pandemonium.

CHAPTER 2

Catherine's illusions disintegrated. The roses littering the floor at her feet shifted and twisted into ropy red serpents that slithered away from her and into the crowd. Screaming rippled out from the spot where Catherine stood, aghast at the sudden eruption of her spells.

Freddy's crown and sword disappeared in sprays of lightning. He flinched, throwing his arms up to cover his head.

The hairs on the back of my neck lifted just before the French doors near my alcove exploded, raining glass across the floor.

An enormous creature of brine and smoke swept past me. Something thin and insubstantial trailed behind the shadow like wings, their tips brushing my cheek in a brittle kiss. It must have been illusion, wrought by the failed spell-path, though I'd never before witnessed an illusion so real, with both heft and smell. The flickering lights of the chandeliers and hundreds of candles lining the wall sconces melted together in a rising wall of flame around the creature.

Fire flooded the room, an illusion so bright I shut my eyes against the pain of it.

Then everything went dark.

The air filled with screams. I could feel my pulse beating in my wrists and pounding at my throat. A creeping winter chill stole through the darkness. The smell of roses had been displaced by smoke and frost and the acridness of fear.

When the energy from the fractured spell finally spent itself and the lights along the walls relit, it was to the entirely indecorous sound of my father muttering "Confound it all!" My mother's eyes were shut and her hands clasped in prayer. The creature, like the other illusions, had vanished. The members of the Circle, standing in a loose cluster, flicked their hands in the final gestures of a spell. Their foreheads glistened with sweat, their elegant clothing dark and stained with effort.

Catherine still stood in the middle of the room. But her face turned toward me, her expression icier than the winter-cold of the darkness.

Behind her, Freddy also faced me, his eyes wide.

As if Freddy's and Catherine's gazes were some sort of compass, the assembled guests slowly shook themselves out of their horror and turned as one body to stare. In the midst of that wreckage, their eyes did not seek the shattered glass windows, or my sister and her failed charms.

Every eye in the room was trained on me, half hidden behind a flimsy plant.

"Anna! What have you done?" Catherine's wail soared over the crowd.

"Nothing," I said, though I choked on the word. What *had* I done? My shadow self—all the dark desires I tried to keep buried—had surfaced. I had let her rise, riding on a wave of fury. I had wanted to destroy something: in that fractional moment before the illusions shattered and dread swamped me, I had felt something perilously close to joy.

I flung myself away from the inadequate shelter of the potted tree and pushed through the murmuring crowd. The room seemed to swirl and swoop around me, colors melting together as paints on a palette. I took a deep breath, thrusting my arms out for balance. I would *not* faint.

The crowd's eyes were like so many insects on my back, crawling and uncomfortable. I reached the jagged mouth of the broken window, and, after stepping cautiously over the shards of glass, fled into the welcoming night.

※

By the time Papa caught up with me at the far edge of the sculpted lawn, my head was pounding in time with my pulse. Pain spangled at the edges of my vision.

"Anna."

I could not look at him. I did not want to read the disappointment in his face.

"Will you tell me what happened?"

"There's nothing to tell." Trees rustled in the wind, shadows moving against shadows.

"Hmm." He did not press me, as Mama would have. "You

must come in. There's a chill in the air. And the Circle representatives wish to speak with you."

My heart sank. The Circle comprised the most powerful Luminate in England. Though officially tasked with preserving the Binding spell that held our magic, regulating spell-casting, and aiding in national defense, unofficially the Circle had fingers in nearly every branch of government. The same was true of most European nations, though I knew from Papa's lectures that the Circle's strength varied in proportion to the monarch's power. In England, Queen Victoria, a powerful spell-caster in her own right, headed the Circle. In France, where the Circle had saved the nation from Napoleon's depredations, the Circle's rule was absolute, the Bourbons merely puppet kings. And while the powerful Maria Theresa had once dominated the Circle in Austria-Hungary, her Hapsburg descendants had been steadily losing ground to the Circle following her death.

And these were the individuals waiting now to speak with me.

I followed Papa back to his study, resigned to the inevitable. Mama and Catherine huddled together on the settee, Catherine glaring at me with reddened eyes. I guessed the other two individuals to be members of the Circle: an older gentleman with a forehead permanently grooved in a frown, and a dumpy middle-aged woman. Grandmama was not there—doubtless the drama had sent her to bed with a headache.

But where was Freddy? I wished I were back in the garden with him. I wished I'd never agreed to watch Catherine perform.

But I lacked the magic for even one small wish, and so there I stood.

My father hastened to introduce the two members of the Circle. "Lord Orwell, my daughter Anna. Anna, Lord Orwell leads the Coremancer Order."

I curtsied. Lord Orwell cleared his rather phlegmy throat. His watery blue eyes traveled over my person, but clearly found no pleasure in the exercise.

"Lady Berri, my daughter. Anna, Lady Berri heads the Lucifera Order. Lord Eldon, head of the Elementalist Order, could not stay." He did not need to add that Queen Victoria, who headed the Animanti Order, had not been present to begin with. My father's cheeks were still flushed, but the light in his eyes had vanished. I tried, and failed, to read his expression. Was he angry? Afraid?

There were four orders of spell-casters among the Luminate: Coremancers, like Mama and Lord Orwell, capable of discerning and influencing thoughts and emotions. Elementalists, like Papa and Catherine, who manipulated light and nonliving elements. Animanti, who influenced living things and might, depending on their gifts, speak with animals or heal injured tissues. And the Lucifera, rarest and most powerful, who shaped forces: gravity, electricity, magnetism, sometimes even space, as Freddy had done earlier when crafting his portal. I studied Lady Berri with new interest.

"Charmed," Lady Berri said, smiling at me, and then chuckling at her own mild pun. Her soul sign, a sleek leopard, prowled incongruously where her plump neck melted into her shoulder.

An answering smile tickled the corner of my mouth, but

I suppressed it. That three of the most powerful Luminate had come to Catherine's debut meant they suspected Catherine had great promise as a spell-caster. I didn't doubt it: Catherine had studied magic with an intensity most young ladies reserved for their suitors. I glanced at my sister and guilt washed over me. I hoped I had not entirely ruined her chances.

Though in theory most Luminate had equal access to magic through the Binding spell, in practice it was not always so. Casting spells, particularly large ones, required a focus and attention to craft that many people lacked. Thus, Papa was a relatively gifted Elementalist, but Mama had never progressed beyond basic-level spells: her debut spell, her soul sign, common Coremancer charms.

Young men might demonstrate their power during their years at Oxford or Cambridge. But for a young woman, there was really only one opportunity to impress the Circle: at her debut.

Small wonder my sister wept. I squashed an impulse to comfort her; Catherine would not welcome my pity.

In any case, I had greater things to worry about at the moment. Namely, what two of the most powerful Luminate in England sought with me.

"What is this about?" I asked, summoning false confidence. "Of what am I accused?"

Lady Berri smiled at me. "No one has made any accusations yet."

Returning her look but not her smile, I said, "Experience, my lady, has taught me that when I am summoned to my father's study, it is because I am blamed for something."

She laughed—a loud, jolly laugh that turned into a cough when Lord Orwell scowled at her.

"Someone in the ballroom tonight disrupted Catherine's charms." Lord Orwell looked at me when he spoke.

"It was not me." But I remembered the shout that grew out of my terrible anger, and my blood ran cold.

"You were not supposed to be there at all. I *told* you—" The words burst from Catherine like starlings from a bush. "I told you to stay away, or you would ruin everything. And you did. My charms were destroyed, all my prospects of happiness . . ." She trailed off, blinking hard.

Mama put her arm around my sister's shaking shoulders.

Lord Orwell spoke. "It is most unusual. I've never seen charms come unraveled quite so spectacularly. The casting was solid. There was no reason for the magic to come so . . . unbound." His mouth pursed around the last word with distaste.

Spells *were* miscast, sometimes. I did not know much of the theoretics of Luminate magic: my magic lessons had been tacitly dropped after my disastrous Confirmation eight years earlier. But I did know that spell-casters drew power for their spells from the Binding, an enormous and ancient spell that held magic as a dam held floodwaters. The Binding existed in an ethereal dimension that lay over our world like a veil, so Luminates never had to reach too far to summon power. Spell-casters employed spells to draw out the magic, using their words and gestures and will to direct the shape of the charm, as a canal channels the route of water. A spell with insufficient will or inaccurate gestures might misfire, sometimes inconsequentially, sometimes tragically, depending on the size of the spell and the degree of the miscasting. Power, once summoned, had to go *somewhere,* and if the caster could not control it, the magic might take its own form. But Catherine would not be so common as to allow any degree of inexactness.

Something else had happened tonight.

Lord Orwell continued, turning his attention from me to my father. "I cast a survey spell, after the chaos from the broken spell settled. The point of disruption was clearly your younger daughter."

Cold prickled up my arms.

"Impossible." My mother's voice was sharp, but I heard a darker note—fear?—behind the words.

Lord Orwell's eyebrows rose again. Lady Berri pressed her lips together, but the look she cast at me was not unsympathetic.

I turned away, knowing what my mother would say and bracing against it.

"It is impossible," my mother repeated, "because Anna has no magic."

In the darkened glass of the window, the shadowy faces of the others scrutinized me. And there it was again, that doubled reflection of my face, as if I were divided against my own self.

"Has this been verified?" Lord Orwell asked.

Lady Berri said, "The girl's diagnosis is written in our records. Her Confirmation did not take, and the Circle officiate certified the diagnosis of the girl as Barren."

My cheeks burned with the memory. A Luminate's Confirmation was meant to bind a Luminate to a particular order, activating the gift for magic in her blood and enabling her to draw power out of the Binding for use in spells. It was supposed to be a solemn, holy day, the start of one's magical career.

I had been eight years old, like most Confirmands. I had stood at the nave of our local church, my white dress splashed with color from the stained-glass window behind the altar. Catherine stood beside me, almost bouncing in her eagerness. The previous year, the Circle member who was to cast her Confirmation spell had fallen ill, and by the time he recovered, Mama and Papa had decided it would be easier to hold our Confirmations jointly.

The officiating Circle member had been an older man with a thinning beard. He spoke the charm first over Catherine. At the conclusion, a hush fell over the audience. Catherine screwed up her face—and executed a flawless Lumen light, a basic spell all Luminate could master. She cupped the blue glow in her hands like it was some rare sapphire.

The crowd clapped and cheered, and Catherine turned a radiant smile on them. The Circle officiator, pronouncing a benediction on her, named her Elementalist.

Then it was my turn.

I'd felt nothing of his charm-casting—no nudge, no burning, no fizzing up my spine. Just as I'd felt nothing tonight when Catherine bound her spells.

"Cast a Lumen light," he'd instructed me when he finished. I remembered thinking his blue eyes were kind, though I was terrified.

I had lifted my hands, inscribing them through the air in a doubled circle, then cupping them before me. For weeks, Papa had drilled me in the proper form and pronunciation of the rite. I concentrated, folding my lips around the words. *"Adure! Canta!"*

Nothing happened.

My cheeks flaming, I had ventured a quick look behind me. The small chapel brimmed with relatives, family friends, and village well-wishers. Grandmama smiled encouragingly. Mama pressed her eyebrows together and nodded sharply at me. *Get on with it.*

Catherine whispered, "It is not so hard, Anna. You can do this."

I tried again. And again. After my fourth failure, Papa had left the pew and come to stand beside me.

"I think she may be Barren," the Circle officiator whispered to Papa.

I had not understood the word, but the look on Papa's face frightened me. Later, Grandmama would explain it meant I was empty—not of seed, but of magic. An ugly term for a Luminate whose Confirmation did not take.

"If you will let me examine her," the officiant had said, "I must note something for our records."

Papa had nodded, his lips tight. "All right." He'd set his hand on my shoulder, weighting me down.

Fear had squirmed through my belly. Alongside the fear was something darker, resentful and angry. *Why should I be embarrassed before all these people?* But the second wave of emotion only frightened me further: it was both familiar and foreign, mine and not mine. It originated inside me but belonged to a shadow part of me I didn't recognize.

There in the nave of the chapel, as the Circle officiator began the gesture of a new spell, dread clawed at my heart.

My shadow self burst free, fighting against the spell. When the officiant's lips stopped moving, it was as if I'd swallowed a living flame.

"No!" I had shouted, shaking free of Papa's hand and running down the aisle, toward Mama's pale face.

The pain had followed me, heat erupting through me. I wanted to reach the doors, believing somehow if I could just get *out,* I might escape the agony and the fear and the embarrassment of failing at the only important task I'd ever been set.

Just as I'd reached Mama, I stumbled over James. I hadn't seen him in the aisle—in the blur of heat and pain, I'd only seen the square of sunlight in the open doorway. He was so small then, barely four. Perhaps he'd thought my running a kind of game.

We'd collapsed in a heap on the ground, and the wave of invisible fire swept out of me. I remembered James screaming, and then nothing at all until morning, when I woke in my bed to find my nurse sitting by my side.

Everything had changed afterward. It was a week before I saw either of my parents, and nearly a month before I was allowed near James. Catherine blamed me for spoiling her Confirmation, as the fete afterward had been canceled. Mama, never particularly nurturing, had grown even more distant, taking my disgrace as a personal slight.

"What I should like to know," Catherine said, pulling me back into the present, "is how Anna came to be at my ball when she was supposed to be in her rooms."

"Yes, Anna." My father's voice was nearly devoid of inflection. "How did that happen?"

Freddy. I shook myself. I must not betray Freddy. If I refused to answer, I would sound suspicious. "I was curious. I hid myself behind one of the plants in the ballroom."

"Doubtful," Lord Orwell said. "The spell I cast revealed that a portal had been opened near your hiding place. You could not have cast it. Someone must have helped you. Who?"

"Tell him," Mama urged.

"No one. I snuck in."

"It is late, I am tired, and I would like to be in my bed before much longer. If you insist on lying, then I must insist on doing this my way." Lord Orwell began weaving his fingers in front of my face in an intricate pattern that could only mean one thing.

A truth charm.

I flinched away from him and his flickering fingers. The last time Mama used a truth charm on me, it had lit the draperies on fire and I'd had blackouts for days afterward.

"Wait," Mama said. "Don't spell her. Truth charms have . . . unpredictable effects on Anna."

"As you wish."

My relief was momentary.

Lord Orwell grimaced. "Then we must return to the ballroom and reconstruct what happened."

My father led the way, and I followed behind the others. I looked down the long hallway, empty now of guests and servants, and considered slipping away from everyone and running to my room. A reconstruction could not mean anything good for me.

Though Mama was a weak Coremancer, unable to read my actual thoughts (thanks be to all the Saints that Bind), she often picked up unerringly on my emotions. No sooner had the notion of flight crossed my mind than she pinched my elbow.

"Tell them the truth." Her voice was sharp, insistent. "This charade is unseemly."

Catherine, at Mama's other side, said, "Anna can't help it. She must be the center of attention. That's all she's doing—prolonging her moment when this night should have been *mine.*"

Sometimes I wished I could fold up all my unladylike qualities—my obstinacy, my temper, my wanting too much, my inability to stay still and quiet—like a handkerchief and stow it in my valise until needed. Mama and I would both be happier if I could fit the shape society prescribed for me.

But that night, the demon in my shadow self prompted me to respond, "At least no one will soon forget your debut, Catherine. If this is indeed my fault, then you have me to thank."

I thought Catherine would strike me. She brought her hand up as if she would let fly, but Mama's shocked "Catherine!" recalled her. Her hand dropped.

Once in the ballroom, Lord Orwell stalked across the floor to the spot where I'd hidden. The room looked so different now, forlorn and sad. Colored streamers lay trampled on the floor; flowers hung dull and wilted on their stems. The water illusions had evaporated.

As the strongest Coremancer in the room, Lord Orwell cast the spell, pulling the reconstruction from memories lingering in the air. When he stopped gesturing and murmuring the Latin incantation, the faint silhouette of a girl took shape, crouched on the ground behind a tall plant. The air in the ballroom shimmered, and the illusion candles flickered. I caught the faint briny smell of the illusion beast, like an echo of a real scent. Light sparked in the center of the room, then my crouched figure rose up and shouted. Outside of the cheval glass in Mama's room, I only ever saw myself in small mirrors and windows, in bits and pieces. It was strange to see all of me from all angles at once, tall and ungainly. The Reconstruction spell followed the illusion me, walking backward through the events of the night.

I waited for the Reconstruction charm to end there, for the Circle to turn to me with recrimination and accusations. But it didn't.

My illusion self crept away from the plant and held out her hand.

I put my hands together to stop them from trembling, so Catherine would not see I was afraid. There was no help for it now. I couldn't hide Freddy's involvement any longer.

A figure flickered into being beside me, a golden-haired man a few inches taller than I. We stepped backward into a portal.

"That's Freddy," Catherine said. "But why would he help you spoil my debut?"

Mama shot a darkling look at me. She knew. I had been fortunate before that she had been so caught up in Catherine's debut she had not had time to track my errant feelings.

"Where was the portal anchored?" Lord Orwell asked.

I did not want to answer. But the memory of the garden rose up full and fresh in my mind, and Lord Orwell plucked it out of me.

"The herb garden."

I hung back behind the others, hoping to escape once again, but Papa took my hand and gently but firmly propelled me forward. We tramped across the lawn, past the rose arbor, and into the herb garden. Overhead, the stars shone and the night wind stirred through the branches of the trees. It was, impossibly, still the same night that had found me in the garden with Freddy. That moment was beginning to feel so distant, as if it were something in a story.

The reconstructed spell had continued in our absence, so when we reached the garden, we did not see the pair of us entering the portal. Instead, everyone saw our illusion selves embracing on the bench. The kiss that felt like a promise now looked like betrayal. My inadvertent betrayal of Freddy to the Circle. My betrayal of Mama's strict training. My betrayal of Catherine, who glared at me with fury-bright eyes.

And something behind the fury I had not thought to see in my sister—hurt.

CHAPTER 3

After the reconstruction, my mother led Catherine, alternately grieving and raging, to her room. The Circle led me—also grieving and raging in the silence of my head—back to my father's study.

There they proceeded to dissect me, laying bare my motives like the skeleton of some beast. They determined the following: I was in love with Freddy, he had spelled me, and the sight of him in the midst of my sister's charm had so enraged me that I destroyed her spell. *How* I destroyed her spell they had not yet determined.

Set in sharp syllables and indifferent pauses, my motives for the night became sordid and unrecognizable. I couldn't find the texture and feel of the night air, of Freddy's kiss, in their words. My story became instead something silly and shallow. A one-note piece of gossip for the morning papers, the younger sister consumed by jealousy.

"We would like to study her," Lord Orwell said to Papa, sipping from a glass of water mixed with the headache powder most Luminate carried. Depending on the scope, spells were frequently exhausting, sometimes painful. "Discover how someone without magic can disrupt spells. As a scholar, you must appreciate that the more we know about magic and its failings, the more powerful we become."

No.

"What I appreciate in the abstract and in historical records takes on a much different cast when applied to my own flesh," my father said. It took me a moment to untangle his words and realize what he had meant: no.

One did not lightly refuse the Circle. For treason against the Circle, an entire family could be stripped of their access to the Binding, thereby losing their magic. For lesser offenses, the Circle might limit what spells one was allowed to cast. Families that stood publicly against the Circle often found themselves social pariahs, shunned by the highest orders of Luminate society. Small wonder Mama was so anxious. And angry.

Lord Orwell looked thunderous, his brows pulling together. "It is your duty—"

Lady Berri interrupted him. "It is late, and this discussion might be best saved for another time, when we have rested." Her eyes caught mine. "I have a feeling, my dear, that you and I are to become much better acquainted."

※

Morning came too early, all stabbing lights and throbbing in my skull. Then memory rushed in. By the time my maid,

Ginny, came bearing hot cocoa, I had already pulled my favorite walking gown from my wardrobe, a plain green cotton with a black fringe along the wide sleeves and neck. I had to get out. I had to move, or I would perish from too much thinking.

Ginny's blue eyes widened in dismay. "You're not going out? I'm sure your mama intends you to stay in today."

"So you've heard?" Gossip traveled particularly swiftly in the servants' hall. "Did Mama tell you herself I was to stay in my rooms?"

"No." Ginny smiled a little. "She said nothing to me." Ginny was half a dozen years older than I, but she was perhaps the closest thing I had to a friend. She mothered me where my own mother did not, and knew well enough I could not bear confinement.

I nodded decisively. "Good. Then we are going walking."

It had rained in the early hours of the morning after my father's spell had lapsed. The distinctive petrichor of wet stone and earth and the damp slap of my slippers against pavement eased my restless heart. I was free—for the moment. In the wake of the storm, the clouds tore across the sky. Intermittently, the sun shot through the clouds, illuminating bushes like something out of a medieval manuscript or an Elementalist's debut.

Ginny and I walked sedately around our neighborhood, and then less sedately in Kensington Gardens, where I could not keep my unruly legs in line. When we reached an empty pathway, I ran, kicking my legs against my skirts and wishing it were not so unseemly for a woman to wear trousers.

When I returned to Ginny, retying the loosened ribbons on my silk bonnet, she shook ginger curls at me, but a smile split her freckled cheeks, so I knew she was not truly upset. Our walk brought us past Rotten Row and toward a wide grassy area where a crowd gathered: businessmen and lawyers on their way into the City, nurses with their young charges, costermongers, dockworkers, and others. I suspected the gentlemen with tailored coats, shining top hats, and gold watch fobs dangling somewhat askew from their waistcoats were Luminate on their way home from a night carousing, though one could never be sure without the telltale soul sign. Behind them, I could see the beautiful and costly ironworks of Cumberland Gate, in Hyde Park.

We had arrived at Speakers' Corner.

Mama did not approve of Speakers' Corner. Nor, for that matter, did Ginny, who began to tug at my arm and cluck with distress. Here, anyone with a will and a hearty set of lungs might speak his mind to the world. I wasn't sure which Mama disapproved of more: the thoughts that were expressed or the company that collected to hear them.

"Don't be so goosish," I told her, edging closer. "Where is your sense of adventure?"

"Adventure," Ginny said tartly, "is often more trouble than it's worth. As you ought to know!"

I grinned at her, unrepentant. She shook her head, but I did not miss the smile trembling at the corners of her mouth.

Someone was speaking, his red hair raised above the crowd. As I drew nearer, I realized the man was not extraordinarily tall. He stood on a packing crate.

"For too long the Luminate have fattened themselves upon the labor of the working class. It is our work, our sweat, and our blood that make their lives possible." The words sounded unnaturally loud in my ears, as if the man stood next to me; he spoke through some kind of mechanism, a small cone made of metal that amplified his voice. Beside him, a strange-shaped lump lay concealed under canvas.

I stood transfixed by his voice, a faint burr betraying his Scottish origins.

"When was the last time you saw a lord labor anywhere but in the bedroom?"

Loud, raucous laughter burst from the spectators. "Miss Anna," Ginny hissed, her cheeks red. "This is most inappropriate."

My own face was warm, but I did not move. Not yet.

"The Luminate use their money to buy land we cannot afford and magic we cannot practice. Their Circle uses magic to keep us cowed, to break our thoughts of rebellion." The man swept his gaze across the crowd. "Sixty-five years ago, the Circle quashed a rebellion in France for the Bourbons, then lost the kingdom to the Corsican Tyrant for nearly a decade. And Napoleon won solely because his wealth enabled him to corrupt Luminate spell-casters. On the power of their spells, he styled himself emperor. We stand now on the cusp of our own revolution—but if we hope to win, we must recognize this one truth."

What revolution? What truth? My pulse quickened, but I could not be sure if it was fear or the faint electric hum that filled my body. The crowd stirred, muttering agreement. The pair of young Luminate lords discreetly turned and stole away. I should do the same. Indeed, only Ginny's reluctance to cause a scene prevented her from dragging me away. Her fingers tightened on my arm. "Miss Anna!"

I turned back to the speaker.

"We live in a world where Luminate are the only ones

with magic. But it was not always so: once, anyone born with a gift wielded magic. Then the Luminate seized control of magic, trapping it with their Binding spell. They have worked hard to erase any memory of a time when magic belonged to everyone, replacing the truth with their fantasy—that Luminate are born to magic, that this birthright qualifies them to rule."

Something cold and heavy settled in my stomach. I had never heard of a time when anyone other than Luminates had magic, and my own father was a historian. Surely this man was mistaken.

"But Luminate are no more born to magic than you are. It is not bloodlines that determine magical ability, but the Circle. They decide who has access to magic and who does not. They decide what order of magical spells you belong to—and how much magic you are allotted for your spells. And the deciding factor is not whether you have *aptitude* for magic. The Circle does not care if you have a gift for magic not seen in a generation. They only care that you belong to an old, decaying line, and that you can afford their Confirmation spell. It helps if you spend sufficient time kissing the Circle's desiccated arses."

More laughter.

"The Confirmation spell does not activate some innate gift for magic in their Luminate blood—it simply gives Luminate access to magic. Without the Binding trapping magic, and without the Circle's tightfisted control of that spell, *anyone* might be a magician. You might." He pointed at a young man near the front. "Or you. It is only this spell that keeps Luminate in power."

It was strangely hard to breathe. I pressed my hands against my stomach and wished my corset were a degree or two looser. Mama had always taught me that magic was our birthright as Luminates, that our blood called to the magic and justified our superior position in society. If I was Barren, it was only because my Luminate blood was somehow defective.

But what if this stranger were right? The Luminate class system was built on the premise that their magical gifts made Luminates naturally superior. Take away that premise and there was not, indeed, any reason Luminates should dominate society. I did not want to believe him—and yet I could not dislodge a tiny kernel of doubt.

A second, more disquieting thought followed on the heels of the first: if the speaker was right, and the Confirmation did not so much awaken magic as grant access to it, what did it mean that not even a Confirmation was enough to give me magic?

The speaker continued. "We seek an equal world for all—a world where anyone with wit may petition for a seat in Parliament, anyone with will might own and work land, and anyone with aptitude might cast spells."

The crowd cheered. Indeed, I might have cheered myself— was this not precisely what Freddy and I wanted?—were his other accusations not so unsettling.

"Such change is not always peaceful. We demand the end of unjust laws, the unfair perpetuation of magic through the Binding, the inequitable distribution of wealth—and the Luminate may not hear us willingly. We must be prepared to fight!"

The cheering increased to a roar.

Someone shouted, "But how shall we fight against magic?"

The red-haired man turned a blazing look on the crowd. "We will fight with our hands. Our wits. Our swords and guns. And our machines." He gestured and a lackey flung the canvas off the strange shape beside him. I could not see clearly over the milling crowd, but I glimpsed something shiny, metallic. Then I heard a low hum and gasps from those closer to the object. A woman near me crossed herself.

"Sooner than the Luminate can anticipate, their world will collapse. In place of jewels, we will give them stone; in place of gold—fire!"

The red-haired man threw out his arm, and the crowd drew back in alarm. I could see now the metal creature at his side. It was roughly human-like in shape, standing on two thick legs with two armlike appendages. But the face, made of sheets of metal hammered thin, bore the hooked beak of a bird of prey. As I watched, a pair of paper-thin metal wings unfurled and the entire machine erupted in flame.

It advanced on the crowd, which parted like the Red Sea before Moses. Ginny cried out and stumbled, falling to her knees. Beside her, a little girl began to cry.

"Stop!" I yelled, a twinge of fear feeding my anger. "Stop this at once."

The automaton continued to press forward. In a moment it would be upon Ginny. My fury flexed and expanded, fueled by my hurt at Freddy's disappearance, my increasing sense of helplessness in the face of my mother's will. "Stop!" I cried again, trying to push the force of my will into the air around me.

The automaton faltered and stopped. The fire died as

quickly as it had begun. Thank all the Saints that Bind, the red-haired man had heeded me after all. He sprang forward and helped Ginny to her feet, then turned to stare at me, his eyes narrowed.

I marched toward him, furious. "Is this your revolution? Is this how you hope to change the world—by frightening women and children? For shame!" The pounding of my pulse crept up the side of my face. The edges of my vision blurred and sparkled. "Not all Luminate are the ogres you paint them. Not all are so wealthy, or so powerful."

His blue eyes drilled into mine. There was a light in them—not of anger, but of interest. "Who are you?"

Half a dozen tart replies flashed through my brain, fighting against the expanding pain. "Someone who thinks you should know better. And now, if you are quite finished, I have better things to do."

I spun around and the park appeared to spin with me. My impressions grew fuzzy. Mama was *not* going to be pleased I had made a spectacle of myself in public.

Again.

My last conscious sight was of the stranger's sky-colored eyes, open wide with surprise.

)(

Consciousness came back to me in fits and starts. First voices, then glimmers of light. My mother's jasmine scent floated on the air nearby.

"Anna is young, Mária. I'm sure she intended no harm."
My father.

"She is old enough to know she should not meet a man

alone in the gardens at midnight. I did not teach my daughters to behave like . . . like a common trollop. And now this! Escorted home by a strange man—a radical, no less!—after fainting in the park."

"Mr. William Skala," Papa murmured. "Clever enough to be dangerous, but he did the right thing bringing my girl home."

I heard a rustle of fabric and pictured Mama's impatient shrug. "Something must be done with Anna. She cannot be allowed to stay here. The gossip alone would follow Catherine to every event of the Season."

Something must be done with Anna. As if I were a particularly thorny problem, not her child. I kept my eyes closed, though I was fully conscious and my head was tilted at an awkward angle against the sofa back.

"Would you have me take her back to Arden Hall?" Papa asked.

I pictured our estate in Dorset, the green growing fields and the faint salt tang in the air on clear, windy days. I had learned to name birds there, and catch fish with James. Arden Hall belonged to the tightly circumscribed world of my childhood. London belonged to my present, and, I hoped, my future. I did not want to go.

A brief pause, as Mama cogitated. "No. There is only one thing to be done. Lord Markson Worthing must be made to marry her. I refuse to let shame and scandal spoil any more of Catherine's debut."

Hope surged up in me. *Marry* Freddy? I knew this was a routine solution to young women in my predicament, but I had not believed Mama would allow it. Somehow it seemed too much like a reward for bad behavior.

"I do not like it," Grandmama said, tapping her cane. "I do not think he will make my granddaughter happy. Let her come with me to Hungary. I should like to see my country once more before I die."

Hungary? That was half a world away. I could not go.

"Happy?" Mama said. "That is not my concern. If Anna is respectable, she must be happy. And Hungary is too far for an old woman and a young girl to travel alone."

My breath slipped out in relief. I would be happy with Freddy, though perhaps not *entirely* respectable.

"It seems to me," Papa said, "Lord Markson Worthing has something to answer for. What business has a grown man with courting one sister in public and encouraging her younger sister—a girl not yet out—to meet him in secret? And I mislike the Circle's new interest in Anna. Lord Orwell wants to study her. I've put him off, though I'm not certain how long I can do so."

"Perhaps you should let him. We would not want—" Mama broke off. "Anna. I know you can hear us."

I cursed her Coremancer gift, hoping she would not read my surliness in the midst of my lingering pain. I coughed and fluttered my lashes for effect, then sat up slowly. Mama and Grandmama sat on the matched chairs by the window in the Green Drawing Room, where Freddy and I had sat only the day before. Papa stood just beyond them, one arm slung across the marble mantelpiece.

Grandmama smiled at me. "You are better?"

A legion of tiny dwarves were excavating my skull with pickaxes. "Yes," I said, wrestling a smile onto my lips. "I am better."

"Anna," Mama sighed. "I need not tell you your behavior

41

last night was shockingly inappropriate. You shall be confined to your room until we have settled things."

I swallowed the tightness in my throat. Was it such a crime, to kiss the man I loved?

"We will do what we must to salvage things. Your father will speak to Lord Markson Worthing. The Circle willing, he will marry you."

"Mária," my father began. "I do not know that—"

Mama shook her head, the tight curls at the sides of her face quivering. "I will not discuss this further. We will *all* do what we must. You will speak to Lord Markson Worthing, and Anna will marry him."

The door burst open. Catherine stood for a moment in the entrance, temper bringing a high color to her face. She must have been listening at the door. "Anna cost me the moment I have worked for my entire life. And you reward her for this?"

The hard contours of Mama's face softened. "I am sorry, Catherine. If Anna does not marry Lord Markson Worthing, her reputation will be ruined—and yours, by association, will suffer."

Catherine's eyes narrowed. "You are making Anna marry Lord Freddy because she kissed him? Unchaperoned?"

Mama blinked, once, as if it pained her.

Catherine lifted her chin, but she did not seem triumphant, only determined. "Why should Anna have Freddy, then? By your logic, *I* should marry him." Her chin lowered, her teeth flashed white in a smile. "You see, Freddy kissed me first."

CHAPTER 4

Following Catherine's shocking declaration, Mama wept, Papa shouted, and Catherine stood straight and unmoved. She did not once look at me, though I could see in the stiff line of her jaw what she was thinking: *You took from me what I wanted most. Now I will do the same to you.* It did not matter to Catherine, particularly, whom she married so long as he supported her study of magic and her position in society. Freddy would do nicely.

I said nothing and let the tempest rage around me. In the end, Mama decided Papa must speak with Freddy, offering him first Catherine and then me. *One* of us should marry him.

I slipped from the room when the talk turned to logistics: when and where and how. I stumbled upstairs to find James in the corridor by my room with a book of poetry.

"Hello, Jamie, my love." I tugged at one of the dark curls tumbling into his eyes.

He batted my hand away. "What happened last night? Everything feels off today."

I tried to laugh, to lighten James's worry, but the sound caught in my throat. "I snuck downstairs to see the charm-casting and got caught. Mama was quite angry. And then this morning I went for a walk without permission—all the way to Speakers' Corner." I pushed my smile wide, hoping James would think it was all a lark.

A smile finally glimmered on his thin face. "I should have liked to see the charm-casting. What was it like?"

I thought of the shattered roses and the strange shadowy creature. *Freddy kissed me first.* Had he kissed her, I wondered, while they practiced for Catherine's spells? "Being Catherine, the spells were of course flawless."

"What were her illusions like?"

"Roses. The Sleeping Beauty."

James wrinkled his nose. "Typical. But none of that explains why Catherine acts as though her favorite dog died." He lifted an eyebrow at me. "What aren't you telling me?"

I hesitated, wrapping my arms around my middle. *I got caught kissing Freddy. Catherine kissed Freddy. I fainted in Hyde Park. A revolutionary brought me home.* The chilly April air hugged the walls of the corridor.

"I'm not a child," James insisted. "You don't have to protect me."

But I did. I had failed to protect him once, when I had let that magical fire from my Confirmation wash over him, and I would live with that failure all my life.

His health had declined after our collision: already small and thin, he had become what Mama called "fragile," prone to chest complaints and weeks where he could not rouse himself from bed. Even the best Animanti healers could not seem to help him. When James was eight, his Confirmation had been prefaced by a private consultation in Papa's library at Arden Hall. James told me later that the Circle member had not wanted to Confirm him at all, saying it would be dangerous to give such a frail child magic. But Mama, her Coremancer gifts heightened by concern for her only son, had insisted. A compromise was struck, and James was Confirmed, but granted access to such a limited amount of power through the Binding that his spells were virtually nonexistent.

Mama had not said, in so many words, that James's sham Confirmation was a judgment on my disgrace, but I knew. My heart pinged. *My fault.*

"I broke her spells," I said, coming back to the present. My words dropped in the air like stones.

His eyes widened, the pupils narrowing to tiny dots. "What will happen to you? Will Mama send you away? Will the Circle punish you?"

I ground my teeth in vexation. I should not have told him anything. I should have known this truth would only make his anxiety spiral higher. "Nothing will happen. The Circle has already spoken with me. And, as you see, I am still here. Would you like something to eat? I was about to ask Ginny to fetch a tray."

"No, thank you. I must get my studying done this morning. Papa's promised to take me to the menagerie this afternoon." But his eyes, when they met mine, were full of misgivings and not anticipation for the promised outing.

I wished Papa were not so set on sending James to Eton

in the fall, believing invigorating studies would compensate for James's limited magic. But though James was nearly as passionate about classics as Papa was about Luminate history, Papa had forgotten how cruel boys could be to those who were different. Freddy might laugh and insist the ritual humiliation of new students toughened them, but such treatment would destroy James. I knew firsthand how a weak Luminate fared in a world that revered power above all. And I was protected some, because I was a girl and not so much was expected of me.

"James," I said, "you don't have to go to Eton. Mama would hire a tutor, if you asked."

"Papa wants me to go. And I cannot stay here forever." His knuckles were white on the spine of the book.

"But it would be safer—"

James cut me off. "Safe? Maybe you want that—to stay forever at home, trapped with Mama. But I want more than that. I want to learn things. I want to meet new people, see new places. I can't do that if I don't at least *try*."

"I don't want that either," I said softly, but James was already shuffling away. As I watched him go, Catherine's smug declaration slithered snakelike through my thoughts: *Freddy kissed me first.*

How could I shield James from heartbreak when I could not even protect myself?

〤

If I had thought much about it, I should have supposed my first proposal would be a romantic thing: whispered words spoken in a garden, or, more formally, an offer delivered on bent knee in a sunny drawing room.

I would not have expected it to include nearly my entire family.

We were all assembled in the Grand Salon—me, Mama, Papa, Catherine, Grandmama, Freddy. The salon was my least favorite of all the rooms in our London town house, barring only the austere chapel: the white walls with silver trim, the fussy statuary on the marble mantel over the fire, the stiff chairs meant to encourage good posture and discourage comfort. Mama sat ramrod-straight beside me on the cream chaise longue, as though determined to enforce my good behavior through her own rectitude. Catherine sat primly on her other side.

At Mama's orders, I was arrayed in a gauzy white muslin dress, though whether as a prospective bride or virginal sacrifice, I had not yet determined. Papa faced us, as did Freddy. Grandmama sat just beyond me, in a chair near the low fire. I suppose Mama thought it would be more difficult for Freddy to wriggle out of his obligations if there were witnesses.

Freddy had arrived late, nearly a half hour past the time Papa had bid him to call on us. He removed his hat and settled himself easily, smiling at all of us and remarking on the dampness of the weather.

My pulse stuttered under his smile. I still hoped he might find a way to explain everything. Perhaps Catherine had lied, though it seemed unlike her.

"Er." Papa cleared his throat, set one booted foot over his knee, then set it back down again. "Thank you for calling, Lord Markson Worthing."

"Your note said it was urgent."

"Er. Yes. That is—" Papa broke off.

"It is a matter of my daughters' reputations," Mama said, throwing a scornful glance at Papa. "Anna was seen kissing you in the garden. And Catherine says you kissed her. Is this true?"

Freddy's eyes flared wide with shock. I felt sorry for him. It was never pleasant to be ambushed by Mama.

"Catherine—that is, Miss Arden—*told* you?"

My heart dropped. He did not seem sorry for having done it, only for having been caught.

"It is a bad thing," Grandmama said, tapping her cane on the floor for emphasis, "to be misleading two young women, and sisters besides."

"You must do the right thing," Mama said.

"The right thing?" Freddy's voice was light, yet his posture was anything but. His shoulders were rigid, his eyes flickering around the room, landing on everything save my face. He fiddled with the rim of his grey hat.

This was not the stiffness of a man in love, trying to summon his courage. This was the stiffness of a man who would rather be anywhere save here.

"You must marry one of my daughters," Mama said. "Whichever you like."

Whichever you like. I swallowed the hysterical giggle bubbling in my throat. I wished Freddy would cast a Lucifera spell making the floor open beneath me. Heat washed up my neck and burned in my cheeks. I studied the carved lily patterns in the carpet so I would not have to watch Freddy's reaction to Mama's words.

"Ah." A long, uncomfortable silence settled in the room. Freddy broke it at last. "I am, of course, flattered you would consider me as a possible husband for either of your lovely daughters. But, unfortunately, I am not the marrying type."

I am not the marrying type. Each word was a dart, pricking my skin. Taken separately, the pain was slight. Taken collectively, I caught my breath at the sting. I gripped my hands together, my nails cutting into my palms.

"I do not see what that has to do with anything," Mama said, her voice rising. "You have compromised them both. If you do not marry one of them, what man will want them? Particularly Anna, who does not have her sister's beauty or her magic."

"I am sure you overstate the matter," Freddy said. "Miss Anna is a lovely girl. And it was only a kiss. Two kisses. Not a promise."

Sourness bit at the back of my throat. His face was like a Greek sculpture, all perfect lines and curves and achingly remote.

"You may have given your kiss lightly," Papa said, "but I doubt my daughters did. Anna, did you believe yourself plighted to this man?"

Yes, I thought. *Maybe.* "No."

"Catherine, did you?"

"Of course. Do you think I would let him kiss me otherwise?"

Catherine was a terrible liar. But I underestimated my mother's will to have one of her daughters wed.

"Then you see you must marry her," Mama said. "Or we will sue you for breach of contract."

Freddy sprang up, snatching his hat from his lap and shoving it on his head. "This is ridiculous. I can't do this. I won't."

Anger flickered in me. Maybe I had been premature to think he might marry me on the weight of a kiss. But I *had* believed he cared for me. "Can't do what? Court me? Kiss me—and my sister? Or is it only doing the honorable thing that you struggle with?" I shook off Mama's restraining hand and stood and faced him, pausing to give my words emphasis. "I had believed you were so much more than this."

"Anna." The anger slid from Freddy's face, and he looked only tired and a little sad. "I'm sorry. I was foolish, but not malicious. I didn't mean for any of this to happen."

"Did you mean any of it?" I asked.

"I meant it when I kissed you," he said, very low. "It didn't mean anything when I kissed Catherine."

I heard my sister's gasp, but I kept my eyes fixed on Freddy.

"But it was a mistake. I realized that at Catherine's debut. I—I heard people talking about you, after. I can't marry you."

A strange high buzzing filled my ears. "Why?"

Catherine's voice sliced at me. "Surely you must know, Anna. Freddy needs to marry power. And you haven't any."

The flush in Freddy's cheeks confirmed her words.

"So this is to be all?" Mama asked. "You refuse us?"

"I must go," Freddy said, turning toward the door. "You're welcome to bring a suit against me, but I doubt it will prosper. It will only serve to embarrass your daughters." In the doorway he stopped and whirled, his eyes meeting mine. "I *am* sorry, Anna. If there had been any other way—if you had any magic at all . . . I shall always remember you."

Mama began whispering furiously to Papa as soon as the

door fell shut behind Freddy, but I did not hear her. Freddy's words rattled around in my skull.

I did not want to be *remembered*.

I had only wanted to be loved.

)(

Barton's heavy knock on the door interrupted Mama and Papa's argument. Catherine had already fled the room, tears starting from her eyes. Grandmama had taken Mama's place beside me on the chaise longue, her arm warm around me.

The door flung open, and Barton announced Lady Berri and Lord Orwell. Lady Berri was resplendent in a particularly bright shade of yellow.

I dropped my head in my hands. My day had wanted only this.

"We met Lord Markson Worthing on the street. Such a charming young man," Lady Berri said. "Is there to be an announcement?"

"No announcement," Papa said.

"A pity—" Lady Berri began.

Lord Orwell spoke over her: "We did not come here to share gossip, but to examine the girl."

"Oh, do hush a moment," Lady Berri said. "It won't help our task if the young lady is upset." She turned to Mama. "You can rely on our discretion. It is not our intent to create a scandal for your family."

The tightness around Mama's eyes lightened. "That is very kind."

"To business, then," Lord Orwell said. "We've come to examine the girl."

Alarm shot through me. I cast a look at Papa. Hadn't he said no studies?

Lord Orwell held up a sheet of paper, covered with elaborately curving calligraphy and marked by an impressive seal with Queen Victoria's rearing lion and unicorn. "I'm afraid you can't refuse. Circle business."

Grandmama's arm tightened around me.

"On what grounds?" Papa asked. "She's still a child."

"She broke a spell with no apparent effort," Lord Orwell said.

"An accident," Papa said.

"You must see how serious this is. A child who can casually break a small spell might break a much larger spell, with deadlier consequences. And the Binding is not so secure as it once was." Lord Orwell arched his eyebrows at Papa. "But perhaps this has been your plan all along. There are rumors, you know."

Mama moaned. "Oh, Charles."

Papa said, "I'll not deny I think society would be better without the Binding, but I'm not so foolish as to attempt to break it myself—or to urge my untrained daughter to do so! I know our laws as well as you."

Gooseflesh prickled along my forearms. The radical, William Skala, opposed the Binding. That made sense, for one coveting Luminate magic and position. But why should Papa? He had nothing to gain from such a stand, and everything to lose.

"You heretics are mad," Lord Orwell said. "You believe the Binding restricts the use of magic, but that is folly. In fact, the Binding spell strengthens our power by giving us access to magic we might not possess individually. It protects us from injudicious spell-casting and from . . . other threats. Breaking the Binding would only weaken our magic."

"The Binding preserve us," Grandmama whispered, echoing a prayer I'd learned in childhood.

Papa did not look convinced.

The radical's words in the park floated back to me. I asked, "Is it true that magical ability has nothing to do with bloodlines? I heard someone say the Circle only grants magic to families who can afford Confirmation."

"Nonsense," Lord Orwell said. "Magic has everything to do with bloodlines—without Luminate blood, we would have no magic."

Papa opened his mouth to speak, but Mama closed her hand around his forearm and he fell silent.

Lady Berri said, "We believe your daughter may be a danger—both to herself and to others." She swung toward me with the majestic mass of a ship at sea. "Come here, child."

"Anna," Grandmama whispered, "you do not have to do this."

"I'm afraid she does, Lady Zrínyi," Lady Berri said.

I crossed the room to her, though I wanted to face the Circle even less than I had wanted to sit through my parents' proposal to Freddy.

My father wore his scholar face: narrowed eyes, intent focus. Mama looked pale. At some unspoken signal, Lady Berri took my right hand and Lord Orwell my left. They began reciting long, sonorous phrases in Latin. Lady Berri's hand was warm in mine, Lord Orwell's callused and dry.

They stopped speaking, and I concentrated on the silence, trying to hear or feel something of the spell they cast. Nothing.

My eyes followed an insect (a bee, perhaps?) tapping gently against a window. Then warmth flooded me, like the first flush of embarrassment. The warmth intensified, tracing lines of heat through my body.

No. I knew this feeling. I knew what happened next.

The heat exploded into flame, as if my entire body had caught fire from the inside out. Heat flared behind my eyes, across my chest, down my limbs, and into my fingers and toes.

I tried to scream, but the sound was swallowed by the blaze in my throat.

Lady Berri must have sensed my distress, because she released my hand. The flames flickered once, then died. I took a long, shuddering breath and shook my other hand free of Lord Orwell's grip.

"Odd." Lord Orwell's bushy eyebrows pulled together over his nose.

"What happened?" Grandmama's voice was tight.

My body, which had been overhot, was now cold.

Lady Berri frowned. "I . . . am not sure. Usually a soul-scry reveals the shape of one's soul and one's natural affinity for a magical order. In rare cases, a scry may uncover any hidden spells or *geas* that impede spell-casting. But Anna's results are . . . indeterminate. At any rate, I have never seen anyone react so strongly to this ritual, which suggests that something else is at the root of your daughter's condition."

"We'll need to study the girl further, at our offices on Downing Street." Lord Orwell nodded at my father. "Perhaps with a blood sample we could—"

Papa cut him off. "I've said before, my daughter is not some specimen for examination and dissection."

"I'm afraid you may not have a choice," Lady Berri said. A look passed between her and Papa that I could not read. "But I promise you, I will see to it she is safe."

And with that we had to be content.

CHAPTER 5

After Barton ushered the Circle members from the room, Papa sank into his chair. "I suppose that settles it."

"Settles what?" I asked. "You can't mean to let them experiment upon me."

"We'll have to send you away," Papa said.

A great weariness slipped over me. "I suppose you will send me back to Dorset."

"No," Mama said. "You will accompany your grandmother to Hungary. You will be gone some months, time enough for the scandal to die down. It is to be hoped when you return you will behave as a proper lady ought."

"It is to be hoped," Papa said, "that the Circle will lose interest in you during your absence. I care less for the scandal than for your safety."

"You will love Hungary, Anna," Grandmama said. "Such

a beautiful country. And generous people. We can stay with my cousin János for the summer. Eszterháza is a remarkable estate—the Hungarian Versailles, people call it, where Haydn used to compose symphonies for the empress Maria Theresa. I spent the happiest summers of my childhood there. I believe János has a great-niece and great-nephew staying with him. They lost their parents, *szegények,* but I am sure they will be good company for you. And in the fall we can go to Buda-Pest, when the Luminate gather in the cities."

I tried to smile at the joy in her voice, at the already thickening accent. But my heartbeat thundered in my ears. So this was my fate. Instead of marriage to Freddy, I was to be packed off to a country on the fringes of civilized Europe. Why not Paris, if I must leave England? Or even Vienna? Hungary might be Mama's and Grandmama's birthplace, but it was so *far.*

Leaving England would mean abandoning any hope of a debut, a legitimate place in Luminate society, for a society that spoke a language I did not understand and lived by rules I did not know. There were Grandmama's stories, of course, of a paradoxical people who could "weep from one eye and laugh with the other," a people who laughed when they mourned and wept when they were joyful. Stories of a fiercely independent folk who had swept into the Carpathian basin and terrorized Europe before being subjugated themselves, first by the Turks and then by the Austrians. Grandmama's stories of Hungarian history were littered with tragic heroes: I grew up believing that to be a hero in Hungary meant you had to die.

I loved Grandmama's stories.

But I did not know how to live in them.

※

Catherine barged into my room that evening while Ginny was brushing my hair.

"I'm not sorry you're going," she said, crossing to my dressing table and examining a tiny vase.

"I had not imagined you would be." I swallowed. "I am sorry for what I did at your ball. You were rightly angry."

"Papa says you're not to be blamed for your . . . *defect*." She whirled, and the uneven candlelight picked out the shadow in her cheek where her jaw was clenched tight. "Perhaps not. But I *do* blame you for choosing to come there with Freddy. I'm glad he won't marry you."

"I'm glad he won't marry you either." Let Catherine take that how she would. The Freddy I had seen that morning would not have made either of us happy.

That surprised a bitter laugh from her. "I never wanted Freddy. But it stung to think he preferred you. I knew he did, for all I let him kiss me."

She swooped toward me, a cloud of lacy nightdress and vanilla scent. Into my ear, she whispered, "I've not forgiven you yet . . . but do try not to drown on the crossing."

※

Papa came later, as I was shredding the handful of notes I'd received from Freddy and stuffing them into my wastebasket. He did not seem to notice what I was doing, instead crossing my room to stand at the window. A low light burnished the edge of the sky. Above, inky blackness scrolled behind the stars.

"They were not wrong," he said. "The Circle, when they called me a heretic. I have studied Luminate history for a long time. It is becoming increasingly clear to me that the Circle is using the Binding, which they once sought to preserve and protect, to increase their own power. Once, Luminate had access to all manner of spells. Now they have only the charms of the order the Circle decrees for them. This control worries me, as does the widening gap between Luminate and the rest of society. I stand by my beliefs, but I am sorry they have brought trouble on you."

I went to his side, tucking my hand into his as I used to when I was small. "It was not your fault. *I* am the one who broke the spell."

He sighed. "Debutante spells have gone awry before. I am afraid my reputation made them look more closely at you than they might have done otherwise."

I tightened my grip on his hand. "I would not have you change your beliefs just to make things convenient for me."

My father lost some of his tense look and kissed my brow. "You're a good girl, Anna."

I wasn't, but I was glad my father believed it. "I'm sorry I disappointed you."

He was silent for a long moment, his throat working without words. Then: "You could never disappoint me, Anna. I just want you to be safe. And happy."

I understood what he could not say: *I forgive you. I love you.*

I raised myself on my toes to kiss his cheek. "I love you too, Papa. I will miss you. Write to me?"

"Of course."

X

James came last of all, tapping on my door so late I was already in bed, reading by the guttering candle. His eyes were bright with anger. "You said nothing would happen. But you're leaving!"

He evaded the hand I stretched toward him. "I don't want to leave."

"Then don't."

"It's not my choice." I heard the pain in my voice and hastened to add, "In any case, you will be leaving in the fall for Eton. You won't miss me for long."

For answer, James turned scorching eyes on me. His eyes were dark—like mine, like Mama's, like Grandmama's. Hungarian eyes. I realized his anger was not at me, not precisely. He was just coming to realize what I already knew: we were both of us trapped in a course we had not chosen.

His would take him to Eton, to suffer through Luminate contempt.

Mine would take me to Hungary.

CHAPTER 6

The Continent, late April 1847

I stood on the deck of the ship, my fingers tight against the railing, and watched the white cliffs of Dover disappear above the grey water. The wind whipped my hair into my eyes, and the sea salt stung my cheeks. Above me, the air was full of black-and-white guillemots. Their raucous, trilling cry filled my ears.

Ginny stood beside me, offering the support of her presence without comment, for which I was grateful.

I would not see Freddy in Europe. He was bound to England, to his plans for Parliament, and his Luminate life. I would no longer have to confront his loud absence, or wonder, walking in Hyde Park, if I would see him. *This is a good thing,* I told myself.

I almost believed it.

Behind me remained everything I knew, nearly everyone I cared for. Ahead of me—I could not seem to see past the crashing waves. Grandmama assured me there would be society in Hungary, that the Hungarian Luminate would not place as much value on magic as the English. I hoped she might be right, but that hope seemed a tenuous thing.

My fingers were numb when we reached the shore.

A thin, exceedingly elegant Austrian gentleman met us at the docks in Calais, holding up a hand-lettered sign with Grandmama's name: LADY ZRÍNYI.

Grandmama frowned at him. "Where is the majordomo I hired?"

"Alas, circumstances conspired against him. He could not come. I have been sent in his place. My name is Herr Steinberg, and I assure you I will take the best possible care of you." Herr Steinberg adjusted his spectacles and bowed us into a waiting carriage.

※

I sat by the window in our shared stateroom aboard a luxury steamboat and counted German castles as Herr Steinberg named them for me: Koblenz, Stolzenfels, Kamp-Bornhofen, Rheinfels, Katz. After spending our first night in Calais, we had traveled northeast to the Netherlands, where we took a steamboat down the Rhine. Byron's Childe Harold had come this way too, I remembered, exiled and alone. An impoverished German Luminate entertained the passengers with illusions. A ring of fire and a crouching dragon around the largest of the castles, a knight in armor in the air above the yellow crenellation of another. Ginny watched with us and clapped her hands in delight.

Near the village of St. Goarshausen, the river skirted around a jutting rock cliff. At its base, our magician cast another illusion: a lovely maiden sat in sunlight, drawing a comb through her golden tresses. Herr Steinberg explained this was one of the Lorelei, a siren maiden who sang sailors to their deaths. The illusion, naturally, had no sound, but as we passed, a low humming lifted above the noise of the steam engine.

The moment was perfect: the sunshine mellowing the landscape, the murmuring water and the faintest hint of real danger to give the story a thrill. I found myself storing up details to share with Freddy before remembering, with devastating suddenness, that Freddy no longer cared to hear such details from me.

I gripped my hands together, my nails pricking my palms.

A slight catching sensation, as if the air about me had thickened, and the illusion shifted. Like dense fog parting to reveal the brick and balustrades of a building hidden only moments before, I caught a glimpse of something under-neath the lovely bright maiden: another woman, her eyes like embers and her hair tangled around her head like some drowned Ophelia. Her mouth opened, exposing pointed teeth, and I caught an echo of a song, like something famil-iar but forgotten.

I gasped.

Herr Steinberg shot a sharp look at me. "Are you well?"

"Did you see that?" I asked. "The other Lorelei maiden?"

"The *other* maiden?" he asked, removing his glasses to look at me more closely. "But there is just the one Lorelei." He paused for a moment, inspecting my face. His usual pleasant expression was gone, replaced with fierce intensity. "What did you see, Miss Anna?"

I glanced back at the rock, now behind us. I saw only a smiling face and a fall of golden hair.

What *had* I seen?

"Nothing," I said at last. "A shadow."

Herr Steinberg did not allude again to that episode, but in the weeks following, I caught him watching me more than once, a worried line drawn across his forehead.

҉

We arrived at last in Vienna, and Grandmama insisted upon buying me new dresses—lovely, grown-up gowns with full bell sleeves and skirts that swept the floor when I walked. The dresses necessitated the purchase of a new, stiffer corset: when the stays were cinched tight, I could scarcely draw breath.

We attended the opera one night, the opera house as splendid as I had imagined, a riot of gilt and red velvet and heavy curtains over the stage. I smoothed the shell-pink satin of my skirts, unease drawing cold fingers up my spine. What if someone were to recognize me for what I was: a young lady who had been sent from London in disgrace? An impostor? I forgot my fear during the performance, Mozart's *Die Zauberflöte,* but it returned again during the interlude, as a steady stream of visitors came to our box. When none of them perceived anything untoward about me, I began to relax. And when one of Grandmama's old school friends invited us to a ball the following night, it confirmed the evening as one of the most pleasant of my life.

Though I was not technically "out" in society, Mama had given Grandmama tacit permission—that is, she had not forbidden it—for me to attend social events in the hope I might acquire *some* polish.

The next night, Ginny buzzed around our rented rooms in growing excitement, helping me dress for my first ball. Standing before my mirror, an emerald silk taffeta gown pooling about my feet, with heavy lace falls at my throat and wrists, I scarcely recognized myself. The skirt was gathered and tucked into elaborate poufs, and it billowed around me when I walked. A mixture of excitement and terror prickled through me. I fingered my topaz necklace and wondered how much it mattered that I was not also adorned with a soul sign, the social symbol of magical worth.

"You look lovely," Ginny said. "Those German lords will be fighting to dance with you."

I grasped her hand. "I wish you were coming with me."

She shook her head, her ginger curls dancing. "Nay, I'd not fit in with such company."

"Perhaps I shan't either."

"Nonsense. Your blood is just as good as theirs."

But not my magic.

Ginny whirled away to fetch my shoes and did not notice my failure to respond. I may have been born Luminate, but Mama had made it clear to me that though I might be tolerated by society, I would never be embraced.

Herr Steinberg appeared promptly to usher us to the ball,

in a neoclassical mansion near the Hofburg Palace in the center of the walled city. Someone had gone to great effort to construct an illusion guiding guests into the building: either the family was extraordinarily powerful or they had powerful friends. Over my head, branches of gold, silver, and palest green trees stretched brittle fingers. Exotic birds flew from tree to tree: a phoenix with a tail of flame, a gigantic golden eagle, a bejeweled nightingale. Pale fire circled the entrance.

A small crowd of commoners gathered, watching the illusions with wide eyes and open mouths. Two guards stood at the fringes, ensuring no one pressed too close to the Luminate entering the building. A thin girl, only a little younger than myself, darted past one of the guards and rushed toward me, her hands outstretched.

"A *kreuzer,* miss?"

My hand dipped automatically to my reticule. The girl's dress was ragged and her cheeks bore the hollowed-out look of someone who did not eat frequently enough. But before I could press a few small coins into the girl's hands, a wall of air shot past me, striking the girl and knocking her to the paving stones.

I sprang forward and crouched down beside the girl, trying to help her up. She shrank back from my hand, her dilated eyes fixed on something behind me. I whirled to see one of the guards trotting toward us, his mustache quivering. Herr Steinberg followed him.

"Leave her be. The emperor Ferdinand has issued orders that the lower classes are not to disturb Luminate events. This girl should know better," Herr Steinberg said.

"But she's starving," I said. "A few coins won't hurt me at all."

"If you give money to one, we'll have hordes descending upon us. She must learn her place."

He held out his arm to escort me toward the gleaming illusions where Grandmama waited, dismayed. I ignored him, turning back toward the girl, but she had already melted into the crowd. I scanned the faces, looking for hers, and found row upon row of glittering eyes. These people hated the Luminate—and feared us too. *I am worried about the gap between Luminate and others,* Papa had said.

I let Herr Steinberg lead me back to Grandmama. We stepped through the fiery doorway, embraced by light but not heat, and left the streets behind us. Our short, rotund hostess smiled and kissed Grandmama's cheeks in the European manner when we were introduced. Then she turned to me, patted my cheek, and told me I was *ein schönes Mädchen*.

The theme from the entry continued in the ballroom, with lights picking out the shapes of enormous trees on the ballroom walls. Another phoenix swam through the air overhead. I accompanied Grandmama to a chair near one wall and sat beside her. As the music swelled around me and dancers swirled past, I could not seem to shake my encounter on the streets. The divide the guards wanted to enforce between that girl and me was as artificial as the illusions gracing this ballroom: the product of money and magic. But for an accident of birth, I might have been her. She might have been me. I shivered, feeling alien in my own skin.

A spotty young gentleman approached us, before halting a few paces from me, his eyes fixing on the bare spot above my collarbone where my soul sign should have been. Abruptly, he swung around and marched off.

Grandmama put her hand over mine and squeezed. I shrugged. I did not care if a spotty gentleman preferred not to dance with me. The music eddied and fell around me, and my feet tapped to the rhythm. The hostess brought a tall young gentleman to us to be introduced. He bowed, and professed himself flattered, but I marked the way his eyes lingered on my absent soul sign, and he did not ask me to dance.

Only one man asked me to dance, an acquaintance of Herr Steinberg's. He was large and overweight, and nearly as old as Papa. Gentleman or not, his eyes crawled over my body in a way that made my flesh creep. As he had trouble keeping his hands in the right places, I struggled free of his sweaty grip before the waltz had finished and returned to Grandmama. *Better not to dance,* I thought, *than to endure that again.*

I spied Herr Steinberg on the far side of the room, deep in conversation with a man of middling height. As if he felt my eyes on him, the second man looked across at me. His eyes were unusually light for his dark complexion. Even when his gaze had moved on, a curious crawling sensation still lingered between my shoulder blades.

Halfway through the evening, a mild tremor shook the crowd. I sprang to my feet to see the source of the disturbance: a small party had entered the ballroom, and the entire company seemed to drop as one, sweeping deep curtsies and bows. I curtsied too, my mind spinning. This must be the Hapsburg royal family. The eldest gentleman, dripping with gold medallions on his coat, must be Emperor Ferdinand, who had given the order that the lower class was not to disturb Luminate events. Beside him was a handsome boy about my age. I asked Grandmama who he was.

"That's the archduke Franz Josef. He'll be emperor after his father and uncle."

Grandmama added that the rather square-faced gentleman behind the emperor was Prince Metternich, the head of the Austrian Circle and the driving power behind the Hapsburg throne for nearly forty years. I shivered a little, resolving to do nothing to draw the prince's attention to me. I had thus far escaped the notice of the Circle in Europe. I intended to keep it that way.

I turned my attention back to the young archduke. What must it be like, I wondered, to be so young and have your future written so clearly? The Austrian empire was perhaps the most powerful nation in Europe, stretching from the Illyrian coast to northern Italy, across Austria and Bohemia, and into Hungary and Poland, almost to Russia. This boy would someday rule all of it.

I knew a sharp, savage prick of envy. I wished my own future were so certain.

A pair of society matrons walked past us. A tall, thin woman in a silver gown said, "I cannot comprehend why Lady Isen allows such a thing in her home."

"Shocking, indeed. Barrens should be kept away from decent society. We know they exist, of course, but no one wants to have their existence paraded before our eyes." The second woman, in a pink taffeta gown much too young for her, fluttered a fan at the sausage curls by her ears.

69

My blood seemed to freeze, then flooded my face with a rush.

Grandmama squeezed my hand again. "The Austria-Hungary I remember was not like this."

She was not alone in overhearing the insult. A young red-haired man approached us, his blue eyes blazing with indignation. Unlike the others, he spared no glance at my missing soul sign. He walked directly to me, caught my hand, and pulled me into the waltz just forming without waiting for a proper introduction.

"You!" I said.

"Me," said William Skala, the Scottish radical from London. His tone was lightly mocking.

"What are you doing here?" I thought of the crowds kept back from the gala by Luminate guards. "How did you get in?"

"I've been trying to find you for weeks. I asked about you after our encounter in Hyde Park. I heard you broke your sister's spells. And that day in Hyde Park, you broke mine." He laughed at the surprise in my face. "Yes, for my sins, my father was a minor Polish count. I was Confirmed like the best of the Luminate, and I admit I find small magics useful purely for showmanship. As I *am* technically Luminate, I'm grudgingly allowed through the doors. But the Luminate world and I have no great love for one another."

He had asked after me—and found me in the heart of Europe. If he could find me so easily, could the Circle? The ballroom, which had been mildly warm, closed around me. I tried to pull my hand free, but his fingers tightened on mine.

"Don't go. I need to talk to you. We could use someone like you. Every revolution in the last two hundred years has failed, except Napoleon's conquest of France. Do you know why?"

Of course I knew. "The Circle keep us safe," I said. It was a prayer I'd learned in childhood. "The Binding preserve us."

"The Circle doesn't merit your prayers. There's nothing divine about it."

"What do you want from me?"

"You break spells. I want to see if you can break the Binding."

I nearly stumbled. Only Mr. Skala's grip kept me from crashing to the floor. "Even if I could do that, what could you possibly hope to achieve?" I said before remembering that Papa thought society would be better without the Binding too.

Mr. Skala curled his lip. "You've been brainwashed by the Circle like every other Luminate child. I'd hoped for better from you—I've heard your father is a man of sense."

He swirled me past Herr Steinberg, who watched us with a slight frown. "Understand this: the Circle uses the Binding to restrict who has access to magic, and its members use that control to rule as despots everywhere. Even in England, though the Queen tempers them some. The Circle wants you to believe that magic belongs solely to noble bloodlines. But this is not true. If magic were strictly hereditary, it would have made its way beyond Luminate families by now, through marriage outside the class or infidelity. But we see magic just within Luminate ranks. Why? Magic doesn't care who—or what—wields it.

"But the Circle does. Somehow, the Binding spell pulls magic from everyone who might have inherited a gift for it, Luminate and commoner alike. The Circle uses its power over the Binding to control even the Luminate, shunting them into Circle-approved orders, so no individual Luminate is powerful enough to challenge it.

"Think. Only the American colonists have won independence from a Circle-governed nation, and then only because the Circle never did figure out how to anchor the Binding spell across the ocean. In the colonies, magic is a matter of aptitude, not wealth."

Mr. Skala spun me in an energetic whirl, and I struggled to keep up both mentally and physically. "But why does no one speak of this?"

"They do—in my crowd." He grinned. "In Luminate society, the only ones who care are too cowed by the Circle to speak."

He continued. "You must see the Binding is key. Without the Binding trapping magic, power could belong to anyone, irrespective of wealth or bloodline. If we break the Binding, we strike at the heart of the Circle's power. That would be the very advantage we need to overthrow them: here, in Hungary, in Poland, in France, in England."

I glanced sharply around. If anyone had overheard us, he risked imprisonment for treason. Or worse. "How do you know all of this?"

"You don't believe me, do you? I've studied for a very long time." A lurking smile lit his eyes. "Also, I've spoken with your father, and others like him."

"My *father*?" The kernel of doubt he'd planted in Hyde Park was growing now, swelling in discomfiting ways. If I had been lied to about Luminate magic, what other lies did I unwittingly believe? And why had Papa spoken so frankly with Mr. Skala but hid the truth from his own children? Was he, as Mr. Skala charged, afraid of the Circle's repercussions? Or perhaps his silence was Mama's doing. "Even if you were right, the Binding can't be broken—least of all by someone *without* magic. If you've asked about me, surely you know that too."

"I heard the rumors. But I don't believe them. Whatever you are, you're not without magic. Not as they would have you believe."

"You know nothing about me." I met his gaze with a challenge in my own. "I heard your speech, you know. But no matter how thrilling the idea of an egalitarian society, I don't believe you can do it, not without more destruction than your cause is worth. Even if I could help you, I wouldn't. I don't wish to overset Luminate society—I want to be part of it."

He glanced around the ballroom, at the men and women who had shunned me because I bore no soul sign. He lifted one eyebrow, and I flushed.

"Not society like this, perhaps, but there might be others. . . ." I trailed off, feeling suddenly ridiculous.

"They won't make you one of them, you know. No matter what you sacrifice."

The fact that he was likely right infuriated me. "I don't want to discuss this."

Mr. Skala twirled me out with a flourish. "As you wish," he said, turning the conversation to unexceptionable things until the waltz finished.

Mr. Skala returned me to Grandmama with gentlemanly

correctness, but any pleasure I had in the ball was ruined. When I asked to leave early, Grandmama did not demur.

As our carriage rattled away through the darkened streets, Herr Steinberg said, "You ought to be more careful, Miss Arden, whom you associate with before a roomful of Luminate. Radicals like William Skala could ruin you more surely than any lack of magic."

)(

Our route from Vienna into Hungary wandered through wooded hills before skirting Lake Fertő and emerging onto a marsh known as the Hanság. As the road threaded through spindly thickets, I watched a goshawk circle over the rushes before plunging toward its prey. A mile or two farther, and a purple heron moseyed long-legged among the reeds. My heart sank. Besides the birds, there was nothing here.

No society.

I was to be immured at the edge of nowhere. Somehow, such isolation seemed all the more painful coming on the heels of my failure at the ball in Vienna. I had not given up my hope of finding a way into society, but such an event seemed increasingly unlikely.

I fell asleep to Grandmama pointing out sights to Herr Steinberg and woke to the sound of our carriage wheels bumping down a poplar-lined road. My eyelids felt made of fine grit.

Eszterháza is not an estate one approaches by slow degrees, winding down a long driveway before bursting through the trees and beholding the house in all its glory. Instead, our carriage rattled directly to huge iron gates covered with a flourish of leaves.

Beyond the gates, two great semicircular wings curved around either side of the courtyard, leading to an immense, four-storied façade. Two flights of marble stairs swept up to a balcony. A large clock was set into a triangular wall above the third floor, beneath a profusion of figures and flags and weapons. I tried to count the windows blinking at us in the setting sun, but gave up well before one hundred.

I turned an astonished face on Grandmama. She had called it the Hungarian Versailles, but I had discounted that as the kind of benign exaggeration Grandmama often applied to things she loved.

"Prince Miklós—János's great-uncle—expanded his father's hunting lodge eighty years ago to rival the palaces of the French princes. People believed he was unwise, pouring his money into a swampland. But he built this."

The carriage skirted an empty fountain and drew to a stop before the double staircases. Herr Steinberg leapt out to help us exit. As I emerged, it became clear this estate was not what it at first appeared. Pale gold plaster flaked from the walls, and the trim around the windows needed paint. Weeds pushed their way through cracks in the stonework around the courtyard, and a goat munched a particularly large bush near the steps. My first awed impression faded.

Herr Steinberg led us to double doors set between the stairs and knocked.

For a long moment, we waited. Herr Steinberg knocked

again. I watched Grandmama with concern, seeing how tightly her hand gripped her cane, how deep the grooves in her cheeks were. I linked my arm through hers. Why was no one answering? Surely they knew to expect us.

At last, a scuffling sounded behind the door, then it creaked open. A young maid stood in the doorway, not the butler or footman I had expected for such a large estate. Though the girl was pretty, with fair hair and blue eyes, her clothes were extremely untidy. Large streaks of dust marred her once-white apron, and the black dress she wore beneath the apron was tattered at the hem. I could not help thinking Mama would never have tolerated such slovenliness, and was surprised when such a prosaic thought hurt. After a month away, I missed even Mama's sharpness.

"Ach, Himmel!" the girl said in German to Grandmama, and I remembered that most of the Hungarian Luminate were bilingual, governed as they were by Austria. This close to the Austrian border, no doubt their servants were bilingual too. The maid continued in German, "You must be Lady Zrínyi." I watched a blush rise in the fair cheeks. At least the girl had some sense of appropriateness. "Come in, please."

We stepped into a large, shadowy room with high, rounding walls and delicate floral reliefs. An arched glass door led into another, larger room beyond. From a nearby corridor came ecstatic barking, followed by the sharp click of canine nails on parquet floor. Then a rusty streak barreled directly into me, and I fell to the floor in a tangle of skirts.

An exuberant canine stood over me, his forelegs on my shoulders and his hind legs on my skirts, preventing me from rising. The animal breathed gustily into my face. It seemed scarcely possible to feel any lower than I did then, buried underneath a small mountain of dog. I wondered which of my rustic cousins owned him.

The maid squeaked an appalled "Oroszlán! *Nem!*" She clapped her hands, and the dog retreated. I sat up cautiously, rubbing my stinging elbow.

"I am sorry," the maid said, her face nearly scarlet with embarrassment. "Oroszlán, you see, loves visitors. We do not have many."

Herr Steinberg helped me to my feet. Grandmama was laughing, though she tried to hide it in a cough. The dog—Oroszlán?—bounded over to Herr Steinberg and put his paws on the man's shoulders. Herr Steinberg looked discomposed but said nothing, merely lifting one paw at a time off his person and then excusing himself, saying he would be more comfortable in a nearby *csárda,* but he would return the following day to see how we got on.

Grandmama watched him leave, then turned back to the girl. "It is a very handsome animal," Grandmama said in German. "Is it yours?"

"Yes." The maid laughed. "He thinks he is a lion, a king of everything."

The serving maid keeps a dog in the house? Mama would never have allowed such a thing. Nor would she have permitted a maid to keep her guests talking in the entryway when they were newly arrived from a long journey.

I squared my shoulders. I was tired, I was hungry, this palace was both dusty and smelly, and if Grandmama would not say anything, I would.

"Bitte," I said, using the German a decade of governesses had drilled in me. "Will you tell the family we are here?"

The maid turned her blue eyes on me in astonishment, her chin lifting. "Oh! I am sorry. I supposed you knew. I am your cousin Noémi."

CHAPTER 7

I stared at the girl. How could this dusty, disheveled creature be my *cousin*?

Noémi flung herself around and marched, shoulders stiff, through a doorway and up a twisting staircase fringed by a wrought-iron railing. We trailed behind her. The staircase terminated in a relatively plain hallway: I caught a glimpse of gilt and mirrors in something that might have been a ballroom to my right, but my cousin was already disappearing down the hallway and through a series of high-ceilinged rooms. Many of these stood empty, the plaster of the walls chipped and peeling, only a few chairs remaining from the last century, their woven covers faded and worn.

I'd stepped into a fairy-tale enchantment—a kingdom waiting for a hero to awaken it from its curse. This house had been beautiful once. Grandmama had told me the entire Viennese court had come here with Empress Maria Theresa to listen to Haydn play. Now it appeared nearly abandoned.

At last we came to a small parlor, the walls lined in pale green brocade. Unlike many of the rooms we'd passed through, it was well cared for. A ceramic stove dominated one corner, its mock marble finish and gilt flourishes gleaming in the fading light.

In a corner near the stove, an older gentleman with an impressive mustache puffed away at a pipe, his arms resting on the round bowl of his stomach. A pair of Lumen lights hung in the air beside him. He set his pipe, still smoking, on a side table and greeted Grandmama with an old-fashioned kiss on her hand.

Grandmama introduced him as her cousin János, and then they began chattering together in the Hungarian of their childhood. As Mama had deemed German sufficient for foreign tongues, I knew only a few homely phrases in Hungarian from Grandmama. I stood awkwardly near the door until Noémi gestured to a high-backed chair near my grandmother. I removed my bonnet and sat, wondering at my cousin's look. The mulish cast of her lips suggested she was still upset with me, perhaps because of my unintentional slight at the door. But it was a silly thing to take offense at. Anyone might have made that mistake.

"Noémi," János said, switching back to German for my benefit, "send word to Cook we want something to eat, now our company has arrived."

Noémi cast a quick glance at me, a blush rising up her neck and into her cheeks. "János *bácsi,* it is Cook's half day, remember? I will bring some bread and cheese, if you like."

"No need. Send the maid for it."

Noémi only nodded and disappeared from the room.

János watched her leave with a bemused expression. "I cannot seem to persuade her that she does not need to do the maid's work."

"Of course she does." A new figure breezed into the room. "When one of the maids is down with the toothache and the others have gone home to prepare for *Pünkösd,* what else would my sister do but help?"

"Mátyás! Dear boy. Come, meet my cousin, Lady Irína Zrínyi, and her granddaughter, Miss Anna Arden." János smiled, the waxed tips of his mustache quivering. "My grand-nephew, Mátyás Eszterházy."

Mátyás turned around to face me, and I got my first good look at my distant cousin. He was tall and broad-shouldered, wearing a light wool coat with embroidered seams, and no more than a handful of years older than I. He was not unpleasant-looking, with his high, broad forehead and strong chin, but the slightly rounded cast of his cheeks and his sleepy-looking eyes made him seem somehow childish and unformed, despite the golden mustache he bore. If I had harbored a faint hope that flirting with Mátyás might drive away any lingering longing for Freddy, I was disappointed. This was not a face to haunt my dreams.

I stifled a sigh.

Mátyás bowed, loose-limbed and graceless. "Welcome to the heralded family estate," he said, sitting down at János's feet. His German was flawless, better far than mine. "How were the roads from Vienna? Interminable? Marshy?"

I smiled. At least, if not precisely a scintillating wit, my cousin had a sense of humor. Grandmama answered Mátyás's question at length, describing our route, the hotels we'd visited, and the lovely time we'd had at Vienna.

Sometime during Grandmama's discourse, Noémi returned with a serving platter filled with breads, cheeses, and some dried fruits. She handed me a plate, and I attempted to apologize in careful German. "I am sorry, cousin, if I offended you earlier. I had supposed you were the maid."

Another of those unreadable expressions flickered across Noémi's face. "Please do not apologize. Do not patronize me because you are the fashionable English lady and I am the poor cousin." She pulled a small packet of letters from her pocket. "These came for you."

Then she moved on to János. Watching the stiff line of her back, I marveled I had ever mistaken her for a servant.

※

Ginny ran a brush through my snarled dark hair. Her fingers were gentle, the repetitive motion soothing.

My eyes swept the high arched ceiling with its delicate tracery of roses. The room was grand enough, but the furnishings were sparse. A four-poster bed, a small rug on the floor, a vase of dried lavender on a bedside table. The vanity where I sat was carved with rococo exuberance, but the gold paint was beginning to flake and the wooden legs were battered.

Ginny set my brush on the vanity and squeezed my shoulder encouragingly. "It will come right, Miss Anna. You'll see. I have a good feeling about this place."

I smiled at her, more from politeness than agreement.

Ginny left, and I settled into my bed and picked up the letters, reading them by the fitful light of a small kerosene lamp. How could I shatter Catherine's spells and yet be incapable of carrying even a Lumen light?

There were two letters from James, both very short. Another letter, a bit longer, from Papa, adjuring me to enjoy my first glimpse of the world. He described meeting with Lady Berri and Lord Orwell, who asked where I had gone. *I returned a vague answer that you had gone into the country,* Papa wrote. *But be watchful. They might yet come looking for you.*

Gooseflesh prickled up my arms. I was nothing in their world—if I could break spells, I knew neither how nor why.

So why this continued interest?

)(

There was rain that night, hammering like a fusillade against the glass panes of my window. I lay on a stiff feather mattress, staring into the darkness. I had passed the point of exhaustion and could not sleep. This room, *my* room now, smelled strange to me—of sage and lavender and dust.

Scenes played over and over again before my eyes, like a finely crafted illusion. Freddy, in the garden, leaning in to kiss me. The unraveling spell in my parents' ballroom. Catherine's smile when she announced Freddy had kissed her. The red-haired William Skala predicting a Luminate fall in Hyde Park and then confronting me in Vienna. And the last: the hollow-eyed, sharp-toothed woman I'd seen beneath the Lorelei illusion.

Around and around my head they danced. The familiar

faces stretched, becoming monstrous through overexamination until I no longer recognized any of them.

Ж

A wild, unearthly music splintered the air, riding on the echoes of pealing bells.

I jolted upright in bed, my heart thumping. I was still trying to catch my breath when Ginny nudged open the door with a breakfast tray.

"What is it?" I asked.

Ginny smiled. "It's Whitsunday. There are Gypsy musicians in the courtyard, and most of the village has come for breakfast. Your grandmama tells me it is customary."

I settled back against my pillows. Whitsunday, the seventh Sunday following Easter. At home there would be fetes and a special sermon. I swallowed down a sting of homesickness and let Ginny help me dress.

Later, after I drowsed through a Hungarian sermon, the villagers spilled onto the bit of green lawn before the Romanesque church, wearing their holiday finery: the men in brilliant white shirts with dark, embroidered vests and wide trousers, the women in blouses with puffed sleeves, wide skirts, and aprons covered in floral handwork. Some wore kerchiefs over their hair. In my dark green gown, with its pointed waist and moderate sleeves, I stood out among these colorfully dressed folk like a crow among peacocks.

Wooden trestle tables groaned with food in the sunshine. I scanned the offerings, but they were mostly unfamiliar: rich meat dishes with savory sauces, potatoes with cream and herbs, sausages, miniature dumplings, and so many pastries. I settled on pastries as the least likely to disagree with me. I stripped off a glove and reached for a golden brown morsel. My mouth watered at the sweet smell—until I bit into something with the taste and texture of grit.

Mátyás watched my face as I tried to chew and swallow. He laughed. "Poppy seeds."

When Mátyás was not looking, I rolled the remainder under the trestle table for a bird to find.

"I wonder why you are here if you are determined to dislike everything," Noémi said in German beside me. I started a little—I had not seen her approach.

"I—" I stopped. I doubted my prickly cousin was interested in either Catherine's broken spells or Papa's fears for my safety. "Grandmama wished to come."

"And did she warn you? About Whitsun night?" The brim of her hat cast her eyes into shadow.

"There's nothing to warn of." Mátyás frowned.

Noémi ignored him. "Tonight is a night of unrest." A chill pricked me, as if that word, *Unruhe,* were enough to rouse the ghosts of the nearby cemetery. "In Germany, evil spirits walk this night. In Bohemia, not so very far away, *rusalka* are stronger now than at any time, able to leave their watery graves and crouch in trees, or hide in the fields, luring innocent victims to their death. And here the *lidérc* watch for unwary sleepers."

I knew the *lidérc* from Grandmama's stories: a midnight lover, hatched from the first egg of a black hen. A demon lover in some tales, a hoarder of gold in others. The *rusalka* was, perhaps, Slavic—I did not know it.

Noémi smiled, a stretching of her lips that didn't reach her eyes. "Did you know our Hungarian word for nightmare is *lidércnyomás*? That feeling when you wake suddenly from sleep and cannot breathe for the pressure on your chest." She raised one white hand to her own chest to demonstrate. "That is the *lidérc* sucking the life from you."

"Stop trying to frighten her," Mátyás said. "*Lidérc* and *rusalka*—they're just stories to scare children."

"I'm not frightened," I said.

"Very well," Noémi said. "But I'd not walk alone tonight."

$$\text{X}$$

I could not seem to shake the uneasy prickling from Noémi's words, even through an afternoon of games in the fields beyond the churchyard, including a horse race for the Whitsun King crown—a role that brought no kingdom, but a year's supply of beer and wine at the local *kocsma*. Mátyás won easily, breezing through the finish line to rowdy cheers. Noémi tossed a poppy chain across his horse's withers.

Mátyás dismounted and turned a face full of boyish delight to me. I extended my fingers, meaning simply to shake hands, but Mátyás caught my hand and pulled me into a tight embrace. He smelled of sweat and sun and made me feel hot and cold together.

Perhaps he felt my rigid surprise, for he released me almost at once. He turned to view the crowd gathering around him and pumped his arm in the air. *"Hajrá!"*

The crowd echoed back, *"Hajrá!"* A few scattered voices added, *"Éljen Mátyás úr!"* Long live Lord Mátyás!

A second cry ripped through the crowd, and the cheers died. In the middle of the field, a stocky man snapped his whip down on a young man in the white linen trousers of a servant. A dark horse limped a pace forward and collapsed behind the boy.

I knew the sound of a whip, of course, the sizzle and sharp crack. But somehow, the sizzle and crack and slap against human flesh was like nothing I'd heard before. My stomach twisted.

The boy flung both hands over his head. Even at this distance, I could see his white sleeves crisscrossed with blood.

"Stop!" Mátyás shouted, in German and then in Hungarian, struggling through the crowd. The others whispered and some of the women cried, but no one else moved. Mátyás pushed forward until he was next to the two figures.

He did not, as I expected, shove the stocky man back. Instead, he stood beside him, talking quietly, his hand outstretched. The man with the whip nodded and folded the whip under his arm. He offered the bridle of the lamed horse to Mátyás.

The boy still knelt huddled between them. Mátyás did not look at him or speak to him. The stocky gentleman backhanded the boy, knocking him into the mud of the churned-up meadow, then stalked off.

When the man had disappeared, Mátyás finally turned his attention to the boy, helping him stand and escorting him to an older woman wailing nearby.

My cousin came back to us looking grave. "It is a bad business. The horse will need to be shot, I think."

"The *horse?*" I asked. "What about the *boy?*"

"The squire," Noémi said, her voice tight, "needs a bridle more than this animal."

"The horse was injured while the squire's boy was riding him. The squire had money hanging on the race, and to lose the horse also . . . Well . . . he blames the boy."

"But to *beat* him?" My stomach was tight with the lingering horror.

"The boy belongs to him," Noémi explained, though her mouth twisted. "He is a serf."

A serf was little better than a slave. I swallowed something sour. "Why didn't anyone stop the squire?"

"And who should? The Circle excuses him because he is Luminate, and because under Hapsburg law, he is the local magistrate. Here in Hungary, we are entirely subordinate to the Austrian Hapsburgs, just as they are subordinate to the Austrian Circle. And why should they care what becomes of a serf?" Mátyás looked back at the field, where the horse was struggling unsuccessfully to rise. "I must put my horse down."

"*Your* horse?" Noémi echoed in surprise.

"I bought it from the squire. It was the surest way to stop the beating."

"But how will you pay for it?" Noémi caught his sleeve as he stepped away from us. "Not gaming. Mátyás, you promised."

Mátyás shook her off, a frown starting between his brows. He stalked toward the field without looking back.

※

Dinner that night was quiet and uneasy, all of us sitting at a long, formal table in a room too large for so few. The white

walls had been painted in the Chinese style, an elaborate or-
namental garden sketched in blue, with warriors and sages in
exotic costumes strolling through it. I studied the peaceful,
frozen scene and wished I might step into it.

János said, "There are likely to be Gypsy musicians tonight, Miss Anna. You'll want to keep your distance."

No one spoke about the beating in the field.

After dinner, Ginny helped me into my favorite new dress,
purchased in Vienna: an amber-colored gown with double
rows of ruching above the hem and blond Brussels lace falling at the neck and about my wrists. I was dismayed to arrive in the entry hall and discover we were not to drive to
some nearby estate but to *walk* back to the green outside the
church. Once there, my heart sank even lower as I studied
the assembled dancers.

I had hoped this dance might redeem my failure in Vienna. I knew how to sweep into a ballroom, my skirts held
just so. I knew how to curtsy to the appropriate degree—
when I chose to. But I did not know how to sweep into a
dance conducted outdoors, on a patch of earth. I did not
know how to keep my long skirts or fine shoes from getting soiled by the grass and the dirt. The women's skirts,
cut high to show an expanse of ankle, seemed much more
practical—if a touch scandalous.

And the dances! I'd expected dances that one might find at
any society ball: schottische, polka, quadrille, waltz, Roger
de Coverley. Each of these I knew. Mama, for all she doubted
my future in polite society, had seen I was properly drilled.
And truth was, I loved dancing—the music, the twirl and
swish of dresses, the color and energy.

But I did not know these strange round *csárdás* dances,

these whirling dances to energetic but discordant music. So as Noémi and Mátyás were drawn, laughing, into the swirl, I stood alone, watching. Herr Steinberg, who lingered still in the village, asked me to dance, and the two of us tried to fit the steps of a polka to the music playing. It was an ill fit, and I was less than cordial when we parted.

János took center stage during a cessation in the dancing. At his signal, the Gypsy musicians took up a mournful tune, and János flung his hands upward. Water droplets materialized in the air around his head, each lit with a tiny flicker of colored light. They danced through the air, swirling above the entranced crowd. The music crescendoed, and the water droplets coalesced to a horse-shaped wave, galloping across the night sky. A final flourish, and the horse shattered. A fine mist settled over the assembled crowd, a cooling kiss after the exertions of the dance. Three cracks of lightning split the sky, the finale to his Elementalist spell, and János bowed to much applause.

Then it was Mátyás, whistling two high notes in the air. A murder of crows descended from the sky, their wings inky against the gold horizon. They circled above his head before diving toward the crowd, who shrieked and ducked low. Mátyás laughed, and the birds lifted, their raucous cries echoing his laughter. Other birds followed: white egrets with their yellow feet, red-backed shrikes with their grey heads and masks, short-eared owls with banded tails. They swirled through the air in an intricate dance, weaving in and around one another in response to Mátyás's silent persuasion. He clapped his hands, and the birds vanished as swiftly as they'd come. A tiny piece of my heart went with them, and I coveted my cousin's gift.

The crowd turned expectantly to Grandmama, who laughed, waved her hand, and protested she was too old. So the crowd turned to me.

I shook my head, anxiety crawling up my throat. The villagers clearly expected some kind of Luminate performance. But what could I do? Ask János to cast another illusion so I could break it, perhaps sending fire through the fields? Unthinkable.

Noémi, Grandmama said, would not be asked to perform. Like Mátyás, she was Animanti, her magic working on living things, but she had focused on healing spells, which were not suitable for display.

With a kind of collective sigh, the musicians struck up again and the crowd returned to dancing. I sat beside Grandmama to watch, but a movement caught the periphery of my vision.

I squinted into the shadows between two houses. Like the other Hungarian villages we'd passed, the village near Eszterháza consisted mostly of houses strung along a rutted main road, like shells on a bit of twine. Behind the houses spread fields, silent and fathomless under the star-bright sky.

There. Something *was* moving. My first thought was some kind of animal—a cow or horse, perhaps. But no animal would carry that faint nimbus of light.

My heart leapt into my throat. I remembered Noémi's words: a night of *Unruhe,* of restless shades and shadows. Who was in the field? Whoever it was moved erratically, the light blinking in and out of sight.

I set my lips together. Probably some villager.

No. Something about the light wasn't right: it was neither the flickering gold gleam of a lantern nor the steady, otherworldly blue radiance of a Lumen light. It looked, in fact, as though the stranger were wearing gloves of moonlight, a steady silver glow limning his hands and spreading up his arms. I'd never seen a Luminate illusion like that—and it seemed odd that a spell-caster would waste magic on that kind of illusion rather than the simpler Lumen light.

I inspected the dancers and the crowd beyond. Mátyás and Noémi still danced with the others. Herr Steinberg stood at the far edge of the crowd, a drinking mug in hand, while János sat at Grandmama's far side. The squire was there too, though I noticed the villagers made a wide berth around him.

Whoever the light-bearer was, he was not one of the local Luminate. Likely, it was a Luminate stranger passing through, wandering the fields on foot. I edged toward the field, my curiosity piqued.

He might be a ghost, Noémi's voice whispered in my ear. I brushed the idea away as one might a bothersome gnat. Ridiculous.

I glanced around once more. No one paid the least attention to me: even Grandmama was enthralled by the dancers. I slipped into the shadows, hiking my skirts up to an unseemly height as soon as I reached the field beyond the houses. The light bobbed in the distance, silver against the tree line.

I frowned. Something about the situation nagged at me, a piece that would not fit. Why should a Luminate nobleman skulk about a relatively insignificant field at night? Why not call on the local landowners? Surely, he was up to nothing good.

An improbable idea struck me, momentarily robbing me of breath. What if the man in the field were not Luminate at all? Mr. Skala said people from all classes had once practiced magic. What if someone had found a way around the Circle's restrictions? It seemed impossible—and yet I could not shake a growing hope.

Whatever the source of this light, I had to know for certain.

I stepped into the field. In the spring night, the plants—whatever they were—had not yet achieved their full growth, for which I was grateful. Even so, in my dainty dancing shoes, I slipped and lurched on the loose earth.

For a moment, I lost the moving light. I stood motionless in the quiet field. Overhead the stars shone and the moon cast a faint tracing across the ground like hoarfrost. In the distance, the echo of the fiddles sounded plaintive, almost lost. I considered going back.

But no, there was the light again, in the copse of trees ahead. I plunged forward, weaving my way through the trees, my eyes fixed on the soft glow. My skirts caught on some kind of thornbush, and I wasted several moments trying to free myself without ripping the delicate fabric. At last, my patience at an end and fearful of losing my way, I simply tore free.

To my right, I could hear the gurgle of water. Between the dark bars of trees, silver moonlight glinted off the surface of the stream. My mind filled with images of drowned maidens, their hair spread like a veil across their faces. I touched the rough bark of a nearby tree and looked up, but the canopy of new leaves was so thick it blotted out the stars from the night sky. My shoulders tensed as I moved forward; if a *rusalka* or *lidérc* crouched in the tree above me, I would not know it till she sprang upon me, her nimble fingers tearing at my face and throat.

I cursed Noémi under my breath. If she had not succeeded in scaring me earlier, she had succeeded now.

I lost the light-bearer again. In the fitful darkness, I felt the first real stab of terror—not the almost-pleasant frisson of alarm that came from scaring myself with fancies, but gut-wrenching fear. I could feel my shadow self stirring in panic and let her rise. What did it matter now if I were less than perfectly behaved?

Something seemed to snag in the air around me, as though I had walked into a spider's web. But when I batted at my cheeks, I could feel no silk filaments. I shuddered, imagining the creature somewhere on my body, skittering beneath my clothing.

I could not see the way forward; behind me, the trees were closing ranks and I could not see the way back either. I could still hear music, distantly, but it seemed to come from all sides.

A soft hissing like wind in the trees sounded behind me—but there was no wind. I froze, hardly daring to breathe. My heartbeat thrummed in my ears. I glanced around, squinting into the gloom.

There.

Something stirred, a subtle difference of shade on shadow. Something with a sinuous, nonhuman movement. I stepped forward, setting my foot down with the precision of a dancer, trying to stay silent. One step, then two, then three.

The shadow-that-was-not-a-shadow crept forward too.

I took a few more steps, and the thing kept pace with me. It was *following* me.

I had lost the glowing stranger entirely now. The darkness gathered around me like a living thing, waiting to spring. I pressed forward, keeping the gliding shadow in the edge of my vision. I knew, somehow, with the certainty one gets in moments of high emotion, that I had far, far more cause to be frightened of the thing behind me than whoever was before me.

By the time I'd made it out of the trees, into the comparative brightness of a moonlit meadow, I was ready to weep. The thing following me was still there, though it had made no attempt to draw closer. As I moved out into the meadow, I watched the rim of trees. A shadow detached itself from the grove and crossed into the moonlight. The vaguely human shape had no features I could make out, only a mouth like a gaping wound.

"Free us."

A breeze caught the words and tossed them against my ears, tangled them in my hair. Then the shadow multiplied into one, two, three, four shadows, all of them melting toward me in the meadow, with tendril-like arms outstretched. But there were no hands on these arms, and no fingers.

"Free us."

I screamed then and began to run. I slipped and stumbled across the field, dragging at my skirts, and staggered up a slight hillock. I continued to run even as the earth dropped away beneath me.

As I fell, I glimpsed a young woman emerging from a thread of silver water with a face straight out of my nightmares: immense dark eyes studding moon-pale flesh, dark hair clinging in drowned clumps to the sides of her face.

Rusalka.

CHAPTER 8

I tumbled down the far side of the hillock. Small and not-so-small rocks banged against my body as I slid, coming to a gasping halt at the water's edge. My throat hurt from screaming.

The creature by the water cried out too, her voice eerily human, the way a cat's cry at midnight sounds like a baby.

More lights blossomed along the bank. Dark shapes massed and ran toward us.

I tried to stand, to flee, but my ankle pulsed with pain and would not hold me. I collapsed back to the ground.

The shapes drew nearer, and I saw they were nothing monstrous, just people, their lights only flickering torches. Some were men, hatless in the night. Others were women in long, striped skirts and clinking necklaces: Gypsies.

This should have alleviated my fears—after all, Gypsy

musicians had played at the procession this morning and again for the dancing. But lost as I was, my mind was full of warnings: Grandmama, telling me not to speak with the musicians; János, more bluntly, adding Gypsies were not to be trusted; and a half-remembered scene from Miss Austen's novel *Emma,* where Emma and her friend Harriet are attacked by Gypsies.

An argument was unfolding on the banks of the river, an older woman shaking her fists at the girl—it was only a Gypsy girl bathing in moonlight after all, not a *rusalka.* The fists spoke a language I knew: *You should be ashamed of yourself.*

The girl hung her head, her arms sliding protectively around her wet torso. But then she straightened and flung her hand in my direction, and dozens of eyes fixed on me.

None made a move to help me. The girl slipped away, no doubt stealing back to camp and drier clothes. Chanting rose on the air, and music. I could see now the distant yellow glow of campfires across the stream, the pale outline of tents.

I shut away the memory of the things that had followed me. Surely I had made shadows into monsters, as I had turned a Gypsy girl into a *rusalka.* But my ears still held the echo of those haunting cries.

Free us.

I tried again to stand, and failed. I held my hand out toward the crowd. *"Bitte helfen Sie mir."* Help me, please. They shifted and muttered, but no one approached me. I could not tell if they did not understand me or chose to ignore my plea.

I swallowed, trying to ignore the burning in my ankle. The night air pricked at my face, cold where the sweat dried against my cheeks, the nape of my neck.

The music ceased abruptly. I heard angry shouting. Those

nearest me turned toward the sound, their faces tight. The crowd began to melt away, slinking toward the camp. I thought of the long, impossible walk back to Eszterháza—I no longer knew in which direction—through shadow-infested woods, and sniffed. I would not let myself cry.

A girl slipped through the crowd and crouched beside me, laying her hand on my arm. "Shh." A dark-patterned kerchief covered her hair.

A young man followed her, carrying a small lantern. He spoke to the girl in a language I didn't recognize, touching her temple lightly and then lifting a strand of wet hair from beneath her head covering. *The girl from the water.* In the light of his lamp, his face was all angles and shadows and almost unbearably beautiful—the words of a Byron poem come to life in a wild midnight spell.

Then his burning eyes fell on me, and the whole aspect of his face changed, hard and cold. He spoke to me first in Hungarian, and then, when I didn't respond, in German. "What are you doing here?"

"I lost my way." I lifted my chin so this Gypsy wouldn't think me pitiable.

"You should not be here. You are *gadzhi*—a foreigner. You're unclean." His dark eyes swept down my dress and then he turned away as if he were ashamed of what he saw, as if I were a loose woman in Covent Garden with her bodice cut low and her skirt hitched high, rather than a young lady decently covered by a rather lovely Viennese gown (if now the worse for wear).

A spark of indignation lit me, warming me in the evening air. How dare this *Gypsy* accuse *me* of being unclean!

"I hurt myself." To prove it, I pushed myself upward. Pain

99

shot through my ankle, radiating up my leg, and I crumpled. The girl rushed to my side, slipping a thin arm around me and supporting my weight on her shoulders.

As I caught my balance, I glimpsed an old woman watching us from the stream bank. She flicked her hands toward me, palms down and then up, as one does when shooing off crows in a field or a feral dog. Her words were unfamiliar, but her meaning was clear: *Go away.* The young man turned and called something to her. His words were calm, placating.

The girl beside me sighed. She said something in Hungarian, and when I did not respond, pointed to my leg, then looked a question at me.

Does it hurt?

"A little," I answered in German. "I should go." The pain ratcheting through my body was now augmented by increasing social discomfort. I was not wanted here.

The girl ignored me and whispered something under her breath, catching my right hand with hers.

A stone bracelet at her wrist began shining with a silver light. The glow spread across her palm and lined her fingers before sliding across our joined hands like gloves of moonlight. A slow warmth suffused me, the pain in my ankle beginning to recede. A healing charm? In London, only trained Animanti could cast such spells, as a healing charm took considerable power and mastery. A poorly spoken spell could intensify rather than erase the pain.

My heartbeat quickened, and not from my pain. I was right. There was magic here—and non-Luminate magic at that. Perhaps my adventure had not been so ill guided. If *Gypsies* had found a way to use magic outside of the Binding spell, surely I could do the same. "Please—how are you using magic?"

The young man turned back at my words and sprang forward, grasping the girl's arm and tugging her away from me, breaking the charm. His voice was sharp with disapproval.

My weight crashed onto my ankle, and I nearly toppled before the girl caught me.

I ignored the stab of pain. "Can you teach me your spell?"

Her eyes were wide, uncomprehending. I wished desperately that my Hungarian was better.

The older woman was shrieking now, her voice tinged not just with anger but with fear. A shudder swept through me. At once, I wanted nothing more than my plain bed back at the palace. "Please," I said, "can you help me home?"

"I will take you." The young man's German was clipped and hard. He called to a pair of men still standing nearby, watching. One disappeared into the shadows and emerged a moment later with a horse, a long, leggy creature with a dark coat. The young man swung himself up in a single fluid movement, and the girl helped me toward the horse. The young man reached down, grasped my arms, and yanked me up in front of him. I cried out in surprise and some not-inconsiderable pain, and then we were cantering forward.

"Thank you," I said stiffly. I was not used to being man-handled. Or to riding bareback.

"Pull your skirts down," my rescuer said.

My skirts bunched around my legs, exposing an indecent amount of skin. Cheeks burning, I tried to tug them down. I straightened and wound my fingers in the horse's mane, praying we'd be home swiftly. "I'm Anna Arden."

Grandmama would be horrified that I introduced myself to a Gypsy, but I had to say something to fill the silence straining between us, and my name seemed a small thing to give him for his aid.

"You should not have come here," he said, ignoring my introduction.

To your camp? Or to Hungary? I swallowed a ridiculous urge to laugh. Of course I should not have come.

"Did no one tell you what night this is? It is not safe to be abroad alone."

Noémi had. I had not believed her.

"Might I know your name?"

A long pause. Then, "Kovács Gábor." He gave his name in the Hungarian way, surname first.

The faint fall of the horse's hooves and the slow breaths of my reluctant rescuer boomed in the silence between us. His arm was secure around my waist, his chest warm against my back. He smelled nice, of green things and sunlight. From the rigid way he held himself, I gathered he was no more comfortable with our proximity than I was.

Our route took us within hailing distance of a copse of trees. I turned my head toward the fields, so I would not see the shadows that were not shadows. A faint breeze stirred the moonlit plants around us. Everything looked peaceful.

Then I heard it again, the faintest suggestion of words. Almost, I could pretend it was only the sighing of the wind, but the words were too distinct. *Free us.* I released the coarse hair of the mane and clapped my hands over my ears.

Gábor stilled. The horse beneath us kept moving, but I could tell the rider's attention was elsewhere. Could he hear it too?

His breath was warm on my neck as he bent forward. "Hold on." The muscles in his thighs flexed alongside mine as he spurred the horse forward. His arm tightened around my waist.

I turned my head so my cheek lay against his chest and tried not to see the blackness streaming across the field, shadows against the moon-pale earth where nothing existed to cast a shadow. Our heartbeats hammered counterpoints to one another.

Free us.

A shadow snaked across the horse's coat, sending the poor beast sidestepping wildly for a moment. A second shadow curled up my arm and slid across my cheek before withdrawing. Fear tasted sharp and bitter in my mouth.

And then we were past the field, riding onto the rutted road to the village, and the shadows, whatever they were, dissipated into the midnight air. The streets were quiet, but Eszterháza, when we approached, was ablaze with light. My heart contracted. I had not considered how my absence would distress Grandmama.

Gábor stopped just beyond the ring of light cast by the Lumen lanterns at the front door. He swung himself down and helped me dismount.

"Can you walk?" he asked.

I tested my ankle. It hurt, but held. "Yes."

He swung back into the saddle.

"Won't you come in?" I asked.

"No." The monosyllable was like a slap. His hauteur, forgotten during our shared run of terror, was back.

I fought an unladylike glare. "I'm sure my grandmother would wish to thank you."

"No. I'll take no thanks for a duty that brings no pleasure. Next time you choose to go slumming, my lady, pick a time and place less likely to get you killed."

While I struggled to form a coherent response, he whistled sharply and was off, the horse's hooves clattering against the cobblestones.

CHAPTER 9

Grandmama pressed her hands against her heart when I entered the parlor, where she waited with the others. "Thank all the Saints that Bind! What happened? Are you all right?" She frowned at my dirty and torn dress.

"I'm fine. I got lost and I fell."

Noémi's eyes bored into me, but I would not give her the satisfaction of knowing her stories had any effect on me.

A maid came into the room with tea, and under the cover of the clatter, I buried my face in Grandmama's shoulder. The shock and pain and exhaustion of the evening came crashing down on me. Grandmama stroked my hair with gentle fingers. "Are you sure you are all right, *szívem*?"

I was quiet for a very long time, trying to swallow the childish plea bubbling up inside me. I failed. "Please, can we go home?"

The gentle fingers stilled. Grandmama sighed. "Not yet. Your mama does not wish us to return until Catherine is safely betrothed."

That might be ages yet. I stood, wobbling a little on my ankle. "If you'll excuse me, I should like to retire."

"Noémi, can't you do something for her?" Mátyás asked.

"I am afraid I have exhausted myself dancing." Noémi looked up from the cup of tea she nursed near the fire. "But I will bid you good night, cousin. Sweet dreams. Be sure you do not count the corners of your room."

"I beg your pardon?"

Grandmama hushed Noémi, a fine line of irritation drawn on her forehead. "Only a silly folk custom: if you count the corners of your room, you will remember your dreams."

)(

Grandmama followed me to my room and sat on my bed, watching my face in the mirror while Ginny brushed out my hair.

"You mustn't let Noémi get to you, *szívem.*"

"I make it a point not to mind unpleasant people," I said, wincing as the brush caught in another snarl.

Grandmama shook her head at me. "She deserves your pity more than your scorn. It has not been easy for her. Her father gambled away their estate, her mother's dowry, her own portion—everything. Then he could not live with the shame, and he shot himself. Her mother died shortly after. She lived with her Eszterházy cousins for a time in Vienna, while Mátyás was at school, but—it is not easy to be the poor cousin.

When János invited them here, to help with the estate, they came gladly. But this is not the life either of them sought."

I looked down at my hands, still dirty and scraped from my tumble down the hill. I knew how it felt to be thrust into a life you did not want. I promised myself to be kinder to Noémi.

Ginny helped me undress and settled me in bed. "I'm glad you're home safe." Her smile wrinkled her nose. She bobbed a curtsy at Grandmama and left.

Grandmama sat beside my bed with a collection of Hungarian fairy tales. She had read to me nearly every night as a child. Somehow, the familiar cadence of her voice in this unfamiliar place raised stinging tears in my eyes. I blinked them back.

"It was long ago," Grandmama read, "and far away, over forty-nine kingdoms, beyond the Operentsia Sea, beyond the glass mountains, and beyond that to a kingdom beneath a pearl sky." She described a beautiful reed maiden, the king who loved her, and the wicked girl who trapped the king in marriage. Her voice soothed my fraught nerves.

After she left, I stared at the ceiling of my room, the carved rose vines dimly visible in the moonlight sliding between my half-drawn curtains. *I should close them.* But my ankle throbbed and I was disinclined to move. Noémi's words rang in my ears: *do not count the corners.*

One.

This was ridiculous. There was no reason for my breath to hitch as I began counting. No reason to feel that something beyond mere curiosity drove me. I did not need to remember my dreams, not after that night.

Two. Three.

I would not do it. It was clear Noémi was only toying with me, trying to frighten me. I could not decide if she was malicious or ignorant or both.

Four.

Nothing happened. The moonlight streamed serenely through the curtains, pooling on the floor. The shadows stayed put, as well-regulated shadows do. Eventually, I drifted off to sleep.

Hours later, I woke with a start. There was a pressure on my breast, as if something heavy weighted me down. I threw the blankets from me, but the pressure did not abate. I sat upright, both hands flying upward to settle on the warm, bare flesh at the base of my neck. Nothing. There was nothing there.

And then I remembered.

In my dream, a creature had crouched on my breast, long, tangled hair framing its face, two burning pits where eyes should be. The feet that pressed so heavily into my chest were goose feet, a mundane detail made all the more terrifying by its incongruity.

Lidércnyomás. Nightmare. The pressure of a *lidérc* before feeding.

The blood-red lips opened, revealing a mouth of needle-sharp teeth. I cringed, anticipating the creature's foul breath and the sting of pain. But the breath was sweet, like honey.

And the only thing that came from the creature's mouth was a word: *"eloldozva."*

)(

When I asked Grandmama in the morning, she said the word meant "free." Or perhaps "unbound." She wanted to know, where I had heard it.

"I dreamed it." I stirred some honey into my tea. "I counted the corners of my room."

Grandmama looked up from a bit of bread and jam, her forehead pinched with concern. "Some say you will dream truth if you do. What did you see?"

A creature out of folklore. A story. "Nothing," I said.

⽊

While my ankle healed, I was confined to the palace and its grounds. I slept most of the first two days, exhausted by the journey across Europe and the terrors of Whitsun night. By the fourth day, my gait had improved noticeably but my temper had not. I was bored.

"Why don't you show Anna about the place?" János suggested at luncheon, tipping his pipe toward Mátyás.

I should like that. I glanced up at Mátyás with a slight smile.

"It's tiring," Mátyás complained, tugging at a small ornamented cross he wore around his neck. "Wouldn't you rather go into the village for a pint? I've a year's worth of winnings to drink through."

I wouldn't—and so we set off to explore the palace. Noémi's vizsla romped behind us, sniffling at our heels and then bounding off into darkened rooms before darting back. In English, Mátyás told me a little of the history, how the house was expanded in the late eighteenth century and then largely abandoned.

"Do you know why?" I asked.

Mátyás shrugged. "Who can say? Perhaps it was too expensive to keep up—perhaps the family merely decided it was too far from Vienna, too unfashionable. Miklós's grandson—one of János's cousins—moved most of the furniture and paintings to Eisenstadt."

"But you live here."

Mátyás quirked one eyebrow, the corners of his lips curling. "Yes. For my sins, I live here. János came here perhaps ten years ago, when his pension proved insufficient to Viennese life. I believe he asked to come—he had fond memories of the place as a child."

I smiled. "Grandmama shares those memories. Do you like it?"

For a moment I worried I had asked too much. A muscle flexed in his cheek, and my hitherto good-humored cousin looked grim. Then his face lightened. "It's not so bad. János was lonely before, and he enjoys having us. And of course, now you're here, it's infinitely better." He winked at me, and, to my disgust, I found myself blushing.

We followed a curving staircase down and wandered through a small room unaccountably full of the most exquisite china—all of which, he said, was used when Empress Maria Theresa had visited. The shelves were lined with Sèvres vases, Chinese urns, and delicate Dresden figures. The most valuable had been taken to the family's primary holdings at Eisenstadt, and yet a lord's ransom remained. On one shelf I discovered something odd: a wooden sculpture of a web-footed boy stuffing a frog into his mouth. He looked wholly feral.

"What is this?"

Mátyás grinned. "Our local legend. He was found in the Hanság and brought to Eszterháza, but he escaped and was never heard from again. Some say he lives in the marsh still."

More monsters.

We passed out of the china room into the vaulted entryway, and crossed through a pink marble doorway into a large, multiwindowed room. The floors here, like the one above in the Banquet Hall, were of white marble. Painted silver and green flower garlands, only slightly faded, adorned the walls, and cherubs gamboled overhead with roses. Three other doorways, each framed by pink marble, led out into the ruined gardens. The middle set were open, letting a spring breeze into the room.

"Behold the celebrated Sala Terrena," Mátyás said, gesturing into the room.

Something moved in the far corner. Several somethings. The strong scent of livestock was not, as I had supposed, wafting in through the open windows.

"Those are sheep," I said faintly. "In the house." Oroszlán gave a sharp, delighted bark and sprang into the room, chasing the sheep toward the far wall and scattering hay beneath him. Some escaped through the open doorway.

Mátyás grinned at me. "Well, the barns are disreputable, and János never uses this room."

I wondered if Grandmama knew.

"Keeping sheep in the house is also marvelous tonic for overinflated self-esteem," Mátyás added, and I choked on a laugh. "Come." Mátyás took my arm and tugged me toward the set of large doors opening onto the gardens. We dodged the sheep—and sheep droppings!—and found ourselves looking out at the garden that had once been the pride of Hungary. A series of paths branched out from a central fountain, most of them lost into shaggy foliage.

"There, at the end of the garden. Do you see those buildings?"

I nodded. The buildings were a smudge of darkness beyond the green.

"One was an opera house, another a puppet theater. Now they're mostly decayed, unused. Sometimes vagrants sleep there, though don't tell my sister that. And yet sixty years ago, Haydn lived here. Operas were performed monthly in the opera house. *'My name is Ozymandias, king of kings: Look on my works, ye Mighty, and despair!'*" He laughed softly. "Behold how the mighty are fallen."

"You know Shelley?" I asked, too startled by his familiarity with the English poet to make a witty comment on the fall of modern empires.

Mátyás flashed his grin, a dimple flickering into being in one cheek. "Of course. My education has included all the essentials. How to identify a fine vintage. How much to wager at the racetrack. And of course, how to seduce pretty girls through poetry."

Seduce? Only as he said this did I realize how close he stood to me, trapping me against the wall beside the door. Mátyás put one hand on the wall and cupped my chin with the other. Even Freddy had never stood quite so close as Mátyás did now, so close I could feel the heat of his body and see the fine gold stubble on his chin. So close he loomed over me, taller, broader, denser, more physically *present* than Freddy ever had been.

I froze. I did not want Mátyás to kiss me.

A tiny bloom of excitement unfurled in my stomach. Did I?

Before I could make up my mind, his lips were on mine, butterfly soft. The fine hair of his mustache tickled my skin, not unpleasantly. Feeling surged in me, a yearning I had almost forgotten since Freddy's kiss in Grandmama's garden. It was thrilling and terrifying at once. Mátyás pressed his lips more firmly against mine, and pleasure sent fireworks pinwheeling through my body.

No, I thought, my rational self reasserting control over the boiling stew of emotion. I put my hands on Mátyás's chest, fighting the urge to curl them into his shirt and pull him closer. Instead, I shoved. Mátyás staggered back, nearly tumbling over a sheep.

"Don't," I said, wishing my breathing did not sound so ragged. "Ever. Do that. Again." My entire head burned, even my ears. Mátyás, to my chagrin, appeared utterly untouched by our encounter. His color was smooth, his smile steady.

"I won't," he promised. A beat, then his dimple flashed. "Not until you ask me."

CHAPTER 10

I passed a bakery, the smell of yeast and fresh bread heavy in the air, my heart thumping. Any moment now, I expected someone to question why I was in the village alone, for Grandmama to notice my absence and send Ginny after me. But no one approached. I walked by the *kocsma* with its usual collection of afternoon drinkers lounging on the wooden benches. Surprisingly, Mátyás was not among them. A thin man in a fine suit turned swiftly away, though not before I'd caught the glint of spectacles. Herr Steinberg? Surely he'd returned to Vienna already.

Beyond the chapel and the row of whitewashed houses with their thatched roofs, I left the road to cross the open field, heading west and south—toward the Gypsy camp. As I walked, I kept one eye on the dark fringe of trees at the edge of the field. The trees, I had learned, marked the edge of the Eszterháza estate. Rationally, I knew I had nothing to fear from the shadows of Whitsun night in bright daylight.

But I watched the trees all the same.

Insects hummed lazily. An unfamiliar bird fluttered past me, exotic in its black-and-white-banded wings, its orange crest. I paused at a glinting stream to splash water on my face and neck before following the stream bank past a gentle rise. I could smell campfire now. A short distance beyond the hillock and I spotted the first of the tents, simple sheets of fabric draped across a pole held upright by two more poles.

The camp bustled with activity. Women stirring cook pots, children running between the tents, dogs rolling around underfoot. I could not see many men—only one or two, in the distance, grooming a horse.

My feet halted. This was madness. My welcome last time had been less than cordial. What would happen if I were discovered now, without the excuse of injury? Being yelled at was unpleasant enough.

But I could not turn back. If the Gypsies had a way to use magic without being Confirmed, I had to know it. The Circle officiant had told Papa I was Barren, empty of magic. But when I had told Mr. Skala as much at the ball, he had not believed it. And indeed, if Luminate drew all their magic from the Binding, then my inability to perform spells might only mean that my Confirmation spell had not worked. If there were other ways to use magic, perhaps they would work for me. At the least, they might work for James.

A couple of children spotted me and came running. They tugged at my sleeves and laughed and held out small brown hands. My first instinct was to pull back, as if they might pollute me. I shook myself. The children, though poor, were clearly well cared for: their cheeks glowed with health, and their lack of self-consciousness around strangers bespoke someone's loving solicitude.

The older child, a boy with a bare torso and long pants, tugged at my sleeve again and held out his hand, palm upward, with an imperious gesture.

Did he want money?

I pulled out my purse and dropped a small coin into his hand. He laughed and sprinted off, holding the coin high. The smaller girl watched me with wide, unblinking eyes. I gave her a coin as well, though Grandmama's warnings echoed in my ears.

Within seconds, I was mobbed by a group of small children, all shouting and jostling for place and grabbing at my skirts. I emptied my purse of coins, but the children did not leave until one of the larger children took the purse from me and shook it upside down, demonstrating it was indeed empty.

So much for a subtle approach.

The adults watched me openly now, their faces guarded.

I was about to turn back when the young woman from before approached me. She gestured at my skirt, smiling. Then she bent and tapped her own ankle, and looked a question at me.

I mustered a smile. "My ankle is well, thank you," I said in German. I had spent my convalescence collecting Hungarian words for my current errand, but I hadn't prepared anything about ankles. I took a deep breath, trying to steady my jangled nerves. "Anna, I am," I said in Hungarian. I tapped my breast and smiled.

"Izidóra." She returned my smile.

"*Kérem*. I ask nicely, teach me? Magic?"

Something flickered in Izidóra's eyes, and she cast a quick glance over one shoulder, as if she were nervous.

"No magic. I want to learn. You help me?"

Izidóra ran off.

I watched her go with some consternation. I didn't know if I should wait for her, or read her disappearance as refusal. I glanced around, looking for an answer. A small cluster of children still hovered nearby. When my eyes fell on them, some giggled and darted behind the tents. The others continued to stare. A very small boy toddled past, entirely naked, and a young woman darted after him, laughing.

I blinked, heat creeping up my neck. The English were not so casual about nudity.

"Hallo?" Gábor had approached while I was watching the children.

I thought I had imagined his face—that the angles had been enhanced by the moonlight into something impossible. But I found in daylight I had not imagined him, and my heart gave a peculiar thump. His face was all lines and shadows, his eyes large and dark. If there was a physical imperfection to be found, it was that the angle of his cheeks was perhaps too sharp, the line of his mouth stretched a hair too wide and too thin.

Also, that the heavy brows arching over his eyes were drawn together in irritation.

Heat crept from my neck to my cheeks. He must think me a dolt, staring at him so. And then I remembered his final disdainful comments, before riding away, and even my forehead burned: *Next time you choose to go slumming . . .*

I wished Izidóra had chosen anyone but this man to speak to me.

Gábor took two steps toward me, crushed me to his chest—and kissed me. Hard.

Again that flame gusted into life inside of me. I pushed it down, appalled at my own reaction, and struggled free. My embarrassed glance flickered toward Izidóra, who only grinned.

Was there something in the water here? First Mátyás, now this stranger. And even I seemed inflicted by some peculiar madness.

My fingers itched to slap him, but I reminded myself I was here to beg a favor, not cross swords, and slapping my host—no matter how provoking—would scarce suit my purpose.

Gábor scowled at me, his look hardly fitting a man who had only moments before kissed me with such intensity. "Well? You've gotten what you came for. You may leave now."

He thought I had come for a kiss? "What are you talking about?" I answered him in the German he'd used with me, sure my meager Hungarian was unequal to *this* conversation.

"You *gadzhe* women are all the same. You think it romantic to be wooed by a Gypsy lover. Do you think I have not seen this before?"

"I didn't come for a kiss. I came because I wish to learn about your magic." There. That sounded calm, even reasonable.

"No."

"I would of course pay you."

"No."

I was surprised by his outright refusal of money but soldiered on, feeling decidedly off balance. Each time I supposed I had the measure of this man, he surprised me. I tried channeling Catherine, casting my eyes down and then up, softening my voice in a confiding way that irritated me but seemed to please men. "I would be very grateful to you."

He snorted. "I'm sure you would." He bent toward me, until his face was inches from mine. "Ask one of your own kind to teach you."

I swallowed the anger pressing hot against my throat. "But I *saw*. . . ." I looked beyond him to Izidóra. "I saw her with light in her hands. And she started to heal me."

"By your laws, what you say is impossible. Only Luminate possess magic."

I was no longer certain that was true. "You don't understand. I might be Luminate born, but my Confirmation did not take. I'm Barren." I watched one dark eyebrow rise slowly, and wished I'd kept the word unsaid.

"And you think we can sell you magic?" he taunted. "Is magic a game? A bauble for rich girls to wear as they hunt an even richer groom? You ask for it so easily, as if you were asking about the fashions this season." His words were educated—eloquent, even—not something I'd expected from a Gypsy.

Angry words burned my tongue, but I swallowed them. I lifted my chin, determined to preserve the appearance of pride even as my words stripped me of it. "I don't think magic is a game. Without magic, I don't belong in my own world. But I'm nobility, so I'm not allowed to apprentice to

119

a trade either. I am useless. I *need* magic—even if I have to beg to get it."

Something in the severity of his face softened, and hope fluttered briefly inside me.

Then he shook his head. "I'm sorry. We cannot teach you what you want. What you ask is forbidden by law."

He caught Izidóra by the hand and turned away, hauling her behind him. She kept glancing back, as if she wanted to say something but lacked the right words.

My fingers dug into my skirt. Clearly, I did not have the right words either.

)(

In the days that followed, I was in a mood for mischief.

I rode a sluggish pony in the mornings on the Eszterháza grounds and tried to spur him to gallop in the field beyond. He balked, and I returned to the house muddy and baleful. I tracked herons in the grasses and laughed when my approach drove them to terrified, ungainly flight, though normally I was fond of the long-necked birds.

I hurled half-ripe apples at the Bagatelle, the ridiculously named and ridiculously expensive temple rotting in the gardens, and imagined that Gábor's face was my target. My temper was deadlier than my aim.

I played cards with Mátyás and trounced him with vicious pleasure—until Grandmama caught sight of my face and sent me to my room to calm myself.

To Mama, I wrote, *I have met an astoundingly attractive man. He is, unfortunately, Gypsy and penniless, and seems to despise me, so you need not worry about me scandalizing you yet again. Your loving daughter, Anna.*

But since my mood was not yet for self-annihilation, I tore the letter into tiny pieces and scattered them over my cold grate.

)(

Mid-June passed, and with it my birthday. Mátyás gave me a horse: a lovely, leggy mare the color of burnt wood with a blaze on her forehead. I christened her Starfire. The Circle alone knows how Mátyás paid for her—and I did not ask, afraid to learn he had pawned some of the prized Eszterházy porcelain, and I would be morally bound to give her back.

One morning, I snuck to the stable in the grey light just before dawn and saddled her. Together, we flew past the gate at Eszterháza, down the poplar-lined avenue, and into the fields beyond. We found tracks through the woods and raced across meadows, stopping only occasionally to rest and for Starfire to drink from shadow-dappled streams.

It was the nearest I had come to flying.

On horseback I was free from all expectations, free from Noémi's silent critique and Mátyás's quicksilver moods. Starfire did not care that I was Barren, that my seventeenth birthday had come and gone and instead of ordering dresses from Paris for my debut, I had traveled to Sopron with Grandmama for a village-sewn gown with red poppies spooling across a pale green silk. She didn't care that my only gifts from home were letters: a short one from Mama reminding me I had not outlived my scandal, a longer one

121

from Papa describing his research, a card with an insipid painting of flowers from Catherine, and nothing at all from James.

Starfire did not know that James was the type of boy whose happiness boiled over into words and whose silences meant he was hurting, retreating like a wounded beast to its den. She could not see how guilt pricked me, constantly repeating the refrain *I should be home*. Mama fussed over James without understanding him, and Papa rated James as he did the rest of us: a tolerable distraction from the real work of his research. Caring for James had always been my responsibility—just as his fragility was.

That day, I pushed my gloomy reflections aside and raced the wind into oblivion.

Only now I had come to the edges of a swamp, and I could not tell which direction I was facing or which direction to return. The trees had petered out, giving way to grasses and here and there the glimmer of water among reeds. Small hillocks pushed themselves up from the swampy earth, crowned with alders and willows. The Hanság.

I had gone too far.

The sky was overcast, making it difficult to get my bearings. Soon Grandmama would be missing me—and worse, discovering I had ridden out alone.

Ahead of me, a great white egret picked its way along the marsh, and beyond that, two dark figures crouched beneath a cluster of trees, a horse grazing nearby.

I took a deep breath. Perhaps they could help me.

The figures looked up when I drew near: a boy and a young man, both swarthy. With a hammering heart, I rec-

ognized the elder as Gábor. The younger boy was a miniature copy. His brother, no doubt.

I groaned. Why did it have to be *him*? My luck was decidedly out, to keep stumbling across the one Gypsy who hated
me above the others. My lips burned with the memory of
his angry kiss.

But there was no help for it. At least I knew he spoke German. I slid down from my horse.

He scrambled to his feet. "What are you doing here?"

"I was riding and became lost." I winced. I had said much
the same thing at our first meeting. He must think me a
ninny, to so often lose my way. *I do not care what he thinks.*

"Eszterháza is that way. You can see the church if you
look." He gestured behind me.

I followed his gesture and flushed. Now I knew where to
look, I could see the faintly glimmering spire. I swung back
to him. "Thank you."

His brother knelt on the creek bank, fishing something out
of the water. I recognized the movement: I'd seen James do
it often enough. Somehow, the familiarity of frog-catching
both charmed me and sent a wave of homesickness crashing
over me.

"Are you catching many frogs today?"

Gábor shook his head. "Fish. My mother thinks frogs are
unlucky. But how does as a lady know of frog catching?"

I smiled. "I have a brother at home, about your brother's
age. James. Will you eat your catch?"

"No," Gábor said, watching my face with a challenging light in his eyes, as if daring me to laugh. "I plan to
study them."

I lifted my brows in surprise. "*Study* them?"

"I hope to be a naturalist." He lifted his own brows in a distorted echo of mine. "Do I surprise you? You think because I am Gypsy I am illiterate and ignorant of science?"

"No, I——" I stopped. That was precisely what I had been thinking. "People can be many things, not all of them expected." *I should know better than most. I have spent my whole life failing at being the daughter my mother wanted.*

When his eyes flared wider, I realized I had spoken aloud. The tight-pressed line of his lips softened with something that might have been humor. "Tell me about your brother. Is he also a naturalist?"

I shook my head. "No. He wants to be a classics scholar. But he loves fishing and hunting for frogs, and I would go with him sometimes so I could watch the birds." Bird-watching was genteel enough that Mama did not object overmuch to my frequent outdoor excursions.

His gaze flickered behind me, and I twisted my head to see the egret still searching for food. "You like birds?"

"When I was young, our groundskeeper taught me to recognize them. I know most English birds by their call or the shape of their wings in flight or their coloration. But many of the Hungarian birds are new to me. Outside of my horse, I believe it's my favorite thing about Hungary." I watched the egret for a moment longer. When I turned back, Gábor was smiling at me. A real smile—the first he'd given me. My cheeks burned, and I looked away, unsure what to make of the sudden tightening in my chest.

"The Hanság is a great place for them. Kingfishers, rails, bitterns, goshawks—all kinds." His voice lifted with enthusiasm, and his posture lost its stiffness. "Someday I hope to make a full study of them." His eyes fell on his brother, who was trying unsuccessfully to stuff a silver fish in each pocket, and he laughed. "But today it is fish."

His eyes were full of affection for his brother, and my heart beat hard with a sudden, impossible hope. I said to Gábor, "You know, my brother is much like you."

Some of the stiffness returned to Gábor's shoulders. His eyes, when they met mine, were guarded.

I plunged on. "He also wants to do more than is expected of him. He goes to Eton in the fall and wants to study classics at Oxford when he is finished. But my brother has very little magic. He will be a weak Luminate in a school with little toleration for weakness. You . . . you might imagine what it's like. As a Gypsy." He must have encountered considerable prejudice. Perhaps even cruelty.

A grimace crossed his face, but his eyes did not leave mine. "I am Romani. *Gypsy* is a *gadzhe* name, not ours."

"I'm sorry," I said, committing the word *Romani* to memory. I knew something of how it felt to be named by other people: *Barren.* "I didn't know." I swallowed. "I asked you once and you refused me—but I beg you to reconsider. Please. Teach me magic. If not for my sake, then for my brother's. If there is a way to use magic outside of Luminate spells, I could teach him. He would not need to fear his differences."

"I told you before, it's forbidden." The muscle in his jaw flickered, relaxing.

"But no one need know! Surely we could be circumspect."

A long moment of silence fell between us. The wind shifted the trees. The water burbled inches away from my feet, and the toneless clattering of a nesting stork sounded above the woods. Hooves pounded the turf from somewhere nearby.

"I don't—" Gábor began.

"Stop!" A crisp, High German voice rang out. "Move away from the lady!" Both of us swiveled to find a hunter bearing down on us, his gun alarmingly aimed at Gábor. I recognized the florid complexion: the squire who had beaten the boy on Whitsunday. Gábor pushed his brother behind him.

The squire sneered at them. "Filth. How dare you approach a lady?" His gaze shot to me, his eyes flashing down my body and lingering. I stiffened. "Are you harmed? Has this creature dared touch you? Steal from you? I'm the local magistrate—I'll have him hanged before sunset if you like." He began whispering under his breath.

Tell him what he wants to hear. I opened my mouth. "He—" I clamped my lips together, fear sparking in my gut as I recognized the Persuasion spell. "Stop that at once! I am an Englishwoman. You've no right to spell me!"

"I've the rights the Austrian Circle vested in me. I'm the sworn servant of his majesty King Ferdinand. I do what I like here."

"Then you're a fool. Have you any idea how dangerous this is? Spells have a nasty habit of misfiring around me. You might have hurt yourself."

The squire paled a little. *Good.*

"And this man has done nothing save give me directions. At *my* request." Inside, I was sick, both at the squire's temerity and at the way Gábor's face had turned to stone. Whatever rapport we had shared earlier was shattered now.

The squire was already backing away, clearly unnerved. "Ahem. If you are quite all right, then I shall be going." He wheeled around.

"Are they all like that?" I asked as the squire's wide backside receded.

"Who? The local Luminate? Mostly. Your great-uncle's kind enough, but the majority have let their power go to their heads. The Austrian Circle encourages it, and the Hapsburgs do little to restrain them."

I shivered. Eszterháza seemed so sleepy and remote it was easy to forget how widely the Circle reached. I had heard rumors that the Hapsburg family I'd seen in Vienna were more governed by the Circle than the Circle by them. It seemed the rumors were true. Queen Victoria would never allow such impertinence.

"I'm sorry to hear that," I said, not sure whether I was sorry for the government's corruption or the poor reputation of my own kind. Perhaps both.

I turned back to Starfire, meaning to head home, and stopped, staring in dismay at my sidesaddle. I hadn't thought, when I slid down to ask directions, how I was to remount without a groom or a mount.

Gábor blew out a breath behind me. "Let me help you." Rather than cupping his hand for me to step into, like a gentleman would, he set his hands on my waist and lifted me to the saddle. The pressure of his fingers sent a jolt of electricity through me.

"Thank you," I said. "You've been kinder to me than I deserved."

I was not like Catherine, to see admirers in every male I met. But there was something about Gábor, something rarer than mere attraction.

Were he not Gypsy—no, *Romani*—I thought we might be friends.

Gábor's eyes lifted to mine. "Not kinder," he said, a rueful twist to his lips. "I've been as quick to judge you as you have me. I'm sorry for that." He shut his eyes for a moment, as if conceding something, then opened them. "I'll do it."

"I beg your pardon?"

"I'll teach you what you want."

My heart jumped, beating in my ears.

"But it must be on my terms, when I can arrange for us to meet safely. And your cousin must come with us."

"Noémi?" I asked, surprised he would consider the proprieties.

"Mátyás. I know him, and I trust him."

That anyone would *trust* Mátyás defied nearly everything I knew of him. But I was too relieved at Gábor's acquiescence to protest.

CHAPTER 11

After my encounter on the Hanság, it was a relief to slip into the familiarity of teatime rituals, to trade the discomfiting role of supplicant for the polish of civilized conversation and the soothing clink of china. János nursed his tea as he worked through a pile of pastries, and Noémi ignored me. Mátyás was conspicuous by his absence. I wondered if he were already drinking.

"How was your outing with Noémi, *szívem*?" Grandmama asked.

Over the rim of her teacup, Noémi's china-doll eyes met mine.

"I am so glad to see you are becoming friends," Grandmama continued.

I swallowed and set down my cup.

Noémi did the same. "What outing is this, Irína *néni*?"

Confusion marched across Grandmama's face. "This morning, you . . . and Anna?"

My heart plummeted. If Grandmama knew I had ridden so far unescorted, she'd never allow me out of the palace alone.

Noémi's face cleared—and she laughed. "Oh! This morning! Of course. Anna accompanied me on an errand."

Surprise, then relief, washed over me. Before I could say anything, Mátyás charged into the room. "I've brought a guest," he announced, but there was a note in his voice that meant mischief.

A man stepped through the door behind Mátyás, his confident posture as familiar as his red hair. My hand jerked, and the saucer on my lap clattered against the cup. Mr. Skala was obnoxiously persistent, and I disliked the ease with which he'd found me. Again. Perhaps Eszterháza was not as safe as Papa supposed.

"William," Noémi said, the smile falling from her face as if she'd been slapped.

My racing heart slowed. Maybe he had not come searching for me after all. Noémi's curt welcome hinted at some history between them. Noémi would never tell me, but I suspected I could pry the truth from Mátyás.

William bowed. "Miss Noémi. Your radiance puts the sun to shame. As always."

Mátyás said, "William, this is my great-uncle János, my great-aunt Lady Irína Zrínyi, and my cousin—"

"Anna Arden," William interrupted. "We've met."

All the eyes in the room turned toward me. William smiled. I winced.

He turned back to Noémi. "It has been a long time."

"Yes." Her single syllable was cold, unyielding.

A tense silence settled over the room. William watched Noémi, who smoothed her hands across her lap. Everyone else watched William.

"Mátyás says you have lovely gardens. Will you show them to me, Miss Noémi?" William shot an irritated look at Mátyás, who was trying to smother laughter with a cough.

"If you like your gardens ragged and unkempt," Mátyás murmured.

Noémi crossed her arms. "I should prefer not to. I have nothing new to say to you. Unless your situation has changed?"

William didn't answer.

Noémi's eyes were very bright. "I thought not." She picked up her teacup and stared fixedly at it. My heart tightened in sympathy at her obvious distress.

William stilled for a moment, then swiveled toward me, his face already taking on his familiar energy. "Well, if Miss Noémi will not show me the gardens, perhaps you would be so kind?"

I shook my head but smiled, to soften my refusal. "I think you should prefer my cousin. In any case, there truly is not much to see."

The corner of his mouth twisted ruefully. "I suppose I deserved that. Only, I do wish to speak with you."

Grandmama interrupted her sotto voce conversation with János to say, "You cannot have anything to communicate to my granddaughter in private. You can speak with her here."

William's eyes danced. "Very well. I've come to ask your

granddaughter . . ." He paused, drawing out the suspense of his announcement. He was enjoying himself too much, the impertinent wretch. Grandmama frowned, and Noémi looked stricken. Did she think he meant a marriage proposal? I knew better. ". . . to help me win a revolution against the Hapsburgs and the Austrian Circle."

My stomach flipped. He had said it.

Mátyás laughed. Grandmama looked astounded. "A what?" she asked. "You cannot be serious."

János frowned at his great-nephew. "A revolution is no laughing matter. The Hapsburgs have been kings of Hungary for generations. I own I should like to see Hungary more forward in the world, but the way to do that is through industry, not rebellion. And to stand against the Circle? You should bring war and devastation on us."

"Don't let him bother you, János *bácsi*; he's talking nonsense." I set my cup down and rose, crossing the room to stand closer to William so he needn't shout his conversation at everyone. "I've already made my refusal quite clear."

William crumpled his hat in his hands, a soft thing with a wide brim. "You have. And I thought I'd made *my* answer equally clear. I've not given up hope."

I looked out the window at the decaying gardens of the palace, tamping down flickers of anger—and something that might have been hunger. When I had dreamed of changing the world with Freddy, it was always through words, through salons and impassioned letters and parliamentary debates. But I could not deny a flicker of excitement at the idea of rebellion—of fire and passion and blood—even though I knew it was unthinkable. "Well, you should. I'll not change my mind. I might wish society were more equal, but I've no wish to unmake it."

William switched tactics. "Would you be open to an experiment? There is a place, not far from here, called Sárvár. A very old spell there, connected to the Binding, has gone awry. If you can break that spell, it would confirm what I suspect of you."

"And what is it you suspect of Anna?" Noémi asked, drifting over to join us. Mátyás followed behind her.

William turned the full light of his enthusiasm on her. Noémi blinked and shifted a step closer, dazzled despite herself. "Your cousin can break spells. I think—hope—she might break the Binding."

"You're being irrational," Noémi said. "The Binding was established to protect everyone, to provide a stable pool of energy and keep untrained Luminate from overtaxing their ability and dying. Think what would happen if you broke it: you would be unleashing all that magic, and who knows how it would settle. Or how it might affect the Luminate."

"I always did admire your mind," William said. "But you're wrong. The Binding was established less for protection and more for Luminate self-aggrandizement. Its sole purpose is to ensure that only Circle-approved nobility have access to magic."

Noémi's cheeks burned crimson. "Is this why you've come? To foment revolution in Hungary now you've failed in Vienna and England?"

"Change is coming," William said. "Here, Vienna, England—it doesn't matter. One revolution against the Circle will spark others. Hungary is the strongest of the Austrian states—if she rebels successfully, others will follow. Poland, almost certainly." A beat too late, he added, "I came to see you too. It was fortuitous that the two women I wanted to see most in the world are currently under the same roof."

"Me?" Noémi laughed, but her laughter carried a steel edge. "Don't make me a party to your madness."

"What happened at Sárvár?" I asked Mátyás, ignoring Noémi and William's continued squabbling.

"Countess Báthory—" Mátyás eyed me uncertainly. "That is, nothing that concerns you, because you won't be going."

My temper spiked. "I go where I please. You are neither my father nor my grandmother, and I do not think you have any say in this."

"Oh, do I not? I am far older and wiser—"

"Ha!"

"And I will tell your grandmother to keep you here, by force if necessary."

My fingers curled against the itch to slap him. "You are insufferable. This is none of your business."

"Please be civil, children," Grandmama said.

"It's not yours either," Mátyás said, goading me.

"Enough!" Noémi said, pivoting between William and Mátyás. "I am sick to death of both of you. Because you are men, you think your will should bind us too. No matter if you destroy our country, or break our hearts." Her voice shook, as if she were on the brink of fury or tears. She linked her arm through mine. "I shan't wish you good day. Anna and I are leaving."

When we reached the crumbling courtyard, I had recovered my composure enough to ask, "Where are we going?"

"I have somewhere I must be, and you might as well come with me."

"Why should I?" Perhaps my anger had not entirely run its course after all.

"Because it is better than being trapped in the parlor with two nattering fools." Noémi's cross look lifted when she smiled. "Besides, you owe me a favor."

Noémi led me down the dusty street of the village, to a small hut set some distance from the others. The white-washed walls were grimy with dirt, the thatched roof bedraggled and thin in spots. Noémi stepped up to the door and knocked. I stood back, eyeing the door and the house with considerable reluctance.

Angry as I was with Mátyás and William, I recoiled from following Noémi as she played Lady Bountiful, dispensing unwanted advice to the poor. I'd seen how our tenants looked at Mama, their expressions of gratitude just masking resentment. But Noémi was right. I owed her a favor for interceding with Grandmama, for hiding that I'd ridden away from the palace alone.

The door opened, and Noémi stepped in without hesitation. When I did not immediately follow, she frowned and beckoned me in.

The inside of the house was as mean as the outside—meaner, perhaps, as the only furniture on the packed clay floor was a pallet in the corner, occupied by a woman who moaned and thrashed in pain. The air in the room was rank and close. A small girl with a dirty face watched me with wide, solemn eyes, one thin finger thrust up her nose. An even smaller child clung, wailing, to the woman in the corner. Noémi scooped up the toddler and thrust it in my arms, where it continued to screech. I bounced it uneasily on my hip, and after a moment the screaming slowed. Instead, the child grabbed fistfuls of hair from the sides of my head and yanked.

Tears smarted in my eyes. I tried to set the child down, but it only resumed screaming and I hastily lifted it up again.

Noémi crouched beside the sick woman, stripped off her gloves, and laid a hand against the woman's forehead. She fussed at the woman for some time, feeling the pulse in her wrist, urging her to sip something. The older child remained unmoving, her eyes fluttering from Noémi to me and then back again. Her stillness was unnerving.

As I struggled to balance the feral child in my arms, I watched Noémi's face tighten. At last she bent near the woman, whispering a few words. Her hands flickered.

I set the child down once more. This time, it rocketed on unsteady legs toward its mother, who had ceased thrashing and lay still. Noémi murmured something to the woman, patted the older child on the head, and walked toward the door. I nearly stumbled in my rush to follow her.

"Will she be all right?"

Noémi hunched one shoulder, as if pained by my question. "I don't know. I think she's dying."

"What will happen to her children?" I thought of the small body, so warm in my arms.

"Perhaps a villager will take them when she dies. If they grow up, they will want to remember her."

"*When* they grow up," I said. "*If* she dies. You must think more positively." It was a peculiar habit of the Hungarians to say *if* instead of *when:* if I grow up, if I go home. Their fatalism was built into their language, just as British optimism was built into ours: when I am rich, when I am married. *When I have magic.*

Noémi turned eyes full of despair on me. "Mine is only a small gift. It's not enough. And there is no doctor here. János cannot afford to sponsor one, and the Viennese branch of the Eszterházy family doesn't care. There is a medical examiner in the county. But like most of our Hapsburg-elected officials, he is poorly trained and mainly concerned with maximizing his profit and minimizing his labor."

"So you heal them?"

"I do what I can. I wish I could do more."

Shame filled me. I had misread Noémi on so many counts. "Is all of Hungary like this?"

"There are hard times everywhere," Noémi said. "But it is harder for the peasants in the country. Hungarian Luminate are exempt from paying taxes, so the burden falls heavily on poor farmers. It would be better if Hungary could govern herself, but with the Austrian Circle all but running the country, there is small chance of that."

I smiled a little. "You sound like a revolutionary."

Noémi rounded on me. "Don't say that! I am nothing like William. He is like a stupid old man who believes you can heal a patient by killing him. William and my brother don't see that people have to live in a real world, where compromises must be made."

What compromises, I wondered, had Noémi been forced to make? I took a deep breath. I was not good with friendships. I had never really had a friend, outside of James and sometimes Catherine. Maybe Ginny, though it was scarcely acceptable to be friends with one's maid. I liked Noémi, despite her prickliness, and something about her face, a wistfulness in her eyes belying her words, made me sense an opening. But I had wounded her pride, which meant I would have to offer her my vulnerability.

"Do you know why I am here?"

Noémi blinked at the abrupt change of subject. "No. János is not a gossip."

"Except with Grandmama," I said, and she smiled. "I ruined my sister's debut. I spoiled her illusions. And I kissed the man she'd hoped to marry."

Noémi's mouth fell open. Then, incredibly, she laughed. "You?"

A small, birdlike hope flexed its wings in my heart. "I didn't mean to do it. I thought I was in love. I was wrong."

Her eyes softened. "Why are you telling me this?"

"Because . . . because I think I could like you, if you would only talk to me."

"I do talk to you."

"Yes. About the weather. And today's luncheon."

Noémi laughed again. I had been right—she liked frankness. "Thank you, for coming with me today. It's not easy to bear hard things alone."

"No," I agreed. "It's not."

)(

William Skala was gone when we returned to Eszterháza, on to Buda-Pest to stir up bigger and grander revolutions than our quiet estate afforded. I felt only relief, until Mátyás slipped me the note William had left for me.

Think on my offer.

I tore the note into tiny pieces. I had no patience for his games. I had my own plans to execute.

I told Mátyás of Gábor's offer, and his stipulation.

Mátyás laughed. "Gábor to teach you magic? That's a rich jest, cousin."

When I continued to stare at him, he sobered. "You can't be serious. Do you know what he risks to teach you? Gypsy magic is illegal. Verboten. Gábor could be imprisoned, or worse if the arresting officer wishes to make a point."

Fear prickled through me. "If he doesn't mind, why should I?"

Mátyás's lips curled. "I knew I liked you. I'll come."

⚸

Two days later, a village boy brought me a scrap of paper with a message in an incongruous copperplate hand: *Meet me at Hangman's Hedge in the morning.*

CHAPTER 12

Gábor's hands were in constant motion: clenching, straightening, fingers sliding in and out of one another. I wondered if he was as nervous as I was.

"What do you know about magic?" he asked.

A wind shook through the clearing near Hangman's Hedge, scattering the shadows and sun dapples across our laps. The Hedge was a quiet, sunny spot—Mátyás said a highwayman had been hanged here in the last century, and the locals avoided the spot in the belief it was haunted.

Gábor stilled his hands and waited for my answer, his dark eyes resting on my face. I told him what I knew: the Binding spell served as a reservoir of magic, and Luminate spellcasters called magic from the Binding through rituals. They pushed their magic into spells shaped by word and gesture and will.

Mátyás translated my words into Hungarian for Gábor's sister, Izidóra, who sat in the shadows beside Gábor and turned smiling lips and eyes on my cousin.

A slight frown settled between Gábor's eyes. "I have never understood how you *gadzhe,* with all your supposed education, know so little about your own power. Magic is a by-product of *dji,* the life-force in every creature. Your Binding may gather that force and hold it, but it is not its source. A reservoir is made up of many small rivulets coming together in streams and then rivers; the Binding simply collects the magic that flows from every living thing. Birth and death feed powerful magic into the Binding as well."

I began to feel bewildered. In Queen Victoria's England, children were celebrated and extended mourning indicated one's virtue—but the actual acts of birthing and dying were sterilized and strange. One did not speak of them. "I don't understand how you use magic without having Luminate blood."

"We are Romani," Gábor said, as if it explained everything.

When I only wrinkled my forehead at him, he continued. "*Romani butji.* Our work. We glean from things others discard. You Luminate are too quick to assume you know everything about magic, but even your own spells leak sometimes. We gather that surplus. Your Binding spell is not perfect: like a dam made of stones and mortar, there are places where the Binding is weak, where magic seeps through. We find those places. And there are days and nights, old holy days, when the Binding does not seem to pull magic from our world as well. We collect what we can before it's drawn into the Binding. Sometimes, we can glean magic at birth and at death, when the flow and ebb of life generates excess power. We store the magic in talismans that are enchanted to hold it."

Gábor held out his hands, his fingers splayed wide. On two of his fingers, he wore silver rings with large, polished stones. He touched one of the stones and murmured a word, and the stone came to life.

Izidóra leaned forward to show me her own charms: a necklace resting in the hollow of her neck and a pair of bracelets jangling on one wrist. Mátyás plucked at the necklace she wore, lifting it away from her collarbone. "Are you able to command much power with these?"

"Mátyás," Gábor said, a sharp warning in his voice.

Mátyás withdrew his hand, but he winked at Izidóra as he did so.

"Not much," Gábor said. "Enough for small charms only. Our charms are not like Luminate spells in any case—they could not function if they were, because magic will not respond to Luminate spells cast by anyone who has not been Confirmed. Magic responds to our charms only because we have learned to use it differently. Much like water, how you use magic changes its form: water pushed through a mill is different from the steam that runs the new locomotives, though both generate power."

"Even Luminates are not so powerful. The Circle limits the scope of Luminate magic," Mátyás said. "Once Europe teemed with firesmiths, necromancers, *chimera,* time-walkers."

"And shapeshifters," Gábor added. "Like the *táltos* daughter of Rákóczy."

"Who is she?" I asked.

Gábor glanced sidelong at Mátyás. "You tell her. She was one of yours after all."

Mátyás appeared oddly reluctant to speak. For a moment he would not look at me, only plucked at the grass growing by his feet. "This is a much-beloved story, about Rákóczy Ferenc, a Luminate who led an uprising against the Hapsburgs and their Circle a little over a century ago."

"Did he win?"

Mátyás laughed. "It is not the *Magyar sors* to win battles. He did not win. But we celebrate him as a hero anyway. We love a lost cause, and Rákóczy's was quite desperate. Austrians and Hungarian traitors were undermining his army, urging his troops to abandon him in return for the promise of imperial pardon and lands. They planned to attack his fortress while he was weakened.

"Rákóczy's daughter was a *táltos,* a shapeshifter and traveler between worlds. She transformed into a fly and listened to the plans of the Austrian army. She flew back to her father and told him of the attack, and he was able to escape his enemies."

"Are there still shapeshifters in Hungary?" I asked.

Mátyás hesitated, tearing a piece of grass down its heart. "Shapeshifters were always rare, even here. Rákóczy's daughter was one of the last. It is a difficult spell to master, and the Circle doesn't allow individuals as much power as it once did."

Something unreadable flickered in Gábor's eyes. He shook his head minutely, then pulled a small parcel from his pocket and handed it to me. I unfolded the scrap of fabric to find a bracelet of three intertwined strands of silver holding in place a round, polished stone. Thin layers of purples and blue swirled around the stone. The metal was still warm from Gábor's body. Heat crept up my neck as I slipped the charm over my wrist.

"It's agate," Gábor explained. "For protection. The first thing you must learn is to channel magic into your talisman. Once it is full, you can learn to use the power inside it." He tapped one slim finger against his lips, thinking. "The central difference between Romani and Luminate magic is the relationship between magic and the spell-caster. Luminate magic is about focus and control—about narrowing and limiting the expression of magic through spells and rituals. Our magic is about openness and submission. The way you wield the magic shapes the form the magic takes. Our spells may not be so powerful, but they do not cost as much either, in pain or wasted energy.

"The talismans connect us to other objects, animate and inanimate. To use them, you must be willing to make yourself vulnerable. The charm-caster opens himself to the essence of the thing being manipulated and persuades that object to adapt to his needs."

It sounded like so much mystic gibberish to me. My confusion must have shown in my face because Gábor blew out his breath in frustration.

Izidóra bent toward her brother, whispering and pointing at my ankle. His frown lifted. "When my sister healed your ankle, she connected with the bone and tissue. She used the power in her talisman to persuade the essence of your body to be more itself—for the tissue to attach itself

144

properly, for the bone to be whole. Romani magic can't make a thing other than it is, but we can nudge it to shift itself a bit."

"Fascinating," Mátyás said, looking, for once, as if it were true.

"But you cannot use your talisman until you can call magic into it. And for that, you need to feel the traces of magic around you, the *dji* of the living world. Close your eyes. Listen. Feel."

I folded my hands in my lap and closed my eyes. Having feelings was something I seemed to be particularly good at, but being British, I never quite knew what to do with those sensations except push them away. A twinge of uncertainty brushed through me. I was not sure whether I could undo a lifetime of Mama's training in order to master the requisite vulnerability and openness.

I concentrated on the pulsing red behind my eyelids. A breeze skittered along my skin. The leaves rustled overhead. In the field, an insect hummed, and some distance away a bird called out, high and sweet. *Tu-weet. Tu-weet. Tek.*

But of internal feelings? Nothing, save a growing sense of shame.

"Do you sense any magic?" Gábor asked.

I opened my eyes. "No."

"Perhaps if Izidóra helps you focus?" He translated his request into Hungarian.

Izidóra held out her hand. *"Kérem."*

I set my gloved hand in her bare one. I closed my eyes and tried to focus my attention outward. Mátyás's trousers rustled as he shifted beside me.

There. A faint vibration, as of some giant hand plucking an invisible string.

"I feel something." I tried to keep my voice steady, not wanting to betray the excitement thrilling through me.

"Try to call the magic into your charm," Gábor said. "Find the heart of the charm, invite the magic in."

I kept my eyes closed. All I could feel was the weight of the silver, warm against the band of skin above my glove. I shook my head.

Izidóra whispered something.

"My sister says she pictures the charm-stone as a flower that opens as the magic approaches."

I imagined the roses in my mother's garden, the way the petals slowly opened to the sun. The warm buzz of the magic skittered across my skin, but it slid over the charm-stone like oil on water.

"Something's blocking the magic. Try again. Use a different image this time. A stream bed, or wind sweeping through a ravine."

I tried each image in succession. Nothing happened. With the final image of the wind, I could not even feel the magic. Gábor asked me to repeat the exercise, with varying images, half a dozen times. Still the same result. I opened my eyes, flinching at the brightness.

"Perhaps Romani magic, like Luminate magic, depends on a Romani bloodline," Mátyás suggested.

I did not want to believe it. My fingers tightened around the fabric of my skirt.

"No. Anyone can use our talismans, though we keep them carefully guarded. I'm not sure what's preventing Miss

Arden." Gábor rocked back on his haunches. The movement pulled his trousers taut against the line of muscle in his leg. The muscle of a working man and an athlete. So different from Freddy's slim, aesthete build. Uncomfortable heat pricked in my breast. I turned away, hoping Gábor did not notice my rising color.

Gábor stood, brushing dirt from his trousers. "That is enough for one lesson. You should go now. If you stay, you'll be missed. I'll send you word when it's safe to meet again."

I felt as though someone had offered me a draft of water when I was parched, only to snatch it away. "Why not tomorrow?"

Gábor folded his arms across his chest. "My magic, my rules."

I gave in with poor grace. "You are not very gallant."

He bared his teeth in a wide smile. "No. I am not."

※

In a month, we met a half dozen times in the drowsing summer heat. I did not make much progress, a fact Mátyás bemoaned loudly, but Gábor never remarked on. I could sense the magic, yet I could not seem to pull it into the charms.

On afternoons when Gábor took pity on my repeated failures, he and Izidóra alternated demonstrating how the talisman magic worked. Izidóra cajoled a rose to bloom and then furl back tightly. Gábor raised a small windstorm that tore my hair loose and made Mátyás laugh as I scrambled to find the pins in the tall grass. Eventually, I gave up. Later, I told Grandmama the pins had fallen during my ride.

I watched Gábor more than I perhaps should have, noting his small kindnesses to his sister, his clever hands, his quick wit. And then, becoming aware of my own observations, I retreated behind a prickly austerity that made both Mátyás and Izidóra stare.

The lessons were not a complete failure. I learned enough of the theory to wheedle a ring from Izidóra and enclosed it in a letter to James with detailed instructions on its use. Perhaps he'd have better luck than I.

※

The sun was hot on my head. Not four hours past dawn and already the day was stifling. Sweat beaded my forehead beneath my bonnet and trickled down my bodice. I leaned forward to whisper to Starfire, soothing words meant more for me than for her. I was riding alone to meet Izidóra and Gábor, as Mátyás had failed to appear. I reasoned: Izidóra would be present. There would be no impropriety. *Aside from meeting a pair of Romanies in the first place. And learning their magic.*

A breeze swirled the warm, sweet summer air around me. The towering linden trees near the Eszterházy estate had burst into bloom, thousands of star flowers filling the air with their honey and lemon-peel scent. At night I pushed my window open so the fragrance filled my room and my dreams.

When I arrived at the appointed site, I dismounted and tied Starfire loosely to a low branch. Gábor lounged against a tree trunk, pulling the head off a daisy.

"Izidóra could not come today," he said, tossing the daisy head away.

"Oh." All of my words appeared to have deserted me, along with our chaperones. Breathing was strangely difficult. I wondered if Ginny had laced my corset too tightly.

Gábor's glance flicked behind me. "Where's Mátyás?"

"Gone." I slid my tongue across my lips, trying to call the unruly words in my head to order. "I think he's bored with my progress. Or lack thereof."

"And you, Anna? We don't have to keep going if you're tired."

"No." My pulse hammered in my throat. My given name on his lips was intimate, dangerous. "I want . . . *this.*" My hand swept out, gesturing vaguely at the clearing, at Gábor.

His eyes sharpened, and he took a single step toward me.

My face lit like a fuse. This man had kissed me once, though he had kept his distance since.

And we were alone.

The brook rippled past us. Overhead, the branches laced together, retreated, and then met again in the wind, as if trapped in some ancient courting dance.

My breath caught, and I waited—half hoping, half fearing—for him to take the steps that would close the distance between us.

I wanted . . . What did I want? I did not want this strangely proud young man to kiss me. I could not want that. I wanted magic. I wanted James to be whole. I did not want the dizzy rush and heat of kissing. I did not want another Freddy.

Then why was I so out of reason disappointed when Gábor halted? Part of me, the shadow part I struggled to keep safely contained, whispered wickedly it would not be very hard to close the distance myself, to set my lips against his.

I laid a square of fabric on the ground and settled myself upon it, folding my hands in my lap. Only the lingering heat in my cheeks betrayed my unmannerly thoughts. Gábor sat a safe distance from me, his hands kneading the muscles in his thighs. I watched their movement, fascinated, until I became aware of precisely *what* I did and blushed.

"Have you always been Barren?"

My eyes flew to his, startled by the abrupt question. But there was just curiosity and even a little sympathy in his eyes, so I answered.

"The Circle tested me as they do all Luminate children at their Confirmation. I failed spectacularly." *And I injured James.* But I could not say so to Gábor. "After that, Mama kept me away from everything magical, including most of Luminate society."

Gábor's eyes held none of his usual reserve. They were dark and warm, like a summer night. "I am sorry. It is not an easy thing to feel divided: part one thing, part another, but never whole."

An aching shock of recognition hit me. "You feel this too?"

Gábor plucked a leaf from a nearby bush, holding it up to the light so the veins showed dark. "I've always been interested in the natural world. A clergyman in a nearby village the winter I was nine noted my interest and offered me lessons with the other boys he tutored."

"That was generous."

"I suppose it was kindly meant. But if I had known how it would end—" He broke off.

I waited, silent, willing him to continue. After a minute or two, he began again. "The parents of the other boys complained. I was Gypsy. I was no longer allowed to study with them, but the priest made time for me when he could. When my family moved on, he sent books with me. My mother threatened to destroy them—who needed *gadzhe* learning?—but I begged her not to. Learning—it was like a curse. I couldn't get it out of my thoughts, my blood. I wanted more. Occasionally I could find people kind enough to teach me: sometimes priests, sometimes students.

"Mostly, people weren't very welcoming. A Gypsy to aspire beyond his station? Absurd." He sprang up and began striding across the clearing. "I could have tolerated *gadzhe* scorn. I've heard it my entire life. But then my own family accused me of turning *gadzho,* of thinking myself better than them."

"Do you?"

He turned troubled eyes on me. "I am proud of who I am. There is much to admire about my people: their tenacity, their intelligence, their humor and passion. But sometimes I catch myself seeing them as a *gadzho* might, seeing their superstitions, the difficulties of a nomadic life." His voice dropped. "And sometimes I see myself as they do: a man aspiring to foolishness, currying favor of people who will never value him."

I thought of James, trying to find a place among those who should have welcomed him, and my heart squeezed tight. "At least you know *something.* I've been taught to stitch and curtsy."

Gábor stopped pacing and dropped beside me. My entire left side came alive at his nearness.

151

"Is knowledge always such a good thing? I mean to go to Buda-Pest in the fall to take courses at the university, if I can. Mátyás says he will help me. I believe in what I'm doing—but sometimes it costs more than I can bear. I do not always fit comfortably with my own people—or with the *gadzhe*. Where does such a half creature belong?"

I had never heard this note in Gábor's voice before, and it took me a moment to identify it. Uncertainty. Vulnerability. Odd how openness can make something familiar strange, and something strange familiar. Gábor was only a boy after all, not much older than I was.

"You're not a half creature," I said. "Two ways of seeing should make you better, stronger, wiser. Like the owl, who sees in all directions."

"Perhaps humans weren't meant for such double vision. A woman with a double soul once nearly destroyed the world."

Gooseflesh prickled up my arm. I knew this story: Pandora, the all-gifted by the Olympian gods, given one soul for herself, and one to punish the men who helped Prometheus. "But Pandora was *chimera*. Your dual vision doesn't make you monstrous."

"I wish I could believe that."

One slim brown hand clenched and unclenched against his leg. Before I let myself think, I stripped off my glove and reached out, my fingers closing over his. His hand stilled.

His bare skin was rough and warm against my touch. I had never touched a man's ungloved hand before, save Papa's. And this was *quite* different. "Everyone feels that way who does not fit neatly into the role society gives them. But it doesn't mean something is wrong with you, only that you are bigger than they can imagine." Recognition pulled at me—my words were as true for me as for Gábor. I put them away to study them later. Just then, my attention was all for Gábor. "You know so much. You're kind to your sister and brother. You're patient beyond anything I deserve. You are . . . quite remarkable." My nerves stood alert like soldiers, alive to the perils—and promises—of some uncharted territory.

His eyes lifted to mine, his dark pupils swallowing the brown iris. Perhaps I should not have spoken so freely, but I could not call the words back. Would not.

His hand shifted, capturing my fingers in his, his thumb tracing a slow movement across the back of my hand. The heat sweeping up my arm, suffusing my body, had nothing to do with the warmth of the summer day.

I knew I should pull away, but I did not.

Gábor smiled down at me, and for a moment ringing filled my ears. He was going to kiss me. He wanted to. I could see it in his slightly widened eyes, the way he leaned intently toward me as he spoke, his gaze dropping to my lips, to the skin exposed by the neck of my dress.

But he held back, waiting for me to make some sign.

What would it matter, here, away from prying eyes, if I let him kiss me? Here he was not Romani, I was not a lady. He was Gábor; I was Anna. All it would take was a look, a slight upward tilt of my chin.

But I kept my chin lowered. I dropped my eyes.

I thought of Catherine's ball, how I had traded a kiss with Freddy for months of exile. And I remembered the strange, wild hunger that swept me the first time Gábor kissed me. I did not trust myself. Gábor might be a good man, a remarkable one, but he was still Romani, his life and heritage worlds away from everything I had ever known, everything I had ever wanted.

A current of air beneath the trees shifted. At once I felt watched, exposed.

I pulled my hand away, angry with myself for wanting something I couldn't have, angry at society for dictating those barriers. "I must go." I scrambled to my feet and lurched away. With the aid of a nearby stump, I mounted Starfire and turned her head toward home.

I did not look back.

CHAPTER 13

Nearly a week passed before I heard anything from Gábor. I walked in the gardens with Grandmama, practiced Hungarian with Noémi as I accompanied her on her rounds, rode with Mátyás, and tried to read Gábor's silence. Was he angry? Offended? Perhaps he thought himself well rid of me.

When the summons came, I pressed the scrap of paper to my breast in relief. My lessons would continue, and perhaps I could salvage something of our friendship.

Still, I insisted Mátyás accompany me, both for propriety and as a buffer against any potential awkwardness.

Gábor waited alone at our usual spot, studying the brook a few feet away with an intensity it did not warrant.

I selected a fallen log for my seat and fussed with my skirts, trying to ignore the heat rising in my cheeks at the sight of him. Mátyás plopped down beside me.

"Today," Gábor began with no preliminary greetings, "I'd like to see if Miss Arden can use the magic already stored in a talisman to summon light." Still, he would not look at me.

There was a long silence. *Miss Arden,* he said, but he spoke about me, not to me. My heart clenched tight.

"Miss Arden—are you tired of our spells? We do not need to continue." Gábor's voice was clipped, precise.

I made an effort to speak normally. "I'm sorry. I was wool-gathering. I'll do whatever you ask."

Mátyás waggled his eyebrows at me, and I elbowed him in the side. He tumbled off the log, laughing. Gábor glowered at both of us.

"I'm sorry," I said again. Sorry for Mátyás's folly, for my own. Whatever intimacy Gábor and I had shared, I had ruined.

Gábor held out his hand. Sunlight played across his palm. "Watch." The light in his hands seemed to coalesce, intensifying until he held a miniature star in his hand. I reached out to touch the light, and it splintered apart. "Now you. Reach through the magic in the talisman to the essence of the sunlight."

I closed my eyes, envisioning the magic as a tenuous string linking my heart to the air brushing across my skin, and curled my fingers around the Romani talisman I wore. I needed this to work. That need was a tangible thing, a weight against my breast, a prickling of tears at the back of my throat.

The sunlight warmed my palm. *Essence,* I thought. *Connection.*

I was so focused on my spell that Izidóra's voice near my ear made me jump. I had not seen her coming.

"Gábor! It's Duci. The baby is here, but she is not breathing right. And Mama's spells aren't working." Izidóra's eyes were wet, her face pale.

Gábor sprang up, our lesson forgotten. "My sister's baby. She's come early."

I stood as well. "Noémi will help, I'm sure of it. Mátyás and I will fetch her and bring her to the camp."

He shook his head. "Mátyás can't come with you. Men are not allowed near the birthing mother. It is bad enough we bring *gadzhe* women into camp." He met my eyes at last. "Thank you."

I felt a flash of relief that Gábor was speaking to me again, and then Mátyás helped me mount and we rode headlong to Eszterháza.

Once we'd explained everything to Noémi, she paused only to collect her satchel from the stillroom. I hesitated near the horses.

"I should stay. If you have to cast a spell, I'd only be in the way." Or worse.

Noémi clutched my hand. "I've never been to the Gypsy camp. I can't go alone. Come with me."

With some misgiving, I remounted Starfire. The two of us rode together through the town and into the fields beyond. Gábor met us just outside the Romani camp. The tang of woodsmoke filled the air, and wind hissed through the tents. The camp seemed strangely deserted: no children shouted, the campfires smoldered untended. Perhaps everyone had been sent away, for privacy.

Keening rose above the wind, and I shivered. Or perhaps the Romanies could feel, as I did, the stillness in the air of something gone awry.

Starfire snuffled against my shoulder, and I shooed her into the meadow. "I'll wait here," I said to Gábor and Noémi. I could not risk breaking spells that might save a child and its mother.

Gábor turned to Noémi. "Romani custom dictates only a few women are allowed to be with the mother, to protect the baby. No men are allowed—and certainly no *gadzhe*. Izidóra knows you are coming, but my older sister may be alarmed. You'll need to work quickly. My mother and grandmother have gone to gather plants for a salve, but they will return soon." His warning hung unspoken: *they will not approve.*

I watched as Gábor led Noémi to a nearby tent. He scratched at the side, and Izidóra appeared, her face white with strain. She murmured something to Noémi, who nodded and ducked inside after her. Gábor returned to me, his lips set.

"Noémi is a good healer," I said. "If there's anything to be done, she'll do it."

"I know it," he said. "The villagers all look up to her."

Silence sprang up between us. I tried not to hear the cries spiking from inside the tent. If this is what it meant to birth a child, I was no longer certain I wanted one.

I snuck a glance at Gábor. His eyes were on the horizon beyond the meadow, anxious and unfocused.

I put my hand on his arm, and he jumped. "I'm sorry," I started, then paused. I wanted to undo the stiffness between us, but I could not say *I'm sorry I did not kiss you.* "I'm sorry your sister is suffering."

He nodded in acknowledgment.

A snatch of song carried across the air to us. Gábor stiffened. "My grandmother."

"So soon? But there hasn't been enough time for any sort of spell to work."

"I'll try to delay her. Go warn your cousin."

"But—"

Gábor was already gone, striding through the meadow toward the trees. I looked back at the tent, my stomach cramping.

I couldn't do it. If I interrupted Noémi, I might ruin her spell as surely as if I'd broken it. Gábor would understand that. And as long as he kept his grandmother away, Noémi would not need a warning.

As the minutes crept past, I began to relax. Soon, Noémi would be finished, the child would be well, and it would not matter if Gábor's grandmother returned.

But then a woman emerged from a clump of trees on the other side of the camp, a basket of herbs over one arm. She didn't appear to see me. She strode through the camp, her gaze focused on her destination—the tent where Noémi worked.

I had to stop her.

Propelled by a terrible instinct that something dreadful was about to happen, I started forward.

"*Bitte!*" I called, my feet snagging in the matted grass. "Stop! Do not go in!"

The woman turned a startled face to me, then shook her head in anger. She didn't slow, so I sprinted forward, intercepting her just before the tent and throwing my arms around her.

The tiniest buzz of magic brushed against me and I froze. *Noémi's spell.* The woman shoved me away, and I fell, gasping at the impact as my shoulder and hip hit the ground. But that slight pain dissolved as fear ratcheted through me.

I scrambled to my feet, trying once more to block the woman's entrance to the tent. She scratched at my arms and shouted, but I scarcely heard her.

The buzzing was stronger now, the magic vibrating just beneath my skin, a thousand tiny pricks of pain burning in my blood.

The Circle ends. The spell was starting to fray. "Noémi!" I cried. "Stop!"

Too late. A slight catch in the air, then an explosion of heat and light, a conflagration that seared my eyes, even outside the tent. A brilliant intensity of pain, then the light vanished like a snuffed candle.

Izidóra burst from the tent, a small bundle cradled tight against her. Her eyes were wild, terrified. The Romani woman threw her arms around Izidóra and the infant as if she would shield them.

My legs would not hold me, and I dropped to the ground.

Noémi stumbled out of the tent. "Anna. *Istenem.* Anna!" Her face was white. "Binding Saints save us."

Gábor came rushing toward us. "What happened?" His eyes flickered from his sister to me, curled on the ground. "Are you all right?"

I put my palms against the packed dirt to push myself upright, and my eyes snagged on the talisman I wore.

It blazed with light.

Gábor crouched to brush his fingers across it, then launched a string of sharp-edged words. He turned to my cousin. "Tell me what happened."

"I don't know. I had cast one spell, to ease the baby's breathing, and was casting another to warm her when the spell seemed to snap. All the magic broke from it."

An older Romani woman stumped toward us, her face dark with anger, her breath coming in harsh jags. She stopped before me, her shadow falling across my face and still-trembling hands. In that half shadow, the talisman blazed even brighter.

The woman swooped down and grabbed my wrist, ripping the talisman from my arm. She held it close to one eye, pressed two fingers against it, and then began shrieking. I threw my hands over my ears. I could not seem to stop trembling.

When she'd finished, she shouted something at Gábor, then stumped off again. The other Romani woman—Gábor's mother?—ducked into the tent. A low murmur of voices emerged, one steady and soothing, the other thready and broken.

Noémi helped me stand, then turned to Gábor. "What is going on?"

He would not look at me. "My grandmother believes that an infant's soul is not fully tethered when it is born. That is why only a few people are allowed to attend the birth, so they will not accidentally steal its soul. But the spell you cast—my grandmother believes that when the spell broke, the magic was pulled into Miss Arden's talisman, along with some of the baby's soul."

Noémi's eyes widened with horror. "Surely that's not possible."

Gábor shook his head. "For all that you Luminate say

differently, we still do not know everything about how magic works. I have seen that our talismans gather more magic near births and deaths. Who is to say that the exchange of a soul does not release magic into the world? Or that a soul is not somehow connected to magic?"

Bile burned in my throat. "Do you believe your grandmother?"

"I don't know. Grandmother understands more about magic than anyone I know. If she says it is possible, it must be."

"I'm desperately sorry," I said. "I never meant to hurt anyone. Will the baby be all right?"

Noémi said, "I think she will heal. I can't speak for her soul—I know nothing about that. But why should you blame yourself? You did nothing."

"I—" The words nearly choked me. "I broke your spell. That's what I do. I break things."

"You didn't mean to," Noémi said, her voice so gentle it brought tears stinging to my eyes.

Gábor looked at me as though he had never truly seen me before. "What are you, Anna? No Luminate could break a spell like that, not without casting a spell to counter it."

I crossed my arms across my chest, trying to still their trembling. A terrible fear stole over me. I had hoped the shattered spells I left in my wake were the result of something I did, because I could learn to undo my actions. But if the broken spells were driven by something I *was,* how could I undo my own nature? And what, in all the Circle bound, was I?

"We should go," I said to Noémi.

Something shifted in Noémi's face. "The broken spell—*that's* why William wanted you to go to Sárvár. To break a spell there—maybe even break the Binding."

I nodded. "I won't, of course." Noémi still had not moved, so I started walking away from the tent, toward the meadow where our horses waited.

"Someone asked you to break the spell at Sárvár?" Gábor asked sharply, and I stopped. "Stay away from there. The magic that leaks from that spell is fouled." A muscle in his jaw flexed. "You saw something Whitsun night. A *fene,* maybe, a dark spirit of illness and destruction. I don't believe your appearance along with those creatures is all coincidence. Don't go to Sárvár. If your friend is right and you can break that spell—if you can break the Binding—you could destroy us all."

A rumble of voices stopped whatever else Gábor meant to say and dissolved the tart words on my tongue: *I already said I would not do it.* Gábor's grandmother was returning, a half dozen Romani men behind her.

"No," Gábor whispered.

"What is it?" Noémi edged closer to me, her arm slipping through mine. The group formed a loose circle around us, trapping us among the tents.

"My grandmother has brought the Elders." He listened for a moment. "To judge if we have harmed my sister or her baby."

Gábor's mother emerged from the tent to stand beside his grandmother, her arms crossed.

"Tell them to let Noémi go," I said. "She's done nothing wrong."

Gábor's mother stepped so close I could feel the warmth of her breath on my cheek. *"Csönd legyen!"* Be silent!

Gábor's grandmother spat a tangled string of words I didn't understand and shook the talisman in the air. Gábor translated, but from his hesitations, I sensed he omitted the worst of what was said. "She says you both are without shame or honor, coming to our camp to steal away the baby's soul."

"We came to save the baby," I said. "We never meant to hurt anyone."

Gábor turned back to the surrounding circle of men and started to speak. One of the men cut him off, shouting, and Gábor pressed his lips together, his expression uncomfortably grim. Gábor's grandmother spoke again, and the men listened in silence, some crossing their arms, others fingering their mustaches. When she finished, each man spoke in turn. The eyes they fixed on us were hard and cold. I shivered.

Gábor would not look at us as he translated. "Whatever your intentions, you put the baby at risk. They find you guilty of theft, and you are hereby banned from this camp."

"Are we not allowed to defend ourselves?" I asked.

He shook his head. "I told them you meant only to help. But don't be angry with them—our clan rules exist to protect us from *gadzhe* who have not always been kind, and I went against those rules to bring you here."

His mother wailed as he spoke, a thin, keening sound that slit through my ears and pierced my heart. She must be grieving her granddaughter, as she could not regret our banishment.

Noémi tugged at my arm, her face burning red. "Let's go."

My chest burned too, part angry that Noémi's kindness should be treated so brusquely, part horror-struck that Gábor's grandmother might be right about the baby's soul.

Gábor led us away from the camp. He shoved his hand through his hair and studied my face, his eyes dark and soft and wide with an emotion I could not read. It might have been sadness. Or fear. "The first night you came to our tents, my grandmother was terrified, claiming you would destroy the Binding. I did not believe her. Sometimes she sees true, but her sight is unpredictable when she has been drinking."

Hurt and fear and regret and grief tangled in my heart, and so naturally I covered them with anger. "No doubt you regret everything about me. I would apologize for my very existence, but alas, you can hardly expect me to wish to undo that."

"I don't regret you," Gábor said softly, and an entirely different sort of heat flooded me.

But then he spoiled the effect by adding, "I'm only afraid for you, for what you don't know about yourself. Until you know who you are, your powers master you, not you them. This is why *gadzhe* cannot master Romani magic: they lie to themselves."

"I don't lie to myself," I said, but I knew even as I spoke that I lied. I had hidden from myself how much I wanted to be with Gábor, seeing it only now as I might never see him again.

"I can't teach you anymore. I thought there was no harm in it, as long as we weren't caught. I was wrong."

Noémi stared at me. "What was he teaching you? Oh, Anna. Not Gypsy magic!"

"Not Gypsy," I said. "Romani."

Gábor continued, "It's no good, Anna. I'm sorry."

Anna, he said. Not Miss Arden. I should have been pleased by the intimacy, but all I heard in it was farewell. "Wait." And before I could let myself weigh the consequences, I threw my arms around Gábor. He smelled of sunshine and grass, and I wanted to hold him forever. But Noémi watched, and already his family gathered, waiting for us to leave.

"Thank you for trying to help me," I said.

"I wish I could believe I *had* helped you," he said, holding out one hand. "May you find every happiness."

Trying to ignore my falling heart, I stripped off my glove and took his hand. I wanted to feel the slow burn of flesh against flesh. I held his hand for as long as he would allow me. My fingers were strangely weightless when he let go, as if I had lost an anchor.

I watched Gabor walk away, memorizing the long, lean line of his body and the easy grace of his stride. Regret tasted sour in my mouth. *I should have kissed him.*

Noémi linked her arm through mine. "I am sorry, Anna." The understanding in her eyes nearly undid me. I blinked against tears and lifted my chin. We marched toward the meadow.

Then I stopped. Noémi's horse grazed alone, lifting her head as we approached, her great limpid eyes indifferent to the upheaval we'd left behind. Starfire was missing.

A Romani man stood near Noémi's horse, his arms folded across his chest.

"We've taken back our horse," he said in accented German.

"What? But she was mine—my cousin bought and paid for her."

He continued to stare at me, his gaze uncompromising.

Realization swept over me, and I sighed. Likely Mátyás had not paid anything at all, only purchased her with a promise.

"I'll walk back with you," Noémi said, picking up her trailing reins.

As we headed toward the road leading to the village, I glanced behind only once.

Gábor had already vanished.

)(

I wrote to Papa that evening, smoothing the paper beneath the fitful glow of the lantern. The pen wanted mending, but I hadn't the time or means at the moment. I wished I'd thought to borrow one of Papa's new steel pens before I left England, and hoped he could still decipher my wretchedly scratchy penmanship. I chewed on the feather tip, uncertain. My heart ached at the events of the day. I wanted to ask Papa about the baby, if it was possible I had indeed stolen part of her soul, and if so, what would happen to her. But I was not sure I could bear the answer.

I could not tell him of Gábor, since I could not tell myself what I thought of him, and even Papa with his liberal notions might not welcome my involvement with a Romani.

Instead, I told him of Noémi's healing, as I knew familial magic lines interested him. I described the rides I'd taken and the way the smell of the linden trees filled my room in the morning when I wakened. I sent well-wishes to Mama and Catherine, and asked for word of James. In all, my letter might serve as a model for a dutiful daughter in a conduct manual.

The words were true, but the letter was a lie—it hid the

truth of my life. And then I added a question no dutiful daughter would raise because it could only invite trouble, as I knew the scholar in Papa could not refrain from answering: *Papa, what is Sárvár? I heard mention of a spell gone wretchedly awry. . . .*

CHAPTER 14

An uneasy quiet settled over the village and the palace in the days and weeks following our expulsion from the Romani camp. Noémi spent much of the time in her room, recovering from her spell-casting. Word reached us that the Romanies had packed up and disappeared.

I spent hours rambling through the disintegrating gardens at Eszterháza, the ragged shrubs and tangled paths a fitting reflection of my tumbled thoughts.

I wondered what I ought to do next, since I could no longer learn Romani magic.

I wondered if I would ever see Gábor again.

The aching sense of loss would fade, I knew, as Freddy's loss had. But the very existence of that ache meant I had begun to care for Gábor more than I knew. More than I wished to.

Sitting in the window seat of my room, I read Papa's letter through once, then twice, frowning. He said nothing of my question about Sárvár, only mentioned a few mundane bits about the family estate and his research. Mellow afternoon light pooled in my lap as I turned the letter over in my hands. Then I saw it: a tiny imprint of our family crest—a phoenix—buried in one corner of the paper.

Papa had spelled the letter.

I pressed my finger to the imprint and waited for the spell to recognize my blood.

Papa's voice filled the room, and tears pricked my eyes at its familiarity.

> *Of course I know of Sárvár. It is believed Countess Báthory attempted a blood ritual there. Historians such as myself are still not entirely certain of her aim—to break the Binding spell, or merely to access it herself and circumvent the Circle. Whatever its aim, the spell created a kind of bridge—a way station—between our world and the dimension where the Binding holds our magic. The Circle have tried repeatedly to dismantle her spell, as it creates a weak point in the Binding, but have been unable to do so, in large part because they are unwilling to re-create the blood magic she used to build her spell. Indeed, it's a curious spell, one I have often wished to study from a closer vantage point.*

There was a long silence, and I had begun to think the charm was finished, when Papa resumed speaking.

170

You already know I am a heretic. I believe the Binding should be abolished and magic should be allowed to run free, for use by all with a knack for it. When Charlemagne convened the first Circle and cast the original Binding spell, no doubt he believed it was a good thing. The Binding was crafted to protect spell-casters: too many magicians were dying because they misjudged the power required for their spells and burned themselves out. The first Circle decided to create instead a reservoir of magic all magicians might draw from, limiting that power only to those trained for it, thus protecting the untrained from using a spell beyond their capacity—and everyone else from the ruins of their spells.

But whatever good was begun with it, the Binding has ended by perpetuating injustice. Those with magic began to use their power to promote themselves, restricting the use of magic not to those with training but to those with powerful bloodlines.

I am not always a brave man. I know this. I do not always stand for the things I believe are right. But the more I study the history of magic, the more I come to see we have made a mistake. Magic should not belong solely to those who made themselves powerful at the expense of others. I believe we now know enough about magic to establish protections against the deaths that plagued ancient magicians. Anyone with talent should have access to magic—and to proper training. Imagine what we might learn if all those with talent and inclination could practice magic!

I find I am not so alone as I once imagined. Lady

Berri has, surprisingly, indicated she shares my belief. I took the liberty of showing her your letter, and she was most intrigued. It occurs to us that you might be of use in breaking that spell at Sárvár. Lady Berri is preparing to come to you as I write, as such spell-breaking should not be attempted alone. I send this letter in the hopes it will give you some warning of what is to come. But do not fear—I am confident Lady Berri will keep you safe. She and I have spoken a great deal about the schools we shall build when—if—the Binding can be broken.

In any case, the castle bears an interesting history and is said to be worth the journey.

Your loving Papa

I stared at the letter. Pressing my finger again to the charm elicited no response, so I set the letter down and fell backward upon my bed, my thoughts reeling. Papa's letter only confirmed what William had already claimed: nobles were not Luminate because of some inherent gift but because the Binding made them so, taking power from non-Luminates to augment a reservoir of magic reserved only for those already powerful. Seen this way, members of the Circle were not so much preservers of an ancient spell but gatekeepers arbitrarily determining human worth. This one was wealthy, let him be a magician. This one was not, let him be a serf. My stomach turned.

My thoughts shifted to Lady Berri. Papa had sent me away in part to keep me safe from the Circle, yet now he was sending one of them direct to me—*and* asking her to test my so-called ability? Papa seemed to think that she was also a heretic, that they shared the same goals, hence everything was all right.

But I was not so sanguine. I was not one of Gábor's fish, a specimen for experimentation, regardless of whether everyone around me seemed to see me as such: William, Lady Berri, even Papa. I could not bear the thought of going to Sárvár under Lady Berri's pig-eyed scrutiny. But if she showed up with Papa's blessing, Grandmama would send me with her.

I pushed off my bed and began rummaging in my wardrobe.

Very well, then. I would go to Sárvár. But I would go on my own terms. Instead of running from my abilities, I would see what I was capable of. I had located Sárvár on one of János's maps when William first mentioned it. If I left at night, I could be back before Grandmama noticed me missing.

Gábor's words came back to me. *Don't go to Sárvár. If your friend is right and you can break that spell—if you can break the Binding—you could destroy us all.*

My hand froze on the sleeve of a yellow cotton day dress. Gábor's grandmother had interrupted him before he could tell me how I might destroy us. What did he know that I did not?

I shook myself. Papa was confident the spell might be broken without ill side effects, or he would not send me to do it. Perhaps Gábor's fear was mere superstition.

In any case, he was no longer here. He was not entitled to an opinion on my choices.

)(

That evening, when heavy silence fell over the palace, I climbed out of bed and donned my most sensible gown, a plain navy broadcloth with only two bands of ribbons around the sleeves. Then I crept down the stairs, through the echoing hallways, the sheep-filled Sala Terrena, and the overgrown gardens to the stable.

A snuffling noise outside the stable doors stopped my heart for a moment with improbable fancies: an escaped *lidérc,* a *rusalka.* But it was only one of the sheep that had wandered from its sleeping brothers.

The loss of Starfire hit me anew with the strong smell of horse and leather. Ignoring my aching heart, I found a bridle and sidesaddle and carried them to the stall where Mátyás kept his horse, Holdas. The sidesaddle proved a bit troublesome, as the pale horse had an unusually broad girth. At last I managed by boring another hole in the leather with an awl I found among the stable tools. I led the horse to the mounting block.

The horse rolled an eye back at me. For a brief moment, red seemed to flicker in the eyes, like a still-burning ember. I dismissed the idea, and hauled myself up into the saddle. The horse bounced a little beneath me, as if testing my weight. I tapped his flank lightly with my heel, and we shuffled toward the stable doors.

Only to find the door blocked by Mátyás.

In the moonlight, his gaze took in the full saddlebags on his horse and my light cloak. His eyes widened. "What are you doing? Holdas will kill you." He swayed a little, and my lip curled.

"You're drunk."

"Am not. Only happy. Now get down."

"I need to borrow your horse." I considered trying to ride past Mátyás, but I didn't trust my drunk, feckless, foolish cousin to move out of my way.

"Why?"

"My actions are none of your business."

"They are. It's my horse. And my ancestral home." He swung one arm out, waxing energetic, and nearly stumbled.

"It's not your house. And I'm only borrowing your horse because the one you gave me was reclaimed for lack of payment." I burned inwardly.

Mátyás closed one eye and peered at me through the other. "Where are you going?"

I didn't answer.

"Get off my horse."

I thrust my chin out and stared down at him.

"*A fene egye meg!*" Mátyás stalked toward me. My fingers tightened on the reins.

"I refuse to ride that slug of a horse." Mátyás nodded toward Cukor, placidly chewing hay in a corner stall. "You ride him. I'm riding Holdas."

I dropped the reins. "What—?"

"Daft girl. Haven't you been listening?" Mátyás sighed. "I am *trying* to ensure my willful cousin does not kill herself on a stupid midnight ride."

I blinked at him.

"I'm coming with you."

⟨⟩

It was not quite dawn when our road wound down into the Rába River valley, descending through gently rolling hills before arriving at the heart of Sárvár. Mátyás had worn off the worst of his intoxication (the singing stage had been impressive), and was now merely a little talkative.

"I admire your fearlessness," Mátyás said.

"I'm not fearless." My heart had kept up an uneven thumping all night, and I was beginning to think the line between bravery and stupidity was determined by whether or not one survived.

"Oh? What are you afraid of?"

The summer air was warm, even at the tail end of evening. A night for the safekeeping of secrets—and for sharing them. So I gave Mátyás the truth. "That I will live and I will die and none of it will matter. That I won't matter." Because this truth came too close to laying me bare, I covered it over with poetry, from Tennyson's "Ulysses": "How dull it is to pause, to make an end, / To rust unburnish'd, not to shine in use! / As tho' to breathe were life."

I half expected Mátyás to laugh, or to meet my poetry with a line of his own. But he met my sidelong look steadily. "You already matter, Anna." His eyes darkened and my heart skipped. "There's something I—"

"And you?" I asked, turning the conversation away before Mátyás could say something we would both regret. "What do you fear?"

He was silent so long I did not think he would answer. Then, "Sometimes I'm afraid I will turn into my father, disappointing everyone around me with my life—and with my death. It's easier when no one has expectations."

And so he cracks jokes and resists responsibility. I wondered if Mátyás knew just how revealing his words were. I cradled them to me, wishing I could put my arms around Mátyás as I would James, when he was troubled at heart. But now was not the time or place. We'd come in sight of Sárvár.

We rode beneath the castle, which I found, frankly, disappointing. It was not the fairy-tale castle I'd been spinning in my brain, all crumbling walls and turrets, but a rather squat, sensible edifice clearly built for defense. A short tower rose from one corner.

I knew from my reading that the castle had belonged to the Nádasdy family, one of whom had married the infamous Blood Countess, Báthory Erzsébet. Rumor held she bathed in the blood of virgins to preserve her youth and beauty. I did not know if rumor spoke truth, but Papa had confirmed that she used blood magic. I looked at the moonlight-drenched walls of the castle and shivered. What would I find in this woman's blood–soaked spell?

Mátyás led me unerringly to the remains of an old Roman bath, a small square building with an arched roof, a mile or so beyond the castle, confirming my belief he had been here before. Part of the roof and one side had crumbled away, leaving the bath inside exposed to the elements. A Latin inscription flowed across the keystone over the doorway.

We drew closer, trying to peer into the gloom of the interior. Two men stood near the shadow side of the building, talking softly.

"The Circle guards," Mátyás said. "I'll draw them off."

He darted to one side of the bath, melting into darkness. A crow lifted to the air in his wake, crying wildly. It winged toward the two guards and plummeted down on top of them. They cried out, throwing their hands over their eyes as the bird attacked.

I sent silent thanks after Mátyás and plunged forward into the opening.

The interior of the bath smelled of sulfur and steam. As my eyes adjusted to the new gloom, I found I stood on a tiled ledge running around the four sides of the room. An intricately patterned mosaic covered the bottom of the shallow pool. Outside, the two guards shouted and the crow answered back. I took a half dozen careful steps along the ledge toward the back of the bath, where stars shimmered through the missing roof.

Something brushed against my face, cobweb-light, but when I brought my fingers up to rub it away, nothing was there. Voices echoed in the ruined space, whispers of laughter, the jagged note of a woman crying. Papa had described the spell here as a *way station,* a bridge between our dimension and that of the Binding. I wondered, a shiver convulsing through me, if the voices I heard belonged to my world—or to the Binding.

As I crept forward, the heat in the room intensified, seeping through the soles of my feet to permeate my entire body. I paused for a moment, my eyes drawn to a dark line across the tiles in front of me. What material could leave such indelible trace? Some kind of dye? Surely blood would have washed away long since.

The air around me was curiously dense, like fog on a winter morning. I had the strangest sense that if I thrust my hands forward, they would plunge through an invisible barrier. I lifted my hands: the radiating heat in my body erupted from my fingers, my eyes, my temples. The sharp smell of winter frost rose around me, and that invisible barrier tore open.

The space bloomed with darkness—and something claw-like closed over my wrist.

The clawed hands pulled me forward, and I stumbled, thrusting my free hand out for balance before I could fall into the pool. I half expected my fingers to snag against the stone wall, but nothing was there. Something brushed past me, bringing with it the scent of brine and smoke, and, so faintly I thought I might be imagining it, roses. My heart hammered. It smelled like the creature from Catherine's debut.

Around me in the darkness, the voices crescendoed. The echoes of laughter were gone, replaced almost entirely by screaming. There were words too, but in a language I did not recognize. A cold wind caught my hair.

Still, that relentless grip pulled me forward, slipping and sliding across a stone floor. I could see nothing of my captor. The blackness was absolute—not just the absence of light but a presence itself.

The space around me had taken on the echoey quality of a cavern or cathedral. Though I could not see—even the stars had blinked out—I had the impression the space had expanded well beyond the confines of the tumbledown bath.

Countess Báthory's spell. Somehow, I must have crossed into it.

I tried to look behind me, searching for the seam I'd come through, but blackness closed up my eyes. I took a deep, shuddering breath.

There were other creatures in the darkness with me. I heard faint splashing in water and the wet slap of limbs against the floor. Eyes glimmered briefly before their owners scrabbled away. Some distance from me, lit by a faint glow about his brow, a man with the head and horns of an elk strolled through the shadows. On his arm was a woman, naked except for the spiders skittering across her body, drawing the faintest skeins of silk webbing around her. Both of them wore shackles of silver, hammered to paper thinness. The woman turned a night-dark face to me, a third eye opening like a flower in her forehead.

"You must pay the forfeit," she said before turning away into the blackness.

Her partner spoke, soundless words that curled in my head, intangible as smoke. *You must set us free.*

The clawed hand jerked me forward again. In the dim light from the elk creature, I glimpsed an almost-human monster, all long shanks and bones with scabbed skin stretched taut across a misshapen spine. Something crowded past us, a confusion of fur and scales against my palm and fingers. It hissed and I yanked my free hand back to my chest. A wave of cold washed over me, trickling down my spine, spilling down my throat and freezing my lungs.

My legs, scrambling after my captor, seemed oddly detached from my body. Perhaps the creatures were not real, only illusions cast by the mutated spell, like the illusions in the wake of Catherine's debutante spells.

But I suspected that illusions could not pull me as my captor did, would not feel as tangible as the fur and scales I'd brushed against. Fear battered at the back of my throat, squeezing stiff fingers around my heart. What could this creature want with me? A blood sacrifice, to continue fueling Countess Báthory's spell? Worse—a meal? I tried not to imagine the sudden sting and burn of claws against the soft skin of my stomach, my throat. I tried not to picture monsters converging on my broken body, tearing and slurping in that pit of darkness.

I stopped, throwing my entire weight opposite my captor's forward motion. Whatever the creature meant to do with me, I would not let it happen without a fight.

A star streaked across the space, then coalesced into the form of a man standing before me, smelling of brimstone and brine. My captor released me with a suddenness that sent me reeling back, my arms windmilling. It scuttered away into the darkness, claws clattering along the ground. I caught myself just in time and had a confused impression of multiple faces, sleek and vaguely draconic, and then the light solidified into a single face so beautiful it pained me to look at. Before I could draw back, the man put fingers like brands on my shoulders and set a kiss like a live coal against my forehead.

When I gasped—more out of anger than fear, though the anger might only have been a cover for fear—the creature laughed. The sound of his laugh had a falseness to it—an actor imitating an emotion he doesn't truly feel. He released me, but I could still feel phantom hands burning against my body. Shackles jangled at his wrists.

"Well met, maiden," he said.

I wiped my forehead with my hand and hoped he did not notice my trembling.

"Peace, child. We shan't eat you."

I wished I believed him. I'd caught a glimpse of fangs among the faces that flashed across his.

"We haven't much time. Already this spell unravels, and the Binding pulls us back. We need your help."

I was startled into speech. "Mine?"

"Your magic snagged the edges of Báthory's spell, tearing it enough so we could catch you through it. And this is not the first time you've troubled the barrier of the Binding spell."

I gripped my shaking hands together. My fingers were like ice. Pictures flickered through my mind: the winged creature at Catherine's debut, the hollow-eyed Lorelei, the shadows racing across a dark field. "No."

"We need you to break us free. It's not enough to tear the boundary—the Binding always pulls us back. You must destroy the spell entirely."

I shrank away from him. The trembling in my hands spread to my arms. My legs shook beneath me. "Who are you? How are you here?"

He shrugged, the human gesture hanging oddly on his body. "Báthory's spell created a kind of bubble, a space connecting the Binding spell that holds us and your world. The Binding is thinner here—sometimes we break through, though never for long, and never past this space." His eyes were gold, gleaming like polished coins.

He did not answer my other question.

A tremor tore through the cavern, and something in me surged upward, carried by a wild, unexpectedly sweet longing. I fought my shadow self back. I could not lose control. Not here. Not now. I gripped my hands tighter.

"Release her," the creature said, and the hunger in my shadow self became an ache. I trembled under the strain of holding her. "I must go—but we shall meet again. Hold your heart for me. I shall have need of it." He launched himself into the air, disappearing into the darkness above me. Air gusted into my face, stirred by something sweeping overhead.

Another surge rocketed through the space of the spell. I gasped and opened my hands. At once there was a sense of release, of heat and light and longing and even darkness flooding out of me.

Then nothing.

CHAPTER 15

I heard the voices first, murmuring softly in Hungarian. Sometimes I heard a lullaby, sung in Grandmama's aging cadences. And once I heard Mátyás declaiming poetry, an incongruous mix of Hungarian, German, and even English poets. I drifted then, colors and lights and sounds flashing at the periphery of my consciousness.

When I finally opened my eyes, it was to the dim light of early morning and the raucous call of birds outside the window. I was in a strange room, in a strange bed, in an unfamiliar *csárda*. Noémi drowsed in a chair by the empty fireplace, a book tumbled open in her lap.

I tried to speak. My voice croaked like a foghorn, and Noémi jerked upright, the book falling to the floor with a loud slap.

"You're awake! How do you feel?"

I coughed. "Like a silk gown left out in a rainstorm."

She made a sympathetic face. "So well?" She crossed the floor to my bedside and laid her hand against my forehead. "Your fever has broken."

"What happened?"

"You collapsed inside the bathhouse at Sárvár." She primmed up her lips, as if she were deliberately holding back words. "Mátyás and the Circle guards dragged you out and summoned us."

"Is Mátyás all right?"

"He's fine. The spell seems to have broken before he entered, fortunately. You, however, were not so fortunate. It's been three days, and this is the first time you've been lucid."

I thought of the strange creatures in the bathhouse. Were they only fever dreams, the side effect of being caught in a tainted spell?

Noémi left to tell Grandmama I was awake, and I looked around my room. My eyes caught on a small, dirty mirror mounted against the wall. A glimmer of a twinned reflection, then the two smudged echoes of my face merged into one. I was pale, my dark hair wild around my face. The neckline of my nightdress had slipped down on one side.

Against the skin of my right shoulder, as if branded there, was the faint print of a hand. An indistinct sphere imprinted my forehead, token of that burning kiss.

It had not been a dream. Or an illusion.

The spell had been real. And *I* had broken it.

Papa would be jubilant. As would William.

I should feel jubilant as well—and vindicated. I had set

out to prove what I could do, and I had done it. But I felt neither. My stomach curled tight, and I pressed my arms against my sides, my hands folded protectively before me. It was one thing to be a spell-binder, to shape air and light into illusions, to heal. It was something else entirely to destroy those spells, to turn gifts into curses, to release shadows into daylight.

Grandmama eased into the room. After fussing over me for a moment, she sat down on the bed beside me and brushed a thin hand through my hair. At length, she said, "Will you tell me why you came here?"

When I shook my head, the corners of her eyes drooped. "Mátyás will not say either. But Anna, *szívem,* I am very much afraid you have started something you will not be able to stop."

)(

Someone tapped at the door.

"Miss Anna?" Lady Berri opened the door.

I rubbed my forehead, which was beginning to throb. My life wanted only this: conducting social calls in my bed-chamber when I was supposed to be convalescing. I wished I was back at Eszterháza, amid the familiarity of my own things.

Lady Berri dragged a chair to my bedside and plopped down, a sigh escaping her as she settled. "I have just come from Vienna. You have certainly managed to set a cat among the pigeons, my dear. As soon as word came you had broken the spell at Sárvár . . . Well. I am sure you can guess at the reaction. The Circle is up in arms, fretting you might break the Binding."

She shook her head at me. "Did not your Papa tell you I was coming? We could have avoided all this fuss if you had simply waited."

I flushed. My brave act of defiance seemed foolish in hindsight. "Then why come now, when the spell is already broken?"

Lady Berri fidgeted, her plump hands patting her lap as if she were looking for something. "Do you suppose they serve tea in this abysmal hostelry?" She sighed. "It's clear, child, that you have a knack for breaking spells, though the Binding Saints alone know why. I want you to break the Binding."

"Why?" I was not as surprised as I might have been: Papa's letter had prepared me.

"Because I am a pragmatist. Perhaps you know that Luminate magic is growing weaker. The Binding spell does not hold so much magic as it once did. I believe we weaken it further when we bind it solely to Luminate bloodlines. We need a new infusion of magic, one we can get only if the Binding is broken and magic returned to our world."

I noticed that she made no mention of fairness, as Papa had done.

"Sárvár is the first spell I have broken *after* its casting; every other spell has been broken during the casting. You can't even be sure I can duplicate this, not with a much larger spell."

"I shall help you."

The door opened again. It was Ginny, bearing a tray with

187

two teacups and a plate of *diós kifli,* a crescent-shaped walnut pastry. I accepted the tea gratefully. Ginny grinned at me before dropping a curtsy to Lady Berri and slipping out again.

"Even presuming I can do what you want—why should I? Why should I upset a system that has been in place for a millennium?" No matter what Papa had written, I was not certain I trusted her.

"Your papa wishes it."

"I love my papa very much, but his wishes do not always dictate my actions."

Lady Berri's fluttering hands stilled. "Because I know what you crave: a place in society. Oh, don't look so disbelieving. I was once a girl much like you. I wanted to shine in society, but like you, I lacked something. Only in my case it was not magic and a certain want of manners, but beauty."

The teacup in my hand trembled. I set it carefully in its saucer on my bedside table.

Lady Berri continued. "I found my way, with a little help from a generous mentor, and here I am now. A patroness of the arts, a member of the English Circle, the head of the Lucifera order. And I wish to help *you.* I think with sufficient patronage a place can be found for you in Luminate society. I can introduce you to the right people. Find you a wealthy husband, if that is what you wish."

"Another Lord Markson Worthing?" I asked, lifting one eyebrow. Lady Berri did not know me nearly as well as she believed.

"If you like."

"But if I do as you ask—will there be any society to introduce me to?"

She laughed. "You place too much weight on a spell. Do you think society will remake itself so quickly?"

I swallowed the sourness in my throat and took a rather fierce bite of the sweet pastry, the flaky crust melting against my tongue. My pulse pounded in my temples. "May I think it over? You ask a great deal."

"Of course, child. Rest now, and give me your answer when you are ready." She smiled brightly. "Your grandmama has invited me to stay for some time. So I shall see the famous Eszterházy estate, and then travel with you to Buda-Pest at summer's end, where I have some business. It all sounds quite delightful, do you not think?"

Delightful was not precisely the word I would have chosen. As Lady Berri finally waddled from the room, the headache that had been circling as she spoke settled in my skull. My thoughts spun in time with the pounding in my head. Lady Berri promised me everything I had ever wanted. Her arguments were compelling, and Papa sided with her.

All I had to do was break the spell I had been taught to honor since childhood, the spell that made my entire world possible.

※

I woke from a nap to find Herr Steinberg sitting nearby, scrutinizing me, worry drawing deep lines between his eyes and around his thin lips. His glasses flashed at me in the long afternoon light.

I sat up, clutching the bedclothes to me, alarmed to find

we were alone. Not that I believed the good Herr had any designs on my virtue, only somehow his mild demeanor seemed changed—charged with tension. The hairs on my arms lifted.

"What are you?" he asked.

"I beg your pardon?" My headache had not entirely vanished, and my skull began to throb, my scalp drawn tight against it.

"There were wards set at Sárvár that ought to have kept you out. Yet you walked through the wards as though they were cobwebs, then broke a spell that has been vexing the Circle for centuries." Herr Steinberg stood and began pacing, his hands clasped behind his back. "The most powerful Luminates of a dozen generations have thrown their energies at that spell and failed. Yet you broke it easily, without any demonstrable spells or rites. How?"

I wished I knew. *What are you?* His question rattled around my skull.

Herr Steinberg stopped pacing to look at me, his eyes sad behind his spectacles. "When you broke that spell, did you *see* anything?"

He had asked me this once before, about the Lorelei maiden. Monsters crowded my thoughts: an inhumanly beautiful face with lips like brands, a spider-woman with a third eye open. I gripped my covers, sure now his question was no accident. "Why are you asking me this? What business is it of yours?"

He breathed out through his nose, clearly attempting to remain calm. "It is my business because I belong to the Austrian Circle. I took an oath to protect the Binding, and I have been tasked with watching you—a task I clearly failed, as you were allowed to steal away to Sárvár."

I froze. "But you were our majordomo from England. You arranged the details of our trip. I thought—"

"You thought what you were meant to think. That I was nothing more. But Lord Orwell suspected you might be trouble. When you disappeared from London, he sent word to Vienna, and I was selected to deal with you. It was no great difficulty to track you—one of my gifts, if you must know—and pay off the man intended for your escort."

"You have been watching me this whole time." Had he seen my meetings with Gábor? My veins ran ice.

"Not, it appears, closely enough. Now I will ask you again: what did you see?"

Nothing. My tongue curled around the word.

"Take care. I shall know if you're lying. Did you see creatures, somewhat monstrous in aspect?"

"Yes," I said finally. *And they asked me to set them free.*

Herr Steinberg closed his eyes, as if my answer pained him. "I feared as much."

"But what are they? I thought at first they must be illusions."

His eyes flew open. "They're real. And ancient. The monsters and demigods of folklore once lived among us. But Charlemagne deemed them too dangerous to humans, and they were bound up with the magic in the Binding. If some of them managed to find their way into the spell at Sárvár, we may all be in very grave peril."

The Circle keep us safe.

The Binding preserve us.

These were not vague prayers for the future, but injunctions from the past. The prayers of my childhood hid beasts out of legend. "Why have I never heard of them?" Even Papa's letter had said nothing.

"A decision was made when the creatures were bound not to speak of it. Their existence is better forgotten. Even most members of the Circle do not know they are real. But if you can see the creatures, if they can reach you, then the Binding spell is no longer impermeable. Your ability is perilous, Miss Anna. It's dangerous to you—and to every Luminate. There are some who would kill you to keep the Binding safe."

My hands against the covers were frozen, my knuckles white. "I don't even know how I broke the spell."

"That makes you all the more hazardous. You might break the Binding by accident. Or the heretics might persuade you to aid them. Your father, for one. Lady Berri, for another. I've seen her skulking about this inn. You should know she is not to be trusted."

I pressed my lips together, thinking of Lady Berri and the promises I held like hope in my heart. She had been very persuasive, but I was not at all certain I could break a spell that would unleash monsters on the world, no matter what Papa believed.

"Are you among those who want to kill me?" I had planned to be unmoved, even defiant, but my voice emerged thin and wavering. I was aware of the quiet of the room—and of Herr Steinberg's hands, with their long, corded fingers.

He shook his head. "I am a pacifist, child. I would like to see you live a long life. But I will protect the Binding before all else. When the spell was first cast, it was designed to keep all Luminate out, to guard against this very possibility. But you—you are something else entirely."

I shivered.

"Has Lady Berri asked you to break the Binding?"

I did not answer.

His lips compressed. "I do not think you appreciate the gravity of this. No doubt Lady Berri has assured you that nothing serious will happen. Perhaps she has promised you something for your efforts: wealth, a position in society. She cannot guarantee those promises. Would you destroy your entire world on such thin possibilities? Surely you are not so selfish. The lower classes hate us; if you strip us of magic, they will destroy us. And the monsters from the Binding would be free, slaking their blood lust and ravaging our cities."

I stared at him, chilled by the world he presented.

"Understand this: we are watching you. If you attempt to enter the Binding spell, we *will* stop you. Kill you if we must. I do not wish to do this." He stepped closer to me, patted my hand where it lay lax on my thigh.

I twitched away. I did not want those hands touching me.

"Your grandmother tells me you are heading to Buda-Pest soon. I think this is an excellent plan. Enjoy society life, as a young lady should. Forget about the Binding, for your own sake."

When I said nothing, he left, the door shuddering against the frame. I curled under my bedclothes, my heart racing. Between them, Herr Steinberg and Lady Berri presented me with impossible choices. I might choose to be safe, continuing to live the same circumscribed life I'd always known and abandoning any hope of magic and a real place in society.

Or I might answer the yearning call of my shadow self for a bigger life, a life that meant something. I might break the Binding and upend my entire world. But to do so, I would risk everything that mattered to me: my family, my friends, Luminate society itself.

CHAPTER 16

The stork's shadow crossed me like a bad omen. On horseback, I watched the bird land in its enormous messy nest—imposing, ungainly, and magnificent all at once—and tried to shake the sense of being watched.

Now that we were back at Eszterháza, I felt eyes on me everywhere: Herr Steinberg, finding an excuse to call on Grandmama and ensure I was where I was meant to be. Lady Berri, trundling through the rooms of Eszterháza and appearing at unexpected times in unexpected places, trying to catch me alone (Noémi had come across her more than once in the stillroom). Grandmama and Noémi, both worrying I was not fully healed. Only Mátyás did not watch me, and I could not decide if I was affronted or relieved by his disinterest. In response, I escaped the palace as often as I could.

Before me, the road curled away like a question. I glanced

at the village behind me, barely visible at the edges of the green fields. No one appeared to notice. In the windless afternoon, even the shadows stayed put, wilted by the heat.

I nudged Cukor off the road. Incuriously, he stepped across the field, and within moments I'd reached my destination.

The Romani camp.

Only circles of stone and ash marked where they had been. I dismounted, letting Cukor graze on the grass that had already sprung up beneath the former tent sites.

We were departing for Buda-Pest in the morning, but I could not leave Eszterháza without seeking out my last connection, however faint, to Gábor. The city promised so much: museums and plays and operas and society, university classes for Mátyás, medical training for Noémi. But the city threatened as well. Reading between the lines of Mama's latest letter, I surmised she wished me to acquire social polish there—better still, a husband to take me off her hands. Lady Berri would expect an answer to her demand. And Herr Steinberg would follow me to the city, his presence its own kind of menace.

For the moment, I answered them all with silence—a mute refusal to cooperate. But silence would only work as a delaying tactic for so long.

I pushed such unpleasant thoughts from my mind as I wandered through the campsite, imagining *here* was where I first met Izidóra and *here* I first saw Gábor. And *there* he kissed me—an angry, derisive kiss that had made me hate him until, unexpectedly, I hadn't.

Heat beyond the sultry warmth of the afternoon flooded through me.

And *there.* There I had broken Noémi's spell with an ability I didn't understand. *Selfish,* Herr Steinberg had named me. Maybe he was right.

I turned back toward my horse. There was nothing for me here save aching memories. I should not have come.

"Anna."

The voice from beneath the clump of alders behind me was so unexpected I let out an unladylike screech, then clapped my hand to my mouth in mortification. I whirled around, my heart thumping. Hoping, *hoping* . . .

I was not wrong. Gábor stood in the shadows of the trees, watching me. Strangely, I did not mind the weight of *his* eyes.

"You left," I said stupidly.

He crossed the campsite toward me. "I helped my sisters to Buda-Pest, where they will stay for the winter. And then I came back."

For me? I wanted to ask, but swallowed the words. My entire body was a lit fuse. Whatever this knot of feeling in my chest was, I could not tangle it further by inviting confidences I was not ready to hear. He was Romani, and whatever I was, I was not that. And I could not bear another Freddy: another set of intentions and veiled promises and heated feelings and disappointment.

"I had business with your cousin," he said, and I was doubly glad I had not asked.

He studied my face a moment, his eyes lingering on my mouth a heartbeat longer than strictly proper. "Are you well? You look flushed."

I fluttered my handkerchief at my face. "It's this heat."

"I heard you were ill."

"A temporary indisposition. I am much better now, thank you." I could not mention Sárvár, after his warning. I could not bear seeing the concern in his eyes fade to anger, or worse, repulsion.

"I should not keep you," he said. "You have illustrious visitors at the palace, I hear."

I waved my hand. "They don't matter."

"The German herr asks about you in the *csárda*. And Mátyás says the English lady has been hounding you. If she is bothering you, perhaps I can help."

An involuntary laugh escaped me. "You cannot help with this."

His lips tightened. "I may be Romani, but I am not helpless."

"I did not mean that! Only this . . . this is Luminate business."

"What does she want?"

It would be easier to hide truths from him if I cared nothing for him, if the sharp line of his cheek did not distract my thoughts, if my body did not already impel me toward him.

I did not want to lie to Gábor. I said nothing. I balled my hands into fists and did not move.

"You don't trust me." His words were steady, unsurprised, only the faintest tinge of sadness in them to tear at my heart.

"I *do* trust you."

Gábor stalked forward, stopping so close to me I could feel the warmth from his body. So close his breath stirred the hair around my face. "Then tell me."

When I didn't answer, he put both hands on my shoulders.

My skin, even under the fabric of my dress, prickled at his touch.

"Anna." My stomach fluttered at the intensity in his voice, the intimacy of my bare name. "Tell me this: what has the English lady asked of you? And why will you not tell me? Is it something to do with Sárvár?"

"No." It wasn't a lie: the spell at Sárvár was already broken. Lady Berri had no interest in it.

He stared at me but did not release me. "A great English lady, a member of your Luminate Circle, comes to visit you—a girl without magic, who cannot learn spells but who can break them. . . ." He trailed off, horrified. "The Binding."

"I have not agreed to anything," I said, beginning to feel angry. Why was everyone so determined to choose my path for me? I could not see there was much to choose between what Lady Berri offered and what Herr Steinberg did. Herr Steinberg would see me live out the same dull, restricted life I had always lived at the fringes of society. Lady Berri offered change, excitement, a chance to do something that mattered. But what of the costs? How would my world look in the aftermath of the Binding breaking? The American colonists had ushered in a vigorous democracy on the heels of a revolution, but there was no guarantee the same would happen here. What if breaking the Binding only led to bloodshed—or something worse than the Circle rising to power?

"What has she offered you?"

I shook my head to clear my thoughts. "I didn't say she'd offered me anything."

"I know a deal when I see one, and this scheme reeks of it. What has she promised you?"

My cheeks flamed. I pulled a cloak of anger over my embarrassment and jerked away. "Whatever she offers is my business alone. You and I have no promise—no *deal*, as you put it—that gives you any right to question me."

A veil shuttered down over Gábor's face. "If you trust her more than you trust me, then you're right. We have nothing left to say to each other. My apologies for disturbing you." He turned away.

My heart clenched tight. "Wait. Please. I didn't come here to fight with you. I haven't said yes to her."

He paused, listening, but did not turn back.

"Please," I said again. "I am going to Buda-Pest tomorrow. You say your family is there. Will I see you there?"

"And how should I *see* you, Miss Arden?" The distance was back between us in my formal name, in the stiff way he held himself, his arms crossed across his chest, in the bitter tang of his voice. "Shall I come calling at your grandmama's house? Ask you to dance at some fine Luminate party?"

Angry tears stung my eyes. "You need not mock me. *I* am not the one using our differences as a weapon. I don't care that you are Romani."

The stiffness evaporated from his shoulders. He turned back and crossed the space dividing us. "I'm sorry. That was uncalled for." He reached out one lean hand and brushed my cheek. "Please, trust me. Do not do what this woman asks."

My skin came alive beneath his touch. "Very well," I said, not agreeing precisely but buying myself time. I did not want him to leave. "Will you go back to your family?"

"I am not currently welcome, not after what happened."

"You've been banished?" Shock lined my veins with ice.

"Do not judge the elders. Their job is to keep the family safe. They did what they deemed right—as I did." He shrugged, but I could see how his shoulders hunched, as if to ward off a blow. "In time, I may be allowed back."

"But how shall you live?"

"I shall look for work. A clerical position in a small firm, if I am very lucky."

A possibility bubbled up inside me. "I have a better idea." I grabbed his hand. "Come with me."

※

If Grandmama was surprised by my abrupt appearance in the parlor with Gábor in tow, the only sign she made was a small sigh.

"What is it, Anna?"

"I've found a secretary for you," I said.

"A . . . but . . . Anna, I'm not in need of a secretary."

Gábor shifted from one foot to the other, tucking his hands behind him. "Truly, Miss Arden, this is very kind of you, but if your grandmother has no need of my services, I should go."

Lady Berri set down her cup of tea, her small eyes dancing with interest.

"Wait," I said, borrowing Mama's imperious tone. It worked. He stopped shifting. "Grandmama, Mr. Kovács is highly intelligent and well educated. He can write letters for you, tally bills, secure a carriage—anything you'd like."

201

"He's Gypsy," János observed, shaking his head. "He's as like to steal from you as serve you."

"Romani," I said. "And he won't."

"A Gypsy!" Grandmama said, dropping her embroidery. "Anna, really, I couldn't."

"That's unfair, János *bácsi*," Mátyás said, speaking for the first time. He uncurled himself from the sofa and crossed the room to shake Gábor's hand. "Hallo, Gábor." He looked back at Grandmama. "I know him. He's a good man. Honest too. I trust him."

I beamed at Mátyás, who colored faintly. I turned to Grandmama. "His being Romani is precisely the point. He's capable, but who would hire him? He only needs a chance, a good recommendation that might open other doors."

Lady Berri said, "I've found that a good secretary is almost indispensable."

I could have kissed her.

Grandmama sighed again, a luxurious release of air. She picked up her embroidery. "Very well, Anna. Only do not let me regret this."

I crossed the room to kiss her cheek. "You won't, Grandmama. I promise."

Her voice was very dry when she answered me. "I already do."

CHAPTER 17

Buda-Pest, late September 1847

On my eighth circuit of the room, Grandmama set down her reading spectacles and rubbed her temples. "Anna, *szívem*, must you prowl like some caged beast? Have you nothing better to do?"

I stilled obediently, dropping into a chair near the window overlooking a broad thoroughfare in the Pest *belváros*. From this vantage point, buildings blocked my view of the Buda hills, on the other side of the Duna River dividing the twin cities. But restlessness still crawled through my body, and I tapped an imperceptible rhythm against my skirts. Lady Berri had called again that morning, and I had no answer to give her. For the first time in my life, I knew a lurking sympathy for Hamlet, whom I had once denounced to a governess as a waffling, pudding-hearted excuse for a man. I was not normally indecisive, but I could not make my decision about the Binding lightly. Too many lives were bound up in it.

Still, I must decide *someday*. And soon, before my prowling wore holes in Grandmama's carpets.

"You can come with me to the hospital," Noémi offered, winding up her embroidery thread and stowing it neatly in the basket near her chair. "We can always use more hands."

"Another time, perhaps." Most days, Noémi shadowed a nurse-midwife at the hospital, but I did not think I would feel any less restive in the square building on Rókus Street, with its narrow hallways and stench of chlorinated limewater.

Mátyás popped his head into Grandmama's salon. "I'm on my way out. Can I be of service while I'm gone, Irína *néni*?"

Grandmama replaced her glasses. "Yes. Take Anna with you."

Anything was better than staying in Grandmama's salon, fretting over a decision that could unmake my world's magic. I ran upstairs to my room for a light wrap and my reticule. When I reached the mouth of the courtyard, Mátyás waited for me with Gábor.

My heart stuttered. Despite my maneuverings, I had seen Gábor only in tiny slivers of time during our weeks in the city: enough to sting with longing, but never enough to satisfy. If Lady Berri was right and breaking the Binding would make magic accessible to everyone, it would undermine the very class structure that supported my family. No doubt Mama would object to that—but if it erased the gulf between Gábor and me, I could only welcome it. I added a small weight to the invisible scale in my head. One more reason to break the Binding.

We emerged through the gates into sharp-bright sunlight. A fine layer of silt scoured down the street before the small baroque palace Grandmama had rented for the season, blowing in from the plains beyond Pest. Only a little larger than a town house, with walls marching against its neighbors, the palace sounds grander than it was. I coughed and held my handkerchief over my mouth and nose. We walked past the fine shops on Váci Street, before veering off onto a narrow side road, our heads lowered and eyes squinted shut against the dust.

"Are you well, Miss Anna?" Gábor asked me. "That is, you do not look like you feel ill—you look very well. I meant, do you feel well? In spirit?"

It was not like Gábor to be tongue-tied. I smiled. "Yes. Thank you."

Mátyás squinted at me. "I think Anna looks quite ill. Positively dreadful."

I nearly stopped, to try to see my reflection in a window (I had not paused to look at myself before I left), when Mátyás burst out laughing.

"*You* are dreadful," I told him, and he only laughed harder. I turned to find Gábor watching me, a curious expression on his face. "And you, Mr. Kovács?" His full name was stiff on my tongue. "Is my grandmother treating you well?"

"The work is not difficult. It gives me time to study."

"And your family?"

"I have not seen them."

Something about his clipped words indicated he would

not welcome further questions. We fell into an awkward silence, which Mátyás tried to fill with a series of increasingly terrible jokes.

At last we reached a small building, four arched windows beneath a sign reading CAFÉ PILVAX. Despite outward appearances, the café was long and airy, scattered tables set up beneath a series of brick archways. All sorts of people crowded inside, despite—or perhaps because of—the winds: Luminate women in their fine lawn dresses, noblemen in their top hats and embroidered dolmans, a soldier or two with their high shako hats and red feather plumes, students, workers, even a dog lying placidly on the parquet floor.

Mátyás found us room at several small tables shoved together. Somehow, I was not surprised to see William there, engaged in heated debate with a curly-haired young man with a luxurious dark mustache. I ordered coffee in the Hungarian style, sweetened with milk and honey, and listened to the young men around me, mostly students, debate everything from natural history to politics to Jókai Mór's newest play. Though the conversations were mostly Hungarian, I picked up enough to follow, and what I did not understand, Mátyás or Gábor translated.

One of the students asked a waitress for "the tongue of the dog."

I turned startled eyes on Gábor. "Surely they don't eat dog's tongue here!"

He laughed. "No. Wait and see."

Within moments the waitress returned with a long paper, and the student set to scribbling furiously. The curly-haired man who had been arguing with William broke off to peer over his shoulder.

I grinned. This place—everything about it, from the cozy brick walls to the students' energy—was delightful.

The curly-haired man clapped the writer on the shoulder. "Bravo! Well done, lad."

I leaned toward Mátyás. "Who is that?"

He whispered back, "Petőfi Sándor. They say he may be the greatest poet of our generation. I read you some of his poetry while you convalesced."

William, deprived of his sparring partner, looked around the café. His eyes lit on me. "Miss Anna Arden!" he cried, leaning across the table toward me. "Mátyás told me of your excellent work at Sárvár! Have you come to join our cause?"

Gábor stiffened beside me, but when I risked a glance at him, he did not look surprised. Mátyás must have told him what happened.

I shook my head gently. "I've made no decisions."

William accepted my rebuff affably enough, and he and the poet fell back into a friendly argument as to the most compelling reasons to break from Austria. The poet said, "The Hapsburgs dictate our laws, our schools, who our spell-binders might be, even our wars. They've deprived us of all our natural rights."

William shook his head. "The Circle is more your enemy than the Hapsburgs. They are the ones who limit your magic, who encourage the Hapsburgs to limit your rights for fear you will grow strong enough to challenge them."

As Mátyás translated their words, my sympathy grew. I knew what it was to have your life determined for you. In their complaints, I felt all my old chafing against my mother's strictures.

I asked Mátyás, "Are they not afraid of the Circle, or

government censors?" Any of the Luminate in the café might be a spy.

Mátyás laughed. "The Circle members are fools. They think all plots require secrecy and midnight meetings. They see no danger in our open discussions." He sobered. "Perhaps they should. There is suffering enough in Hungary to rouse even the faintest heart."

"It's not only the Hungarians who suffer," Gábor said to me. "It is still legal to take a Romani child from her family and raise her to an apprenticeship far from her home."

A young woman sitting near me said, "Kossuth Lajos hopes to see such laws changed. He would abolish the serfdom, and make proper concessions for the Romani. And Jews. And anyone else who suffers under current laws. But first Hungary must break away from Austria and the Circle's power. At present, we are entirely subordinate: we lack our own government, our own laws, our own Circle. Not even all our aristocracy are Luminate, because the Austrian Circle will only allow Confirmation to the wealthiest of Hungarian nobles."

I warmed to her immediately. I liked the calm intelligence of her voice, the openness of her face, and—it must be confessed—the elegance of her gown, brightly embroidered with the stylized flowers of Hungarian *kézimunka*.

"Kossuth!" William scoffed. "He is a tame sort of radical. All fuel and no fire. He won't challenge the Circle."

"He is still our best hope." The woman's cheeks flushed.

Gábor added, "I think Kossuth's policy is best: we should exhaust diplomacy before we fight."

Petőfi shook his head and tapped his chest. "*We* are Magyarország's best hope. And so far, talk has achieved nothing. We must act: drive the Circle from Hungary, demand our independence from Austria."

"But in the months I have spent in Buda-Pest, all you have done is talk." William's lip curled.

Petőfi frowned. "We wait for the right moment."

"You don't wait for a moment; you *create* it." William looked at me. "Miss Arden could help us, if she would only break the Binding."

Could I? If William were right, breaking the Binding would weaken the Circle, perhaps destroy it outright. The Circle's control and maintenance of the Binding was their primary source of power. Without it, though they might attempt to continue regulating magic, they would lose that leverage. An influx of magic *outside* the Luminate class could well shift the balance of power away from the Circle. Without the Circle to support it, the Hapsburg government in Vienna must release its stranglehold on Hungary, on the people and places I was coming to love.

The poet followed William's gaze, his mustache twitching as his lips turned down. "A girl?"

I crossed my arms. "You should not dismiss me because I am only a female. Even a small dog can bite. And," I added, remembering a scientific conversation I had overheard between Mátyás and Gábor, "a microorganism smaller than the head of a pin can kill a grown man."

"Brava!" The young lady beside me clapped her hands.

Gábor murmured, "But having power does not always mean using it. The Binding is a large spell and a dangerous one. My grandmother believes that it contains monsters. She may be wrong, but breaking a spell without understanding what you unleash is madness."

Monsters. A woman with a third eye, a golden man with shifting faces, shadows scuttering across a field, clawed hands dragging me through darkness. For a moment, Gábor's doubt set my mental scales trembling. Herr Steinberg had also warned me. Then I thought: *none of the creatures harmed me.* Likely, Gábor's warnings stemmed only from Romani superstition. And Herr Steinberg was less than trustworthy: his position in the Circle was only as secure as the Binding spell.

Mátyás laughed. "I should rather like to see Anna take on a massive spell."

"We don't have to break the Binding to petition for more independence," Gábor said. "Kossuth—"

William cut across him. "Nonsense. Consider the evidence of the past centuries. Petitions alone have never spurred change. The Circle simply ignores them. We haven't the leverage we need to make them listen. But we would be strong enough if the Binding was broken. Only look at the colonists."

"If there are monsters," Petőfi added, "and I have never heard of their existence, they cannot be worse than what we already face."

Gábor looked as though he wished to argue further, but Mátyás stood up. "This has been an invigorating discussion. But it's time we returned for tea."

I swallowed a slightly hysterical urge to laugh. Because tea was, of course, the appropriate response to an afternoon's talk of treason and monsters.

As we rose, the young woman rose with us. "Wait," she said, accompanying us toward the doorway. "I am Károlyi Karolina. You may call me Karolina. I very much admired your speech earlier, and I should like to know you better. May I call on you?"

I nodded, strangely shy. I could count my female friends on one hand, and they were all either related to me or in my employ. "I should like that."

"And you must all come to the ball my sister and I are holding next Monday night at the Redoute," she added.

"That's kind of you," Gábor said, "but I am not certain your friends would welcome me."

"Nonsense," Karolina said. "If you care for Hungary, you are welcome."

"But," Gábor said, frowning, "perhaps you do not realize I am Romani."

"What should I care for that?" Karolina said, stepping through the doorway and swinging up her parasol. "We are building a new world, are we not?"

A dark-haired man on the far side of the street watched us as we emerged, his pale eyes intent on my face. Something familiar about him nagged at me, but I could not place it.

His scrutiny shook me. Herr Steinberg had said the Circle would be watching me. Was this man one of their spies? *If you attempt to enter the Binding spell, we will stop you. Kill you if we must.* A heavy weight settled on the negative side of my scale. Did I value this cause enough to risk my life for it?

)(

Karolina called the next morning. When Ginny brought her card up, both Noémi and Grandmama straightened in shock.

"Is she not respectable? Ought I not to have invited her?" I asked.

"Nothing like that," Grandmama assured me. "Her family is very old and well regarded. One of the Zichy sisters, you know. Married to Count Károlyi. Only, I didn't know you knew her."

Karolina burst into the room, a whirlwind in a simple white cotton dress. Hungarian made, she explained, settling herself onto the sofa beside me. She greeted Grandmama and Noémi. She asked me about my family with genuine interest. When I mentioned that James was at Eton, her expressive face grew pensive.

"My husband speaks of sending my eldest to Vienna soon, but I am not sure I wish to send him. Surely he can be as well educated close to home in his mother tongue. Better, perhaps, away from Hapsburg influence."

"Yes." Grandmama nodded, though her eyes were stricken. "It is good to keep a child close to home."

"And how is your brother faring? Does he like the school?" Karolina asked me.

"Many of the boys are cruel, mocking him because he can barely muster the simplest of Luminate spells."

Karolina sighed. "I think it is in the nature of boys to tease one another, whether or not magic is involved. Your brother will find his place, I am sure of it."

"I hope you might be right."

"I am always right. My sister would tell you so, if she were here. But this is a dour topic for a morning call. Tell me"—

212

Karolina leaned forward, her dark ringlets falling across her cheeks—"do you read poetry?"

At the end of an energetic discussion, Karolina sprang up. She had stayed nearly an hour, well past the quarter hour allotted for polite calls. I walked her down to the entryway, where her maid waited.

Karolina kissed my cheek in farewell. "I was right," she said. "You *are* a dear. We shall be good friends."

"Yes," I said, warmth rising from my toes. It was a novel sensation, to find someone who liked me for myself, with no expectations attached. I rather fancied it.

I opened the door for Karolina, and found Lady Berri perched on our doorstep.

My happiness evaporated.

I introduced the two women. Karolina curtsied and left.

"You've been avoiding me," Lady Berri said. "Why? If your papa supports our plan, what hesitation can you have?"

I had many, but I could not list them on my doorstep. I settled for the one I thought her likeliest to understand. "Herr Steinberg said there are members of the Circle who would kill me if I touched the Binding."

Lady Berri laughed. "Herr Steinberg always did enjoy talking like a villain in a melodrama. You needn't worry about him, my dear. I can keep you safe." She patted my cheek and surveyed the sky. A storm brooded over the horizon, already pushing dust down the street. "I shan't come in just now. But don't think you can put me off forever. When you decide, find me at the Hunter's Horn."

)(

On the evening of Karolina's ball, I passed Gábor in the hallway, on my way to the drawing room. He carried a sheaf of papers toward the study, but he paused when he saw me. A shadow flickered across his face.

"Well? Will I do?" I held out my skirts in a mock curtsy. Ginny and I had spent the better part of two hours preparing for the ball. Karolina had warned me that everything was to be in the Magyar style, so I had commissioned a dress that laced across the bodice, golden ivy climbing beside the laces and sprawling across the full green skirt.

"Anyone would be honored to dance with you." His lips tugged upward in a smile that did not quite reach his eyes.

Would you? I wanted to ask. I could not read the look in his eyes, and it troubled me. I wanted him to admire me, to say something more to me than the bare dictates of politeness. His plain trousers and light cotton dolman registered. "You're not coming? Karolina made sure to invite you."

Gábor's lips curled again, that smile that was not a smile. "It's best if I stay."

All afternoon I had entertained visions of the two of us sweeping across the ballroom together. Those visions crumbled, and a sharp, stabbing ache took their place. "You shall be missed," I said, careful not to let my words betray too much, then swept past him to the drawing room where Noémi and Grandmama waited.

Mátyás and Noémi were arguing about Mátyás's sporadic attendance at the university.

"They will expel you," Noémi said, digging her fingers into the sleeves of his coat. "What is so important that you risk your future? Sitting in cafés talking about revolution?"

Mátyás shook off her hand. "This *is* my future. What future does any Hungarian have, restricted as we are by the Hapsburgs and the Viennese Circle?"

"You have options," Noémi said. "You're Luminate. You can study in Vienna. Or Paris."

"And what sort of patriot would I be to abandon my friends and my country? Hungary deserves better than this."

"And your sister? Do I not deserve better? What kind of future shall I have when you are killed?"

Mátyás didn't answer. He marched out of the room with thinned lips to see if the hired carriage had arrived. It had, so he returned to escort us downstairs and help us in—nearly dropping Noémi in the process—and we were off.

The vehicle carried us beside the raised walkway of the Korzó along the Duna. Buda Castle soared above us on the far side of the river, lit by some Luminate spell: the elegant rococo façade of the central wing rising up over the flanking wings, the endless rows of windows reflecting blank eyes across the water. Behind the castle, the Buda hills slumbered like folds of black velvet.

Eventually we reached the Quay, the semicircular row of white stone buildings in the Italian style, with their classical pillars and porticoes. When I descended from the carriage before the Redoute, the public ballroom ornamented with baroque lavishness, my entire body was taut like a violin string. I could not bear a repeat of the ball in Vienna.

Mátyás put an arm around me. "Don't be nervous, Anna. I'll dance with you, even if no one else will."

I forgot my nerves in trying to bat at him. Mátyás laughed and skipped out of reach.

The walls of the ballroom were draped with great swags of Hungarian colors: red, green, and white knots everywhere. Even the dances reflected the nationalist theme: the orchestra played circle dances, like the quadrille and a *csárdás* much like the one I'd danced with Mátyás at Whitsun night. The entire evening I did not once hear the strains of an Austrian waltz. The guests spoke Hungarian almost defiantly, and the few conversations I heard begun in German were quickly hushed.

There was no overt magic here, not like the wild phoenix at the Viennese ball. Only minor charms to keep the air circulating and cool, to keep the flowers from wilting and to heighten their scent. The women wore gowns, like mine, covered in exquisite Hungarian handwork; the men were resplendent in traditional embroidered dolmans and satin-lined mentes.

Thanks to Mátyás's student friends, I did not lack for partners. I danced with a banker and a doctor, an apothecary and an aspiring valet. I even, daringly, danced with a young Jewish man. After supper, I whirled across the floor with the poet Petőfi Sándor, who apologized for doubting me at Café Pilvax. I told him how much I enjoyed his poetry, and we ended our dance very well pleased with one another. Mama would certainly not approve of the egalitarian mix, but I liked it. No one marked my missing soul sign. Here I was like any other young lady, dancing with a string of charming suitors.

"Are you enjoying yourself?" Karolina asked me halfway through the night, sliding her arm through mine. Her tousled chestnut curls bore witness that she too was enjoying the dancing.

"Very much."

"I am glad," Karolina said, smiling. A golden falcon necklace, wings spread wide and diamond crusted, sparkled around her throat. Petőfi had worn a similarly shaped pin in his neckcloth.

My gaze swept the room, workingmen and workingwomen swirling through the dances in company with poets, artists, and Luminate. I had dreamed of something like this once. As the dancers flashed past, I noticed what I had not before: how very common the falcon motif was, nearly every third gentleman sporting it on his coat.

"The falcon?" I asked, nodding at Karolina's necklace.

"The turul bird. He led our first parents to the Carpathian valleys and a new empire—and, God willing, he will lead us to victory and independence again. Here." She unfastened the chain and held it out to me. "I want you to have it."

I stepped back. "I could not take it from you."

"I think it belongs with you—as you belong with us. A true Magyar patriot."

William had told me in Vienna I would never be accepted by Luminate society. Perhaps he was right. But this night had shown me there were other societies, better societies, that might welcome me and others like me, and James, and Gábor. A ballroom was not the real world, I knew, but it reflected real possibilities.

Something kindled in my heart, stirred by the memory of a starving girl on the streets in Vienna repulsed by magic, a Luminate squire willing to use magic to kill a Romani boy, a woman dying in poverty, a serf boy whipped in a field. Something gallant, perhaps reckless.

This time, when Karolina held out the necklace, I took it,

fastening it about my neck and letting the still-warm gold settle against my skin.

These people—*my people*—wanted to remake the world into something better, something more egalitarian and open. And I could help them do it, without violence or bloodshed. *You are something else entirely,* Herr Steinberg had said. He was right.

I *was* different.

But that difference did not mean I was weak or helpless. I had learned to fear my ability to break spells, but it did not have to be a curse. I could choose to see it as a gift. I could embrace my own power.

I could change the world.

The weights in my head shifted, then settled.

CHAPTER 18

Approaching Lady Berri's hotel the following afternoon with Ginny, I felt rather more like the faltering hero of an epic poem—Byron's Childe Harold in the shadows of the Alps—than a young lady paying a call on her country-woman. My courage of the night before had evaporated. And though the Hunter's Horn was a staid, neoclassical hotel located in a mew off Váci Street and the afternoon was warm and bright, darkness seemed to cling to the cornices of the building.

I took a deep breath and entered. A red-uniformed porter led me up to Lady Berri's room, on the second floor of the building. Ginny waited in the lobby below, fortified with a dog-eared copy of one of Mrs. Radcliffe's novels.

The room where Lady Berri received me was almost overpoweringly opulent. Gold leaf bloomed across the carved ceiling above my head, and the gold was echoed in the vivid yellows and browns of the Turkish carpet beneath our feet. Plush red velvet covered the chairs and couches, and crimson-and-gold brocade curtains hung by the windows.

"Tea?" Lady Berri asked, holding up a white porcelain teacup with a delicate pattern of forget-me-nots. The subtlety of the design appeared out of place in the bold room.

"Thank you." I doubted my ability to swallow anything, given my suddenly tight throat, but the prosaic activity of holding a teacup might help me stay grounded. That is, if I did not spill it all over myself.

When I had seated myself on a high-backed chair, Lady Berri said, "How may I help you, my dear?" Her small, cat-like smile suggested she already knew why I had come. The words were only a formality. "Have you decided?"

"Nearly." I began ticking off concerns on my fingers. "Papa says spell-binders used to die because they burned up too much of their own magic. If magic returns to individuals, how will you stop that?"

"Better training," she said promptly. "And your Papa and others have begun to theorize alternative ways to hold magic so it is not as dangerous."

"What happens to the Circle if we break the Binding? To Luminates?"

"Nothing so very dreadful. I imagine the Circle shall have to relinquish some of their authority, but I cannot see that as a bad thing, though I am one of them. And the Luminates shall go on as they always have—only they shall have to share magic with others, which may force them to open their ranks. Also a good thing, in my opinion."

Lady Berri must have read my doubt in my face, for she laughed. "Come now. What else?"

Well, then. "If I help you, do you swear you can keep me safe?"

The humor vanished from her round face, and she leaned forward, her gaze sharp. "I swear it. I am powerful enough to face anyone the Austrian Circle might choose to send against me."

I released a long breath. "Very well. Show me the Binding."

Her eyes grew round. "*Show* you?"

"I know the Binding exists in a realm other than ours, but there must be dimension to it, if it holds magic." *And monsters.* "I need to see what it is you want me to break, and what I shall release in breaking it."

"There's nothing to release," she began, "only magic . . ."

"Herr Steinberg swears there are monsters. And I . . . I spoke with them inside the spell at Sárvár. I want to be certain I am not unleashing something terrible on the world."

Her mouth creased with vexation. "If you saw something in that spell, they were only illusions, meant to deter people from the spell. The stories of monsters were only ever that—stories."

"They did not feel like illusions."

She grunted. "Very well. I believe I can build a Portal spell that can let you cross into the Binding, though it shall take some time to set up. Will that satisfy you?"

"A spell? Are you not worried I shall break that as well?"

"As to that, I have an idea. You'll simply have to trust me."

I nodded. "Will the Circle know we have touched the spell?"

221

"If anyone is paying attention. But members of the Circle touch the Binding spell all the time, to refresh the wards on it and strengthen the barriers. I doubt it shall be marked. And I shall take steps to ensure no one is watching us."

Our talk turned to idle pleasantries. I finished my tea, and Lady Berri stood, shaking crumbs from her capacious lap. She put her arms around me, and I stiffened for a moment before relaxing into her softness. She was comforting in a way my mother had never been. "You're a good girl, Anna. Don't be afraid. I shall call for you tomorrow evening."

※

I did not sleep much that night. My dreams were threaded through with nightmares. Images from my past: the golden-eyed man at Sárvár with the burning touch, the pale strangeness of Herr Steinberg's hands when he threatened to kill me if I tampered with the Binding. Worse still, nightmares of my future: a city overrun with creatures thirsting for blood, as Herr Steinberg warned; a world scoured bare by a sudden onrush of magic; the pain in Gábor's eyes when he realized I had disregarded his warnings.

I woke panting. Had I made a mistake? No, not yet. I would do nothing until I had been inside the spell, until I knew unleashing the magic from the Binding would do no harm—or at least, less harm than good.

In the morning, a letter arrived from James. It was only a

handful of lines wrapped around a new novel, *Jane Eyre* by Currer Bell, but I hugged the letter to me. *I have not much time to write as I am busy studying. I am determined to be first in Latin and history. And I must say, that magic bauble you sent me is top-notch. The other boys are impressed that my spells are beginning to hold, though my tutor is puzzled at how I accomplish them. Still, I think I can keep him suitably flummoxed till the term is over. Yours, James.*

I wondered what James would think if he knew my evening plans might lead me to entirely remake the magic he studied at school. Then I shuddered, and pushed the thought away from me. If I overthought what I was to do, I would lose my nerve.

)(

I watched globes of lamplight spin past me as Lady Berri and I followed one of the main arterial roads away from the city. Pest was full of the thin darkness of early evening, the sun only a remembrance of light above the Buda hills. A pale-eyed man stood beneath one of the lamps, watching our carriage as it rattled past.

The lamps fell away abruptly. We passed a ring of factories, windows lit red by the fires within, smoke still rising from chimneys. Then the city was gone, swallowed into a maw of darkness, and the countryside spread out before us.

"I shall open a portal for you when we arrive," Lady Berri explained. "Not your typical Portal spell, from one known location to another, but more of a gate."

"And how shall I get out again?" I was only beginning to

realize the enormity of what I'd committed to—entering an unknown spell, with no real security I'd return. Lady Berri seemed unworried, so I clung to her confidence.

"The portal will remain open. Just don't get lost—I'm not certain I can hold the gate open if I come in after you."

We pulled up at last, and Lady Berri climbed out, her flickering fingers summoning a Lumen light. In the pale blue glow, a hill rose gently before us. "Attila's Hill," Lady Berri explained. "A ley line crosses near here; the ground has historically been sensitive to magic. My spell should be stronger here."

She began climbing the hill, and I followed, alternately lacing my gloved fingers together and releasing them. When we reached the crest, I glanced back at the carriage, gleaming faintly in the starlight.

Lady Berri paced a circle around the top of the hill, muttering under her breath and waving her arms in the intricate pattern of a master spell-binder. Something shifted, the quiet air around us taking on an almost sentient quality. I shivered and rubbed my arms. The night was not particularly cold, as the day had been gloriously warm, one of those fall acts of defiance against encroaching winter. But there was something in the air that made me think of cold things: of midnight gusts of wind, ice in my washbasin on January mornings, snowfall at New Year's.

When she had finished, she beckoned to me, pulling a small flask from a pocket in her gown. "Drink this."

"What is it?"

"A bit of wine, laced with laudanum. It should calm your nerves enough for you to enter the gate without breaking it."

I swallowed, choking a little on the bitterness of the drug. Within a few moments, a curious sense of well-being settled over me like a wool blanket on a cool night.

A tiny smile curled across Lady Berri's mouth. She handed me a thin knife and directed me to stand in the center of the roughly trod sphere.

"Go on, child. The spell won't hurt *you*."

I thought, a bit fuzzily, that I ought to be worried by the implication that the spell could hurt someone else, but nothing seemed to dent the calm spreading through my blood. I lifted my chin and stepped into the center of Lady Berri's spell.

The night swung around me, as if the earth itself was moving. I dropped to my knees, wondering if Lady Berri had miscalculated the dosage of laudanum. But instead of coming up against dried grass and hard-packed earth, my hands and knees encountered a fragile resistance that tore away almost immediately. I plunged through the flimsy barrier.

I fell down into darkness. Stars tumbled, burning across the sky, and then winked out. In my veins, fire blazed up and then froze.

I screamed—and hit the ground. When my stunned vision cleared, I found it was daylight. My fingers, closing around the earth beneath me, found a light, springy substance, and when I lifted my hands, they were full of violets, their tiny, imp-dark faces winking at me.

I sat up. Flowers carpeted the earth around me. With a growing sense of wonder, I pushed myself to my feet. Violets spun out in a circle, reaching to the edge of the mound where I stood before giving way to impossibly green grass speckled with daisies and bleeding hearts and chrysanthemums, with cheerful disregard for seasonal rules.

At the base of the hill, I spied a pathway winding away into a wood of thin-branched trees lifting leaves like silver pennies to the sky. Beyond the wood, the spires of a city soared into the blue vault of heaven. The Binding was nothing like the dark, closed world of the way station in the bathhouse at Sárvár. Rather, it was something out of a fairy tale.

Long ago, and far away, over forty-nine kingdoms, beyond the Operentsia Sea, beyond the glass mountains, and beyond that to a kingdom beneath a pearl sky . . . so Grandmama's tales had always begun. My heart spiraled upward, and I hummed under my breath as I headed toward the city. After all, a city implied people, perhaps creatures.

The road was smooth beneath my feet. I reached the shadows at the fringe of the wood when a voice interrupted me.

"Has no one told you, child, not to wander in unfamiliar woods? Have you not read your fairy tales?"

I whirled around to find myself face to face with the man who'd kissed me inside the spell at Sárvár, his curiously inhuman eyes glowing gold.

I fingered the knife Lady Berri had given me and wondered, If I were killed in this dimension, would I be dead in the other as well? But the creatures would not harm me: they needed me too much.

Behind me, the wind sang through the trees. A glance over my shoulder revealed only the sun-dappled shadows of a quiet wood.

"Who are you?" I glanced at the silver manacles he still bore at his wrists.

A smile slithered across his face, transforming it into something unnaturally, painfully beautiful. "I have many names. Some call me Hunger. I bear other names too: Need, Want, Desire." The smile slipped, as if he was unused to holding it for long. "And you are Anna Arden. I know you. I know your need."

My heart thumped, a beat too hard and too fast. "I am not afraid of you."

His eyes fixed on mine, and he laughed. "Of course you are not. But was it wise, my dear, to come into the Binding with drugs burning in your blood?"

"*Is* this the Binding? It looks like no spell I've seen."

"Its like has never been cast, before or since. It is prison and sanctuary, world and shadow," he said.

Riddles. "You asked me to break this spell. Do you know how?"

Those golden eyes kindled brighter. "The spell was bound with blood and will break with blood."

More riddles. I ground my heel. "Speak plainly if you mean me to help."

"You will have to sacrifice at the heart of the spell. You must pull the power of the spell into your own heart and let your heart break with it." He tapped the turul necklace I wore, and I fancied I could feel the wings fluttering against my skin. "You will need blood."

A breeze whispered across my neck, raising gooseflesh on my arms. "A blood sacrifice? Will I die then?"

"*You* shall not die. The spell-caster must live to hold the spell."

I nodded, relieved. "Can you show me the heart of the spell?"

He bowed. One pale hand sliced through the air, inscribing a circle, and a giant sphere rose around us like a bubble raised in the kitchen sink when the maids did the washing.

I watched the ground fall away from me, my spirits lifting as the bubble rose higher. Once, as a child, after watching a goose launch itself from the surface of the pond, I'd tried to do the same. Instead of flying, I had nearly drowned. Catherine, who fished me out, intoned I would never fly— our family (Elementalists and Coremancers) hadn't the right magic for it. Then I'd seen the great air balloons in London, and Mama forbade me to try them. But this soaring required no magic (at least, no magic of mine), and no one was here to forbid me.

I looked up from my inspection of the miniaturized world below me to find Hunger watching me with a curious expression, his cheeks hollowed and his eyes incandescent. The shadowy wood passed underneath us, cut by a silver strip of water. Past the trees, we flew over an open plain, an ocean of grasses waving in an unseen wind. A creature that seemed made of pure light gamboled across the grass, and delight sparkled through me.

We drew closer to the outer wall of the city, bastions of glass and fine-carved stone spiking into the sky. The sphere drifted lower. In a private garden, young women, each more beautiful than the last, danced to a faintly heard melody. Near the heart of the city, where a fountain spilled over gold-veined marble, a maiden sang to a reclining knight, her pale fingers tracing love runes through his hair.

Our sphere floated by the castle. Inside I glimpsed paintings of dreamscapes, stained-glass windows, and long, vaulted hallways filled with creatures in gorgeous gowns. In an airy room in the highest tower of the castle, imps twirled around a small laughing child. Every gurgle of laughter lifted the child into the air. In response, the imps kicked up their heels to impossible new heights, and the child's giggles lifted it even higher. Everything was touched with wonder.

Relief swept through me: Gábor's fears were groundless. Releasing these creatures into the world would harm no one.

And yet.

I glanced again at the silver at Hunger's wrists. "Does the spell hold you here?"

"Yes."

"If I break this spell, what will happen? Will you go free?"

"Who is ever truly free? We trap ourselves with bonds of our own making: duty, love, desire." The last word hissed from his lips, and he ran a black, glistening tongue across them. "But if you mean, will we leave this place? Yes."

My thoughts were tangled with unpleasant memories: the suffocating weight of my mother's expectations, my painful rejection at Lady Isen's ball in Vienna. Luminate society, much as I had longed for it, brought its own rules and limitations. James, trapped at Eton by those same rigid rules. Noémi held virtual prisoner at Eszterháza by her poverty. There were so many ways of being trapped in my world. This spell should not be one of them.

I began to ask another question, but the words were torn away and the bubble shattered into a million shards of brightness around me. Then I was falling, falling, and finally gasping on the winter-hard earth of Attila's Hill.

Lady Berri's round face bent over mine, her brow creased with concern. "Are you well, child? You weren't supposed to be sucked in so quickly. Something else—something from the other side—was shaping the spell, twisting it away from me. I couldn't let you stay in that other realm. It wouldn't be safe."

"I was in no danger," I said, pushing myself upright. There was nothing in that world to harm me.

Except your own need. A pair of golden eyes rose in my mind, and I trembled.

Lady Berri looked away from me, her expression lost to the darkness. She said only, "I'm glad you were not hurt," before loading me into her carriage and whisking me home again in silence.

All that long, dark drive I found myself reliving the spell-bound world in my mind. Something sharp lodged in my heart, and I could not shake the pain of it. So Eve must have felt after being thrust from her garden: exposed by her desires, tethered by her need.

"I must go back," I said. "To break the spell, I mean."

Rising elation bubbled up in me. I would go back to the Binding. I would break the spell, and nothing terrible would happen. I should be doing a good thing—perhaps a great thing, the most important thing I had ever done. Papa would be pleased, so would Mátyás and Karolina and the students at Café Pilvax. The thought of Gábor's and Noémi's disapproval dimmed my joy—but only a little. When the Binding had broken, they would see we were right.

Lady Berri nodded. "Good girl. Now I must study the Binding spell a bit more. This night's work has shown me I am not as prepared as I ought to be, nor are you. I must devise counterspells to protect you, and we must plan how you are to break the spell. Come to me again in one week."

CHAPTER 19

Grandmama's palace was shrouded in darkness when I entered. I had told Ginny not to wait for me. I lit a candle and mounted the stairs. The sphere of light cast by the flame rose with me, my shadow long and wavering beside it. In my room, I set the candle on a small table near my bedside, shivering as my hands went to the buttons at my throat. The effects of the laudanum were fading, a heaviness replacing the euphoria that had burned through me inside the spell.

A deep voice spoke out of the darkness.

"Isten áldja meg a lelked!" God bless your soul. The voice was unfamiliar, the intonation eerily like a prayer one might say over the dying.

There was a man in my room.

Terror spiked through me, setting my heart racing and sending new energy into my exhausted body.

"Who are you? Why are you here?" My voice emerged high and tight.

A shadowy figure pushed away from the far wall. In the fitful light of the candle, his face was indistinct, framed by dark hair. I heard a murmured Latin phrase, followed by a flare of light.

The spell burst over me in a cascade of pain, stars dancing against my eyes, flame spouting down my back. Agony crackled through my heart. I was going to be killed—not by some half-forgotten beast in the Binding but by a Luminate assassin in my bedroom. Herr Steinberg must have sent him, to punish me for going into the Binding.

Lady Berri had not protected me after all.

Dark spots danced at the edge of my vision. I fought to breathe.

No.

I was not going to die so easily.

Everyone believed I could break spells. I would break this one.

Think, Anna.

What common thread linked my previous experiences breaking spells? I struggled against the blackness clouding my mind. I had been angry with Catherine at her debut, afraid when Noémi's spell in the Romani camp brushed me, and in Sárvár there had been a longing so sharp and sweet I still ached with the memory of it. Somehow, that emotion was key. But I couldn't feel anything now except pain drilling through my bones and a dullness where the laudanum had been. Tears leaked from beneath my closed eyes.

I burrowed a little deeper. *There.* My shadow self hovered, a knot of longing behind my heart. I called to her, and she surfaced in a wave of terror-induced rage.

My shadow self scrabbled against the distant pull of the spell, catching and then tearing.

In a silent explosion of light, the spell ripped wide.

I heard a startled "Mária!" across the room as I tumbled against my bed, gasping for breath. My eyes flew open, the aftereffects of the spell hanging in my vision like the after-image of a harvest bonfire. My attacker stumbled backward, his head slamming against my vanity table. A sickening crack sounded, and then he lay still.

I heard a long, shuddering breath that caught on a sob—mine—and did what I should have done when I realized there was a man in my room.

I screamed.

X

Gábor was the first to reach my room, his trousers hastily pulled on beneath his flowing nightshirt. "Anna!" He crossed the room to me, and drew me upright, his hands warm on mine. His released me almost at once, his fingers flashing upward to brush against my shoulders, then my cheeks. His eyes searched my face. "Are you all right?" His hands stilled, one thumb caressing the corner of my mouth.

I stared at him, eyes wide. The tingling left in the wake of his touch made it difficult to think. I swayed toward him, dizzy with relief and a sudden rush of blood, and Gábor slipped his arm around me to keep me upright. The longing of my shadow self still lingered in my body like a fever.

The door was flung open again: Noémi, rushing to my side in a flurry of red-silken robe and lacy nightdress.

Her eyes flickered from me to Gábor, her expression wavering between shock and reluctant understanding. Then she registered my gown. "Why are you still dressed?"

Words tumbled through my mind and tangled my tongue. Instead of speaking, I pointed across the room. Noémi squinted in the direction of my finger. She whispered a spell, and a Lumen lantern bloomed in her hand. "The Circle keep us safe! Who is that?"

"I don't know. I think he's hurt." *Or dead.* I put one hand to my head, which had begun pounding.

Noémi set her lantern against the foot of my bed and scurried toward the prone figure.

Mátyás burst into my room, still in his evening clothes. His collar was askew and his coat wrinkled, as if he'd only just shrugged it on. He scanned the room, his eyes running first across my face and Gábor with his arm still around me, and then to where Noémi crouched by the intruder. "Good Lord. What's going on?"

Noémi looked back at us as Grandmama and Ginny pushed into my now-crowded room. "He's unconscious, but his pulse is steady. He'll live."

Gábor discreetly pulled his arm away from me. The sudden removal of his warmth made me shiver, and the pounding in my head intensified. I sat down on my bed.

"*Who* will live?" Grandmama asked, her voice cross. Like Noémi, she'd seen my cloak and gown. "Anna, where have you been? Is that a *man* in your room? I promised your Mama . . ." Grandmama took a half dozen steps toward the unconscious man and stopped. "*Istenem!*"

Her body wavered like a candle flame. Mátyás sprang toward her, catching her before she could fall. "Pál," she said, the word a slow exhale.

"You know him?" Mátyás asked. "Who is he? Should we call the police?"

Grandmama shook her head. "No. We must keep him here till morning. Someone will be along to look for him."

"But who is he?" I asked.

"And why was he in Anna's room?" Mátyás asked, scowling.

"He tried to kill me," I said. The earlier part of the evening felt remote and dreamlike.

Grandmama stared at me, her face white as undyed cotton. "*You?* But he—why would anyone want you dead?"

I closed my eyes, briefly, gathering courage. I had kept so much hidden from Grandmama. It was hard to undo the habit of silence. "I went into the Binding." An image flashed in my head, a being of pure light dancing in a field.

"What?" Noémi said. "Anna, are you mad?"

"You dabble in magic you don't understand," Gábor said. "You're lucky to have come out unharmed."

For a moment, hovering above that pristine world, I had not wanted to come out at all.

"Anna," Grandmama said, her brows tucked together in dismay. "I had no notion. I thought you had given up your obsession with magic."

My heart tightened at their disapproval, but I lifted my chin. We were right to seek to break the Binding. I tamped down the niggling doubt at the back of my mind.

"Surely none of that matters now," Mátyás said. "Anna is

safe. She did *not* break the Binding. But this man most assuredly tried to kill her. Suppose we deal with that?"

"Grandmama?" I asked.

Grandmama swallowed once, twice. Her hand closed convulsively over mine. "Have you ever done something terrible, something you wished you could undo but could not?"

Yes. I thought of James, of the Romani baby whose soul I might have stolen. "Grandmama, who *is* he?"

Grandmama shut her eyes tightly, as if our hovering faces were a bright light she could not bear to see. "He wears his father's face. He is my son. Your uncle Pál."

※

I gaped at the inert figure on the floor. I studied his face, seeing now the strong bridge of a nose, like Mama. Like me. No wonder his face had seemed familiar when I had seen him watching me outside the Café Pilvax. I remembered now where I had first seen him—at Lady Isen's ball with Herr Steinberg in Vienna. I shivered. All this time, the Circle had been watching.

Mama had spoken of a brother, but only a handful of times. I had always assumed he died as a child, his death the tragedy that made Grandmama's face whiten when he was mentioned.

Mátyás frowned at me. "Did you know he was your uncle?"

I shook my head. It had been *Mama's* name the man said before the spell collapsed, not an appeal to the Catholic Mary. Anxiety unspooled in the pit of my stomach.

Had he known who I was? If so, why had he attacked me? "Grandmama, what happened? Why was I never told about him?"

She was silent for so long I began to think she would not answer. At last she sighed. "Pál is a Coremancer. His abilities were unprecedented; even the Circle was astounded at how deftly he cast scrying spells immediately after his Confirmation. But, perhaps to compensate for such gifts, he has not been quite . . . right in other aspects. When the Circle came for him—to teach him, so they said—your grandfather was relieved. And I . . . I had no wish to quarrel with your grandfather, so I let him go. I told myself it was right."

I tightened my fingers around hers, sensing some of the things she was not saying. I had never met my grandfather, but I knew from what little Mama said that he had been strict, and sometimes unkind. "How old was Pál?"

Another silence. "Nine."

My heart twisted, both for my grandmother and for the young boy Pál had been.

"You understand, *szívem,* Luminate magic is costly. I know you suffer because you are Barren, but I . . . I have been glad. I believed it meant the Circle could not use you." Her voice shook, stricken. "But if the Circle has sent Pál for you, I was wrong. So very, very wrong."

Noémi stood from her examination of Pál and joined us. "Irína *néni,* you've had a shock. You need rest."

"But . . ." My gaze swung to my uncle on my rug.

"You can sleep with me," Noémi said, linking her arm through mine.

"Or me," Mátyás said, winking. His grin stretched wide as both Noémi and Grandmama immediately protested.

"We can't leave him here on the floor!" I said, ignoring the heat in my cheeks. I refused to let Mátyás bait me.

"Ginny can bring a blanket to cover him, and Mátyás can set an Immobility spell on him," Noémi said, already ushering Grandmama from the room. "Everything else can wait until morning."

While Mátyás set the spell, Gábor walked me to Noémi's room. His hand lifted, as if he would touch me again, then fell. "Will you be all right?"

The gentleness in his voice, more than anything else that long evening, made me want to weep. No one else, not even Grandmama, had thought to ask about my well-being after my revelation about the Binding. Gábor might not agree with what I had done—with what I would surely attempt to do—but here, now, in the silence and shrouding darkness of the hallway, none of that mattered. Only the bare concern of one friend for another.

"Yes," I said. *You are here.* "I will be all right."

⟊

My first thought on waking was of the world in the Binding: the wild, unearthly beauty; the pure, unbridled joy. Its absence ached like a bruise on my heart. *I must go back.*

Coming swiftly on its heels was a memory of last night. I had thought I would not sleep after Grandmama's revelation. Yet I had fallen into dreamless slumber nearly as soon as Noémi had found me a spare nightdress and settled me

239

in her bed with a mug of tea. Surveying now an empty bed and a room full of sunlight, I realized Noémi must have drugged me. I suppressed a flicker of anger and pushed away thoughts of the Binding—my energy would be needed for other things—and gathered up my cloak and dress from the chair near Noémi's wardrobe. I walked back down the hall to my room, tapped gently at the door, then eased it open. The room was empty, the bed neatly made up. My uncle no longer sprawled across the floor.

For a moment I feared he'd escaped—then I realized my room would not be so orderly if he had done so. Doubtless Mátyás had simply moved him. I rang the bell for Ginny and hurried to dress.

Ginny's white face looked as shocked as I felt. "I can hardly believe it, miss." She pulled a brush through my hair, her hand trembling. "I've always admired your grandmama, but this . . . how could she give away her child?"

"Don't judge her," I said. "People do terrible things when they are afraid."

"Yes, miss." Ginny began twining my hair into a knot. "Is it true what you said, that you went into the Binding?"

I started to nod, then caught myself. Ginny wouldn't appreciate it if I undid all her work with my hair. "I mean to break it. I mean to let everyone have access to magic."

Her hands stilled. "I believe," she said slowly, as though picking her words with care, "that would be a mighty fine thing, miss."

When Ginny finished with my hair, I rose and, on impulse, threw my arms around her. "Thank you."

She laughed, astonished. "Whatever for?"

"For believing in me."

I heard voices in the drawing room as soon as I reached the landing from the stairs. Despite the unseemly early hour, there was quite a gathering. My cousins and Grandmama sipped their tea while my uncle sat empty-handed on a narrow wooden chair, his hands loose in his lap. Lady Berri spread her bulk across a chaise longue, and Herr Steinberg stood against the wall nearest my uncle.

I nearly ducked back out of the drawing room. But I was ravenously hungry and could smell the pastries from the doorway. I squared my shoulders and marched into the room. I collected a plate full of food from a sideboard before squeezing onto a sofa between Mátyás and Noémi. My cousins' warmth made me feel marginally less exposed.

"Welcome, cousin," Mátyás said. "We're in the midst of a rather brilliant confabulation about your future."

I glared at him. "*My* future? I was not the one in a stranger's bedroom after midnight attempting to murder her with a spell." Grandmama always said the best defense was to attack.

"Too true," Mátyás murmured. "And therein lies part of the scandal. Where exactly *were* you, Anna, when you were supposed to be abed?"

I elbowed him. He knew well where I had been. I had told him. Then I took a bite of a walnut-filled *rétes* and turned my attention to Grandmama, who spoke with Herr Steinberg and Lady Berri. Her back was stiff, her voice full of militant politeness.

"This is unconscionable," Grandmama said. "That *you,* Lady Berri, should have coerced my granddaughter into participating in dangerous magic, and that *you,* Herr Steinberg, should take it upon yourself to punish her!"

"Notice the prodigal daughter bears no blame in this," Mátyás murmured.

"Mátyás!" Noémi warned.

He grinned at me.

The door opened, one of the maids with a fresh tray of pastries, and Gábor slipped in behind her to take up silent vigil beside the door. He caught my eye and smiled reassuringly.

"I very much regret the necessity for Pál's actions," Herr Steinberg said. "But I cannot allow risk to the Binding, and your granddaughter broke her promise."

"Surely that is for the Circle to decide, not you," Grandmama said. "Surely she is entitled to a trial, at the least. And why is Anna to be punished, and not the spell-binder who drove her?"

Herr Steinberg glanced at Lady Berri, his gaze flat with loathing, and said nothing.

Lady Berri laughed. "What the distinguished herr means to say is I outrank him. He cannot touch me." Her voice turned serious. "But I do very much resent what he tried to do. It is only the mercy of God Anna was not hurt."

I stiffened, affronted. I had been saved through my own efforts, not divine intervention—though it was not, perhaps, the best moment to say so.

"And to use her own uncle against her . . ." Lady Berri's voice trailed off.

I glanced across at my uncle Pál, who fiddled with the cuff on one sleeve. As if he felt my gaze, he looked up. His

242

eyes were incongruously pale against his dark hair and skin. There was a light in them that was not quite right. Fear skittered across my skin.

"I did not realize," Herr Steinberg said gruffly, "he was her uncle."

"Zrínyi is not a common surname," Grandmama said. "You might have guessed."

"I would not have killed you." Pál's pale eyes drilled into me. "I know what you are."

My heart pounded. Beside me, Noémi gripped my hand in hers.

"What did you see?" Herr Steinberg asked. His eyes were on me, so he did not notice the look Pál unleashed on him: dark, cold, contemptuous.

"Nothing," Pál said. "And everything. She will break the world, as her kind has done since the beginning."

A wave of ice flashed through my body. *My kind.* What *was* I?

"And the Binding?" Lady Berri asked.

"She could break it if she chooses." Pál shrugged, as if it did not matter to him whether I undid the spell or not.

Lady Berri looked pleased, Herr Steinberg grim.

I thought of going back into the Binding, and a frisson that was equal parts pleasure and terror shivered through me.

"She must not be allowed to do so," Herr Steinberg said.

"I should like to see you stop her," Lady Berri said, her chin high.

Herr Steinberg sprang to his feet, his glasses trembling on his nose. He lifted his hands, his fingers already weaving the beginnings of a spell. "Watch me."

My body flashed cold. *No.*

Lady Berri surged upward, her own fingers flickering.

"*Hajrá!* My money is on the thin one." Mátyás leaned forward, his eyes bright.

Grandmama pounded her cane on the floor. "Enough! I won't have you quarreling over Anna as if you were a pair of mongrels and she a bone between you. Now, I think you should leave."

Herr Steinberg dropped his hands, two spots of color appearing high in his cheeks. His cravat had come askew, the first sign of sartorial untidiness I had ever seen in him. "But the Binding?"

"I think you may trust me to keep my granddaughter away from that spell, and from Lady Berri. But I will not allow you to stay in my house, threatening my flesh and blood. Anna is a child still, and under my care." I wondered if anyone else saw the sliver of a glance she shot at Pál, the shadow of pain that flashed across her face. "I won't shirk my duty."

Herr Steinberg looked as though he would protest, but Lady Berri nudged him. "Come, you heard the lady." She did not look in the least discomfited at being thrown out of Grandmama's house. Her lips curled, catlike. What was she plotting?

Lady Berri apologized once more to Grandmama and departed, leaving behind her a message that sounded in my ears with a puff of air: "Herr Steinberg will send for reinforcements from Vienna who will try to stop us. I must go into hiding until the Binding is broken. Watch for my letter."

Herr Steinberg took my uncle away, and we all breathed a sigh of relief.

But Herr Steinberg returned four days later with a sealed letter from Vienna.

Grandmama tried to have the butler turn him away at the door.

"Circle business," said Herr Steinberg, flashing the seal and nodding at the two Austrian soldiers who'd accompanied him, and the butler let him in.

To Grandmama, who sat with lips pursed and arms tightly folded, he said, "The Austrian Circle appreciates your concern for your granddaughter. But you must also appreciate that we cannot let her become embroiled in any plots to break the Binding. I have come with a solution."

He held out his hand, revealing a ring in his palm: a hideous gargoyle with a faintly glowing green stone in its open mouth. "I know that spells cast around Anna are sometimes unpredictable, so I have asked Pál to cast a spell on this bauble. It will register where Anna goes and what spells are cast around her. If she goes into the Binding, the spell will immobilize her."

"No one will be hurt?" Grandmama asked.

"No one. Though the ring, once worn, cannot be removed save by the caster, and if Miss Arden attempts it, it will pain her. And if, by chance, she breaks the spell on this ring, we will have no alternative but to keep her under personal supervision."

"Imprisonment, you mean?" I asked.

"Nothing so crude. House arrest, rather."

I thought of Hunger waiting in the Binding: prison

was prison, no matter how appealing the bars. "I won't wear it."

"My dear Miss Arden, you have no choice."

I looked at Grandmama, who shrugged sadly. Herr Steinberg plucked up my hand and slid the ring on my smallest finger. It hung on my hand like a tumor.

CHAPTER 20

The wind frolicked down Kerepesi Street like an untrained vizsla puppy—it pushed its impudent nose at my skirts, tugged at my hair, and then darted off for long moments before returning to pummel me. The first leaves of autumn danced down the street before us. Buda-Pest in fall was much like a piece of music played on a cello: sweet, mellow, restful, but with unaccountable hints of melancholy.

It was good to be out, striding down the street with a purpose. William had invited Mátyás to his workshop, and Mátyás had extended the invitation to Gábor and me. It had been nearly a fortnight since my foray into the Binding, a week since Herr Steinberg put the spelled ring on me. I had spent the time mostly hiding, alternating between Grand-mama's drawing rooms and the shops in Váci Street, debating the merits of lace versus ribbon for my new dress, as though I were only an ordinary girl who wanted ordinary things. If the Circle was determined to watch me, I would bore them into inattention. I tried, once, to break the spell on the ring, but all I had won for my efforts was a pounding headache and blistered skin beneath the ring. Pál must have spelled it particularly to resist me.

I had heard nothing from Lady Berri.

Gábor had charmed us before leaving the house, a Romani casting that drew shadows to us and turned away attention.

"Won't the ring register your spell?" I asked. If the Circle caught us casting a spell to go unnoticed, that would draw their attention far more effectively than doing nothing.

"I doubt it," Mátyás said. "It's not a Luminate spell. Probably the Circle doesn't think anything else counts as magic."

"Persuasion, not force," Gábor reminded me. "There's no ritual for the ring to recognize."

I was tired of shutting myself up in the house, so I let myself be convinced.

Before me, Mátyás whistled tunelessly, his arms swaying with his long-limbed gait. Gábor walked beside me, close enough for his fingers to brush mine every few steps. With each grazing touch, warm prickles shot up my arm and into my stomach. But he did not look at me, and I could not tell if the contact was accidental or intended.

"Miss Arden, I have wanted to talk with you," he said, speaking low so Mátyás would not overhear. My heart thumped. I wondered, for a wild, hopeful moment, if he meant to say something of his feelings for me.

"I am sorry for what happened. The Circle forcing their will on you must be intolerable," he continued, and I blushed at my own foolishness. Now he did look at me, or rather, at the ring currently making an unsightly lump beneath my gloves. "But if this impels you to abandon a destructive path, it can only be a good thing."

I stared at him. "It is a good thing to be trapped? To have someone else dictate your actions?"

He met my gaze evenly. "It is never good to be bound by rules not of your making. Any Romani could tell you that. But we still have choices. We can choose safety. Family. Life. You do not have to break the Binding. We can find other ways to create change."

"And this revolution you plan, this is safe?"

"I am not a revolutionary. I want change, a society where Romani voices have a chance to be heard—something that will never happen so long as the Circle and the Hapsburgs rule together. I would prefer diplomacy, but I will fight if it comes to it. Change is never without cost."

Ahead of us, Mátyás stopped to speak with an acquaintance. We paused a half dozen paces behind him.

I could have stomped my foot with frustration. With Herr Steinberg's ring effectively preventing me from doing *anything,* Gábor's arguments were particularly provoking. "You think I do not know that? Of course breaking the Binding is a risk—but I believe the risk is worth it for the change it will bring."

He pressed his lips together, a dark flush staining his cheeks. "You don't know what you risk. You can't calculate its cost."

A tremor of disquiet passed through me. I believed what I said. And yet—I could not be entirely sure how much of the certainty was my own, how much drawn from my lingering need to return to the world of the spell. I knew that Gábor would pounce on any sign of doubt, so I covered it over with anger.

"Then tell me! Don't make vague allusions to a disastrous future. Respect me enough to assume I am an intelligent creature." I could not bear it if Gábor patronized me as Freddy had. "You say there may be monsters. Have any of your people seen these creatures? Do they *know*?" Gábor had not seen the world of the Binding, as I had: the creatures of light, the dancing, and the laughter. Whatever I was releasing, it was not the destruction he feared.

"No," he admitted. "But there may be other effects. The magic from the spell must go somewhere. Surely you haven't forgotten what happened to my niece? Or to you, for that matter. Mátyás says you were unconscious for days after Sárvár."

My words strangled in my throat. I had not forgotten. "Is your niece all right? Was it . . . was it truly her soul I pulled into the talisman?"

"She's growing. But it's early yet to know about her soul. My grandmother says it is."

My fist closed around a handful of fabric from my skirt. I could not undo what had happened to Gábor's niece. But I could—I hoped—make the world she grew up in easier for her. In any case, the situations were not the same. I had broken Noémi's spell as she cast it, and the spell at Sárvár had been corrupted. The Binding spell was already cast. Its breaking would not be like the others. "Surely Lady Berri or Papa would have warned me if they feared that breaking the Binding would release destructive magic."

250

Gábor shook his head. "I'm not sure they see past their own interest."

"Lady Berri, perhaps, but not my father. Please," I begged, "trust me to make the right decision as I trust you."

"I care about you, Anna." Gábor's voice was pitched so low I strained to hear it. He glanced at Mátyás, but my cousin was still deep in conversation, oblivious to our exchange. "But I am afraid to trust you in this. I could not bear it if you were hurt."

My heartbeat thundered in my ears. Something tremendous hung in the balance between us, something fragile as glass and poised to shatter.

"Please," he echoed my plea. "Do not break the Binding." Lower still, "You will break my heart."

Words hammered against my throat, words of longing, words that could frame the way my pulse beat so sharp and hard when he spoke to me.

But I could not give him the promise he wanted. If a way could be found around Herr Steinberg's spell, I would break the Binding. I had not come to my decision lightly, and I would not be one of those women who remade herself and her beliefs for the attention of a man, even for Gábor. He would have to love me for myself—or not at all.

Mátyás's friend moved on, and Mátyás filled the remaining distance to William's workshop with harmless chatter. His noise covered the sharp-edged quiet that had fallen between Gábor and me, for which I was grateful. Gábor had taken my silence for answer and pulled away from me, his face pale and his lips set.

There was no more accidental brushing of hands. Despite

my brave thoughts, *not at all* loomed as a terribly real and bleak prospect.

In Gábor's silences I heard what he did not say: so long as the Binding remained intact, so long as the Circle governed society, there was no place in the world for a Romani and a lady to be together. But if I broke the Binding, I would lose him just the same.

It was a false choice. I was damned either way.

)(

At length, Mátyás halted before an empty lot full of weeds and wind-blown leaflets. I frowned, confused, until he stepped forward and knocked three times on a door that seemed to have appeared from nowhere. Only then did I see the large, unornamented building attached to the door. The structure looked sturdy, but bore signs of neglect in the boarded-up windows and weed-choked walkway.

I heard footsteps, then the sound of someone struggling with a lock. After a moment of fumbling, William flung the door open. "Welcome!" He cast a swift glance down the street, and then shut the door behind us and locked it. "There's a warrant out for my arrest," he said cheerfully. "I've a Hiding spell on the building, but that only works as long as the police don't know what they're looking for."

He led us into a narrow, well-lit room bearing witness to its dual use as an office and living area. A small stove stood in one corner, opposite an unmade bed. In between, every available surface area was layered with drawings and papers so covered in scribbled notations they appeared to be bleeding ink. We forged onward, emerging into a vast, high-ceilinged room beyond the living quarters. I gasped.

Looming over us, metal sculptures in various stages of completion filled the room. Those closest to us resembled fantastic creatures: a manlike figure with four arms and delicate horns curling from his skull; a creature that was all trunk, with a small face—mostly eyes—perched atop a great cage of a body, underslung by two sets of wheels. Another sculpture appeared to be a woman, the hammered planes of her face alien and beautiful at the same time. Her hair, made of tiny, jointed arms, reminded me of a medusa.

"What are they?" I asked. "They're beautiful."

William grinned. "My secret weapon. You are the first— and so far, the only—to see them. Some men fight with weapons, some with magic. I fight with machines. Well, and a bit of magic. A man can stand inside each of these figures, protected from gunshot and anything other than direct cannon fire. I've improved the firing range and accuracy on the weapons built into these machines too."

"They're incredible." They truly were—intricate form married to deadly function.

William thrust one freckled hand through his hair. "The Bourbons are slaughtering Italian revolutionaries in Palermo. They've summoned the Circle, and the Circle has infiltrated the people's army. The Animanti go invisible behind enemy lines to tamper with their weapons and poison their food supply. They set flocks of ravens and starlings on them, spooking the men, blocking their guns. The Lucifera spoil the aim of their artillery and swallow entire cannons with the ground. The Circle uses Elementalist illusions to terrify the fighters and Coremancers to amplify their fear. The same will happen here, unless we have tools to fight."

"That won't happen here," Mátyás said firmly. "Your machines will help—and you know there are those among us who are the equal of any Circle member in power and ability."

"Fighting isn't the only way to change," Gábor said.

"Of course not. Perhaps Kossuth will succeed in Vienna in persuading the Hapsburg government to grant independence to Hungary and Poland and Bohemia. But I find it unlikely, and we must be prepared to state our case more strongly." William turned to me, grasping one of my hands in his. His thin fingers were surprisingly strong. "Anna. What news of the Binding?"

"Bad news, I'm afraid." I tugged off my glove to show him the ring and explained.

"That is unfortunate. But we shan't let it stop us from fighting if we must."

I replaced my glove. "Shall you succeed, with the Circle drawing on the full strength of the Binding?"

William didn't answer. He didn't have to.

I knew that the Austrian Circle was unlikely to let Hungary go, even with the shrewdest diplomacy. Hungary was too big, too important to their empire. But an outright rebellion was a poor alternative. The students would be slaughtered. Already, I could see them: Gábor and Mátyás and the others from the café, strewn across the streets of the city like autumn leaves, bloody and broken.

Heat sparked inside me. If I could only find my way around Herr Steinberg's ring, I could break the Binding and undermine the Circle's power, giving my friends a chance to make their case with minimal fighting. I would not let the Circle's threats dictate my actions.

I had to speak with Lady Berri. There must be some method of circumventing the ring's restrictions.

We took a hansom cab from William's workshop to Café Pilvax to celebrate the completion of William's mechanical warriors. Before leaving, William cast a minor illusion to darken his bright hair and prematurely age his face, should anyone be watching for him.

To my delight, my new friend Karolina was at the café. While Gábor, William, and Mátyás joined Petőfi and the other students to debate accounts of the revolution in Italy, Karolina and I enjoyed a wide-ranging discussion involving the new play at the Hungarian national theater, the unexpected beauties of the Hanság, even fashion. When it came time to leave, shortly after Karolina's departure, I had successfully put aside the gnawing worry about the Binding, the swirling uncertainty of revolution.

The street outside was quiet, only a handful of carriages rattling down neighboring roads and a scattering of pedestrians before us. The wind had died down.

Abruptly, shouting rent the air. A cluster of young men tumbled out of a nearby *kocsma,* fists raised high in the air. I could not make out what they were crying, but I saw Mátyás tense.

"What is it?"

"Croats," Mátyás said, his eyes fixed on the young men in front of us. They were mostly thin and dark-complexioned, their black eyes flashing in the half light of the overcast day.

"*Szabadság!*" one cried, throwing his arms wide. Freedom. "Let us govern ourselves!"

Others shouted words in a language I didn't recognize.

"We should leave," Gábor said.

"Why are they so angry?" I asked.

"They want independent standing in the empire; they are tired of being considered part of Hungary." Mátyás said this without a trace of irony. Did he not see that the Croats were only echoing the Hungarians' own cry?

Students tumbled from the café behind us, drawn by the shouting.

"Hungary for Hungarians!" A young man with blond curls and a loosely tied red cravat ran into the street, coming to a halt just before the Croats.

One of the Croat boys spat in his face. The blond youth erupted toward him, fists swinging. Mátyás started for them.

"Mátyás, don't," Gábor warned. "We can't be involved in this."

At once, there were young men fighting everywhere. A student flew past me, crashing against the brick wall to my right, the soft felt hat favored by the radicals tumbling to the ground. He slumped down to the pavement, and I winced in sympathy. He blinked at me, dazed.

A Croat boy charged toward us, and Mátyás pushed him away. The boy snarled and shoved a fist in Mátyás's face.

I scarce had time to wonder if Mátyás was all right when something—an elbow?—slammed into my cheek, and I stumbled back, my left ear ringing. Gábor cursed and swung me behind him. "Fools."

Gábor hurried me around the corner. When the shouting had receded behind us, he probed the injury on my cheek. "Does it hurt much? We're not far from the hospital."

"I don't need a doctor." I wished, stupidly, that my wound were more severe, so his hands would linger.

Mátyás peered over Gábor's shoulder at my face, wiping the blood dripping from his nose on his sleeve. "You'll not want to go about for a day or two."

"Me?" I asked, looking at the blood now smeared on his cheek.

"You're going to have a black eye."

I tried to imagine Grandmama's reaction to *that*, when Gábor grasped my hand. "Move," he said. "Soldiers."

Flickers of blue and red flashed in the street beyond, followed by the thudding sounds of students fleeing. I hoped William got away safely.

"They're making arrests. Go!"

Between Mátyás's face and my already-swelling eye, it might be difficult to prove our innocence. Gábor took my arm, and we followed Mátyás as swiftly as my cumbersome skirts allowed.

When I got home, I snuck upstairs to my room and found a crisp card with Lady Berri's sprawling signature lying on my pillow. I assumed Ginny had smuggled it up to me. I flipped the card over.

Lady Berri had written simply: 8 o'clock, with an address scrawled beneath it.

)(

I was not entirely easy when I arrived at Lady Berri's rooms with Ginny, this time in a more modest establishment. A perfectly circular white carpet lay over the floor. In the center of the carpet stood a stone table, and on the table rested two shallow bowls, one silver and one bronze. Blood-red drapes guarded the windows.

"Good heavens, child." Lady Berri peered at my eye, which was nearly swollen shut. "What on earth happened?"

"A street fracas. Some students were fighting, and we got caught in the middle of it."

"What are they fighting about this time?" She sent Ginny downstairs to wait and gestured for me to sit.

I stripped off my gloves and set them to the side of the silver bowl, where they lay limp, like corpses.

"Freedom," I said, sitting and fingering my ring. *Szabad-ság,* the Croats had shouted, but they attacked Hungarian students who wanted the same thing.

Didn't they?

She tsked. "The Hungarians want to be free of the Austrians, I suppose. Well, that's their business. I hope you've sense enough not to get caught up in it."

I said nothing. The turul necklace Karolina had given me hung heavy at my throat.

Lady Berri handed me a tray of sliced bread with salted butter. "Eat. You may need your strength."

I took the tray but did not select anything. I surveyed the shallow bowls on the table with misgiving. "What is this?"

"A minor grounding ritual. I need something of you—a bit of blood—to craft a spell to protect you in the Binding. You needn't fear this spell. It won't harm you. It touches your flesh, not your soul."

This looked nothing like any *minor* ritual I had seen. "Herr Steinberg will know what spell you cast," I told her, showing her the ring I wore and explaining how it worked.

She pressed her lips together until they had disappeared entirely. "Well. That is most vexing. I suppose we can forgo the protection spell—though I shall have to cast other spells in its place. I cannot risk Herr Steinberg finding me at the present moment or suspecting anything of our plans, which he will certainly do if he discovers this spell."

I selected a piece of bread and nibbled at it, considering. When I came out of the Binding, Lady Berri had said that something held me there. A part of me was there yet, a dull yearning that never eased. Had Hunger spelled me, sealing me to the Binding spell with my own desires? Had it been a side effect of the laudanum? Or something else, something deeper, truer? "Can you still find a way for me to get back into the Binding?"

She frowned. "I believe so. I will need to complete some minor spell work before we attempt it again." Her eyes met mine. "Three nights from now, I shall be along to fetch you. Be ready."

Ready? I nearly laughed. How does one prepare to end the world? To start anew? Even with years to prepare, I imagined I could not ever be ready.

But to go into the spell again? Ah. For *that,* I was more than ready.

CHAPTER 21

Ginny brought in the mail with my morning tea and set the tray beside me in my bed. For a wonder, there were three letters, including one from James. I slid my finger beneath the seal, curious to find how his Romani magic was progressing.

The letter was to the point. *Someone ratted me out, and the magic tutor discovered my ring and your letters. I've been sent down. They were asking me where you got the ring, but I wouldn't tell them anything. Be careful.*

I dropped the letter on the covers, my fingers suddenly numb.

Ginny, who was laying out my dress for the day, noticed my stillness. "Is everything all right, Miss Anna? Bad news from your family?"

"James has been sent home from Eton."

She smiled a little. "A prank, no doubt. I shouldn't worry. Boys will be boys."

"No." It was strangely difficult to force the word through my lips. "It's worse than that. He's done something illegal."

Something I told him to do.

I did not want to read the other letters. I knew what they said. Mama would find a way to blame James's failure on me, though James would not have told her the truth. Papa might suspect my involvement, but he would speculate instead how James had come by the talisman, and his careful nonblame would hurt more than all Mama's railings. I set the letters down and flung my covers aside. The need for action was already building in my limbs, energy fizzing through my blood and into my brain.

I could not bear to think of James. The only solution was to cram my mind so full of other things there would be no time for reflection.

)(

I had meant to show the letter to Gábor, to give him notice if there was anything to James's warning. But he was not anywhere in the house. I begged Mátyás to accompany me to Café Pilvax, hoping to find Gábor there.

"I'll come too," Noémi said. "I'm not expected at the hospital until this afternoon, and there won't be many more fair mornings."

Mátyás and I exchanged a glance. I suspected Noémi might not like what she found at the café: conversations about revolution—and William.

Indeed, Noémi spotted William almost as soon as she had crossed the threshold. She stood in the gathering light from the large window facing the street and scowled. "What is *he* doing here?"

Neither Mátyás nor I answered. I scanned the crowd for Gábor, the familiar set of his shoulders, the dark curl of his hair. I had not realized, until my heart sank, how much I depended upon finding him.

While Mátyás and Noémi secured spots at a nearby table, William cornered me.

"Well, Miss Arden. Have you found a way to break the Binding?"

I did not mean to tell him—I had planned to break the Binding in secret and let the students challenge the Austrian government in the wake of the Circle's collapse. But William must have seen something change in my face.

"You have! Come, this is encouraging. Tell me when it is to be, so we may be ready."

I did not want the blood of boys on my hands, if it came to a fight. And this was so soon.

"You know I am fully capable of bivouacking on your doorstep and following you everywhere until I discover your secret." He snapped his fingers. "Or perhaps we should begin our revolution at once, and when it fails, you will carry the guilt of our failure on your shoulders for the rest of your life."

He would do it too. "You are detestable," I said, and he grinned at me. I sighed, and told him what Lady Berri planned. We would break the Binding if we could—the students might as well prepare for it.

"Was that so difficult? You've done well, Miss Arden. I must tell Petőfi at once." He scurried off to fetch the poet from an argument in the back corner. They conferred animatedly for a moment, Petőfi gesticulating and William nodding.

His eyes shining, Petőfi rushed toward me. He grasped my hands in both of his. "Most noble lady, thank you. You have given us precisely what we need: a moment of crisis, a time to change everything. For weeks, months, we have deliberated with no clear plan, but you—*you!*—have given this to us. Words are easily come by, but it takes more to rouse men to action."

I blushed, uncomfortable under his scrutiny and flowery prose. I did not feel particularly heroic. Rather, I felt flattened, pricked by worry for James and nagged by doubt. I believed I was right to break the Binding, but I feared for my friends if it came to open battle with the Circle.

After shaking my hands once more and pressing a kiss on my knuckles, Petőfi swept past me to Mátyás. "We'll need you to go to the soldiers at Buda Castle, mislead and confuse them. Infiltrate their ranks. Mimic their leaders."

Mátyás froze. "I've no training as a spy."

"You've unprecedented gifts, William says. You should use them." Petőfi clapped a hand on my cousin's shoulder. "You'll be the hero of Hungary when this is through."

"I've no desire to be a hero. Surely there's something else I can do? What you ask . . . it isn't easy for me."

Petőfi's eyes flashed. "And you think this should be easy? What we do demands sacrifice, demands blood and honor and sweat and tears. You will do this for us because we need you."

Mátyás nodded, but his eyes were uneasy and sweat beaded about his temples. None of this felt real, these boys arguing about their fight to come. They sounded precisely like James, playing at Napoleonic spy games. The poet moved on, murmuring instructions to others in the crowd: what weapons to gather and where to meet.

I crossed to Mátyás. "What was that about? What is it Petőfi wants you to do?"

Mátyás folded his arms. "I don't wish to speak about it." He cut his eyes at Noémi. "I hear you've agreed to break the Binding."

His attempt at distraction worked. Noémi sprang up and plucked my ringed hand. She thrust it in my face. "Have you forgotten what the Circle will do to you if they find out?"

I pulled my hand back. I had not forgotten. Fear tightened in my gut, but I had chosen to trust Lady Berri. I had chosen to believe we were right to break this spell. The skin beneath the ring itched and burned, and I rubbed it absently, trying to ease the discomfort.

Noémi cast a scornful glance around the café, her eyes coming to rest on William, who was helping the poet organize the students. She stalked over to him, jabbing one finger into his chest. "And you! How can you suppose you will succeed against trained Austrian soldiers? Against the *Circle*? It will be a slaughterhouse."

"Noémi," Mátyás said, rising from his seat and putting his hands on her shoulders. "It will be all right."

"It will *not* be all right!" she said. "When you fight, people *die*. You've seen nothing of death. I have."

"Some things are worth dying for," William said, his eyes

burning. "'Only this thought haunts me, that I might die in my bed, slowly withering like a flower.'"

The bittersweet words caught at my heart, but Noémi scoffed at them. "Oh yes. I've read Petőfi's poem. One expects such thoughts of poets. But I had hoped you were rational men. There's nothing heroic about dying."

"We won't die." William smirked. "Have Mátyás bring you to my workshop. I'll show you."

"What makes you think I want anything to do with this?" Noémi asked. "I'd stop you if I could. But I—"

She broke off as a wiry man with thinning hair pushed his way through the crowd of students. "The Circle is rounding up Gypsies in Tabán! They mean to enforce the Hapsburg prohibition against non-Luminate magic. Should be quite a show."

A show. Because of course punishment was only entertainment for those not involved. My heart shrank. Is that where Gábor disappeared? Then the knot of my heart twisted tighter. *James's letter.* Was this the result of my folly? I had to do something. "Where is Tabán?"

"By Gellért Hill, on the Buda side," Noémi said. A beat later, she realized my intent. "But, Anna, you can't go there. Not today. Not ever. Even on a good day it's not safe."

"Someone must warn him. Them."

Noémi shook her head and put her hand, very gently, over mine. "But not you."

I hitched up my skirts and climbed onto a chair, pitching my voice to sound over the crowd. My Hungarian was rough, but it carried. "Please. Listen to me! Today, it is Romanies. But who will it be tomorrow? The Magyar? The

265

Circle have already shown that they do not value anyone not like them. You must stop them!"

A half second's shocked silence met my words, then the room erupted with jeers.

"What's all this buzzing? Is a *woman* speaking?"

"She's not even Magyar!"

"They're only Gypsies!" a student cried. "It's not our fight."

"My girl, you shouldn't be worrying your pretty head about our politics. I've got a much better idea of how you can occupy your time!" This last comment was accompanied by pursed lips and a very vulgar gesture.

I continued to stand for a moment, my chin held high and my cheeks burning. My stomach boiled with frustration. How could these men accept my help with the Binding—and then reject my plea? Because I was a girl did not mean I was witless.

I clambered down. "Mátyás, you must come with me. Gábor might be there."

"There's nothing we can do. What's happening in Tabán has already begun."

A scream burned in my throat. "How can you claim to be willing to sacrifice everything for a revolution—for an idea of justice—and be so unwilling to sacrifice anything for a *friend*. Are you afraid?"

He shook his head, though a shadow passed through his eyes. "If we act now, we'll draw the Circle's attention too early. That will spoil any advantage we have of surprise. Sometimes you have to sacrifice small things to win great ones."

"Gábor is not a *thing*, and you cannot win a revolution on cowardice," I said. As soon as the hurt registered in his eyes, I hated myself a bit. But only a little, because under the cover of my fury, the river of my fear ran deep, deep, deep. I had to find Gábor before the Circle retribution against the Romanies swept him up too.

Mátyás tightened his lips as if he would protest, but said only, "I'm taking you home. The streets may not be safe."

Then, flanking me, Mátyás and Noémi marched me home like a prisoner.

They deposited me in the drawing room with Grandmama, very much as if I were an unwanted parcel. I knew they escorted me into the room solely to make it more difficult for me to slip away and find Gábor. I sent Mátyás a black look as he left, but he only grinned.

"Did you have a nice time with your friends?" Grandmama asked.

"Yes." I choked down a half-hysterical laugh. *A nice time.* We plotted revolution while the Circle rounded up Romanies in Tabán. What would they do to the Romanies they found? Confiscate their talismans, certainly. Execute them? The idea made my heart cold.

Noémi took a deep breath and straightened her shoulders, as if gathering her resolve.

"Irína *néni*," she began, crossing the Turkish carpet toward Grandmama. "You must reason with Anna."

No. Grandmama couldn't know. She would only worry— and forbid me to act. "Noémi, don't."

Noémi paused to look back at me, her eyebrows pinched together, her eyes troubled. "Anna, I must speak. You live by your conscience. I must live by mine." She swung back to Grandmama. "Anna and Mátyás's ridiculous student friends are determined on a revolution. They think they can take down the Circle on the strength of a broken Binding."

Grandmama turned concerned eyes on me. "Is this true?"

I lifted my chin, fury burning hard and hot in my chest. "It's true." The reproach in her eyes was hard to bear, but I bore it. "Without the Circle controlling magic, *anyone* might cast spells. It won't matter so much if I can't use magic, if James can't, because magic won't be the only thing determining one's worth. Beyond that, without the Circle bolstering the Hapsburgs in Vienna, Hungary might finally be free. I know you love this country. Can't you see that this is the right thing to do? Papa believes it; so does Lady Berri. And so do I."

Grandmama's face softened a fraction. "When?"

I did not answer, so Noémi spoke for me. "Tomorrow night."

Grandmama set her cane against the floor and tried to push herself upright. Her hand trembled, so she could not maintain a firm grip. Noémi and I both started for her, but Noémi reached her first, helping her to stand. I was only a few paces away when Grandmama said, "Anna, I understand why your heart is in this—but you cannot do it. I forbid it. I will not betray your mother's trust this way."

I set my teeth against the pain in her eyes. I did not like to disappoint Grandmama, but I had given my word.

"I will stop you," Grandmama continued. "I will set wards around your room."

I could break a ward, if I must.

Grandmama added, "And if the wards fail, I'll set a footman to watch you."

I swallowed my words of protest and turned on my heel. I marched down the hallway toward my bedchamber, seeing neither the patterned wallpaper nor the ornately framed pictures. I saw instead Gábor's face, and James's. I knew Noémi and Grandmama only acted out of concern for me, but that knowledge did nothing to stem the hot anger coursing through me.

⟨

Once in my room, I paced the floor. I threw myself onto my bed and screamed into my pillow. And then I looked at the bedclothes beneath my hand.

It only took moments to strip the bedclothes from the bed and fashion knots between them—heaven knew knots were the one thing for which my embroidery skills prepared me. I eased open the window. I had never escaped this way, but heroines did it all the time in books.

Someone tapped at my door, and my heart leapt into my throat.

"Anna? May I come in?" *Noémi.*

"I've no wish to speak to you." Let her think I was sulking.

A deep sigh. "I want to help."

"You don't want to help. You want a world where things go on the same. I don't."

"I do want change. But not your way."

I had to send her away. It was not hard to let bitterness

infuse my voice, to craft an edge sharp enough to draw blood. "I liked you, Noémi. I trusted you. But now I wish I'd never met you."

A long pause. A faint shuffling, then silence.

She was gone.

I steeled my heart against guilt and threw my makeshift rope out the window.

CHAPTER 22

In books, the heroine never has any difficulty escaping through her window. I ran into trouble almost immediately: between my corset and my petticoats, I could not fit. I stripped off some of the petticoats, but I could do nothing about the corset or the narrow sleeves of my gown without summoning Ginny to help me undress, and she would feel duty-bound to tell Grandmama.

After much maneuvering, I managed to get out of the window, skirt and lower limbs first. The stitching beneath my sleeves tore, and the rope itself gave way when I was still a good six feet above the ground. I landed with a bone-jarring thud in the garden courtyard at the center of Grandmama's rented palace and limped through the back gates toward the mews behind.

I hired a fiacre to take me to the Duna and crossed the

pontoon bridge into Buda after paying a small toll. Normally, Luminate did not have to pay the toll, but with my torn dress and lopsided skirts, no one would believe I *was* noble. The boats beneath the planks rocked as I crossed on unsteady feet. Buda Castle hovered above me on the hillside, the banners of the Hapsburgs flying briskly over the ramparts. The hills around the castle were transmuting into a rainbow of gold, ocher, crimson, and umber.

On the far side of the river, I stopped to ask directions of a middle-aged woman. She eyed me askance, but pointed obligingly.

Tabán, as I approached it, was not as I'd expected. I'd pictured a collection of narrow streets full of squalid buildings. But though the streets were indeed narrow and largely unpaved, the single-story houses lining the roads were for the most part clean, their walls scrubbed and freshly whitewashed.

The streets were empty, dry leaves scuttling across the packed earth, though I sensed eyes on me through the occasional cracked door or narrow window. Shouts rang out ahead of me, and I followed the sound, my heart thumping against my breastbone. The noise brought back the horrible afternoon when Noémi and I had been barred from the Romani camp. My steps slowed, but I forced myself onward.

As the noise grew louder, I clung to the whitewashed buildings, at last finding a narrow alleyway to slip through. It opened onto a larger, unpaved street, which in turn gave way to an open space that might be called a square, were it more properly formed. I proceeded cautiously down the street and positioned myself behind a wall of bystanders.

The square was full of people: Romanies, Circle members, onlookers. The handful of Luminate were easy to identify by their fine clothes. There was not much to choose from between the Romanies and the bystanders, most of whom wore plain, patched clothing. But the darker-skinned Romanies were being herded to the far side of the square, and their faces bore tracks of tears and tight-twisted mouths. Some invisible spell seemed to hold them in place. The onlookers reminded me of nothing so much as crows gathered around carrion. Were I an Elementalist, I'd have cast a Wind spell to knock all of them onto their rears in a fine patch of mud.

Two rough-looking men emerged from a nearby street with a thin Romani girl in tow. Desperate, she bit one of the men and kicked the other in the shins. They released her with matching howls of pain, but when she turned to run, the man nearest her hauled her back by her hair.

My breath caught. *Izidóra.*

At a gesture from a tall Luminate woman, the men shoved Izidóra toward the mass of Romanies. I scanned them, but there were too many. I could not see Gábor, though that meant nothing. If his family was here, no doubt he was nearby.

My heart sank. I was too late. Yet I felt compelled to watch, to witness whatever might be happening for Gábor's sake, for his sister's. They were my friends.

A second Luminate woman wove through the captive Romanies, collecting their talismans in an enormous sack: rings, brooches, necklaces, and bracelets. I rubbed at my wrist, at the phantom memory of the bracelet Gábor had given me.

In the center of the square, two Luminate men stood, setting the grounding for a spell. Herr Steinberg was one, his glasses flashing in the low light. The other crouched down, placed a coil of rope on the ground in a precise circle, then straightened. His light-eyed gaze swept the crowd, as though looking for something. I started.

Pál did not see me, or whatever he searched for. He closed his eyes and sniffed the air. I pressed back against the nearest building, slouching down so I was hidden from view by the people in front of me. Pál's eyes snapped open.

His voice carried across the square, even over the muttering noise around me. "There's a Gypsy woman nearby hiding her newborn. Bring them here."

A dozen eager citizens peeled away from the crowd, disappearing into side streets. My stomach cramped. I knew how sacred the Romanies held the privacy of the newborn. To thrust both mother and child into the dirty public square would be the worst kind of violation. I wondered if Pál knew as much. I hoped he did not: I hoped he was only ignorant, not malicious.

The crowd stirred restlessly. I ignored my neighbors, concentrating instead on the Romanies. Still no sign of Gábor. I hoped he had escaped. I hoped he was far away. But my heart hurt for those who remained, the young mothers with terrified children clinging to their skirts, the older men and women wearing looks of stoic resignation. Izidóra gripped her mother's hand. A woman near them dropped to the ground, wailing, pounding her hands fruitlessly against the dust. A young boy who looked much like Gábor's brother darted, toward a gap between the Romanies and the Luminate, only to recoil hard against an invisible barrier.

At last a young woman was pushed forward into the square, her hair hanging wild around her face, free from the kerchief every Romani woman wore in public. It was not Gábor's sister with the baby I had cursed—but I ached for her anyway. She held her baby against her breast and keened: a high, horrible sound as if her heart were being turned inside out.

Herr Steinberg took the baby from her with gentle hands. The tall Luminate woman put an arm around the girl and led her to the other Romanies. But their very gentleness made their actions the more abominable—they *knew* they were doing a terrible thing and wished to lessen the horror of it.

Herr Steinberg spread a bit of cloth on the ground before Uncle Pál and laid the baby upon it. The infant thrashed tiny limbs and wailed a high, thin note, nearly lost in the growing murmur around me. The crowd was uneasy, disliking this new turn when they had hoped for blood. An innocent provided poor sport.

I closed my eyes briefly, praying for courage, and then shoved my way through the crowd. I did not know precisely what Pál and Herr Steinberg planned, but a tight certainty in my gut told me they must be stopped. The two men looked up in surprise as I emerged in front of them. I waved my hand at the child and the bound Romanies. "Don't do this! These people are no real threat to you. Let them go."

Herr Steinberg readjusted his spectacles. His brows pinched together. "As distasteful as this may seem to you, civilized society must be governed by rules. And rules demand consequences. The Gypsies have been using magic reserved for the Luminate, a practice punishable by law."

He nodded at Pál to continue. My eyes flickered from the baby, whose lips and fingers were already blue with cold, to the young mother who threw herself repeatedly against the Holding spell.

"Please stop." I brought my icy hands together in supplication. Did Lady Berri know the Circle had planned this? Then I remembered—she was in hiding. Of course she couldn't know. She was not like these men.

"Be silent, or I will silence you." The look Pál cast me was chillingly indifferent. "The spell is begun." He crouched beside the baby and touched its forehead with a finger. The baby stopped wailing. Pál pulled a small, wicked-looking knife from a pocket in his coat, and I cried out.

Pál did not look at me, but slid the knife in a practiced gesture across his own wrist. His blood dripped onto the baby, crimson rivulets running down its cheeks. The baby began crying again. Behind the bar of the Holding, the mother screamed at my uncle.

The spell is begun. I scrabbled for the anger that had let me break Pál's spell when he entered my room. The air seemed to catch, as though I had snagged the edge of the spell. The ring on my finger blazed white-hot, and I gasped, my concentration shattering. The ring must have been charmed to prevent my breaking not only the Binding but *any* spell.

Pál stood. The tall Luminate women rushed forward with a strip of white cloth to bind his cut. When she finished,

Pál extended his hands and began intoning in Latin, a sharp phrase that bit the air. Beside him, the Luminate woman chanted a counterpoint to his: high when his voice was low, low when he was high, their two spells mingling to become something stronger, more powerful.

At once the square was silent. The screaming mother, the crying women and children, the angry fathers—all still. I looked at them in surprise. Their faces were blank with horror, as if the blood on the child were the child's own blood and not Pál's.

Of all the Romanies in the square, only the baby continued to wail.

The tall woman scooped up the baby and returned it to its mother, who wept and kissed its head and opened her mouth to speak but no sound emerged. The Romani nearest her edged away. Others dropped to their knees.

I found my voice. "What have you done?"

"A minor Blocking spell," Herr Steinberg said. "The practice of magic requires that one both sense magic, to pull it into one's soul, and speak the words of ritual. The spell put a buffer around their souls, blocking any possible ability to sense magic, and silenced their vocal cords."

"They cannot speak," I echoed, sure I had misunderstood. "Not to each other. Not to anyone. How could you do this?" I wanted to weep.

"My blood sacrifice brought me strength; profaning something the Gypsies hold sacred made them weak," Pál said, mistaking my question. He wavered, his knees buckling. Herr Steinberg slid a supporting arm around him, and Pál cast a look at him, resentment just masked with gratitude.

Pál's words twisted in my head. He knew about Romani birthing practices, knew that what he was doing was a profanation. Did he know that their magic did not require words? Blocking their connection to magic was one thing; stealing their ability to speak was gratuitous cruelty. My own knees trembled.

Herr Steinberg must have read my contempt in my face because he hastened to add, "It's quite humane, really. None of them will be imprisoned. None will be forced to leave their home or their family."

"But they cannot use magic," I said. "And they cannot speak."

"Well. Yes. That was rather the point." He smiled, and I saw for the first time the malicious edge to it. "I understand we have you to thank for pointing us toward them. Count yourself lucky your family is deemed too important for your punishment to be the same."

Those *damned* letters.

Already the crowd dispersed around us, their lust for blood blunted by the disquieting spell. The Holding spell lifted: the Romanies left the square in driblets, leaning on one another.

I could not stay. I had been told the Binding protected us from monsters. But monsters existed outside the Binding as well.

I swung away from Herr Steinberg and my uncle, my body braced for a spell that never came. The Circle made no attempt to stop me.

They had already done what they came to do.

A Romani family brushed past me, a father and mother herding two small children between them. My eyes stung.

I suspected that some, perhaps most, had never practiced magic as the Circle charged. I wondered what they would do now.

I paused to search the square behind me. The Circle had vanished. There was no sign of Izidóra. But a half dozen paces away, I spotted a Romani bracelet, trampled and half buried in mud. I dug it out and slipped it into my pocket, with some half-formed idea of cleaning it and returning it to Gábor's family. It was not atonement, but it was a start.

I stripped off my now-filthy gloves as I walked. Turning a corner into a shadowed roadway, I strode directly into someone. I had a confused impression of a man, taller than I, wearing a green wool dolman of considerably nicer cut than most of the people in the square. Likely Luminate.

I recoiled. "I beg your pardon!"

The owner swung around. "Anna?"

X

Gábor's hands were trembling, but not at my nearness. His eyes were wide, drowning in a film of tears. I had never seen him look so *gutted*. Without thinking—not of how it might look, not of my own horror—I threw my arms around him, feeling the soft wool of his collar against my ear. His heart thumped an uneven rhythm.

"Anna," he said again, his cheek coming to rest against the top of my head, his hands tangling in my hair. A spasm seized him, and his tall frame seemed to collapse on me, folding in on itself, sliding through my arms until he was kneeling before me in the dirt, his head resting against my abdomen.

He sobbed, a great heaving gasp that shook both of us, and I cradled him in my arms and kissed his hair and wished I could leach some of the horror from him through my touch. A fierce protectiveness welled in me, something I had not felt since James.

I could not tell him it was all right. It was not.

But I could hold him tight. I could grieve with him.

We clung to each other for a long moment, the only still points in a turning, tottering world.

"Oh, Anna. This is my fault." His voice was muffled against the damp front of my dress.

I swallowed against my constricting throat. "How is this your fault? The Circle bears blame for it." My arms tightened around his shoulders. *My fault.* I should never have written those letters. I should have broken Pál's spell as he cast it. I should have done *something* more than I had.

"I should have stopped it. But I did nothing. I watched—and I *did nothing.*"

"What could you do?" I asked. "If you had acted, they would have spelled you as well. You survived. You did what you must to fight again another day."

"I was not being heroic. I was frightened. *You* were not. I saw you." He lifted his head. His eyes were bloodshot and his nose red and dripping, and still my heart contracted.

"I was terrified," I admitted. His words twisted in me. He did not know the extent of my guilt—and I could never tell him. He would hate me. "I could not stop them either. Only the fact I am Luminate prevented them from punishing me with your family." I hesitated. "But we *will* act. And soon. When I break the Binding, we will—"

"Don't," Gábor said, laying his fingers against my lips. "Don't say it. Don't do it. It won't save my family. It might not save any of us."

I heard his words, but they seemed distant. Against all reason, I wanted to kiss his fingers. Despite the horribly inappropriate time and place, I wanted to slide my hands into his hair and press my lips against his.

I stared at him. Gábor fell silent, his eyes fixed on mine. They were dark and warm, like buckwheat honey. Something flickered in them, and he looked away, dropping his fingers from my mouth. My lips felt chilled and exposed.

Gripping my arms for balance, he pulled himself upright. "Thank you." As soon as he was stable, he released me. He glanced down the street, where the last of the Romanies straggled past. "You should go."

No. He was pushing me away again. I could see it in the tight set of his lips, the way his eyes refused to meet mine, the darkening flush high in his cheeks. "I want to be here. With you. I want to know you will be all right."

"I am fine. I must see to my family."

"I'll come with you," I said. "Perhaps I can help."

He shook his head. "It's better if you don't. They would be embarrassed for you to see them like this."

I moved in front of him so he was forced to look at me, and set my bare hands to his cheeks. My stomach trembled, but my fingers were steady. "I will not think less of your family for what happened to them. That's what friendship is—what *love* is. People who love you will not think less of you for grieving. *I* do not think less of you."

Gábor set his hands over mine and drew them away

from his face. He stared down at me. "What is it you want from me?"

I want you to forgive me for what I've done. Heat scalded my cheeks and washed down my throat. I willed myself to return his gaze. *I want you to love me.* "I wish you would let me be your friend. Let me help you."

I took a deep breath, my heart hammering. Well-bred girls did not say what I was about to say. I thought ruefully of my escape from Grandmama's house. Perhaps I was not so well-bred either. "I know this is neither the time nor the place for this discussion, but you seem determined to say nothing, so I must. I care about you. I might even love you. But I won't know unless you allow me closer—and you are always so careful, so guarded."

His beautiful dark eyes clouded. "Anna. You are a lovely young woman: pretty, witty, strong-hearted, brave." His fingers tightened around mine.

I heard the unspoken "but" and turned my face away, tugging my hand free from his. My face burned with mortification. I had misread everything. Gábor did not care for me in that fashion. His silence now was only because he searched for the right words to let me down gently.

"You've said enough. I understand." I whirled around, my eyes already filling with tears.

And then Gábor stood before me, blocking my path. He put his hands on my shoulders and drew me to him, bringing his lips down firmly on mine.

His lips were warm and surprisingly soft. I leaned into the kiss, desire and relief and hope surging through me. And then the kiss was no longer gentle, but something powerful—shot through with longing and a dark thread of sorrow. I didn't know if it was love or fear or desperation or all three that drove us together, but I welcomed it. I slid my fingers behind his head to stroke the soft, fine curls at the nape of his neck. He released my shoulders, his hands moving in slow circles down my spine. Energy fizzed through my body, filling me until I thought I should burst with it.

He pulled back to rain kisses on my face: along my brow line, down the curve of my cheek, the corner of my mouth, before finding my lips again. My skin flared beneath his touch. I kissed him back, marveling at my temerity, thrilling that I *could*. He was here, he wanted me like I wanted him, and the miracle of this fact transcended any magic I knew.

Gábor pulled away first. I blinked at him, unsteady on my feet, shocked to find myself still standing in a muddy street in Tabán.

"How could I not love you?" he asked, his eyes fierce but his voice tender. "You are the bravest, kindest, most infuriating woman I've ever met."

My heart expanded. *He loves me.*

Gábor continued, releasing my hand and stepping back a pace. "But try as I might, I cannot see a future for us. I see a lovely Luminate lady who will return to England and marry one of her own—and I see a Romani man who hopes at best to aspire to a small clerical or scientific position. There is nothing for you in this."

"Must we have a future to be together now?" My voice sounded wistful, even to my ears.

Gábor's gaze was steady. "You are not that kind of woman."

A wind kicked up, whistling down the alley. I rubbed my arms, chilled in the weak sunlight. My mind understood his words, but my heart protested. I remembered *Jane Eyre,* the book James had sent me. Sometimes love can't be had even when both lovers want it. I had adored Jane's dark, bittersweet story, but I did not want it for mine.

"I am, and always will be, your friend. But I do not see how we can be more than this." He held his arm out to me. I took it, his warmth and nearness firing electricity up my side. "Let me take you home. I'll see to my family when you are safe."

"I could try to break the spell on them," I said, though I was fairly certain the ring would stop me if I made the attempt. But I had to offer.

Gábor stopped moving. "That is kind of you. But I don't think it's a good idea. You might free them—but in breaking the spell, you might cause other damage."

His words stung, though he had not said anything I did not already know. The specter of his niece hung between us.

We walked down the hillside to the Duna and crossed the pontoon bridge. We followed the Korzó until we reached Rákóczy Street, and then turned into the heart of Pest. At Grandmama's doorstep, I emptied my reticule and gave him all the money I could find inside it.

"It's not enough," I said. The infant's thin wail against the sudden silence of the Romanies still rang in my ears. Money couldn't atone for that. "But please, see that your family has everything they need."

Gábor hesitated. "Thank you."

Then it was my turn to hesitate. "You should know, I mean to try to break the Binding tomorrow night, with Lady Berri. I believe William intends to launch a revolution against the Hapsburgs after the spell is broken. Possibly I will fail. Perhaps we all will. And maybe the monsters we release will be dangerous. Maybe the magic released will be destructive."

I took a breath. I could not unsend my letters to James. I was not even certain I could undo Pál's spell, since, as Gábor charged, my control was unpredictable. "But I must do something. The Circle is as dangerous and destructive as anything in the Binding. I cannot let people like my uncle and Herr Steinberg use the power of that spell to abuse and control others."

Gábor went very still.

"Will you try to stop us?" I knew that Gábor resisted the idea of a violent uprising.

"No," he said. "The Circle must be stopped. I had hoped we might do it by other means; I saw today that they do not speak a peaceful language. Here, as in Austria, the will of the Circle and the will of the Hapsburgs are one and the same. To fight one, we must fight both."

Tears stood in his eyes. I could not tell if they were tears of rage or of grief.

"I still do not agree with breaking the Binding."

I wrapped my arms around my torso, chilled. After all this, he still meant to argue?

Gábor reached out to brush my cheek. "But if you think it right, then you must do it. I will pray you are right and I am wrong."

He dropped his hand and turned away. I watched him until he reached the far end of the street and disappeared around the corner, heading back toward Tabán. I pressed my fingers to my cheek. Gábor's touch felt like hope—and forgiveness.

CHAPTER 23

Ginny was waiting for me inside the back entrance, a basket of mending by her feet. She looked up from her sewing as I shoved the door open. "Your grandmama wishes to speak with you in the parlor. Miss Anna—what were you thinking? To leave like that, and your room all a mess."

My stomach dropped. I hadn't thought of anything but Gábor.

Grandmama too was waiting. She held no book, no embroidery. She sat in one of the burgundy high-backed chairs, her spine ramrod straight, her hands folded over the top of her cane.

"Have I failed so with you, *szívem,* that you would lie to me? That you would not trust me?"

My heart twisted, but I lifted my chin. "I had to do it, Grandmama. I'm sorry I worried you, but Gábor—Mr. Kovács's family was in danger. I had to see if I could help."

The stiff line of her mouth softened a fraction. "Are they all right?"

"No. The Circle—" I broke off, remembering. "They've stripped the Romanies of their magic. And their voice."

"Rettenetes." Terrible. Grandmama's horror was genuine. "And Mr. Kovács?"

"They didn't catch him, so he wasn't part of the spell. He's gone to help his family." I crossed the carpet to Grandmama, sinking down beside her and taking her hand in mine. "Grandmama, the Circle—they're all wrong. We must stop them. You must let me help Lady Berri."

Grandmama lifted my hand, studying the gargoyle ring. "Anna, it's not safe. I understand what you wish—why you wish it—but your mama would never forgive me if something happened to you."

I was not so sanguine about Mama's reaction, but I would not hurt Grandmama by saying so. "Papa would wish it."

"Your papa is a good man, but about some things he is quite foolish. Young, untrained girls have no business messing around in spells like this. Even with the aid of an equally foolish member of the Circle."

"Please. Let me go."

"I cannot risk you. I'm sorry, Anna." Glancing at the mutinous line of my mouth, Grandmama added, "And do not think you can climb out the window again. I've had the house warded. You'll not be able to leave without sounding an alarm."

"You might trust me," I said.

One delicately shaped eyebrow lifted, and I flushed. "As you have trusted me?" Grandmama said. "I shall let Lady Berri know you've other plans for tomorrow evening."

288

※

I did not see the message Grandmama sent Lady Berri, but I saw Lady Berri's answer. I returned from a morning visit with Noémi to Karolina's to find a note with Lady Berri's crest, a sleek black panther, on the salver in the parlor. I flipped it open and scanned the short missive: *I am sorry your grandmother forbids your assistance, but I will not encourage filial disobedience. I hope I may still call on you. Your friend, Lady Margaret Berri.*

Grandmama bade me read it out loud, and I did so, puzzling at it. *Filial disobedience?* But Papa had been the one to encourage me to help Lady Berri in the first place. Then I realized Lady Berri had no intention of heeding Grandmama's request; she meant for me to obey Papa. I did not know what she planned, but I would watch, and wait.

※

I cornered Mátyás and Gábor in the hallway outside Grandmama's salon, as afternoon ebbed away into evening. They wore dark dolmans over plain clothes; a small, silver falcon pin winked on Mátyás's collar. Though they had said nothing of their destination, I knew. They were going to meet William and Petőfi and the others.

"Tell William not to do anything rash," I said. "Lady Berri may not come for me tonight. Grandmama has forbidden it. Don't let him start a fight he cannot finish."

"May as well tell the sun not to rise," Mátyás said, smiling and kissing his cross for luck. Was this a lark to him? I swallowed against something sharp.

"We'll tell him," Gábor promised.

Grandmama invited me to join her in a game of piquet after supper, but I had no heart for it. Instead, I retired to my room, sending Ginny away when she came to help me disrobe. I picked up a book of Browning's poetry, but my mind skittered across the words and I set it down again.

I was peering out my window at the courtyard below when a faint susurration sounded behind me. I whirled to find a faintly glowing seam in the air. Lady Berri's voice echoed through the gap. "Come, child, we haven't all night."

In a moment—before I could think, before I could risk breaking the spell with my sparking anxiety—I was through, the hair on my arms standing upright from my passing. I emerged on the stones on an unfamiliar street. Lady Berri waited in a dark barouche drawn by four black horses, its hood folded back. The night air bit my cheeks and I shivered, wishing I had thought to bring a cloak.

"The Circle was watching your home," she said, waving the driver on before I had even settled in my seat. "I had to bring you out another way. But we must hurry—the portal may have drawn their attention."

"Then why not simply open a portal to Attila's Hill?" I asked.

"It's not so simple to cast a spell across that distance, and I'd prefer to conserve my energies for necessary spells. We shall have to do something about your ring, but I prefer to wait until just before you enter the Binding. Otherwise, we risk drawing the Circle's attention too soon. As it is, we shall have to hope they did not notice the portal. Or pray that we can outrun them."

Neither of us spoke as the carriage drew swiftly out of the inner city, past the sleeping white-pillared National Museum. I listened to the huff of the horses' breath and the *whump-whump* of the carriage wheels. But as we neared the outskirts of Pest, Lady Berri sat upright, her eyes sweeping the darkness around us.

"We're being followed."

I craned my neck, peering into the darkness. I saw nothing but an empty expanse of street. I closed my eyes, listening. Still nothing. *Wait.* Then I heard it, a faint echo of our own carriage, the muffled thud of horses' hooves beyond our four. They must be Hiding, which meant they must also be Luminate.

Panic pressed against my throat, stopping my breath.

Herr Steinberg.

"Can you stop them?"

"Not here. Wait."

I studied the narrow and crowded row houses pressing up to the street around us and wondered why this environment was so wrong for spell-casting. The row houses gave way to factories, and the factories to empty fields and scattered cottages. In a matter of minutes, we were beyond the city.

As we crossed a stretch of road bare of houses on either side, Lady Berri spoke again. "Now."

She stood in the carriage and turned, flinging her hands out toward the darkness, and shouted, *"Terra plica!"*

The road beneath us rippled once, as if testing its strength, and then the whole landscape heaved upward. Someone cried out behind us, a note of fear hanging in the dark air.

The sky fell toward us. The fields shook.

Behind us, the road folded over on itself, like a bit of kneaded dough.

The cry cut off.

The horses whinnied in terror, but before they could bolt, the road finished its contortions. One final shudder, and it settled down, flat and rutted in the moonlight. I peered behind us at the silent stretch of road.

Whoever had followed us was gone, swallowed by a suddenly animate piece of earth.

I turned wide eyes on Lady Berri. I knew she was Lucifera, like Freddy, but I had never seen anyone fold earth as though it were only a bit of flour and water.

"Is he dead?" My heart galloped through my chest.

Lady Berri settled back in her seat, straightening her skirt as if earth-folding were an everyday occurrence. "Most likely. I've never had occasion to use that particular spell before. But needs must when the devil drives."

A chill settled around me, more biting than the cool night air. *Are we safe?* I wanted to ask, but nothing seemed safe anymore. Not this errand. Not the suddenly strange lady beside me. It had been easy to trust a grandmotherly woman who wanted the same things my father wanted. But Lady Berri was not that woman.

I wondered if she ever had been.

"Let me see your ring," she said.

I held out my hand. Lady Berri summoned a small Lumen lamp and examined the grotesquely grinning creature around my finger.

"I don't like this spell," she said, frowning. "This is not Herr Steinberg's work. His spells are crude things, easily enough undone. But this . . . Someone powerful cast this."

Uncle Pál, I guessed. "Can you undo it?"

Her frown deepened. She muttered a phrase, and pricks of light danced over the ring. She dropped my hand as if burned. "No." She blinked rapidly and licked her lips.

I stared at her. I had never seen Lady Berri even mildly discomposed. The worry in her face sent fear spiraling up my throat. "We don't have to do this," I said. William was waiting on my signal. We could plan again.

She shook her head, her eyes bulging slightly. "We're too far gone to turn back. A drive they might forgive, but not a death. We'll have to risk it."

"But I cannot break the Binding as long as I wear the ring. It burns me if I try."

"Are you certain it prevents you? Or does it simply pain you to try?"

"It—" I stopped. I had not actually tried breaking a spell beyond the point of pain. "I don't know."

"You must try. The pain of the ring will be nothing to what happens if we do not succeed tonight."

I swallowed sourness at the back of my throat and sat forward in my seat, wrapping my arms tightly about me. Despite Herr Steinberg's horrible threats, I had never imagined I could actually die.

But at that moment, death seemed a terribly real possibility. Perhaps the Circle had already sent others after us, when their scout vanished. If they hadn't, they would. Soon.

Once we arrived at Attila's Hill, it took some time for Lady Berri to stage her spell. The earlier spell had worn her, and she kept pausing to breathe deeply. My own breaths were fast, shallow, frightened. *Hurry,* I thought. At last, Lady Berri set two fingers against my forehead and against my collarbone. Heat flared beneath her touch, sending a faint buzzing through my skull. "For protection," she said. She pressed a bone knife into my hands. "Remember, you may need to feed the spell some of your blood. It was forged in blood—it must be broken with it."

I reminded myself why I was here: for magic, for James, for Papa. For Gábor and the Romanies and justice. For Hungary.

Because a man had been swallowed by a fold of earth and now I had no choice.

I took a deep breath and stepped forward.

Heat prickled around me. A thin film of resistance.

The ring burned hot against my finger, a bright point of pain. It blazed higher, searing through my body, across my scalp. My breath caught at the sting. "I can't."

"You can," Lady Berri said.

Even my blood was burning. I took a deep breath, bracing myself for immobility, as Herr Steinberg had promised. Would the Circle find us here, frozen? Or would Lady Berri bring my body back to Grandmama?

No. I would not be so weak. Anger brought my shadow self surging upward, and I released her. I would do this. I would not let the spell or pain block me.

The pain was sun-bright now, a whiteness at the edge of my vision. I cried out, and my shadow self flooded my entire body, riding the agony to my fingertips, and beyond.

I dropped to my knees. The air around me seemed to catch, and then split wide.

A thunderclap of pain so intense I thought I had died.

Then I was falling.

Air screamed past me, dousing the fire in my blood. I

waited for the threatened Immobility spell to catch me, my muscles already tensed against the sudden cessation.

Nothing happened, save the wind in my eyes and my stomach somersaulting inside me. Had I broken the spell on the ring? A brief memory surfaced: my uncle's eyes when he looked at Herr Steinberg. Had Pál even cast the Immobility spell?

I had just begun to wonder if I would ever stop falling when I landed.

A dense carpet of flowers spread across a familiar hillside. Only this time, the carpet was not violets, but Queen Anne's lace, the filigree clusters of tiny white flowers bobbing on the wind. I plucked a stem and wrinkled my nose at the rank, parsnip-like smell. Not Queen Anne's lace. Hemlock.

I curled my fingers around the handle of the bone knife and stood. I shook my hand, and Herr Steinberg's ring tumbled to the ground with a faint thud. I smiled grimly at the discarded gargoyle. I had work to do.

Find the heart of the spell, Hunger had said. I looked around. There was nothing in the peaceful vista around me that suggested sacrifice, that demanded my blood or my broken heart. A gentle breeze tugged at me, urging me toward the forest of shimmering leaves. Hunger had told me not to wander in strange woods alone, but he was not here. And I must go somewhere.

A shadow fell across my face. I tipped my head back to see a falcon slicing through the air, half again the size of my beloved peregrines, golden striations across the back and tail. I brushed my fingers against Karolina's necklace. A turul bird? A good omen, in any case.

I followed the bird along a faint trail through the flowers to the edge of the wood, then stopped. Shadows shifted between the close-packed trees, and I shuddered, thinking of the *fene* on Whitsun night. If I died here, in the center of a spell, would anyone know? Lady Berri might suspect when I did not return, but my body would be lost to the Binding spell.

Courage, I thought.

Inhaling deeply, I plunged into the shadows.

CHAPTER 24

The road I followed was deeply scored and narrow, over-grown by weeds and choked with dead leaves. I imagined once it was a busy trade route, now abandoned. By whom and for what reason, I could not fathom. Unease nagged at me.

The woods were quiet.

Too quiet.

I heard no trills of familiar (or even unfamiliar) songbirds. No rustle of small animals in the underbrush. No distant cawing of crows. The falcon had disappeared above the trees. And though the silver leaves twitched and stirred, I heard no rushing wind through the branches. The only sound in all the shifting wood was the crunching of my feet against dry leaves. I told myself it was just the interior of a spell, but that was small comfort. In the millennium since the Binding was created, anything might have evolved within it.

A flashing movement tugged at the corner of my eye. I glanced over my shoulder, squinting into the darkness between the pale trunks. Nothing. But I caught a flash again from the other side, and my heart began to thump too strong and too loud against my breastbone.

I stepped forward in time to the pounding of my heart.

Thump, thump, thump.

Then I heard something. A faint, high keening to my left. A woman's voice, caught in a perfect pitch of agony. The sound was picked up on my right, louder and closer.

My heart sped up. So did my feet.

Another flash of movement in the woods. This time I glimpsed a figure, moon white against the darkness, pale hair tangled around a ruined face. *Rusalka?* Or *vadleány,* a wicked forest sprite from Grandmama's stories? Perhaps something nameless but equally horrifying. The creature kept pace with me, following but not yet approaching.

A thrill of fear shot through me.

A second figure joined the first, and then a third, even closer, on my right side. With cries that sent needles of pain into every pore of my skin, they converged on the road.

I picked up my skirts and ran.

My corset dug bone fingers into my ribs. Each breath sawed through my lungs.

The creatures with their curious loping gait were gaining on me.

I ran faster.

My shoe caught on one of the deep scars in the road and flung me forward, hands and face scraping against the hard dirt. My knife skittered across the road and was lost in the shadows beyond it.

At once the first of the creatures was upon me, her weight like a gravestone on my back. She wrapped her fingers in my hair and yanked, the sharp pain pulling tears into my eyes. A second creature crouched in the road before me. She smelled of wood rot and places damp with mold. *Boszorkány.* Wood witch.

She jabbed a long, waxy finger at my right eye, and I flinched. She flicked my closed eyelid with her finger and laughed.

"Poke her eyes out," she said.

The first shifted on my back. I could scarce breathe under her weight, but when she released my hair and slipped her tomb-cold fingers around my neck, my heart nearly stopped. I struggled to throw her off me, but her body was a dead weight, her hands like stone.

"Choke the life from her," the second said. The clasp of my necklace broke; the fine chain slithered down my neck.

"Tear the skin from her." The third creature joined her sisters, kneeling at my side and scratching a jagged fingernail along the exposed skin at my wrist. Beads of blood followed the line of her finger. Gooseflesh prickled up my arm.

"No! Please." I remembered Hunger had asked me to break the Binding, and the strange not-shadows I'd seen on Whitsun night had pleaded for freedom. "I'm here to break the spell. If you kill me, I can't set you free."

At once my lungs expanded with air. The creature on my back leapt off, joining her sisters before me. I pushed myself upright.

"Is she lying?" the second one asked.

The first, the oldest to guess by the deep grooves in her face, sniffed at the air. "She has the stink of magic on her."

"No Luminate has come here for ages." The third grinned, baring sharp teeth. "And we ate that one."

"I'm no Luminate spell-caster. I've no magic of my own. But I can break spells." I hoped I spoke truth.

"Let her try," the first said. "If she fails, we kill her then."

"Kill her then," the others agreed.

I took a deep breath, as deep as my corset would allow, and tried to swallow the lump clogging my throat. "Do you know where the heart of the spell is?"

The three women shifted as if agitated. Were they afraid?

The first one muttered to her sisters, and the third pointed down the path. "We will take you as far as the end of the wood. But you must face the castle alone. We are not welcome there."

I slid the broken necklace into my pocket and found my knife at the side of the road. I began walking again, flanked this time by my otherworldly guard. Now that I was no longer in imminent danger of dying, I found their presence curiously comforting. At the least, it meant all lesser predators would stay well away from us.

I tried not to think about *greater* predators, or whatever had spooked the sisters about the castle beyond their wood.

True to their word, the sisters left me at the edge of the wood and faded into the shadows. Before me stretched the great golden meadow I remembered from my first visit. The road from the wood continued, but it took a curving path around the edge of the field. Directly across the meadow the crenellations of the castle wall thrust toward the sky. With growing confidence—there was nothing *here* to threaten me—I strode forward into the waving grass.

And immediately drew back. The blades of waist-high grass were, in fact, blades—their edges strewn with serrated teeth. My skirt now in tatters and stinging cuts on my hands and forearms, I kept to the road.

There had been a creature in the meadow, I remembered, an incandescent being that made me think of unicorns, though it was unlike any unicorn I had seen illustrated. As I skirted the meadow, I watched the undulations of the deadly grass and hoped I would see the creature again. After the darkness of the woods, I needed a sign my mission was not foredoomed to failure. Something light would do.

The grass erupted.

There it was: a being of light, as if a ray of sunlight had suddenly become animate. It moved through the meadow with the muscular grace of a great cat I had seen in a London menagerie, with the speed of a long-limbed horse.

The creature ceased its dance through the meadow and whipped its head toward me. I looked away; meeting its gaze was like trying to look directly on the sun. With a roar that shook the bladed grasses, the creature twisted in on itself, stony arms erupting from liquid limbs, darkness spooling in uneven tendrils from its incandescent core. The metallic smell of blood wafted across the meadow. My stomach twisted, and I hurried toward the castle gates, desperate to be inside before the creature decided to pursue me.

I had longed to return to this world, feeling its absence like a toothache, a constant dull throb. And yet today there was nothing here but horror. What had Hunger shown me, that first time in the Binding? The truth? Or only the reflection of my own desires?

The streets inside the castle gates were nearly empty, the cobblestones torn and ruined. A young knight wandered alone. His face was vacant, empty sockets where his eyes should be. I trembled, tried not to speculate what had happened to his mistress, and crossed to the far side of the plaza.

I peered through an archway shrouded with roses. Here was the cloistered garden I remembered, full of dancing women. I thought with relief of their bright colors and their glad looks, and pushed my way past the roses. But when I found the center of the garden, the fountain ran with blood and the women were all dead, their throats gaping wide.

I rushed back to the street and dropped to the stony ground, retching.

A breeze drifted down to me, carrying the incongruous scent of roses and charred flesh, and I was sick again. The delighted laughter of a child drifted down from the castle tower above me.

No. My heart beat hard and fast. *No.*

When the child began screaming, I put my hands over my ears, and still the screams echoed through my bones. I crouched down by the bile-soaked stones and clenched my eyes shut. I wanted nothing more than to escape, to be back in the star-studded darkness with Lady Berri on a hillside that smelled only of dead earth. Not here, not in this nightmare of bone and blood and dying children and charnel-scented roses.

Yet when I opened my eyes at last and took my hands away from my ears, I was still in the middle of the cursed city.

Still in the Binding.

I did not know where the heart of the spell was.

Or how to reach it.

But I knew someone who might.

I rose on shaky legs and made my way to the main plaza before the gates. I braced myself against a stone fountain and closed my eyes, summoning up my strongest desires: magic, belonging, Gábor.

When I opened my eyes, Hunger stood before me.

"You should be careful with such desires," he said. "They might rouse creatures less friendly than I." He looked around, his eyes glinting. "How did you come here? You're not meant—" He broke off.

"Not meant to what? To see this? To set you free? You showed me a pretty lie when I came last," I said. *And I believed it.*

"Are our desires a lie? I showed you what you wanted to see."

Yes. I had wanted to believe his vision because it made breaking the Binding the right choice, the easy choice. I should have known better. I shook my head and swung my hand around at the ruined city, the forest beyond. "If I set you free, is this what I unleash on the world?"

Hunger's gold eyes met mine. "This spell draws power from the creatures it binds. If you break the spell, you free the creatures. But who can say, when you give a creature freedom, what he or she will choose? What will your world look like when you give all individuals the same rights? Can you say with certainty each person will use that power for good?"

I was silent. My thoughts twisted through my head. But one idea emerged clearly: I could not break this spell, not if it meant unleashing monsters like these on the world. The evils of the Circle seemed to pale in comparison.

"I cannot do this."

Those golden eyes were unwavering. "I know what you are."

My heart jumped. "Tell me!"

"Break the spell."

"No," I said. "I won't."

"Then I will not tell you. And I cannot let you leave."

Panic spiked my throat. I curled my hands, digging my nails into the flesh of my palm. *The grounding.* Lady Berri had anchored her spell to a ritual—and to me. Something of that anchor must be here. I rushed back to the archway, to the bloody cloistered garden, and stuck my fingers deeper into the earth, questing. But my fingers met only tangled grass roots and soil.

Hunger stood in the archway behind me, laughing. While I searched fruitlessly for a way back, he sauntered toward me and knelt in the grass.

Setting his hands over mine, he stilled my fingers. The silver manacles jangled at his wrists.

He pressed his lips against mine.

Heat ripped through me. I pulled away, gasping, my lips scorching.

"I see your heart," he said. "Your desires bind you here. To this spell. Even if you leave now, your need will bring you back."

"No." I pushed him away and he let me.

The spell needs blood to break. I drew my bone knife across my palm and gasped at the sting. When the blood welled up, I dipped my fingers in it. I swiped my fingers across my forehead and my collarbone, where Lady Berri had set her protective spell. For good measure, I brushed blood across my lips. Then I thrust my bloodstained fingers into the earth again. This time, beneath the flowers and matted grass there was nothing. Not dirt, not clay, not sand. Only a thinly woven mesh, much like the one I'd broken through on my fall into this world.

With a mighty thrust, I pushed myself through the grass and found myself falling, illogically, down again.

CHAPTER 25

When I blinked, my eyes were full of starlight, and I was back on the hard earth of Attila's Hill. A star flew overhead, dying incandescent. A cold fury burned in me. Hunger had lied to me about the Binding. So had Lady Berri.

I pushed myself upright, my mind already shaping the words I would hurl at her: *You did not tell me the spell draws power from the very creatures it holds, the creatures you dismiss. You did not tell me the creatures were terrible and I should unleash them on the world.*

I will not break the Binding.

I cannot.

But the words died on my tongue.

We were not alone on the hill. The light I had seen was not a falling star, but a spell. Lady Berri stood a dozen paces from me facing a handful of dark figures, her normally neat hair wild about her head. A red glow enveloped her, and she stumbled back. She swung her hands and shouted, and the entire hill lurched.

I dropped to my knees, biting my tongue. The metallic tang of blood filled my mouth, reminding me of the blood-drenched city I had seen, and I remained on my knees for a moment, dizzy and sick.

Though I wanted only to curl up on the brittle grass of the hill and pretend none of this was happening—not the beasts desperate to escape the Binding, not the fight before me—I knew I could not. I forced myself to my feet again.

"Lady Berri," I called. A hammer of air hit me in the face, knocking me to the ground in an explosion of pain.

"The Binding," she said, her words coming in gasps and puffs. "It's not—"

"I couldn't do it." I harbored a thin hope that my words might carry to our assailants, that they might halt their attack. I stood, wiping a thin trickle of blood from my nose with the back of my hand. A brutal wind picked up, whipping at my face. I dodged a flying branch.

"Never mind that now." Her voice was grim. "You must get out of here. I'll hold them."

A slit appeared in the air beside me, dark against the darker night. I hesitated. Fear and despair washed over me, so thick I could taste their bitterness, so heavy my arms hung limp at my sides. Some part of my mind recognized it as a Coremancer's work, and I struggled free of it. "I can't leave you."

"You're no good to me here. Go!"

I went.

I emerged on the street before Grandmama's house, and the slit sealed shut behind me.

X

The heavy wooden gates to Grandmama's courtyard hung askew on their hinges. Shock held me immobile for a moment. I had been gone only a few hours. What had happened? I sprang up the stairs leading off the courtyard, my skirts clutched in my fists, and stopped in the vaulted entryway.

The silence in the house was tangible, a crouching beast with glowing eyes and sharp teeth. The lovely parquet floor of the entry hall was charred and buckled. Here and there small fires flickered in the gloom.

Grandmama. My heart stuttered. *Ginny. Noémi.* I gathered up my skirts again and picked my way across the ruined floor before rushing up the stairs. *I should have been here.* My single-mindedness had left the people I loved exposed, unguarded.

Grandmama's drawing room was empty, and I raced up the stairs to her bedchamber. It was also vacant, though ash was tracked across the carpet and chairs overturned. I released the breath I held, a slow hiss of air between my teeth. Perhaps Ginny saw her safely away before the attack came.

But whose attack? Was this the Circle, punishing me for my temerity? Or William and Petőfi's revolution, gone horribly awry?

I had not broken the Binding. There should have been no signal for a revolution.

I pressed down the hallway to my bedchamber. Clothes were strewn across the floor. The round cheval glass over my dressing table had been flung down. Glittering shards winked up at me from the rug.

Noémi's room bore similar signs of ransacking.

"Anna?" I heard, and paused, my hand on the door. My cousin wormed her way out from underneath the massive four-poster.

"Noémi." I rushed to help her up. "Are you hurt?"

"I'm fine," she said, though her face was pale, her curls in disarray around her head. "Only a bit shaken. Where are the others?"

"I've seen no one else." I put my arm through hers and helped her out of the room.

"The servants fled as soon as the men broke through the door."

"Luminate?" I asked, heading toward the library.

"No. They were young. Workers mostly, I think." Her voice was bitter. "Part of William's mad revolution, no doubt."

"This isn't what we planned." Had Petőfi started the revolution without waiting for a signal?

"Some people need only a small excuse to spread violence," Noémi said. But she didn't sound vindicated, only sad and tired.

I fell silent, my heart not in the argument, and pushed open the door to the library. Ginny lay facedown on the rug.

With a cry, I dropped to my knees beside her. I could see no blood—and her chest still rose and fell. Together, Noémi and I turned her over. I took a cushion from a chair and placed it under Ginny's head. Dark blood, still oozing sluggishly, matted her hair to her temple. Her face was so pale, so still. While Noémi tore a strip from her petticoat to bind the wound, I fetched some blankets from my room to cover her. *Had I not come to Hungary, Ginny would not have followed. She would not have been hurt.*

I pushed the thought away. I did not have time to tally all my guilt: James, the Romanies, now Ginny.

"I must find Grandmama," I said, returning to the library and handing the blankets to Noémi. "Where was she when you last saw her?"

"In the drawing room."

I raced down the hall, shivering. The house was cold. The fires had gone out, and I did not know how to relight them. Only servants and Elementalists knew that.

I scoured the drawing room, examining scuffed, ashy footprints on the Turkish rug, righting fallen chairs, putting Noémi's tangled embroidery skeins back in her basket. Grandmama's customary chair had fallen at an odd angle, held up a few inches from the floor as if by magic. I pulled the chair upward and frowned at the floor. Something shifted, a trick of shadow on shadow. A faint rasp sounded, out of tempo with my own breathing.

I stooped, reaching for the carpet.

But my questing hands never touched it. Instead, I felt the plush nap of velvet. Patting upward, I touched the cool, paper-texture skin of Grandmama's hands. Exploring still further, I found her face, the smooth coils of hair behind her ears, the faint, warm puff of air as she exhaled. My first response was a welling of profound relief.

But my hands looked as if they were shaping air.

Invisible.

Grandmama was invisible—and I had never known she had such magic. If I had thought of her magic at all, I thought her to be a Coremancer like Mama, though one who disliked magic and never used it. But she was Animanti, like my cousins. What other secrets had she kept from me? Rather, not secrets—what questions had I failed to ask? Because she had always been so constant in my life, I had failed her in the worst of ways: I had not seen there might be something to her beyond the needs she met for me.

I had to get her somewhere safe. Karolina Károlyi's home was perhaps a half mile distant. I had walked there only a few days previous with Noémi.

I slid one arm beneath Grandmama's head, another beneath her legs, and awkwardly hoisted her upward. I staggered back down the hall, to the library, where I had left Ginny and Noémi, which was marginally warmer than the drawing room with its shattered windows. I set her gently on the floor beside Ginny and borrowed one of Ginny's blankets. Beneath the covering, the familiar set of Grandmama's contours took shape.

"I found her," I said. "She'd gone invisible."

"Really?" Noémi looked interested, kneeling beside Grandmama and putting her hand to Grandmama's head. "The spell she used will wear off eventually. Her biggest danger now is taking cold. I'll keep her warmed."

"We cannot stay here," I said. "I'll see if Karolina has a place for us."

"The streets aren't safe," Noémi said, her eyebrows contracting.

I swallowed. "There is no one else to go."

The streets were dark—the usual lamplighters had not been out. But I knew the way. I could hear distant shouting, and once I had to draw back into the shadows of a doorway as a troop of Austrian soldiers trotted down the empty roadway. Aside from that, I saw only other single travelers who paid little mind to me, being as eager as I to reach their destinations.

There were still lights on in the Károlyi palace when I approached, and I sighed with relief. The ornamented iron gates were closed, but a pair of footmen stood sentry just inside.

"Is Lady Károlyi within?" I called in Hungarian.

One of the men approached the gate, his eyes sweeping my gown, torn and stained from the Binding and the fight on the hill. Doubtless the dress and my accent made me suspect. "Please, I must speak with her. My name is Anna Arden. My grandmother is Lady Zrínyi, my cousin Eszterházy Noémi."

Apparently the names were sufficiently prominent, for he lost his doubtful look. "I'm sorry, but I've orders to open the gate to no one."

"Will you at least tell Lady Karolina I wish to speak with her?"

He nodded shortly and disappeared into one of the twin entrances flanking the gate. I slid my hand into my pocket, my fingers questing for the golden falcon. But it was gone—lost somewhere in that night's madness.

A few minutes later, Karolina rushed out to the gate, wearing a traveling gown and hat and pulling on her gloves as she crossed the cobblestones to me. "Anna! Why are you still here?"

"You're leaving?"

"Something has gone wrong. The revolution has turned; it is no longer for us. My children are already away. I stayed only for word of my husband's safety. You should leave as well."

"My grandmother has been hurt. She needs help."

Karolina shook her head, biting her lower lip as though she were genuinely troubled. "I'm so sorry, Anna. I can't help you. I wish I could. The carriage is already waiting. I must think of my family first."

Rage and grief boiled in my stomach, a bitter kind of alchemy. "Please."

Karolina fished in her reticule, then pressed a handful of notes through the bars of the gate into my hand. "I wish your grandmother well. Truly. *Isten áldjon!*" God bless you! She picked up her skirts and swept back the way she'd come, leaving me staring after her.

I didn't want her money. I dropped the notes on the ground and spun on my heel.

CHAPTER 26

I wept tears of rage all the way back to Grandmama's. I was furious with Karolina—and with my own helplessness. I had no means to send for a doctor, and no assurance one would come could I summon him. I wished I had not been so quick to spurn Karolina's money, satisfying as the gesture had been.

Across the street from Grandmama's, I spotted a solitary figure lighting a pipe, the flare burning in the darkness. Though I reasoned a Circle spy would not betray his presence so carelessly, the sight sent barbs of fear up my spine.

I climbed the stairs in silence and darkness. I could not stay here: it would be the first place the Circle hunted for me. But I could not leave Noémi alone to tend to Grandmama and Ginny while they were still so weak.

In the library, I curled up beside Grandmama and listened to her labored breathing. I watched her form, initially invisible save for the drape of the quilt, gradually take on color. She looked pasty and waxen, not like a real person at all. And eventually, against every expectation, I started drifting. The corners of the room swam around me—one, two, three, four—and I closed my eyes.

I found myself in a strange forest, surrounded by tall pines. They filled the air around me with their clean scent. My heart lightened, as if all the horror of the night were only a dream and this were real. I followed a path between snow-drops, their white petals blazing in the gloom cast by the towering trees. The path led eventually to a clearing, where a lady sat plaiting her dark hair. At my arrival, she looked up and smiled a welcome.

The Lady was a stranger to me. I had never seen anyone who shone so brightly, her entire body emanating light as if she were made of sunbeams. Yet there was something famil-iar about her. Maybe it was her smile, which held all the ma-ternal warmth I had longed to see in my own mother. Maybe it was the clarity in her look. She stood and came toward me, her long gown scarcely bending the grass beneath her. A great gold falcon perched on her shoulder, much like the one I'd seen in the Binding. The turul bird.

I stood still, trembling. Hope can sometimes feel very much like terror.

"Well met, daughter." She cupped my face in her hands, and the warmth of her touch pushed away the fear and ex-haustion I carried with me. "Be at peace. You have traveled far, and the hardest road is still before you. But remember there are those who love you. You shall not be alone, nor forgotten. Who you are, what you shall do, all these matter."

Her words fell like balm against cracked skin. They stung

a little, with their reminder of hardship to come, but they healed too. A hard kernel of fear, buried so deep I had almost forgotten I carried it, softened and dissipated. I was loved: by Grandmama, by James, by my cousins. By Gábor too, though he fought it. I mattered. With a gentle finger, the Lady wiped a tear from my cheek before bending forward to kiss my forehead. A flicker of warmth built against my skull, radiating down to fill my entire body.

"I set my blessing on you," she said, releasing me.

"Thank you." I met her star-bright gaze without flinching.

"Have courage. We are both of us bound in different ways. You are bound by your fears—but do not let them shackle you. You are stronger than you know."

I studied her serene face, like a Madonna in a Renaissance painting. "You are bound? Where? How?"

"In the same Binding spell you troubled so recently. I can only reach you thus in dreams." She touched my cheek again. "That spell contains a host of creatures, just as your world does. We are not all of us dark, or all light. I am the *Boldogasszony*." The Joyful Woman. "Once, before I was bound, I was mother-goddess to Hungary."

"But the creatures—" I began. A sound like a gunshot fractured through the dream. The Lady's face began to waver, cracks of light splintering across her. "Wait," I said. "Don't go."

"Anna." Noémi was shaking my shoulder. "Someone's here."

And then I was wide awake, blinking in the first grey light of dawn, my heart pounding an erratic rhythm in my chest. I sat upright. Noises drifted up from the entryway below. Voices. Footsteps.

Noémi scrambled to her feet. "Perhaps it's Mátyás."

I listened for a moment. I heard crashing, then the lilting refrain of a spell. "No. The Circle."

"What have you done?" Her face turned the color of bone. "Surely I would have felt the Binding shatter."

"Lady Berri killed someone." *And where was she now?* I stooped to gather Grandmama as best I could. "Help Ginny." My maid was awake but weak still.

The three of us staggered down the hallway to the back of the house, then descended the narrow servants' stairs to a door at the back of the courtyard. We struggled through the rear gate and into the mew. Light though she was, Grandmama was not easy to carry. My muscles pulled and burned.

Please, I prayed as we stumbled toward the street. *Please let there be a carriage.* Behind us, I heard a door slam, then shouts.

As if my prayer had conjured it, there was, indeed, a vehicle in the street. But it was a farmer's cart, worn and slow moving. The farmer in question was unloading jugs of milk.

"We need a ride," Noémi said without preamble. She released Ginny, who wavered a bit but did not fall, and unclasped the fine gold chain she wore. She marched to the farmer. "Here. Take this for payment."

The farmer set down the jug he carried and promptly helped us into the back of his wagon. "Where to, miss?"

I sat beside Grandmama, her head pillowed in my lap. Noémi and Ginny crowded next to us, the bare planks of wood hard beneath us.

"Anywhere," Noémi said. "Please, just drive!"

He clucked at his horses and they shuffled forward. I groaned. At this rate, the men behind us could outrun our wagon *on foot.*

Noémi closed her eyes and began whispering. I recognized a spell from her hand motions, and edged sideways, my arms pulling beneath Grandmama's weight. *Calm,* I whispered to my fluttering heart, to my shadow self stirring beneath it. *Please be calm.* I could not afford to break another spell.

Noémi's eyes flew open. "That should buy us some time."

"What did you do?"

"The only thing I could think to do. I set a plague of boils on them—in, um, a location that should ensure they do not walk, run, or ride horseback easily for the next short while." Her cheeks were pink, but a suggestion of a smile played about her lips.

I sagged back against the side of the wagon. "That is the best news I have heard all week."

⚭

At my direction, the farmer drove us toward Café Pilvax, where we hoped to find word of Mátyás—and of Gábor, though I did not voice that wish. Ginny waited in the wagon with Grandmama while Noémi and I went in.

The interior was unusually empty—a single patron in the back, a stout man rubbing a cloth over the glass display cases near the front. He looked up at our entrance.

"Ladies. You should not be here."

"We're looking for someone," I said. "Eszterházy Mátyás? A student, middling height, curling brown hair."

"The students who were here are all gone. Rounded up by the Austrian police for treason." He plucked a paper from a nearby table and held it out.

"What?" I gasped, snatching at the circular. Beside me, Noémi dug her fingers into my arm.

The paper smelled of ink, fresh from the printer. I unfolded it and stared at the German headline, my entire body tensing.

The Circle Restores Order to Troubled City.

I scanned onward. *Last evening, devastating plans were set in motion to raze the city and bring down the Hapsburg government. Thanks to an informer, Luminate spell-binders and armed Austrian soldiers were prepared for just such action and were able to thwart the rebellion shortly after its onset, with only minimal damage to property in Pest.*

I thought of Grandmama's house, and the blistered and peeling front of the Pázmandy mansion, which we'd passed in our circuitous route through Pest. What had happened when I failed to give the signal for the Binding that evening? Such destruction had never been part of our plan. Of *my* plan, I realized: I did not truly know what Petőfi and William had planned.

I had been as willfully ignorant of their plot as I had been to the Binding, choosing to acknowledge only what I wanted to see.

No citizens were killed, though some Luminate were unfortunately driven from their homes. It is now believed safe for their return.

The fracas was not without bloodshed, however. Some rebels were slain. And it has been confirmed that Lady Berri, erstwhile head of the Lucifera order in England, was shockingly found supporting revolutionary measures and was killed while fighting against the very Circle she purported to sustain.

Lady Berri. Images flashed across my mind: her eyes alight

319

with secret amusement, the strangely imposing fashion with which she moved her stout body through rooms, the grim set to her mouth when she told me to flee.

She had died saving my life.

Noémi took the paper from my nerveless fingers and skimmed through it. One hand flew to her mouth.

I snatched the paper away, my heart thudding. *The following have been apprehended as traitors. Executions are set to begin in two days' time, a fittingly swift and just end for all such rabble.*

With trembling fingers, I turned the circular over. A list of names was appended. My eyes flew down them, dread thick and bitter in my mouth. The letters swam before me, making it difficult to sort out the names. There were dozens of them. I recognized two as young men I'd met at Café Pilvax, one I had conversed with at Karolina's, several I had danced with.

And there—William Skala. I pictured William as I had seen him last, his face radiant with the possibilities of revolution. In all his plans for the future, had he seen this?

Let there be no more, I prayed, guilty with the relief I'd feel if it were only William's name. Or Petőfi's.

But no. There it was, the name I'd been fearing to see from the moment I spied the list. Gábor Kovács.

And a few lines later: Mátyás Eszterházy.

The sensation was like the moment when ice across a winter pond no longer holds your weight: only a second's warning and then you are falling, gripped by a cold so deep and enveloping you cannot breathe.

I choked. How could a list—a string of letters on paper—be so deadly?

Noémi turned a tear-streaked face to me. "This! This is why I pleaded with you not to fight."

My stomach flipped over. "Did you tell the Circle? You said you would stop us if you could."

"You think I would betray my own brother?"

A voice cut across us, "But *someone* told them. Was it *you*?" Petőfi staggered toward me, waggling his finger in my face. I had not recognized him in the gloom of the café. His rollicking gait made one thing quite clear: he was drunk. He began reciting in a singsong voice:

> *Why should I love my homeland?*
> *Or care for her travails?*
> *Her troubles will pass . . . eventually—*
> *I'm a Magyar noblewoman!*

His voice dropped to a normal register. "Your cousin had let me hope Luminate could be selfless—could be patriots. He was wrong. You're self-serving wretches, and you women are worst of all. So concerned for your gowns and your society you can't even follow through on a promise. Where was your broken spell? Where was your signal?"

Spittle flicked my cheek, and I flinched away. "I couldn't break the Binding. I won't loose the monsters it holds."

A flash of remembered touch, ghostly against my cheek. The Lady was bound too. I grieved for her—but I could not let the others free.

"Selfish," the poet sneered. "Weak. Frightened."

"You cannot simply blame me," I said. "If the signal didn't come, why did you fight?"

"Because we were surrounded. Because someone betrayed us." His eyes were flint. "And now my friends will die."

"No," Noémi said. "We can't let them."

"We have to do something," I said. "Fight back."

"We *did* fight. We failed."

"But there are others who escaped, surely?" I asked. "And others who will want to help. I know where William kept his mechanical armor. We can use that." I did not know precisely *how* we could use it; I only knew a rising desperation that somehow we had to free Mátyás and Gábor and the others. As long as they lived, there was still hope.

"If there's anything left of it," Petőfi said, but he followed us out to the wagon.

CHAPTER 27

I stood in the middle of the cavernous room housing William's workshop, my mind reeling. The room looked as if someone had pummeled it with a giant fist. Nothing remained of William's mechanical creations but fragments of metal, glinting in the dim light. The metal woman with the medusa hair was smashed into a corner, her face a flattened sheet of metal, her wild hair slivers of silver on the floor.

Beside me, Petőfi swore.

A cold wind whipped through the shattered windows, pulling at my loose hair. I shivered, glad the others had chosen to wait in the wagon.

This was not random looters or revolutionaries, not the violence that wrecked Grandmama's house. Nothing of value had been taken. The metal pieces were still here, simply bent beyond recognition and use. The thoroughness of the attack—nothing in the workshop had been left unscathed—suggested deliberate planning.

How had the Circle known that the machines were here? Only a few days earlier, William said he had not shown them to anyone else. William. Mátyás. Gábor. Me. Had one of *us* betrayed everyone? I could not believe it. William would die first. Gábor too. And though Mátyás had his share of weaknesses, I did not see him betraying his friends.

That left me.

I had not said anything—but the Circle had been following me. Had they followed me here?

The Circle ends.

My ring. Even if the Circle had not sent someone after me, they knew where I had gone. Herr Steinberg himself had told me the ring tracked me. I already knew it did not work precisely as Herr Steinberg had said: it had not kept me from the Binding. But what if it had other functions? If it could read the spells cast in my presence, could it also record what was spoken? I would not put such a spell beyond Herr Steinberg, who had never trusted Lady Berri.

I thought of all the conversations I had heard in the café, of William boasting he had designed these mechanical creatures to withstand the Austrian armies, of Lady Berri's plans. If the Circle had heard, they would have known everything: when Lady Berri meant to fetch me, where to attack Lady Berri while she waited for me to break the spell, where to find the students as they gathered for revolution.

It was only luck—or perhaps surprise—that the Circle had not caught us before we breached the Binding. But I suspected that was not the case with William and the others.

No doubt the Circle and their soldiers had already been in place, watching as William and a roomful of students began to don the mechanical creatures, planning to catch them in the very act of treason. I'd bet Herr Steinberg enjoyed watching the students' faces turn from exhilaration to horror, when they realized they were betrayed.

I fell to my knees, my stomach twisting like laundry wrung dry. I was the worst kind of fool. I had thought of the ring only in relationship to the Binding—and to me. I had resented it for curtailing my choices. How could I not have seen that my very presence endangered everything, everyone I cared for? I believed I was clever, invincible, important.

I *had* been important. Only to the wrong people. And for the wrong reasons.

Petőfi looked at me with some concern. "Are you well?"

No. "I think it was me," I said. "I think the Circle heard everything through a ring they forced me to wear." I stared at my now-bare finger, heartsick.

"*You!*" Petőfi glowered down at me, the tips of his mustache trembling with his passion. "You betrayed us?"

"Not intentionally." But I had betrayed them all the same.

He was still for a long moment. Then, "I am sorry about your cousin, and your friends. They are my friends too. I will do what I can for them. But you—you are treacherous. I want nothing to do with you."

He stalked from the room.

I pushed myself up and stood for a moment on trembling legs. Without the mechanical creatures, we had almost nothing. Even if Grandmama and Noémi were willing to lend their magic to our cause, it would not be enough to free Mátyás and Gábor. What were invisibility and healing against a legion of Circle-trained soldiers? Even if I could break a few spells, it would not be enough.

I swept a despairing glance around the ruined room before turning away, retreating through the accumulated detritus of William's life and out to the street beyond.

⋊

Grandmama was awake. Despite the pallor of her face, her voice was firm when I climbed into the wagon. "Noémi told me what has happened—that Lady Berri is dead, that Mátyás and your friends are imprisoned."

"There is something else." I told her what I had surmised of my ring, of the role I had played in this devastation.

"We need Pál," Grandmama said. "He can open a conduit to Vienna. I have friends there who might help us."

"I thought he was a Coremancer," I said. Only Lucifera could open conduits.

"He is many things," Grandmama said. "As he gained power in the Circle, they granted him greater magic."

"Will he help us?" I asked. "He works for the Circle." I thought of his chilling expression when he spelled the Romanies—and then of his flickering contempt as he looked at Herr Steinberg. I shivered. Which of those faces was his true face? Was he the obedient puppet of the Circle—or something more?

"I hope so. I believe there is a part of him that remembers being my son."

I was not so sanguine. But what other choices did we have?

"Will your friends be able to help in time?" Noémi asked. "The executions begin tomorrow."

Grandmama's shoulders sagged. "I do not know. We can only try."

X

It was not yet the hour for fashionable visits when we arrived at the modest house where the Circle kept Pál. Ginny waited outside in the traveling carriage Grandmama demanded we hire, after finding the wagon less than satisfactory. Grandmama had also insisted on sending Ginny back to the house to bring us all a change of clothing, for which I was out of measure grateful.

A crow circled overhead as we climbed the stairs to the front door. I chose to see it as a good omen.

Grandmama spelled me before we entered—a Misdirection spell that turned away the eyes of those who looked toward me. Anyone determined to see me would do so, but we hoped the subterfuge would suffice. I could only pray the Circle was busy pursuing me elsewhere, not believing me capable of overt confrontation.

A butler led us up a narrow flight of stairs to a simply furnished salon. The drapes were drawn tightly, giving the room a dank and dusty air. A small fire burned in the grate, casting flickering lights over my uncle and Herr Steinberg, seated in the center of the room as if they were holding a royal audience. Two footmen stood at attention by the door, though I suspected they were not servants but Luminate guards.

Their careful arrangement raised the hairs on my arms. They had been expecting us.

After a few pleasantries, Grandmama spoke directly to Pál. "We need your help. We believe that my cousin's grand-nephew was wrongfully apprehended. I wish you to open a conduit for me to speak with Prince Pál Anton Eszterházy, or his son, Prince Miklós."

Herr Steinberg raised an eyebrow. "Wrongfully? We have evidence of treason against him and the others who were apprehended."

"But why execute them so summarily? Why not give them a trial?"

"The Hapsburgs wish to send a firm message. Unlike the Bourbons, they have no wish to deal with recurrent rebellions. The crown has every right to execute known traitors."

I was not supposed to betray my presence, so I swallowed my retort: *You mean the Circle wishes to send a firm message.* The Circle ruled the Hapsburgs, not the other way around. I might not agree with the means William and Petőfi had chosen, but I still believed their aim was right: to free Hungary from Hapsburg law and Circle control.

"But what appears to be treason in one man may be patriotism when seen through another perspective," Noémi said. "They only acted as they did for love of their country."

"I've no doubt. But I will not stop the progress of the law. It should give you some comfort to know that your cousin and the others will be seen as martyrs for their cause. You Magyar love a good martyrdom."

"We would rather they lived than died martyrs!" Noémi's cheeks brightened with anger.

Herr Steinberg removed his spectacles and polished them

with a handkerchief. "I am sorry, my dear. But there is nothing I can do. And your pleas to your cousins will be equally fruitless. They will not help you. The Circle will not tolerate any Luminate interference."

My heart plummeted. Was this it? Was there nothing more to do but hope Petőfi could manufacture an army? I refused to believe it. I would storm the prison myself before I would give up on Gábor or Mátyás. The Circle would have to bury us together.

He looked directly at me. "You may drop the façade, if you please. I know Miss Arden is with you."

I returned his gaze. "Did you spell my ring so you could hear my conversations?"

"Most illuminating they were too. Thanks to you, we have quelled a rebellion and rid the world of a dangerous heretic."

Lady Berri deserved more. "At least she had *some* standards. Eavesdropping on the private conversations of a girl? Surely that was beneath even you."

His eyes flashed cold. "You insult me. I serve only my Circle and the Binding. There was nothing prurient in my intent."

"Very likely," I said. "What happens now?"

"You will be tried before the Circle. If you are lucky, they will look kindly upon your assistance in the matter of the revolution—and they will let you live, under close supervision. If not, you will hang with your cousin."

I jerked in surprise.

"Thank you for bringing her to me," Herr Steinberg said to Grandmama and Noémi. "Your cooperation will be noted. Guards—"

He never finished his sentence.

Pál muttered something and stood, flinging his hands out, his fingers curled.

The salon seemed to explode, a wall of foggy air sweeping through it with hurricane force. Wind tore at my hair and the hem of my dress. An enormous vase shot across the room, smashing into the far wall with a tremendous clatter. *Grandmama.* I could only just see her beyond the whirl of mist and broken crockery, crouched low to the ground. I tried to cross to her, but the wind was too strong.

I clasped my arms protectively over my head. Shards of glass and porcelain sailed past me, slicing across my exposed knuckles. I prayed Grandmama and Noémi were all right.

The wind began by degrees to calm. When it was just a sluggish breeze, I put my arms down and looked around the room. Only four of us were mobile: myself, Grandmama, Noémi, and Pál. I rushed to Grandmama to help her rise.

Herr Steinberg and the two guards were flat against the floor, unmoving. One of the guards bled from a rather nasty cut in his head. Noémi started toward him.

"Leave him," Pál said. "Someone will find him soon enough. But we must go. The Circle will come hunting as soon as they discover I am missing."

"You will have a price on your own head now, *fiam*," Grandmama said.

Pál bared his teeth. "Then let there be a price. I am tired of being a kept magician."

)(

The carriage rattled through the city streets of Pest and then bumped along the rougher dirt roads leading toward the village of Szentendre. We had escaped Herr Steinberg's house with the aid of Grandmama's Invisibility spell, which she used to hide Pál. To anyone watching, we would have appeared simply as three ladies leaving a morning call.

Grandmama had been the one to decide on Szentendre. We knew we could not return home, or anywhere the Circle might think to look for us.

As the miles rolled past, we discussed our options.

"We cannot simply let Mátyás and the others die," Noémi said.

"Petőfi told me he will try to help," I said.

"The poet?" Noémi looked incredulous. "How can he hope to succeed where Will—where so many others did not?"

Pál's pale eyes rested on me, unblinking. "He will need Luminate aid."

"Why are you helping us?" Noémi asked. "We may be family, but you scarcely know us."

Beside Pál, Grandmama stiffened. "It's true. Pál has much to forgive me for."

I wanted to wrap my arms around her, but wedged as I was between Ginny and Noémi on the opposite seat, I could not reach her.

"What's past is past," Pál said. "The Circle taught me much about my powers I could never have learned at home—but I do not owe them anything. They saw me only as a weapon, best kept close and shut away when not in use. They forgot that no caged thing loves its captor. You wish to bring down the Circle. So do I." He turned to face Grandmama. "You taught me, as a boy, to love my country. If you mean to free Hungary from the Circle, I will help."

Grandmama laid her hand on his, her eyes bright. Her son, lost for so many years, had come home. I wanted to ask Pál if we could trust him, but I did not know how to ask that without wounding Grandmama. Instead, I prayed he would deserve her trust.

Something Pál had said earlier about Luminate aid nagged at me. "But even if you and Noémi help Petőfi—that's hardly enough against the Circle," I said.

"I meant you, Anna."

"You know I cannot cast spells. And I cannot predict or control which ones I break."

"You are far more than that."

His words stirred a memory. The morning after he attacked me in my rooms, he had said, *I know what you are.* Not I know *who* you are—but *what* you are.

"And what am I?" I held my breath, not sure I wanted the answer.

"You are *chimera.* Two souls in one body."

Silence exploded in the carriage.

Perfectly composed, Pál continued to watch me. Ginny edged away from me, as though my dual-souledness were catching. Noémi looked out the window, as if Pál's words exposed a secret shame and she wished to give me privacy. Grandmama's hand fluttered up, like she might reach for me, then fell back to her lap.

Chimera.

Like Pandora, who had broken the world.

I shuddered, unease prickling my skin. *Two souls.* I had always thought of myself as Anna: impassioned, restless, stubborn, sometimes contradictory—yes, all those—but still

Anna. Still one entity, at heart, one soul that would eventually die and, perhaps, stand before her God. But *two?* Two souls made me monstrous, inhuman. The doubled reflection I had seen all my life began to make sense, though the sense was hardly comforting.

Pál continued, oblivious to my distress. "A Luminate spell works as the caster draws the magic into his soul before pushing it into his charm with his will. But as you have two souls, when you draw magic into your souls, they repel one another, much as magnets pushed same side together. A spell with such instability at its heart cannot hold. Thus, you cannot cast spells, and the Circle believed you Barren."

"How, then, do I break spells?" I could scarcely choke the words out.

"When you were Confirmed, you were connected to the Binding, and that connection creates an innate longing for magic. Oh yes," he said, seeing my surprise, "your Confirmation *did* take. That's why you can reach the magic to break spells. But you cannot wield magic; thus your souls constantly thirst after it. When you are strongly moved, you instinctively grasp for the nearest magic. If a spell is being cast, you pull the magic from that spell into you—and of course the spell cannot hold, and it shatters."

A series of shocks burst through my body. *This.* This is how I destroyed Catherine's spells. Why I had nearly killed Gábor's niece. How I broke the spell at Sárvár. And how I might break the Binding. This is why the Circle feared me, why Lady Berri had sought me out.

"Why did no one tell me?"

"No one else could have known. No one *sees* as I do. And there has not been a Luminate *chimera* for centuries."

A second question, quieter. "Why did you not tell the Circle?"

Pál smiled, but it was a smile like Hunger wore, as though he were not entirely certain how humans ought to smile. "Why should I tell them? I owe them nothing. Besides, I rather think I should like to see what a broken Binding unleashes."

I turned away, trying not to see my faint doubled reflection in the glass as I watched the houses and fields flashing past. All I could think of was my extra soul, like an invisible twin trapped in my body. My skin crawled. I scratched at the flesh exposed above my glove. Had I been alone, I would have torn my clothes off and scraped at my entire body. The hand rubbing at my skin felt like that of a stranger.

All my life I believed being Barren was the worst curse one could wish on a Luminate.

But I was wrong. There was something worse.

Chimera.

CHAPTER 28

I do not know what the others discussed to fill those long miles while I wrestled in my heart and soul—*souls*—to understand Pál's revelation. When we stopped at length at a small *csárda* in Szentendre, I went straight to the room I was to share with Noémi and lay down upon the straw mattress. I wanted to weep, to wash away the strangeness of it all, but my eyes were dry and my heart cold.

Ginny brought me a bit of bread and meat, which I did not touch. Instead, I watched the shadows creep across the floor, and when darkness filled the room, Noémi came in and lay down beside me.

"Anna."

I said nothing.

She propped herself up on one elbow so she could look at me. "Anna. It's all right. There is nothing wrong with you."

Except for my extra soul. Could one be twice damned with two souls? I didn't move.

"Anna." Noémi tried again. "I'm sorry."

This time I did look at her, rolling onto my back to stare up at her. I had never heard Noémi apologize before. "For what?"

"I'm sorry I didn't trust you. I'm sorry I've been so prickly." Noémi let her breath out in a sigh. "The truth is—you are the closest thing I have to a sister. And I don't want whatever has happened to fester between us. I need you. And I think you might need me too."

Something broke in me. The tears I'd wanted earlier came gushing, spilling down my cheeks. I sat up, and Noémi held me while I cried and she cried with me, and then, as suddenly as the tears had come, they ceased, and we both began to laugh helplessly. Anyone hearing us might have supposed us mad. But if I were to label the feeling in that small room, I would call it relief.

Whatever happened next, we would not have to endure it alone.

Ж

While Noémi snored softly beside me, my mind whirred. Petőfi might be able to rouse a few hundred or even thousand to fight, but without Luminates it would not be enough. Tomorrow, the executions would begin. A thick dread clutched at my heart and stomach.

I thought of the Binding. I could break it—I could do as Lady Berri had wished, as Papa wished. And what would I unleash on the world? I remembered the imps in the tower, the snarled sisters in the wood. But if I did not act, could I let the others die? We needed an army, and I could think of only one way to raise it: barter with Hunger, an army of creatures in exchange for their freedom.

In the darkness of my room, I stared down the smallness of my soul—my *souls*. There was no courage, no hope, only a wretched sense of self-preservation. I wanted to curl up in my bed, pull the covers over my head, and wake to a restored world. I wanted to be safe and comfortable. I did not want to decide anyone's life or death. I told myself it would not be my action that killed them—but I could not hide from the succeeding thought: *if my friends die through my inaction, I am still at fault.*

I let myself scream into my pillow, once, twice, at the injustice of it all. This was not supposed to be my life. My story was not supposed to end this way, with a deadly, impossible choice. I was supposed to find my way back to society, to sweep triumphantly in on the wings of revolution to some greatness.

Not fail miserably in the quiet of a rented room.

Tears stung at my eyes, but I blinked them away. Words floated back to me, my conversation with Hunger the second time I'd tried to break the Binding: *If I set you free, is this what I unleash on the world?*

Who can say, when you give a creature freedom, what he or she will choose? What will your world look like when you give all individuals the same rights? Can you say with certainty each person will use that power for good?

His words echoed in my heart.

I brooded over the terrible creatures in the Binding, the blood and destruction I'd seen and heard in the walled city. But I remembered also the warming gentleness of the Lady who'd visited my dreams, and I contrasted her with the terrifying chill I'd felt when Pál's spell silenced the Romanies.

Who can say, when you give a creature freedom, what he or she will choose?

The creatures were capable of terrible things. But so were humans. And perhaps captivity had warped the creatures into something they were not meant to be.

Who was I to make this decision for anyone—for any*thing*? Was I not also something monstrous? A *chimera* who could break the world, if Pál was right.

I had never questioned that women and men of all classes ought to have the right to determine their own lives. Yet I had thought I could make that decision for creatures much older and more powerful than myself.

The awful sense of my own hubris struck me as a physical pain, radiating through my stomach and into my heart. The problem of the Binding was much bigger than Hungary's independence from Austria, much larger than the Circle's control of magic. I curled up, wrapping my arms around my knees, and tried not to wake Noémi.

All through that long night, I considered what I ought to do. When hunger pangs struck me about midnight, I devoured the bread and meat Ginny had left on the bedside table. Then I began pacing the room, measuring my thoughts with agitated steps.

The Circle-run Binding was a flawed system, maintaining the Luminate in power, perpetuating injustice, allowing

Austria to dominate a country I had come to love. I knew it. Papa knew it. Others would come to see it too.

I could not ignore the external factors—the threats to me and to those I loved. But stripped of those externals, the question was a simple one: should every individual (man, woman, creature) be free to decide their own course?

By the time the first grey light of morning seeped through my window, I knew what I must do.

)(

I went to wake the others. Noémi looked shocked. "Are you certain?" We were gathered in Grandmama's room, huddled close in the chill air.

"Yes," I said. "It's the right thing to do. The Circle has used the Binding for too long as a way of keeping people under their control—they can't be trusted not to abuse that power. The creatures who are bound deserve a chance at freedom, just as we do."

"Simply breaking the Binding won't free Mátyás and the others," she pointed out.

"I know." This uncertainty was a cold weight in my breast. "But it will weaken the Circle, and I think I can bargain with the creatures to fight with us in exchange for freedom. This is our best chance."

Grandmama listened quietly, then nodded. "I trust you, Anna. And—this is my heart's country. I will fight for her."

My heart warmed at her faith. I described the spell Lady Berri had used to root us to Attila's Hill. "Do you think you could re-create such a spell?" I asked Pál.

339

He nodded. "The Portal spell is straightforward enough. But I don't understand why Lady Berri chose that site."

"She said that it was sacred, that ley lines ran near there and would strengthen our spells."

"Then why use it for an *Unbinding* spell? With all due respect to your Lady Berri, sometimes her faith in her own knowledge prevented her from perceiving certain realities. Symbols can add powerful resonance to spells. We need a site of breaking and desolation."

"A cemetery?" I asked, wrinkling my nose. It was not that I found the graves particularly distasteful, only that spell-casting there seemed blasphemous. "I know that death is powerful magic, but surely there are better sites."

Pál shook his head. "No. Cemeteries are sacred places. They breathe death, yes, but death is more a remaking than an unmaking. We need a profane site."

"A defiled church?" Was there such a place in the city?

"A railroad?" Grandmama asked, her mouth pursed in distaste. Noémi and I exchanged a look. Only Grandmama would find trains profane.

"A symbol is more powerful if it has personal meaning."

"I know," Noémi said. "Eszterháza."

※

I did not want to make the return trip to Eszterháza and waste the little time remaining to us. It would take two days to reach the country palace at a good pace, and I was not sure Grandmama could survive the journey. By then, the executions would have already started. But Pál agreed.

The decaying estate was an ideal mix of personal and symbolic dissolution.

"You needn't ride all that distance," Pál said. "I can open a portal."

"But then you'll lack the strength to open a gateway to the Binding." I recalled Lady Berri's exhaustion after she'd folded the earth.

Pál's light eyes glinted. "I have strength enough."

I returned to my room to stuff my few belongings in the small valise Ginny had prepared for me. In the bottom of the valise was a small, oddly shaped package. I unwrapped the brown paper and stared, chilled, at the bone knife Lady Berri had given me to break the Binding. Beneath it lay the Romani bracelet I had snatched from the square.

Noémi brushed by me. Seeing my stare, she said, "Oh. Ginny found those among your things. She believed they might be important."

How had Ginny known? Perhaps this was fated to be. I slipped on the bracelet, and the agate glimmered in the shadows.

)X(

It did not take Pál long to cast the Portal spell, a thin slit appearing in the doorway. Through it, I could see the hazy outline of one of the Chinese-style salons at Eszterháza, the blue inked figures dancing across the wall.

Pál held his arm out toward Noémi. "After you."

Noémi took one step through the archway. For a moment, her outline seemed to blur and smudge out, then she reappeared in the salon. Grandmama followed her. Then it was my turn. I looked back at Ginny, who sat on the bed, weeping. Pál refused to bring her through the portal, as she would contribute nothing to our fight. She was to depart alone for Grandmama's house in Pest and wait for our return.

She waved her soggy handkerchief at me. "Godspeed, Miss Anna."

I darted away from the portal to hug her, then stepped through.

A rush of heat enveloped me, pinching at my eyes and mouth and nose. I willed myself to stay calm. Then I was through, gasping in the warm air of the Eszterháza parlor.

A moment later, Pál emerged from the portal, and a few moments after that, Noémi's vizsla erupted into the room, barking to raise the dead. Or at least, to raise János, who came stumping into the room shortly after, swearing under his breath.

※

It took only a little time to acquaint János with the circumstances. When he heard of Mátyás's imprisonment, he turned a ghastly shade, and Noémi ran to the kitchens to find some tea. After he revived, János set wards on the house to warn us if the Circle was coming, and we got to work.

As the sun broke fully across the horizon, we gathered in the Sala Terrena, the great ballroom turned sheepfold. The sheep paid us no mind as Pál grounded the spell, treading a circle across the floor and murmuring incantations. Noémi tried, unsuccessfully, to shoo them from the room.

I watched and waited, a yawning coldness swallowing me. What was I doing?

I thought of Gábor and Mátyás and William, and the dozens of others imprisoned with them, awaiting execution. And the creatures, imprisoned for centuries in a different kind of jail. Something like peace swept over me, nestling under my heart. The fear didn't vanish entirely—I could still feel it stirring in my middle—but it was gentler now, less hungry.

A crow cawed from the shaggy garden beyond the empty-eyed windows. Distantly, bells rang.

János started. "The wards!" He stumped toward the pillared opening at the far end of the room.

"Another portal?" I asked, fear leaching through my body. How had the Circle found us so quickly?

Noémi, Grandmama, and I swiveled toward Pál. He stood with his eyes closed, arms extended, fingers splayed. Light winked off a heavy signet ring on one finger.

"You are my son," Grandmama said. "Why should you help us and then lead our enemies here?"

Pál opened his eyes, the unearthly blue blazing. "I have not been your son since I was nine years old. And I want to see Herr Steinberg's face when he knows I have betrayed him. I want him to see that in me he has wrought a tool that will destroy everything he values."

If we survived this, I would kill Pál myself.

Grandmama stood shrunken, her shoulders bowed under the weight of a new disappointment. I wanted to throw my arms around her and tell her if Pál was not the son she yearned for, I would be a granddaughter to make her proud. But she was too far away. I hadn't time.

Footsteps pounded across the marble floor beyond the room. János stumbled and cried out.

"Anna, go now!" Noémi hissed at me.

I hesitated. "But the spell—it could be anything."

Pál's eyes flashed. "The spell is sound."

I would have to trust that his desire for revenge on the Circle was greater than his desire to betray us. I stepped toward the Grounding spell and closed my eyes, preparing for the imminent falling sensation. Instead, an electric shock ran through my entire body. My knees collapsed underneath me, and I found myself staring at the vaulted ceiling covered in writhing rose vines, wondering why my arms would not stop shaking.

Grandmama cried out.

I gritted my teeth and struggled upright.

Four men stood in the doorway of the Sala Terrena. Three were masked. Herr Steinberg was the fourth, his hands extended before him in a spell-caster's stance.

Deep lines scored his face, though his mouth was set. I knew he did not want to be here, did not want this confrontation.

I also knew he would kill me if he could.

The fear I had pushed aside gushed outward, flooding through me. I scrambled to my feet and pulled Grandmama backward, away from the portal. Behind me, I heard the crackle and hiss of electricity. Something exploded, sending a pulse of light through the darkening room. The sheep moved, finally, surging around our feet and heading for the broken glass doors. I pushed Grandmama toward a crumbling sculpture.

Grandmama trembled on her feet, but would not move. "I will not hide."

"But you might be *killed*."

"So might we all. I am an old lady. And you have a spell to break."

I stared at her, my heart racing. Grandmama took my hand, rubbing her papery fingers against mine. "Anna. All your life, your mama and I have tried to fit you into a shape too small to hold you. But you are two souls, not one, and you have always been meant for greater things. Let yourself free. Be who God intended you to be. Now go. We will hold them."

She withdrew her hand, and her outline blurred and became transparent.

I darted back to the portal. A ball of fire shot toward me. At the last moment, I leapt aside and tumbled to the ground. The fireball exploded scant inches from my head. I struggled to rise from the tangle of my skirts.

The light abruptly winked out as something vast and shadowy passed between our small group and the arched ceiling. Then it swooped down, a rush of wind and something cool like mist. I had a confused impression of long, dagger-sharp teeth before one of the men began screaming.

"An illusion!" Herr Steinberg shouted. "It is only an illusion! Hold fast!"

A flash of light illuminated the dark room. For that half second, the world seemed shrunk to a small, bright sphere: Noémi's pale face, János's determined one, Herr Steinberg's grim one. The light faded, and I blinked against the afterimages, trying to regain my bearings. Grandmama and Pál had both vanished.

Another flare of light, this one racing toward me. Just before it hit me, I was struck from the side by something warm and solid. I fell, and Noémi's weight landed across my legs.

Her eyes, when they met mine, were bright, and her face twisted with pain. She took a deep, ragged breath.

"Anna, you must *go*! No one can help us if you are killed." She rolled away from me as I stood once more and ran.

The explosion of a second fireball lit the room behind me. I heard János's cry and my heart twisted, but I did not stop. I dove into the middle of Pál's anchored spell and closed my eyes.

CHAPTER 29

I braced myself for impact with the ground, but the impact did not come at once. When I opened my eyes, I was falling through a field of stars.

When I landed, at last, the Binding was both strange and familiar.

There was no grass-carpeted hill, no flowers, no distant turrets rising above a silver-leafed wood. Instead, I found myself standing in a narrow valley, great rock mountains rising all around me, their tops shrouded in mist. Fir trees sprouted from the mountains at improbable intervals. The ground around me was strewn with rocks, boulders heaved from the mountains by storms or heavy snows. Or giants. Winds howled, tugging at my hair, keening in my ears.

I'd never seen this aspect of the Binding. Was this the heart of the spell—or had Pál's spell merely taken me to the part of the Binding nearest Eszterháza?

I needed to find out. The only vantage point in all that windswept valley was a great stone slab. I made my way toward it.

I struggled to remember all I knew of breaking the Binding. Before, it had seemed enough that I was *chimera,* that if I drew the spell into me, my very nature would shatter the spell as it had at Sárvár. But walking through a lonely valley, dwarfed by solitary mountain pines and rocks, I felt acutely how foolish we had been to think this might work. How could I pull something so vast into my souls?

Though I walk through the valley of the shadow of death, I will fear no evil.

The slab had not appeared far away when I began, but it began to feel as though I had walked for hours. My legs wobbled, sweat stuck my bodice to my skin, and I struggled to hold on to what little courage and composure I possessed. I could not think of Grandmama and Noémi and János, out-matched in Eszterháza behind me. I could not think of what might face me when I returned. I could only move forward, one heavy foot after the other.

I stooped, cringing as a shadow passed over me. It was only a crow, landing several paces ahead of me.

A curl of hope lifted my heart. Ravens were good omen birds—at least in Hungary; surely some of that luck would attend its cousin. And I was no longer alone.

As I moved forward, memories began sliding through my mind. I did not consciously call them; something about this wilderness dragged them into light.

I remembered Hunger, the first time I had seen him in the bathhouse at Sárvár. *I might have need of your heart,* he'd said.

Then later, the first time I'd gone with Lady Berri to Attila's Hill: *You will have to sacrifice at the heart of the spell. You must pull the power of the spell into your own heart and let your heart break with it.*

All magic had a price. I knew that. It cost time, energy, will—the imprisonment of ancient creatures. It had taken a blood sacrifice to craft the Binding; it would take a blood sacrifice to break it. My fingers curled around the bone knife I carried. I doubted my courage.

Hunger had promised I would not die. I clung to that promise as I walked.

I halted and raised my face to the sky. I let all of my frustration and fear and longing swell inside me: for my family, for Gábor, for a world I might not live to see. And for a world that might be changed beyond recognition by what I was about to do. I closed my eyes and whispered, "Hunger. I need you."

When I opened my eyes, he stood before me, his golden eyes glinting in the sunlight. My heart fluttered, moved by something that might have been fear. Or desire.

"I have come to break the spell," I said. The wind picked up my words and tossed them in the air, mocking me. In this land of stone and shadow, my will was a fragile thing.

Hunger cocked one eyebrow at me in amusement. "So you have said, my fairy-tale maid." He began walking toward the stone slab, and I fell in pace beside him.

The crow led the way, winging silently before us.

"If I break this spell, will you promise me something?"

"Anything. Break me out of this world, and I will remake your world in your image. I will bid the stars sing out your name and the shadows guard your slumber. Break me out of this world, and I will even make you my queen."

"No." I shuddered. I knew I should thank him, but his offerings left me cold. "I need an army. If I set you free, you must help me free my friends."

Hunger stopped walking and regarded me for a long moment. "You shall have one. You have my word."

His golden eyes, full of dark shadows, caught mine. Fear skittered down my spine. *What sort of bargain have I wrought?*

The stone slab, when we reached it at last, was larger than I expected, and smoother. Veins of white and pink ran through the dark grey rock. Something translucent caught the sunlight overhead and cast a net of stars back into the air above the stone.

The scent of roses hung thick in the air, rising from low bushes surrounding the stone.

I turned to Hunger. "What must I do?"

"Can you feel the spell?"

I concentrated. I felt the tips of my fingers, which were cold, and the wind that whispered along my neck. I heard the shushing of the trees swaying at the foot of the mountain and the dry rattle of winter grass. I heard the caw of the crow and the rustle of its wings as it settled on the rock before me. I felt the sunlight on my cheeks. But I felt nothing of the spell.

I shook myself free of the memory of summer afternoons with Gábor, failing at spell after spell. I could not fail here.

Just as despair reached clinging fingers into my heart, I sensed it: a faint pulsing that came from the stone itself. I opened my eyes to find Hunger watching me.

"Look," he said, nodding at my hand.

The Romani bracelet I wore glowed faintly, vibrating against my skin and skimming the excesses of a powerful spell as it was designed to do. If I could reach the spell through the stone, somehow, and pull it into me . . .

I reached outward, or tried to. Nothing happened.

I could sense, dimly, the tremendous thrum of power all around me. But it was as if I were separated from it by an impenetrable glass. I wanted to weep.

"What sacrifice have you brought?" Hunger's voice was rasping, jarring, but it pulled me out of my despairing reverie.

I held out my hands. "I brought myself."

Hunger frowned. "If you die with the spell, the Binding will not break."

My heart squeezed into a tight, painful ball. "Lady Berri said my blood would be enough."

"Then your lady doesn't know this spell. The spell needs heart's blood—and you cannot give that and break the spell."

"You've lied to me before. Why should I believe you?"

"I would not lie about this. The spell was bound in heart's blood, with the power only death magic can bring. It must be broken with the same."

I pressed my hands together. Somehow I knew that, had known it since I stepped into the spell, but I had been hiding from the knowledge. "Is there no creature—" I began, but Hunger cut across me.

"No creature here can provide what you need. We are part of the Binding."

The crow fluttered down from its perch to land at my

feet. With a tremor that passed through its entire frame, the crow lifted its wings and expanded, blossoming into a man-sized shadow. As the blackness bled away from the shrinking wings, I saw it was no bird at all, but a shapeshifter.

"I will be the sacrifice," Mátyás said.

Hunger's eyes lit with interest. "A *táltos*. I did not think your kind existed anymore."

A shapeshifter. Once, on a sunny summer afternoon, Mátyás had told me the story of a Hungarian shapeshifter, how a *táltos* could travel between worlds. I remembered now the crow that had attacked two guards at Sárvár. The crow had been Mátyás himself, not just a bird moved by an Animanti spell.

"Why did you never tell me?" I asked.

"I did not want you to look at me differently," Mátyás said. "Those who know always do."

I stared at him, my heart filling with a terrible hope and a terrible despair, before flinging my arms around him. He smelled of sweat and something bitter, and I did not want to let him go.

"You can't do this," I said. "You will . . ." I could not bring myself to say the word *die*. Mátyás's heart thumped beneath my cheek. He knew.

"And what if I do not? Then the Binding does not break, the Circle goes unchallenged, and William, Gábor, and all my friends will die."

"They might die even if you do."

Mátyás nodded at Hunger. "He promised you an army. I don't believe even Luminates could stand against the creatures here."

I shivered. I did not say, *How am I supposed to set a knife*

352

against your heart, to thrust it in? I hugged Mátyás once more, then let him go.

I was not eager to begin the spell that might end with Mátyás's death, however willing he was, but I did not know how much time had passed in the real world. I explained to Mátyás everything I knew. It did not take long.

I did not know nearly enough.

Mátyás rubbed one hand over his jaw, thinking. "You cannot perform spells because the double souls in you repel spells—but you cannot reach spells unless you are angry or strongly moved." He looked at me. "Are you angry now?"

I *was* angry, a simmering fury at the unfairness of the situation. But it was not the raw, overwhelming anger I'd used to break Catherine's spell. "No."

"Even if she were to draw the magic in, her soul would begin to break it down immediately, before she could hold the entire spell," Hunger said. "It would be like unraveling a weaving. It might take weeks."

"We don't have weeks," I said.

"If we could separate your souls somehow, maybe you could draw all the magic into one soul and then bring the souls back together. . . ." Mátyás rubbed his face again.

The beginnings of an idea glimmered. "How does your shapeshifting work? Do you change matter, or something else?"

"I change matter. Usually my own, but I can sometimes shift things I touch."

I thrust my wrist out to Mátyás. "Could you shift one of my souls into something else? Into power that might be drawn into this?" The Romani bracelet jangled.

He studied me for a long moment, his blue-eyed gaze clear

353

and unflinching. "Hold still," he said finally, and took my left hand.

A faint warmth crept from his fingers into mine. But then, as it had done with so many other spells, the heat intensified. It blazed up my arm, following the tracery of blood vessels, and spreading through my lungs like fire. I tried to scream and wrench my hand free, but Mátyás held me fast, and I had no air left in my lungs for sound. I could feel my souls reaching for his spell, to tear it open, and I pushed them down. I must stay calm. I must let this work.

Then something closed around my other wrist—long fingers that were somehow both human in the soft touch of skin and inhuman in the not-quite-right shape. His touch scalded, as it had in Sárvár, but the burning was only a drop to the pain pouring through me. The bone blade fell from my fingers. At my side, Hunger murmured strange words in a lyrical, molten tongue. After a moment, the heat began to leave me, sliding through my fingers into Hunger. His grip tightened. The fire did not go out, but it dampened enough I could bear it.

"Anna, I can't reach you. I can feel your second soul, but it's like a shadow. I can't hold it," Mátyás said.

Grandmama's last words floated back to me. *Let yourself free.* She was right about me. All my life I had been dimly aware of my dual souls, wearing one soul as my public face and pushing everything dark into the other, keeping her, like Macbeth, "cabin'd, cribb'd, confin'd, bound in / To saucy doubts and fears."

I reached beneath the haze of pain and pried the bars of my heart open.

I let my shadow self wing upward, strong and fine and falcon-free. She was not, as I had feared, malformed and dangerous. Only imperfect.

Only me.

"Got her," Mátyás said. Then, "Confound it, Anna, this will hurt—"

The fire flared up, searing through me, tearing through soft tissue, shearing through muscle and bone. And then the final great clap of pain: agony so intense it moved beyond pain into a kind of pleasure, anguish so deep that white sparkled at the edge of my vision, and only the twin grips on my hands held me steady.

As abruptly as it had built, the fire burned away. I was cold, as cold as I could ever remember being. Even the sun on my face carried only a memory of warmth. Mátyás saw me shivering and wrapped his arms around me.

I wept into his shirt.

"It's done, Anna," he said. "Look." With one arm still draped around me, he lifted my wrist with his other hand. The agate blazed—so bright it hurt to look at.

My soul.

And now I could feel the spell around us—not as a faint tremor, but as a living, pulsing thing. It streamed around me in the wind. It shifted in the shadows between the trees. And it danced inside me, warmth blossoming through my body like sensation returning to chilled limbs after a winter storm. *This*—this was the Luminate birthright, the awareness the Confirmation made possible. No wonder the Circle members were desperate to keep it for themselves.

I laughed with relief and threw my arms around Mátyás,

then released him and danced a jig around Hunger. And because I could, I crafted a Lumen light and then sent it spinning off into the sky.

"Careful." Hunger frowned. "This power is not to be wasted."

"I will not," I promised, sobered by the reminder.

My gaze caught on the shifting darkness beyond Hunger, and I discovered that what I had first taken to be simply shadows cast by the trees were not shadows at all, but creatures of every shape and size watching us from the fringes of the wood. Some were of beast aspect, ragged tusks and fur and gleaming red eyes. Others were so beautiful I could not look on them. The Lady blazed like white fire against the green, the golden wings of the turul bird flashing above her.

I would not think about them. I could not afford the distraction.

Closing my eyes, I extended my arms and fingers, trying to put as much of myself as I could in contact with the spell. I cast my thoughts inward, seeking for the calm center where my soul should be.

I found my center, though it was anything but calm. My soul was wild and agitated, the edges raw and wounded, a great, gaping hole bearing mute witness to my missing soul. I closed my eyes tighter and concentrated not on the wounded soul, but on that gap. I reached through it and outward toward the knotted center of the spell. With my invisible sense, I grasped the spell and pulled. One strand of the great spell followed my tug, and I reached for another, then another, and finally too many to count.

When I was full of the spell, so full I could scarcely breathe, so full even blinking hurt, Mátyás released his grip on my other soul.

It slipped back into place, pulled by an irresistible force. The spell inside me creaked and shuddered, an old house caught in the grasp of a strong wind.

A fissure opened across the dome of the sky revealing a band of blackness, night stars incongruous against the blue. The ground trembled, and a handful of boulders shook loose from the rocks above us. One cracked against the stone slab behind me.

A winged creature launched itself from the fringes of the woods, disappearing through the fissure with a cry that reverberated along my bones.

My entire body began to shake, my teeth rattling against each other. The spell fought to free itself, to stay whole, and I could no longer contain it.

The magic flowed back into the Binding spell, and I collapsed on the ground.

"Well," Mátyás said, "I believe that might work."

CHAPTER 30

I could not do this.

I retrieved Lady Berri's bone knife from the ground and looked from the blade to Mátyás's pale face. I did not want to endure that soul-searing pain again. And I could not—I shied away from the end of that thought. The blade hung heavy in my hands.

Hunger caught my eyes with his golden ones. Something flickered deep within them that might have been compassion. "This is the only way."

I took a deep breath and tried to center myself. I thought again of Gábor, of William. I called to mind all the people and places in Hungary I had come to love. If I did not do this thing, I was abandoning all of them to the casual cruelty of the Circle and the Hapsburgs. I would be abandoning all the creatures standing just out of sight, those creatures terrible and beautiful and strange.

Creatures like me.

"Not all of us are monsters," Hunger said, as if he knew my heart.

"It is the right thing," Mátyás said, and took my left hand again. His fingers shook beneath mine.

I took another breath, trying to keep my rebellious stomach in place. I did not want to do this, even if it was the right thing.

"Anna," Mátyás said, dropping my hand and cradling my face with both hands. His eyes were like a spring of water: clear, calm, fathomless. I drank them in. "It will be all right."

I remembered a phrase I'd heard at the café, between students discussing the injustice of Hapsburg rule: *Mátyás is dead, justice is gone.* They were referring to the great Renaissance king, but they could have been speaking of this moment.

If Mátyás dies, how can anything be right?

His eyes held mine. "I chose this, Anna. An honorable death is more than most men hope for. I won't die my father's death." A smile haunted his face. He slipped his good-luck cross from his neck and handed it to me. "Give this to Noémi. She might even forgive me."

My heart twisted as I slipped the cross over my head. "All right." *It is* not *all right.*

As before, Mátyás peeled one of my souls away and forced it into my talisman. The pain crawling through my body was worse the second time, because I knew to anticipate it. Hunger took my right wrist, careful to avoid the bone blade in my hand, and siphoned some of the fire away from me. I called the spell into the emptiness left by my missing soul, and the spell followed, though not willingly.

Magic hummed through my body. Electricity sparked

down my veins, lifting my hair away from my arms, from the back of my head. The slightest touch would shatter me into a million shining pieces.

I looked through that power and pain to Mátyás. He leaned against the great stone slab, his face white, his lips set.

"I am ready," he said.

My heart compressed into a tight mass.

"Mátyás," I said.

There weren't enough words. I wanted to thank him and apologize in the same breath. I wanted to tell him I was horrified and sad and angry and honored all at once to be here with him. I wanted to tell him I loved him like a brother, but those were not the words he wanted to hear, and I could not lie to him. Not here, not now. And Hunger was listening.

So I left the words unsaid and leaned forward, closing the space between us. I kissed him. Into that kiss I put all my gratitude and love and the beginnings of the grief pushing at the back of my throat. His lips moved against mine, our breath mingling for one splendid, wrenching moment.

I blinked against the burning in my eyes and pulled back to look at Mátyás. "I wish . . ."

He shook his head minutely. "No wishes. Just truth. Tell Noémi I love her. And—remember me."

"Always." My voice caught. His face swam before me through a glaze of tears. I wanted to memorize this moment, to engrave it on my mind and heart.

Hunger released my arm, and the full weight of the spell rushed back into me. I nearly dropped the knife. I squeezed my fingers around the hilt and raised it. Hesitated.

"The spell must have heart's blood," Hunger reminded

me, but his voice was gentle, as though he knew what this would cost.

I placed the tip of my knife against Mátyás's breast, above his heart. His eyes met mine, and his fingers, still holding mine, tightened.

"Please." My voice broke. "Close your eyes or I cannot do this."

Mátyás closed his eyes. I studied the tracing of blue veins on his eyelids, the mole beneath his left eye, the way his brown lashes turned gold at their tips.

I looked up at the great cracked vault of the sky, the arching upward thrust of the stone mountains.

I cannot do this.

"God have mercy," I whispered. My hand on the knife wavered.

"The Binding breaks," Hunger said in my ear. He set his hand on mine and shoved the blade home.

⋇

I released the hilt as if it scorched me and shook off Hunger's hand.

Mátyás's eyes flew open. He gasped and dropped my hand, his fingers fluttering up to the hilt protruding from his chest. His legs buckling, he slid to the ground, his back against the stone slab.

I had a brief moment to wonder whom I hated more—myself or Hunger—before Mátyás lost his grip on my soul.

That second soul winged back into its place like a dove to its dovecote.

And—nothing.

I brimmed with power, my veins blazing fire through my body. But the spell had not broken. Mátyás watched me with agony-bright eyes, patient, trusting. Then his head listed, his eyes tipped shut.

No.

"You need more power," Hunger whispered.

But where was I to find more power? My body already contained the whole of the spell. It fought against my souls.

My souls.

My essence.

I brushed my fingers against the Romani bracelet I wore. *Make yourself vulnerable,* Gábor had said, all those weeks ago. *Open your essence to the thing you would persuade.* I had struggled to find magic because I did not know who—what—I was. I knew that now.

I was not powerless.

I was *chimera.*

I had the power to break worlds.

Lumen, I thought, opening my souls to the rushing current of the magic. *Be what you will. Be free.*

And the world fell apart.

The sky erupted—the crack blossoming outward like a firework, a great bloom of destruction. The fissures radiated down to the ground. A thunderclap shook the valley, then another, and chasms snaked toward me through the bent grass and boulders. The mountains trembled and shivered apart, great hunks of rock raining down.

The stone slab broke, the crack down its heart exactly above Mátyás's head.

The Binding breaks.

The Circle ends.

All the maledictions of my childhood coming to fruition on the plain before me.

The creatures at the edge of the woods disappeared, vanishing through the cracks and fissures, screaming their elation.

"We must go, or we'll be trapped here." Hunger wrapped iron fingers around my arm, pulling me toward the nearest fissure. The beginnings of a headache wrapped similarly tight fingers around my skull.

A thin smear of blood trickled down my hand. Mátyás's blood. My eyes flew to Mátyás, huddled in the shadow of the great rock. I struggled against Hunger's grip.

"I can't leave my cousin!"

"He's dead."

"At least let me bring his body!"

"There's no time!"

And Hunger jumped down into a chasm, pulling me with him.

I screamed at him, every curse I could think of. As darkness swallowed me, all I could see was Mátyás dying alone in the shadow of the rock, cradled by a scrim of roses.

CHAPTER 31

I landed, hard, against the cracked marble floor in the Sala Terrena. Pain sizzled up my arms and through my hips. It jabbed pointed fingers in my eyes and glittered at the edge of my sight. I blinked, trying to clear my stunned vision, and stood. Fire radiated from my head, shooting down my spine and flaming through my joints. This, the cost of breaking.

Slowly, as though my bones would fragment if I moved too swiftly, I looked around.

I stood awash in a sea of movement: goose-footed *lidérc,* drowned *rusalka,* hollow-eyed *boszorkány,* the shadow-on-shadow sleekness of the *fene.* And others, creatures I'd never seen: a tawny beast with the face of a boar and a long, wicked horn sloping from his forehead. A manticore with the body of a lion and the face of a man. Serpents of all kinds—

great-winged dragons, snakes with human faces, man-sized roosters with serpent wings and scales. Some—all?—of the creatures had come through the chasm with us.

They raged through the Sala Terrena and burst like a tidal wave into the rest of the palace. From a distance came the faint tinkle of breaking crockery. Nearer at hand was the distressing rip and slurp of something feeding.

I pressed my fist against my stomach, fighting my rising gorge.

What had I done?

Every window in the room was broken, as though some great force had exploded in the center of the room and pushed outward. Outside, it rained, a steady grey drizzle.

Inside, madness reigned. I could not see Hunger, or the calming light of the Lady. The spider-woman with the third eye glanced my way briefly and saluted before disappearing from the room.

"Hunger!" I shouted.

A great boar-headed creature with crow's wings turned at my call, saliva dripping from his thrusting tusks. He sniffed at the air, and his huge lips curved upward in a distortion of a smile.

He sprang toward me, and I ran, dodging a cluster of fae women with flowing hair and ivy-twined dresses. I could not hear, over the cacophony of the room—voices hooting, singing, crying, laughing, cackling, crowing, rooting, roaring—if the monster still followed me.

I tripped and caught myself on my hands on the cracked tile. A sheep curled on the floor before me, asleep. No. Not sleeping. Dead: its throat torn out, its entrails spilled across the floor in bizarre runic patterns, bits of bone and matted flesh strewn around it.

This: the destruction newly released creatures left in their wake.

The room reeked of unwashed beasts and blood and the onset of rot. I struggled upright again, my pulse beating a painful tattoo in my throat. A voice sailed over the crowd, words in a language I did not understand, words with an alien cadence and heavy with age.

The clamor in the room cut off. The silence in its wake was so absolute, my breath roared in my ears.

I blinked and the creatures were gone, winking out of existence as suddenly as they'd come.

My stomach clenched tight as I processed this.

Hunger was gone—and with him, all the creatures.

So much for my promised army. I pushed back at the fear crawling through my belly. I could not despair yet. I had to find Grandmama and Noémi. I had to get to Buda-Pest.

I had to tell Noémi that Mátyás was dead.

My fingers gripped the cross he had given me, its points digging into my palm. Blinking back the tears stinging my eyes, I pressed forward. Dark flashes swarmed my vision. For a moment, I could not move until the pain became bearable.

I stumbled toward the doorway, one hand over my nose and mouth, swallowing against the burning in my throat. My hand smelled of blood and roses—*Mátyás's blood*—and I was sick all over the floor.

After wiping my mouth on my sleeve, I forged onward. A human body lay on the floor near a shattered mirror. I picked my way toward it, trying not to look too closely at the ovine corpses. My head throbbed.

The sightless eyes staring at the arched sky were familiar, though they were no longer framed by spectacles. I crouched and smoothed Herr Steinberg's eyes closed. Though he had tried to kill me, I could not hate him. He had only sought to do what he believed was right.

As I had.

We were both killers at heart—blood the terrible price of our beliefs. I scrubbed tears from my cheeks. The ache in my body was growing, a throbbing mass threatening to splinter me apart.

Another scan of the room confirmed there were no other human bodies. My shoulders drooped a little with relief, and I pushed my way free of the bloodstained room.

The corridors of Eszterháza seemed endless. The pounding in my head kept gleeful time with the shuffle of my feet as I mounted the stairs. I passed through the china room. All the lovely Sèvres vases and Dresden china were shattered on the floor, ground to powder by the passage of cloven and padded feet. Every room was empty. No creatures crouched in the shadows—but Grandmama and Noémi and János were still missing.

I pushed myself up another flight of stairs, my mouth dry. Noémi's room was empty. And mine. I headed toward Grandmama's.

"Anna?" The voice behind the door was faint, but my heart lifted with relief. They were here.

I pressed on the latch, and the door slid open. Noémi and János flanked the canopied bed, Noémi's vizsla circled by her feet. Grandmama lay upon the bed, her arms across her chest.

"Grandmama!" I said, rushing forward as fast as my pain-racked body would carry me.

"Wait—" Noémi said, but it was too late. I flung myself onto the bed beside Grandmama, and one of her arms slid down to her side. Something about that boneless movement made my heart seize up. She was so very still, her face pale as candle wax. The hand curled by her side was cold to my touch.

"Noémi?" My voice cracked. I pulled away from the bed.

"I'm so sorry. She was struck. When I got to her, it was too late." Noémi wiped tears from her cheeks.

"We brought her here to wait for you." János's voice was ragged, grieving.

I dragged my eyes from Grandmama's pale profile to Noémi's face. Something was wrong with her eyes. They weren't tracking right. A bright, angry burn spread up the side of her face and fanned across her nose and eyes. Her eyebrows were gone, and her eyelashes.

"Noémi," I said again, my eyes leaking. "You're hurt." She could not heal herself: few healers could hold a spell through the pain of healing. The fire in my bones was spreading, a lake, an ocean of pain. Grief washed over the fire, threatening to swamp me.

So many dead. Herr Steinberg. Lady Berri. Grandmama. *Mátyás.*

Noémi brushed aside my concern. "I cannot see, only bits of light and shadow, but I will live. Is the Binding broken? We heard a horrible screeching, and there were . . . things . . . in the hall, claws dragging and clicking. They're gone now."

"Yes," I said, wondering why the affirmation felt more like failure than victory. I needed to tell Noémi about Mátyás, but my throat kept closing around the words. The room dipped suddenly. *No.* I struggled to hold on to consciousness, using the pain to focus. "The others?"

"Gone. After your uncle killed Herr Steinberg, they fled," János said.

No caged thing loves its captor. Had that been a warning? The creatures I'd released swarmed the edges of my vision. "And Pál?"

János shook his head. "Gone too. He left just after the Circle fled."

"Did he know about Grandmama?"

János didn't answer, and I wept. For Grandmama, whose son left as she lay dying. For Pál, whose rearing by the Circle had warped something fundamental inside him. For Mátyás.

Noémi turned her unfocused eyes toward me. Her fingers curled and uncurled on Oroszlán's fur. "What now, Anna? Where is your army?"

I could not breathe. Grief and despair were like a massive stone crushing my chest. "No army. I broke the Binding and freed them—and they vanished. They didn't keep their word. And, oh, Noémi." I stopped, sucked in air.

She waited, her hand stilling on Oroszlán. Her skin puckered around her eyes, blistering near her temples, and peeling in bare red patches on her cheeks. I would not let myself look away. Whatever injuries she had sustained, they were on my behalf. Noémi's vizsla, uncharacteristically solemn, thumped his tail against the floorboards.

I said, "Mátyás followed us from Buda-Pest. He flew into the Binding as a crow."

The hope in her face slashed at my heart.

"Mátyás escaped? Where is he?"

I pulled the cross from my neck and pressed it into her hand. "He helped me break the Binding. But he—" I stopped abruptly, swallowing hard. "We needed a blood sacrifice. I could not be the sacrifice and break the spell."

Noémi's fingers curled around the ornament. Her blue eyes flickered and flattened. "He is gone, then?"

"The *szegény* lad," János whispered.

"He wanted you to know he loves you." Tears burned hot trails down my cheeks.

I waited for Noémi to shout at me, to blame me. Instead, she sat silent, shrinking into herself. I shifted away from the bed, kneeling beside her, and put my arms around her. She melted into me, shaking. Oroszlán laid his head in Noémi's lap.

"How did he die?"

"He was stabbed." I rubbed my hand against my sleeve. Noémi could not see the dried blood there, but I feared she might sense my omission: *I* stabbed him.

"Where is his body?"

I saw Mátyás's eyes again in memory: dark with pain but steady before they closed, and then the wall of roses hiding his body as the world collapsed. "I couldn't bring him out. One of the creatures pulled me out before I could reach him."

Silence stretched between us, thick and tangled.

Noémi broke the quiet. "Mátyás sacrificed himself?"

"Yes," I said. "He wasn't like your father after all."

And in a shadowed room beside my grandmother's body,

we sat and wept together. Outside, the rain fell, thin drum-beats against the roof. I was vaguely conscious of János leaving, of him returning later with cups of tea.

At length, I wiped my eyes. "I have to try to save the others. I must go back to the city."

Noémi put her hand on mine, her cold fingers curling around my scratched palm. "*We* must go back. *We* must save the others. You don't have to do this alone, Anna."

Her quiet assurance brought tears once again prickling the back of my throat. *We* was a small word, a tiny one, but its meaning was infinitely expansive.

János cleared his throat. "Beg pardon for disturbing you, but there is something you need to see."

)(

The seam in the corner of the Sala Terrena was scarcely visible against the mottled pink marble of the walls, barely noticeable above the ruin of the room. I had not seen it when I rushed from the room after returning from the Binding, but János had.

"I found it when I came down to inspect the damage."

"Where does it go?"

"A drawing room someplace. I can't tell where."

I peered through the slit, and my heart thumped. I recognized the burgundy chairs, the Turkish rug, and the faint scuff against the molding where Mátyás had kicked the wall.

Grandmama's drawing room in Buda-Pest.

Home.

Pál had left it for us. Why? Perhaps it was his kind of

apology. Or perhaps it fed into some larger plan of his I could only guess at.

It would take two days to ride to Buda-Pest by carriage—and the executions were set to begin today.

We would have to risk the portal.

CHAPTER 32

I stepped into the seam of the Portal spell, my body tight with nerves, anticipating a trap. I exhaled slowly, willing myself calm. Faint heat prickled my skin, and then I was across. A fine layer of silt covered everything in the drawing room, dust blown in through the broken windows.

A heartbeat later, Noémi was beside me. János stayed in Eszterháza with Grandmama's body. Later, when this was over, I would have to return to fetch her for burial. But I could not think about that now.

I had to save Gábor.

Pál had abandoned us; so had Hunger with his army. I was not entirely certain what to do now: Find Petőfi and beg him to help me? Or march to the prison and demand the Circle release my friends? After all, I had destroyed their Binding. I was a woman to be reckoned with.

Or, more likely, a woman to be thrown in the prison and executed with the rebels.

My ignorance pressed down on me like a weight. I did not know what had happened to the Circle in the wake of the broken Binding. Were they confused, anxious, vulnerable? Or already regrouping? When I had envisioned challenging the Circle before, it had always been with allies: Mátyás, Lady Berri, William. We would pit our strength and confidence against their confusion.

But Noémi and I were the only ones left, and Noémi was injured.

Lady Berri and Papa believed that a broken Binding would return magic to everyone with the ability to wield it. By that logic, *some* of the Circle ought to be weaker, as not all Luminate could have a strong innate ability, just as not all people could sing well. And if individuals were the source of their own power, as Papa believed, that would place additional limits on the Circle's power, as they could not draw from the endlessly renewing Binding.

Would it be enough?

The enormity of what I had done snatched my breath away.

When I could breathe again, I gripped Noémi's hands and led her into the hallway and down the stairs. We found Ginny in the kitchen, nursing a cup of tea. After hugging us both and exclaiming, she pressed tea on us, and while I gulped mine down—too hot, too fast—she told us, "There's rebels fighting up on the hill near the castle."

My heavy heart lifted a fraction. Maybe something could yet be salvaged. "And the prisoners? Are they still alive?"

"I don't know. I think so." Ginny eyed me uncertainly. "But, Miss Anna, the fighting. You can't go up there. It's dangerous."

I laughed, not unkindly. "To be safe, I might have stayed at home."

Noémi and I thanked Ginny for the tea, and I led Noémi from the house. The street was carpeted with squares of paper like a printer's snowfall, the leaflets slowly turning to paste in the grim October rain. I scooped one up and read it aloud to Noémi, who helped me translate the Hungarian.

> *Rise, Magyar, your homeland calls!*
> *The time is here: now, or never!*
> *Shall we be slaves—or free?*
> *This is the question. Answer it!*

This was Petőfi's work. I was certain of it. The rebels on the hill must be his as well. He had raised an army through the alchemy of words.

A dozen paces away, a young girl in peasant dress, her hair covered by a kerchief, stood in the middle of the street and flickered on and off like a lantern. She laughed with delight.

Though a dozen errands pulled at me, Noémi and I crossed the street to her. "How are you doing this?"

The glow in her face came and went. "I don't rightly know, miss. Lady. I was midway through my morning chores, and something felt different, like someone had set a charge in me. Then I found I could do this. It's like magic, isn't it?"

The Binding breaks. Already, non-Luminate were feeling the effects: no longer barred by the spell, a girl in the street could draw magic into her soul and channel it. "It *is* magic," I said. "But promise me you won't try a larger spell without help. You could get hurt."

"I won't, miss," she promised, and then turned her attention back to her hands, relighting and then extinguishing them, over and over again.

There would be work to do later, training all these new magicians. But it was not my work.

Half a block from Grandmama's house, we hailed a hansom cab. The driver took us as far as the river.

"Sorry, miss." He touched his cap. "But if there's fighting, it's no business of mine. Nor of yours, I should think."

Ignoring his unsolicited advice, I thanked him and paid him.

Noémi and I crossed the pontoon bridge, though it bucked and twisted beneath us. I gripped Noémi's hands, and we slipped and lurched on the rain-slick boards, grim and determined. The silent pressure of grief accompanied me, pushing against my eyelids and stealing my breath, closing my throat when I tried to form words. But I hadn't the time to do more than look at it askance, to shove the pressure aside and plunge forward.

We stumbled through the streets below Buda Castle. A ragged group of men and women clustered on the steep road before the palace gates, struggling with the Austrian guards. Smoke and gunfire filled the air.

Misgiving seized me. It was one thing to talk of braving the fighting, to imagine the smoke and fire like something out of a Turner painting.

It was something else entirely to stand on the streets, the cobblestones hard beneath the soles of my shoes, the smoke pressing thick against my nose, the taste of it bitter on my tongue. The gunshots echoed down the street and reverberated in my bones.

And the blood. I had not imagined there could be so much blood. I had seen pig killings in the village when I was young, how the blood seemed to go on and on and the pig twitched and twitched before it was finally still.

That was nothing to this.

This was the ruined castle in the Binding. The slaughtered sheep in the Sala Terrena.

A young man fell a half dozen paces from us, his jaw blown off. My stomach revolted, trying to fight its way free of my body.

Noémi made a small, anxious sound, her eyes fixing vaguely on the dead boy. "What is happening?"

I turned my eyes away from the corpse. "A boy was shot."

"Does he live? Perhaps I can help."

I tried to unsee the blood spatter across the stones, the glinting white of bone in raw flesh. "There's no help for him." A bullet winged past us, blasting brick from the wall beyond us. I pulled Noémi down a side street where we would be shielded from the fighting. "And there's no time."

Boys dead in the streets. Mátyás dying beneath a cracked vault of sky. Gábor. I couldn't let him be added to the litany of dead and dying. My heart might shatter.

"We can't go this way," I said. The castle gate was narrow, and the soldiers still held it. We would have to fight our way through the rebels and then the soldiers to reach the prison, and we couldn't do it.

"The Vienna Gate?" Noémi asked, referring to the north-eastern gate leading to the residential streets in the castle district, and the one closest to the prison where Gábor was being held.

"There will be guards there too, surely."

"There might be another way," Noémi said. "There are labyrinths under the castle, rows and rows of old connected cellars. There won't be so many guards at the entrance, not with the fighting drawing them away."

I tucked my arm more firmly in Noémi's. We followed a road as it circled back around the castle hill. On the far side, away from the Duna, we began hunting along Lovas Street for an opening.

"Here," I said, spotting a narrow wooden door set back in some kind of enclosure. I pulled the latch, and the door opened, groaning. I peered into the darkness, but I could see no sign of life. The chill air of the stony corridor wafted out toward us.

"I need light," I said.

"Lumen," Noémi whispered, and a light blossomed in her hand.

We walked into the labyrinth. The darkness seemed to close around us, and I knew a moment of panic. Here, buried under the earth, I had no sense of direction, no idea where we should go.

"This way," Noémi said, tugging on my arm.

I followed. Our footsteps were muffled in the close air of the old cellars. When Noémi stumbled, I put one hand against the stone wall for balance and my fingers came away wet with water. A barrel stood empty in the corner.

Noémi continued forward, her direction sure.

"How do you know where you are going?" I asked.

She paused. "I'm not sure. It's like the certainty of sunlight after a rainstorm. After the Binding—magic feels different to me somehow, Anna. A lit charge, like the girl said. As though I might heal, but do other things as well. I'm following the pull of the magic."

The corridors sprawled all around us, other passageways reaching out to intersect intermittently, curiously shaped rooms periodically interrupting the narrow path we followed. Once, we passed a clump of frightened burghers, arguing about the best way out of the city, away from the fighting.

Just when I had begun to think Noémi was fooling herself with her surety, we came to some narrow stone steps. "Up," Noémi said, and I helped her climb the stairs.

We emerged, blinking, into the grey mist of a street just beyond Saint Mátyás's Church, the high Gothic tower light against a darker sky. I could hear shouting. As we crossed the square before the church, the shouting intensified. Turning a corner, we found the bulk of Petőfi's army. A knotted mass of soldiers and revolutionaries struggled before the rather plain, three-story yellow building serving as the prison, crammed into the narrow medieval street. I could not see any safe way through them, but I moved forward anyway, pulled by an instinct I hardly understood.

As we watched, an invisible hand plucked up a half dozen rebels and flung them against the building opposite the prison with a horrific crack.

Just ahead of us, a young woman crumpled to the ground.

Her neighbor dropped beside her. The utter silence of their falls made them all the more terrifying. A Killing spell? There must be trained Luminate with the soldiers. Only the most powerful Animanti could close the lungs or stop the heart. And the Circle forbade such magic. *Except in wartime.*

I stumbled, nearly pulling Noémi down with me.

The broken Binding had not stopped the Circle. Perhaps it had not even slowed them.

Two more of Petőfi's cobbled-together militia fell. Ten paces before me, a young man in the white linen of a serf broke free of the crowd, his hands alight with fire. With a strangled yell, he thrust fireballs into the air. They smashed against the door of the prison in a glorious shower of sparks. Inspired by his success, he drew on more fire. *Too much. He cannot hold it all.*

I watched the young man lift his arms—and implode. The fire flashed out. A blackened, smoking hulk tumbled to the ground, smelling distressingly of roast meat. The released magic from the Binding might belong to Luminate and non-Luminate alike, but the untrained could not hope to match trained Luminate warriors.

Common Austrian soldiers in white and blue regimentals spilled out of the prison gate, fanning toward us. A Luminate spell plowed over us, a wall of icy air freezing Noémi and me where we stood with the others. A red-haired woman in the black and silver of a Luminate commander allowed her lips to curl as she watched.

My heart shrank. We were too little, too late. The Circle had come, and even a broken Binding couldn't save us. The cold of the spell crept into my lungs, a knife stab of pain each time I drew breath. All around me, the members of Petőfi's army fell with military precision as the soldiers slaughtered them. Frozen as they were, it was as easy as shattering icicles on the eaves in winter.

I raged against the growing ice. I did not want to die. I wanted to feel Gábor's arms around me again. I wanted to see Papa and James again—even Catherine and Mama. I wanted to raise a stone for Mátyás in a quiet *sírkert*, a weeping garden.

I had not killed Mátyás for this.

I remembered the creatures who'd gathered to watch the breaking, and raged again. Curse Hunger and his failed promise. Damn Pál for his capricious games. I needed their help *now*.

I let the anger and need overwhelm me, sweeping through me like ice-laced spring runoff.

The spell cracked. The redhead who had cast the spell looked astounded, then frightened.

As the air shifted around us, I shook my cramping fingers. First a current of warmth, then a tingling in my toes that spread through my frozen limbs. And finally, a yearning so strong it was like physical pain. Noémi's hand tightened on my arm.

My heart lifted with recognition. I knew only one creature who could call this desire.

Hunger.

Light flared through the street, illuminating the rain-drenched cobblestones. Everything wooden caught fire, tinder to an inferno built of need and longing. Hunger flickered into being beside me, his gold eyes blazing.

My army had arrived.

"Why didn't you come sooner?" I asked.

"I'm called by need," Hunger said, his eyes intent on the Luminate before us. "Until your need was great, I hadn't enough power. And the others required feeding."

While the Luminate captain faced the new arrivals, shadows fell across the street, winged beings setting down to slaughter. Luminate and Austrian soldiers alike swung away from their human foes, their startled cries turning to screams as the newly freed creatures pierced their hastily spelled wards. A griffin plucked up a silver-haired gentleman in Luminate colors and sprang to the ornamented top of the palace beside the prison, plunging his beak into the man's chest. I choked and dragged my eyes back to the street before me, where a being of light erupted into stone, crushing a half dozen men beneath his weight. Their screams hung in the close air of the street.

A high, piercing shriek sounded nearby, and one of the *boszorkány* sisters rushed by me, cackling to herself. "Put out their eyes, put out their eyes." She cast me a sly smile as she passed.

A body slumped against a stone wall nearby. A woman hunkered above the corpse, something birdlike about her movements and the careful way she held her head, her arms bent at her sides. Fire flickered down her hair, and her shapely legs ended incongruously in webbed goose feet. Her lips, when she smiled at me, were bloody.

Lidérc. I felt again the remembered night pressure on my chest. *Lidércnyomás.* Nightmare.

This is what I asked for.

There would be time later for an accounting of all my

guilt, but I had a task to do. I scooped up an abandoned knife from the street, trying to block the memory of the last time I'd held a knife. I tugged Noémi with me and slipped to the side of the street, hugging the wall as I inched toward the open prison door.

Though I felt exposed and vulnerable, the soldiers judged two girls no threat to them in comparison with the nightmare beasts. From the corner of my eye, I watched a Luminate soldier lift his hands to cast a spell, then stop, perplexed, to stare at his empty palms. At least the broken Binding had won us that much: not all the Luminate had their former power.

We slid through the doorway into the prison unchallenged. I gripped my knife in my free hand, my heart thudding.

The entryway was gloomy and cool after the heat of the street fire. No one stirred at our entrance—the soldiers must have all been drawn outside. Voices cried out upstairs and we followed the sound, Noémi clinging to the railing of the stairs as we climbed.

I peeked through the bars into the first room.

A man was dead, slumped against the far wall with his throat blown out. His blood splattered the wall in a grim tracery of jagged lace. I recoiled.

I crept, more cautiously, to the second room. There were three prisoners here. They might have been sleeping, but the dark stains spreading across their clothes suggested otherwise. I recognized a friend of Mátyás's who had laughed with me and told me I was pretty. I had not believed it possible for my heart to ache so much, pain piled upon pain.

Noémi caught my sleeve. "I smell blood."

"Someone is killing the prisoners."

"But *why?*"

I had no answer. Perhaps the Circle had planned for this all along, deciding to carry out the death sentences before any rebellion could free the prisoners. Or perhaps the killer acted alone, spurred by misplaced loyalty to Vienna. My legs trembled, and I put one hand against the wall to steady myself. God could not be so cruel, to let me break the Binding and send Hunger's army just in time, only to see us fail.

A distant roar from the street reached us, human screams mingled with inhuman screeching.

A third and fourth cell, on the opposite side of the hall, revealed only more dead. But the blood from some of the wounds still flowed, and one of the men shifted, groaning with pain. Whoever had done this had acted recently.

I hesitated. The need to hurry overwhelmed me—but I could not simply abandon Noémi.

"Go, Anna," Noémi said, reading my reluctance. "I will follow as I can."

The hallway before us was empty. I picked up my skirts, and sprinted back the way we'd come and up a flight of stairs, ignoring the sharp pain in my side as the stays of my corset pressed into me.

I paused on the landing. There—halfway down the hall. A shadowed figure aimed a small handgun through the bars and fired. The report was almost lost in the greater din outside.

I did not let myself consider the madness of facing a man carrying a gun, armed with only my small knife. I padded down the hallway toward the soldier-assassin. He heard me before I reached him and whirled, his teeth bared in a horrible grimace. When he saw me, he laughed.

"And this is the last hope of the resistance? A girl?" His German was precise and clipped.

I closed my fingers around my knife. Words boiled up in my mouth: *I am not any girl. I am* chimera. But I clamped my lips down around them. This was not tea in some fine drawing room. I was not obligated to answer him.

"Fly true," I whispered, and launched the dagger.

I am not sure who was more startled when the blade hit: me or the soldier, who staggered back, his hand coming up to grasp the hilt. He yanked it out of his shoulder. A hit—but not a killing blow. He stalked toward me, a dully gleaming gun in one hand and a bloody knife in the other.

Now I thought of the madness of meeting a gun with a knife.

I fell back a pace, fear drying my mouth.

Behind me, Noémi cried out. Light crackled along the walls of the hall, accompanied by a shouted incantation. The man dropped to the ground, the gun sliding along the floor.

I whirled. Noémi stood at the top of the stairs, one hand tight on the railing.

I did not ask her what she'd done.

Taking a deep breath, I steadied myself. My hands shook. I did not want to approach the corpse, but I needed keys. A hasty patdown of the dead man's pockets revealed nothing, so I picked up the gun, holding it between two fingers.

"Here, lady!" Hands thrust through the bars of the door nearest me. *"Hála Istennek!"* Thank God. "We are saved!"

"Stand back!" I aimed the gun at the lock and pulled the

trigger. The recoil sent shock waves racing up my arm, and I dropped the gun, shaking my stinging fingers. The first prisoner pushed out, pausing only to press a kiss onto my cheek, before scooping up the gun and racing down the hallway, releasing the others.

I followed him, my heart thumping. Noémi trailed behind me.

Bodies surged past us, eager for release.

"Wait!" I cried. "There's fighting in the streets!"

A few of the passing faces turned to me with wide grins, promising vengeance on the soldiers who'd held them. Others seemed scarcely to have heard me. Still others paused long enough to catch my hands and squeeze them, or kiss my cheek as the first soldier had done. They smelled of sweat and urine and sickness, but I found them beautiful.

Noémi slid her arm through mine, and we pressed against the wall to let the prisoners stream past us. A few of the faces were familiar from Café Pilvax, but none of the faces were the ones I sought. *Was* Gábor one of the slumped bodies on the floor below me? I would not believe it, not until I had to.

My eyes flickered from face to face with increasing worry. Then—

"Anna!" William struggled toward me. "I thought I dreamed you." His gaze slipped past me and lit like torches. "Noémi!"

His eyes trailed over her burn scars, but he said nothing, only pulled her to him in a tight embrace. "Forgive me?" he whispered.

I did not hear Noémi's response. A memory flashed through my mind: not Gábor in Tabán, but Mátyás wrapping me in his arms inside the Binding. *Mátyás is dead, justice is gone.*

A wave of grief tore through me, bending me in half and compressing my lungs so I could not breathe. And then warm hands were on my shoulders, a gentle voice saying, "Anna?"

Gábor stood before me, one of the last of the released prisoners. Though the grief did not recede entirely, its grip lessened. I could breathe again. My eyes devoured his face: his large, dark eyes, his sharp cheekbones, and the strong, lean line of his throat. There were bruises on his cheeks. *What had they done to him?*

I flung myself forward. Gábor caught me and groaned, one leg buckling beneath him. I stepped back, frowning. He was hurt.

"It's all right," he said, gasping a little. "It's an old wound." And he folded his arms around me. For the first time in days, weeks, months, I felt safe.

Some small part of me knew the differences between us had not disappeared—but I shut that part away. It was enough, for now, that he was alive. That we were together. That outside in the streets the last of the Austrian army and the Circle's soldiers were being driven away by Hungarian patriots and otherworldly creatures.

Gábor's fingers traced my brow, the tips of my ears, my lips. "I thought I would die without seeing you again."

My hands slid up his arms, my fingers tangled in the curls at the back of his neck. "So did I."

Then he set his lips to mine, and the warmth of that kiss spread through my body like the balmy comfort of tea. Against all the darkness and death and turmoil of the last few days, his kiss was everything light, everything good. His kiss was life, springing up around me. His kiss was hope, radiating out from this still, perfect center of a new world.

I kissed him back.

)(

The street outside the prison, when we finally, reluctantly, emerged was devastating. The Austrian and Luminate soldiers who had guarded the prison were all dead. A handful of Petőfi's makeshift army and former prisoners remained in the streets, gently lifting the dead and carrying them back to the square before the church, where they would be collected for burial.

The creatures were gone—only Hunger remained, looking around at the carnage with a slight smile.

Gábor's arm around me tightened.

"Our bargain is at an end, I think," Hunger said as we approached.

"Yes," I agreed. "And thank you."

He shrugged, a delicate gesture that was somehow disturbingly human and inhuman at the same time. "I paid a debt." His eyes fixed on me, and a tug of longing uncurled inside me. I stepped forward, unthinking, shaking off Gábor's embrace.

As if this were a signal he'd waited for, Hunger swooped toward me, setting his perfectly carved lips against my forehead. Heat seared through me, and when he pulled away, I gasped. I touched my skin, fully expecting to find blisters, but found only coolness. Hunger laughed. "Fare you well. Perhaps we shall meet again."

"Perhaps." I hoped not.

There on the street, Hunger shifted, his too-perfect human form elongating, expanding, growing darker—like daylight dissolving into night. A draconian creature, pieced together of shadows and starlight and smelling of brine and smoke, shook itself delicately, one wing tracing a final caress across my cheek. Those sun-bright eyes met mine for a fraction of a second before Hunger launched himself into the air and vanished.

I could feel Gábor's eyes on me, asking questions I did not know how to answer.

William and Noémi drew even with us in the street. William looked around, frowning, as though searching for something. "Where's Mátyás?"

The Binding breaks—the thought slipped out reflexively. "Mátyás is dead."

"Dead?" Gábor turned to look at me sharply. "But he escaped the prison. We watched him shift and fly through the bars."

"He died saving my life." That was true, though not the whole truth.

We wound our way toward the Duna. The streets around Buda Castle were crowded and noisy—Hungarian hussars, patriots, former prisoners all milling about in a mood of celebration. As we watched, the Hapsburg colors were lowered and the Hungarian tricolor flag lifted to the ramparts. Not all the creatures had gone after all: a great gold falcon soared above the castle. I wondered if the Lady were nearby, watching.

It would take time before the city settled into some semblance of normal life, but the signs were promising.

Already enterprising women and men were mingling among the crowd, offering trays of *rétesek,* breads, meat pies, and drink.

The Binding had broken, and still the world turned on.

Papa had been right.

CHAPTER 33

1 November 1847, Buda-Pest

We buried Grandmama on All Saints' Day.

The whole of the two cities, Buda and Pest, seemed to throng the streets that day. It was a day of celebration—the Austrian Circle was disbanding; its head, Prince Metternich, had resigned; and the Hapsburgs had signed papers recognizing Hungary's independence—and a day of mourning. Fog curled around the Buda streets as Noémi, János, and I walked, candles held aloft, toward the cemetery where Grandmama was to be buried beside my grandfather. János guided Noémi, as her sight had not yet returned, though her skin had healed. The streets were full of others with similar vigils, all those candles like so many stars in the mist.

Temetni tudunk, Noémi had said that morning. We know how to bury our dead. And, indeed, the air itself seemed subdued by grief. No wind blew to brush away the fog, and the moisture clung to our hair, our wool cloaks, our already damp cheeks.

The cemetery was at the end of a cloistered street. We passed through the wrought-iron gate, beneath the trees stretching bare fingers in supplication to the sky. Someone had swept the browning grass free of leaves, and we stood in silence beside the open pit as the grave workers lowered the burnished mahogany coffin into the ground. I wished my family could be with me, but the burial could not be put off any longer. Though Papa was en route to fetch me, on this afternoon, János, Noémi, and I were the only family to pay tribute.

I had not seen Pál since he created my portal into the Binding. I wondered if he knew his mother was dead. If he cared.

I had commissioned a stonemason to carve a monument to Grandmama: an older woman, strong and beautiful in the height of her power, her hands outstretched with a spell. In a few weeks, the monument would grace her grave, but I would be back in England. The mason had also promised to complete a second commission, a young man shifting into a crow. The last *táltos* in Hungary deserved that much.

After a brief ceremony, I sat silent with Noémi in the *sírkert,* the aptly named weeping garden, on a stone bench beneath a chestnut tree, the ground carpeted with fallen nuts. I thought of what I had lost: Grandmama, Mátyás, Lady Berri, those who had died fighting and in the prison. I had gone back to Attila's Hill to look for Lady Berri's body, but there was nothing there. I had heard, later, that her oldest daughter had made arrangements for her burial back in England. I thought of what I had won: the creatures' release, a new future for the country I had come to love, Gábor.

A wind picked up, parting the branches of a nearby bush. In that shifting, I caught a glimpse of leaf-green eyes in a bark-brown face. The creature bared tiny needle-pointed teeth at me in what might have passed for a smile. Noémi murmured something about returning to the hotel where we were staying, and when I turned my attention back to the bush, the creature had vanished.

I wondered how such creatures would fare in our world, free from the Binding. Already rumors were filtering into the cities of strange fae sightings, of creatures with other-worldly voices and the eerie *shush-shush* of giant wings under cover of darkness. But so far, a kind of uneasy truce held: there had been no attacks on humans since Hunger's army came to my rescue outside the prison.

I prayed it would stay that way.

)(

That evening, I swept into the grand ballroom of the Károlyi mansion on Gábor's arm, following Petőfi and his young, dark-haired wife. Noémi and William were only a few steps behind us. Though we were a motley crew by any high society standards—two ladies, a middle-class poet, a Romani man, and a radical—the crowd in the ballroom erupted in cheers as our names were announced. Karolina, our hostess for the night, beamed at us from her station near the entrance to the ballroom.

When the invitation to the ball arrived, I had nearly declined it. I had not seen Karolina since she rejected my plea for help, and I did not want to be in company. I'd rather mourn in private, lick my wounds like an injured animal.

But Noémi had insisted I come. "They want to celebrate you as a heroine. It will give everyone great pleasure and cost you little enough. If I can attend, surely you can."

After that, I could not refuse.

The walls of the ballroom were draped with great swags of Hungarian colors: red, green, and white knots were everywhere. Even the crimson and white flowers filling the room reflected the national theme.

I could not help recalling Catherine's ball, six months earlier, when I had longed to join the dancing and had instead been banished to the schoolroom. Now I was a guest of honor. I wore a gown in the Hungarian style: a tight dark velvet bodice, laced across the breast with rows of pearls, and a flowing skirt. Over the skirt I wore a richly embroidered apron, the gold and silver roses repeating themselves across my full sleeves. Gábor looked striking in his brocaded, silk-damask dolman coat, worn long over embroidered trousers. The coat was not a perfect fit; it was too broad across the shoulders, and I suspected it may have once belonged to Mátyás.

Karolina rushed toward me, pressing my hands in hers and kissing my cheek. "I am so glad you were able to come. I have felt so wretchedly guilty about that night, turning you away as I did. And yet it has all ended well—here you are, a veritable heroine!"

My grandmother and my cousin are dead. I did not speak

the words out loud—to deliberately cloud the celebration seemed churlish. I ought to have been in mourning, but I had decided to put off my mourning clothes until I reached England. There had been enough of death. I would rather celebrate the living and the good memories I had of the dead.

In any case, I could not hate Karolina. She had acted on an instinct to protect the ones she loved. I was no longer so certain that, in her place, I would have done differently.

Karolina waved her hand at the gathering guests in the ballroom. "Our new world, Anna. Now we are no longer Luminate and commoner, countess and serf, master and maid—but we are all Hungarian."

We are all Hungarian. No more "us" and "them," no more solitary "I."

Karolina moved on to greet other guests, and Gábor pulled me forward into a *csárdás*. Noémi and William danced nearby, and as the crowd shifted and flowed around us, a curious lifting sensation filled me.

Happiness.

Despite everything, despite Mátyás and Grandmama and the inevitable cost of the breaking and the revolution, there was still joy in my world. Society was shifting, stretching and growing and becoming something bigger and better— better even than I had dreamed back in the days when I had begun to dream with Freddy. Doubtless there would be growing pains, but I had only to look across at Gábor to know the changes were good.

In a few days' time, Papa would arrive. Shortly after, I would travel back to England and Noémi would return to her Eszterházy cousins in Vienna. Gábor had already found new work as an undersecretary for Kossuth Lajos, leader of the newly forming Hungarian government, whom Gábor hoped to persuade to pass Romani-favorable laws. A letter had arrived, overflowing—in very un-Papa-like style—with emotion. Papa seemed torn between elation and genuine grief at Grandmama's loss. One line I had read over and over again until it was cemented in my memory: *My dear daughter, I am more proud of you than I know how to say.* I should be glad to see him again, and James. I missed even Mama and Catherine.

But I could not think of leaving Hungary—the country of my heart, *hőn szeretett országom,* as Grandmama had always known it—without aching.

Gábor smiled down at me. "Pensive?"

I smiled back. "Thinking of you." I sighed. "Thinking of England."

"I will wait for you," he said. And there, before everyone, he kissed me. I kissed him back, pushing myself onto my tiptoes to reach him better. Fire lit in my belly and spread through my body. *This,* I thought. *This is what I want.*

There were so many things I did not know. I did not know what would happen to the creatures I'd released or what shape magic would take in the wake of the broken Binding. I did not know how the Romanies would fare under Pál's curse. And despite Gábor's promise, I did not know what would happen between us. But, for perhaps the first time in my life, I was content simply to be, to let things unfold as they would.

But I knew one thing. This was my home now, this country with the wide plains and the sere prairies, with the rolling Buda hills and the crowded streets of Pest and the mess of people: farmers, nobles, factory workers, students, and revolutionaries—Magyar, Croat, Wallachian, Austrian, Jew, even Romani.

"I will be back," I said.

The truth of that promise sang in my bones.

EPILOGUE

Long ago, and far away, over forty-nine kingdoms, beyond the Operentsia Sea, beyond the glass mountains, and beyond that to a kingdom beneath a pearl sky, a tree grew between worlds.

Beneath the spreading canopy of leaves, the Lady sat waiting, soft hands folded in her lap, her gleaming face pensive. A young man with curling brown hair lay at her feet. He was neither dead nor alive, neither sleeping nor wakeful. He simply was, and the Lady waited for him to be.

The east wind rattled past them, shaking the branches of the tree and pulling at the Lady's hair. The wind pressed at the youth, filling his nose and mouth and lungs with air from the Upper Realm.

A tremor passed through him.

Author's Note

All history writing is, to some extent, a work of fiction, an attempt to recapture an era that no longer exists, except in the imagination. This is particularly true of historical fantasy. While I tried, where possible, to ground the story in real historical details, I also tried not to let those details get in the way of telling a good story.

The first, and probably most striking, historical divergence is in the Hungarian revolution and the timeline leading up to it. The years 1847 and 1848 were tumultuous ones across Europe, with food shortages and riots and a number of small-scale uprisings. Hungary, in particular, was stirred by a burgeoning sense of egalitarianism and a growing nationalist movement that took pride in all things Hungarian. In March of 1848, galvanized by reports of the Paris revolution, Kossuth Lajos presented twelve points to the Austrian Congress in Vienna, demanding greater independence and rights for Hungary. After reading a printed copy of Kossuth's speech, students and other Viennese citizens rioted in the streets on March 13, clamoring for their own liberties.

When word of this citizen revolution reached Hungary, Petőfi Sándor and the Youth of March took to the streets on March 15, 1848. They commandeered a printing press and printed copies of Petőfi's "Nemzeti Dal" (National Poem), a stirring poem calling for Hungarians to rise up and reclaim their historic glory. That afternoon, Petőfi read the "Nemzeti Dal" on the steps of the National Museum, inspiring the assembled crowd to march on Pest's town hall and then to the castle district in Buda to demand the release of political prisoner Táncsics Mihály. The Austrian government and Emperor Ferdinand, already alarmed by the rioting in Vienna and reluctant to spur more violence, quickly bowed to the Hungarian demands and granted them power to form a separate government. Obviously, my revolution plays out much differently from the actual one, which was largely bloodless. But March 15 still stands as an important day to most Hungarians, and I want to acknowledge that.

Other aspects of the story are, sadly, all too real: the prejudice and mistreatment toward the Romani people were historic fact. They were enslaved in many parts of Romania and the Ottoman Empire until the nineteenth century. In sixteenth-century England, Romanies could be branded and enslaved for two years, and if they tried to escape, enslaved for life. Beginning in the reign of Maria Theresa in Austria in the mid-eighteenth century, it was legal for Romani children to be taken forcibly from their homes and placed with German and Hungarian families, and it was forbidden for Romani families to speak their own language. Though many Romani musicians were in high demand in nineteenth-century Hungary, Romanies, in general, were discriminated against and regarded as pariahs. This prejudice still exists today in many parts of Europe. It can be difficult to reconstruct the world of nineteenth-century Romanies, as literacy rates were low and few kept records. What records we do have were often from outsiders, and either romanticized or tainted by prejudice.

The term "Romani," as used in this story, is in some sense an anachronism—in the nineteenth century, Romanies would have been known primarily as "Gypsies" (*Cigányok* in Hungary). Due to the negative stereotypes attached to the term "Gypsy" and the fact that it stems from a mistaken idea of their origins (it's a corruption of "Egyptian"), "Roma" or "Romani" has been widely adopted as the preferred form of address. I chose to use "Romani" to acknowledge this preference and to reflect the difference between the way Gábor views his family and friends (and the way Anna comes to) and outsider perspectives. Where "Gypsy" is used, it refers strictly to outsiders' perspectives of Romani life.

Some of the characters in the story were real people. Károlyi Karolina, one of two Zichy sisters (her sister was married to Count Batthyány Lajos, who became the first prime minister following the revolution), was an influential force in the growing Hungarian nationalist movement of the 1840s. She and her sister held balls and banquets to raise money for the movement, and spawned the popularity of Hungarian-made gowns and traditional costumes among the fashionable elite. Petőfi Sándor is also real, as is his reputation as the greatest nineteenth-century Hungarian poet. Prince Metternich, mentioned in passing as the leader of the Austrian Circle, dominated Austrian court politics for most of the early nineteenth century in Vienna, and all of the Hapsburgs mentioned were real historical figures (Emperor Ferdinand and Archduke Franz Joseph). The personalities I've assigned to these characters, however, are largely invented.

My thanks to Kovács Ildikó for her help with Hungarian translations, and to Bekefi Miklos, who offered a critical perspective on Hungarian Romanies. If there are faults, they are solely mine.

Some Useful Sources

Curtis, Benjamin. *The Hapsburgs: The History of a Dynasty.* New York: Bloomsbury, 2013.

Gates-Coon, Rebecca. *The Landed Estates of the Esterházy Princes: Hungary During the Reforms of Maria Theresia and Joseph II.* Baltimore: Johns Hopkins University Press, 1994.

Hancock, Ian. *We Are the Romani People.* Hatfield, England: University of Hertfordshire Press, 2013.

Kontler, László. *A History of Hungary.* New York: Palgrave Macmillan, 2006.

Lázár, István. *Hungary: A Brief History.* Budapest: Corvina, 1993.

Lukacs, John. *Budapest 1900: A Historical Portrait of a City and Its Culture.* Grove Press, 1994.

Sisa, Stephen. *The Spirit of Hungary: A Panorama of Hungarian History and Culture.* New Hope, PA: Vista Court Books, 1995.

Stewart, Michael. *The Time of the Gypsies.* Boulder, CO: Westview Press, 1997.

CHARACTER GUIDE

In Hungarian fashion, the surnames are given first, followed by first names, for the Hungarian characters.

Anna Arden: our intrepid heroine
Catherine Arden: Anna's older sister
Charles Arden: Anna's father
James Arden: Anna's younger brother
Mária Arden: Anna's mother
Lady Margaret Berri: head of the Lucifera order in England
Ginny Davies: Anna's maid and friend
Eszterházy János (ES-ter-haa-zee YAH-nosh): Anna's great-uncle; Grandmama's cousin
Eszterházy Mátyás (ES-ter-haa-zee MAT-yash): Anna's third cousin; János's great-nephew
Eszterházy Noémi (ES-ter-haa-zee NOE-ay-mee): Mátyás's sister
Károlyi Karolina (KAH-roy-ee KAH-roe-lee-nah): a young society leader in Buda-Pest
Kossuth Lajos (KOE-shoot LAH-yosh): political reformer and leader of the liberal party in Hungary; inspired and led the revolution of March 1848
Kovács Gábor (KOE-vatch GAH-bor): a young Romani man
Kovács Izidóra (KOE-vatch IZ-ee-DOE-rah): Gábor's sister
Petőfi Sándor (PEH-toe-fee SHAHN-dor): a poet and revolutionary; considered by many to be Hungary's national poet and influential in the March 1848 uprising
William Skala (SKAA-luh): a Polish-Scottish revolutionary
Zrínyi Irína (ZREEN-yee EE-ree-nah): Anna's grandmother
Zrínyi Pál (ZREEN-yee pahl): Anna's uncle; Maria Arden's younger brother

GLOSSARY

bácsi (BAH-chee): loosely "uncle," a term of respect for older men

belváros (BELL-vah-rosh): city center

boszorkány (BOH-sor-kahnyuh) (the final component is voiced as a single syllable): a witch

Buda-Pest (BOO-dah-PESHT): what we now think of as one city used to be two separate cities (they officially joined in 1873). Buda, on the west side of the Duna, was the home of many of the wealthy elite; Pest, on the east side, was a younger, more energetic city.

csárda (CHAR-duh): a country inn

csárdás (CHAR-dahsh): a country round dance with a slow beginning and frenetic finish

Duna (DOO-nah): the Danube River

Eszterháza (ES-ter-haa-zuh): a formerly rich estate belonging to the Eszterházy family, but largely neglected by 1847. The palace on the estate was known as the Hungarian Versailles.

fene (FEH-neh): evil spirits. *A fene egye meg* (uh FEH-neh EH-djuh meg): let the *fene* eat it; similar expression to "Damn it!"

fiam (FEE-ahm): my son

gadzhe (GAH-djuh): Romani word for foreigners. *Gadzho* for male, *gadzhi* for female (also commonly spelled *gadje/gadjo/gadji* as well as *gadže*)

hála Istennek (HAA-luh EESH-teh-nek): thank God

Hapsburgs: the imperial family of Austria-Hungary. In 1847, they were ruled by Emperor Ferdinand. Today, the spelling "Habsburg" is more frequently used, but "Hapsburg" was a common nineteenth-century spelling.

hőn szeretett országom (HOON SEHR-eh-tet OR-sah-gohm): my dearly beloved country

Istenem (EESH-tuh-nem): my god

kérem (KAY-rem): please

kocsma (KOHCH-muh): a tavern or pub

lidérc (LEE-dehrts): a succubus-like creature with goose feet, believed to steal your breath while you sleep

nem (NEHM): no

néni (NAY-nee): loosely "aunt," a term of respect for older women

Pünkösd (POON-kuhshd): the Hungarian name for Pentecost, also Whitsunday

Romani (roh-MAH-nee): referring to Romani culture and language, also to the people themselves

rusalka (roo-SAHL-kah): the spirit of a drowned maiden, believed to lurk in trees and near water to drown unwary passersby

Sárvár (SHAR-vahr): the name of a castle and town, formerly belonging to the Nádasdy family (Elizabeth, or Erzsébet, Báthory, often called the Blood Countess, married into this family). Literally "mud castle"

szegény (SEH-gaynyuh) (the final component is voiced as a single syllable): poor (plural: *szegények*)

Szentendre (SEN-ten-druh): a picturesque village on the Danube Bend, north of Buda-Pest

szívem (SEE-vehm): my heart

temetni tudunk (TEH-met-nee TOO-doonk): we know how to bury (our dead). A Hungarian expression reflecting their familiarity with mourning and funeral rites.

vadleány (VAHD-lee-ahnyuh) (the final component is voiced as a single syllable): literally "wild girl," a woodland sprite known for seducing wanderers and siphoning away their strength

Luminate Orders

Animanti: manipulates living bodies. Common spells: healing, animal persuasion, sometimes invisibility. Less common: shapeshifting, necromancy.

Coremancer: manipulates the mind and heart. Common spells: truth spells, spell re-creation, persuasion, emotional manipulation. Less common: dreams and foresight.

Elementalist (formerly Alchemist): manipulates nonliving substances (light, weather, fire, water, earth, etc.). Most popular order. Common spells: weather magic, illusions, hidings, firestorms, water manipulation. Less common: firesmiths.

Lucifera: manipulates forces (gravity, space, time, magnetism). Common spells: telekinesis, portals, flight. Less common: temporal manipulation.

Acknowledgments

It doesn't just take a village to write a book; sometimes it takes a small army. Thanks to all those who have fought alongside me or for me on behalf of this book.

To my agent, Josh Adams, for believing in this book and for bolstering my faith when it flagged.

To my editor, Michelle Frey, for seeing something in the story and making it even better, and to associate editor Kelly Delaney, copy editor Sue Cohan, and the rest of the amazing team at Knopf. To cover designer Ray Shappell and CG studio Agent BOB for creating the beautiful cover.

To my critique group—Helen Boswell, Tasha Seegmiller, Erin Shakespear, and Elaine Vickers—for reading the first chapter and telling me *this* is the book I should write. And then for sticking around for the rest of a long journey.

To the generous readers who read part or all of early drafts: Jenilyn Tolley, Kendra Santa Cruz, Bruce Collings, Emily Manwaring, Kathryn Purdie, Emily Milner, Naomi Wyatt, Emily R. King, Megan Collins, Angela Ure Cothran, Kel Purcill, Katy Anderson, Sally Pead, Heather Harris Bergevin, Kristine Nielsen, Kimberly Vanderhorst, Virginia Boecker, Danielle Mages Amato, Kip Rechea, Mara Rutherford, Tara Sim, and Summer Spence.

To my writing communities for invaluable advice and support: my Sisters in Writing, the 2014 Pitch Wars Mentees, the Sweet Sixteens, the Swanky Seventeens, and the class of 2k17.

To Kovács Ildikó for making sure my rusty Hungarian was not *too* rusty and generously advising me on phrasing. To Bekefi Miklos for his advice on Hungarian Romani culture. To Dave Lunt for Latin tips.

To my parents for believing I could do this.

To my husband and children for making my nonwriting life richer than I deserve.

Last of all, to readers: you are the reason I write.